THE DISINHERITED

THE

DISINHERITED

By JACK CONROY

Introduction by DANIEL AARON

American Century Series

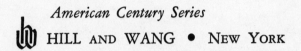 HILL AND WANG • NEW YORK

FIRST AMERICAN CENTURY SERIES EDITION FEBRUARY 1963

Manufactured in the United States of America
234567890

For
the disinherited and dispossessed
of the world

Certain portions of this book have appeared in *The American Mercury*, *Common Sense*, *International Literature* (Moscow, USSR), *The Left*, *The Modern Monthly*, *The New Masses*, *The Outlander*, and *Pagany*.

INTRODUCTION

In December, 1933, a virtually unknown American writer living in Moberly, Missouri, received the following letter:

DEAR JACK CONROY:
I've just read your *The Disinherited*. It's a fine piece of work. I didn't like your language in the narrative part so well, but when you are putting down what your people say you put it straight and salty— so darn few people writing have any feeling for the old English language as we speak it in these parts. The whole thing seemed to me an absolutely solid, unfaked piece of narrative as good as the best of Jack London, and that, in my opinion, is saying a great deal. Congratulations!

And then as an afterthought, the sender of the letter, John Dos Passos, added a characteristic postscript:

For God's sake, don't let them make a "literary gent" out of you. A stuffed shirt is just as much stuffed if it's colored red or white. Your writing has so damned much life to it that the shirt-stuffing artists are sure to be after you from all seven sides of the fence.

Dos Passos's generous greeting was scarcely more enthusiastic than the reviews of the new novel throughout the country. A few critics, both Marxist and "bourgeois," disagreed with the majority estimate, but the book found favor with American and English readers as diverse as Clifton Fadiman, V. S. Pritchett, Upton Sinclair, John Chamberlain, Bonamy Dobree, Michael Gold, Carl Van Doren, and Charles Beard. Even those who disdained its revolutionary message praised its vivid realism, and more than one critic pronounced *The Disinherited* the first memorable proletarian novel of the decade.

Conroy's book appeared at a time when the term "proletarian fiction" had already entered the American literary vocabulary. The long debate* carried on between radical critics in the pages of militant "little magazines" and at congresses of writers held periodically during the thirties never succeeded in fixing the definition of this ambiguous and emotive phrase to everyone's satisfaction. For some, a proletarian novel could only be written by a member of the working class. Others argued that middle-class writers might legitimately employ this fictional form so long as they wrote consciously for a proletarian audience. And still others, resenting such confining criteria, declared that the proletarian novel was simply a novel shaped by Marxian ideology. It need not deal with blue-collar workers nor be primarily directed to them. It was enough if the writer made manifest his loyalty to the working class.

As might be expected, most of the so-called proletarian fiction in the thirties was written by men and women of middle-class antecedents who had lost any lingering faith in the recuperative powers of capitalism and who now as the Depression deepened began to dramatize the "coming struggle for power." Few of them knew about the working class from firsthand experience or were equipped to bridge what Francis Hackett called "the enormous gap between literate and unliterate America." The facts about the people who made up industrial America were and had been available for longer than a half century, but the outsiders who occasionally "reported" them, for all of their sympathy and sensitiveness, never penetrated very deeply into working-class life. Nor was there an audience eager to read about it. Josiah Flynt's studies of tramps, Hutchins Hapgood's sketches of city low life, Walter Wyckoff's disclosures of migratory workers, or Stephen Crane's stories of urban misery attracted comparatively little attention in the early years of the century. The first self-described working-class author of any importance, Jack London, who presented the seamy side of proletarian life graphically enough and

* For the most detailed and informed discussion of this question, see Walter B. Rideout, *The Radical Novel in the United States, 1900–1954* (Cambridge, Harvard University Press, 1956).

who called himself a revolutionary socialist, achieved his public popularity among nonsocialist readers as an adventure story writer or as a purveyor of domesticated pseudo-Nietzschean nonsense—not as the author of *The People of the Abyss*.

Only when the Great Depression of the thirties afflicted the American landscape did the sights and conditions hitherto invisible to the majority of our writers and their readers become legitimate subjects of literary discourse. Now it was virtually impossible for the serious writer to avert his eyes from the unsmiling realities or to rule out the lives of "unliterate" Americans as unsuitable for fiction. Unemployment, strikes, evictions, hunger marches, bank failures, and farm foreclosures confronted him at home; abroad the Soviet five-year plan or the ominous expansion of Nazi Germany seemed to provide topics of greater magnitude for literature than the private and nonpolitical dilemmas of sensitive individualists.

Although no titanic literary figure emerged during the Great Depression with the Balzacian grasp of its details or the Tolstoyan insight to comprehend its social turbulence, the thirties produced in large quantities a kind of tendentious reporting or "reportage," as it was called, and short stories and novels which explored the American jungle. Some of the articles and books were almost literally messages from the pit written by people with names that sounded outlandish at least to old stock Americans. And their subjects seemed unusual and shocking as well: the despair of the jobless; the routine of a worker in an auto factory, a steel mill, a textile plant; the downward careers of box-car hoboes; the techniques of "pearl diving," "rolling" drunks, constructing "Hoovervilles" or "Roosevelt Roosts"; the planning and execution of a strike. These writers, for all of their naïveté and crudity, were uncovering their own lives, announcing what they had seen and done. They added a fresh impetus to the movement of literary realism and helped to break down the barriers between literate and unliterate America.

Jack Conroy, born in 1899 in the coal mining country of northern Missouri, belonged to this new contingent of working-class writers. As a boy living on the fringes of Moberly—one of a family of nine—he had experienced many of the events he later set down in *The Disinherited*. The "Monkey Nest" mine took the lives of his father and two of his brothers, and at the age of fourteen, Conroy went to work in the Wabash Shops. Like his hero, Conroy never got as far as high school, but he took correspondence courses to advance himself, and in 1921, he spent part of the year at the University of Missouri. Whether out of conviction or laziness, Conroy refused to submit to compulsory R.O.T.C. training and quit before the university authorities had time to expel him. From this point until he started his first novel, Conroy worked at a number of manual jobs he describes in *The Disinherited* and bummed around the Middle West. In the late twenties he moved north to Detroit and Toledo where the automobile factories were reportedly offering high wages, but his principal reason for going was to gather material on automobile workers.

By 1931, Conroy was not exactly a literary beginner despite his interrupted education and his itinerant life. His verse, short stories, and book reviews had appeared in both American and English magazines for some time. Since 1929, he had been editing volumes of revolutionary verse and had made an abortive start on a biography of Mark Twain. The Depression, however, gave focus to his experiences and talent and inspired the sketch of hard times in Toledo which he sent to H. L. Mencken. Mencken's conservative social views at this time did not prevent him from publishing young revolutionary writers in his *American Mercury,* and although he scoffed at the "dreadful bilge" Conroy had been editing, he had encouraged him to write the Toledo piece and was happy to publish such "excellent stuff" when Conroy sent it in. Mencken also advised him to write an autobiography instead of trying to incorporate his experiences into a series of sketches. "You have a good story to tell," he told Conroy, "and you will tell it effectively." Tremendously heartened by Mencken's interest (he later considered him "the best friend a young writer ever had"), Conroy settled down in his cottage on Bryne Road, Toledo, and began his book. Shortly after, however, an almost complete shutdown of the Willys-Overland automobile plant where Conroy had been working part time forced him back to Moberly, and there, sustained by checks from *The American Mercury* and by his wife's meager wages from a shoe factory, he finished the book. Fourteen publishers rejected it before one of them, Covici-Friede, promised to reconsider the manuscript if Conroy agreed to transform it into a novel. Conroy did so, and it was published as *The Disinherited* in 1933.

Comrade Jack, the "young working-class author," seemed heaven-sent to left wing critics like the *New Masses'* fervent Michael Gold. Many radical intellectuals at this time still shared the opinion of Trotsky—now the bogeyman of orthodox Communists—that the change from the old capitalist order to the new socialist society would occur too swiftly to permit the evolution of an authentic proletarian literature during the short interim. Genuine proletarian literature would emerge finally after the approximation of the Communist state when "proletarian" would be synonymous with "human." But for Gold and others of the proletarian school, a valid literature written by and for the working class helped to promote revolution. A book like *The Disinherited,* for example, was in itself "a victory against capitalism." And Gold insisted, "Out of the despair, mindlessness and violence of the proletarian life, thinkers and leaders arise. Each time one appears it is a revolutionary miracle." In Conroy, Gold saw a harbinger of a new revolutionary school of writers "arising in the cornlands of the Middle West" who would replace "the tired social-democrats" like Carl Sandburg.

Gold failed to realize at the time that Conroy, although undeniably working-class, did not quite fit the image of the untutored proletarian genius. His mother, so movingly commemorated in the novel, had once thought of becoming a writer, and his father was a man of some education. The young Conroy had found Dickens' novels and Macaulay's "Lays of Ancient Rome" in the family library and had acquired a dangerous fondness for romantic poetry which, to Mike Gold's dismay, he had transferred to his hero, Larry Donovan. "To mouth a few lush stanzas by Swinburne," said Gold, didn't make "one superior to illiterate drill press hands and factory girls." This kind of snobbishness suggested "a subconscious sense of inferiority to the bourgeois world" and usually ended, as it did with Jack London, "in believing *The*

Saturday Evening Post is the eternal standard in literature and that the U. S. ought to annex Mexico." Gold had too much faith in Conroy's authentic revolutionary spirit ever to believe he would go the way of Jack London, but his conviction that working-class boys never quoted sentimental verse was in itself a romantic one.

Very likely Conroy missed the point of these friendly admonitions at the time. He cared little for Marxism in 1933 and knew less, even if the revolutionary conclusion of his novel implied a belief in Marxist eschatology. "Just to look at *Das Kapital* on the shelf," he recollected some years later, "gave me a headache." After Roosevelt's New Deal program got under way, Conroy saw no necessity for violent revolution and dropped out of the left movement without ever repudiating his working-class sympathies.

The Disinherited can be read today as a good example of the American picaresque novel and as a graphic document of the early Depression. Conroy's critics in the thirties, friendly and unfriendly alike, pointed out the obvious literary weakness of his book: its awkwardly hitched episodes, its flat and undeveloped characterization, its pat conclusion. Undoubtedly Conroy might have profited if he had been a more self-conscious writer and had taken to heart Henry James's warning against the "platitude of statement." He adopted a plot pattern, moreover, that was already hardening into a stereotype—the slow awakening of the hero-worker from social unawareness to militant class consciousness. In short, his novel might easily have been as tedious and banal as many of its proletarian equivalents ("valuable only as a transitory report or chronicle," as James T. Farrell testily dismissed it) if Conroy had not possessed his own special distinction.

For all of its imperfections of style and technique, *The Disinherited* is far more than a report. Conroy makes us believe in the genuineness of his experience and the reality of the worker's life he describes, and in addition he presents this world in a way that is by no means characteristic of the proletarian school. His tone is bemused and wondering rather than protesting and declamatory, and he is so intent on rendering exactly the texture of his hero's surroundings that he seems to be constantly forgetting the ideological purpose of his narrative. Perhaps this is what Granville Hicks was objecting to in 1934 when he said that "the strength of the book lies in the pictures of proletarian life rather than in the theme, to which the pictures should be subordinated." From the Marxist point of view, Hicks was right. The writer had no business recording his own life and impressions for their own sake, and less perceptive critics than Hicks (then in his Marxist phase) were mistaken when they read *The Disinherited* as a fictional equation demonstrating the individual's relation to the existing modes of production. For them, Larry was "a graph, a temperature chart, of this march through the years of delusive prosperity to the murderous reality of the great slump."

In fact, *The Disinherited* does not make the reader burn with indignation, nor does it juxtapose fat wicked capitalists and brawny virtuous working men. The casual laborers who appear and disappear in its pages are precisely the men one might have met in the early thirties working in the mines and railroad shops and rubber plants, digging pipelines, hustling bags of beet pulp, paving roads, or scrambling to keep up with the speed-ups in the Detroit assembly lines. They are not splendidly impossible; they are as shortsighted, selfish, coarse, brave, irresponsible, and thick-headed as other Americans, and they speak authentic Americanese —not the tough-sentimental dialect cooked up by class-conscious writers who never really listened to the proletarian vernacular.

Conroy's lack of formal education was by no means an un-mixed blessing, but like Melville, whose Harvard and Yale had been the forecastle of a whaler, or Jack London, reared on the San Francisco docks, his introductory course in hard knocks was not without benefit. "I picked up a lot of education on freight trains, in the shops and in the mines too," he told a reporter in 1933. "It's been a pretty long course." Before he was graduated, he had learned how excessive work brutalizes and breaks down the human spirit and how chronic unemployment can sap a man's self-respect; he learned how "the dissolution of a last pair of shoes" can impair one's morale; and he learned the idiosyncrasies of a dozen grimy and low-paid jobs. Finally, he learned to set down his discoveries good humoredly and without self-pity in plain and energetic language.

Conroy's novel sold about 2,700 copies—a good sale. Most

proletarian novels, perhaps because of their mechanical plots and unsavory contents, repelled the average book-buying American and failed to return the publisher's investment. *The Disinherited* barely paid for itself, but it reappeared in seven translations and brought Conroy into the literary limelight. He did not remain in it very long. His second novel, *A World to Win,* published in 1935, got a cool reception, and a decade or so later, *The Disinherited* had become a collector's item.

This new edition will illuminate as few books can those grim and all but forgotten days when the unemployment figures ran from twelve to fifteen millions and the economic machinery of the world's richest country faltered dangerously. In episode after episode, the vicissitudes of working-class life ordinarily glossed over in the more general accounts of the Depression emerge sharply and unsentimentally; the hieroglyphics of charts and numbers are translated into the lives of men and women. Conroy's novel does not attempt to tell the whole story by any means, but Charles and Mary Beard hardly exaggerated when they observed in *America in Midpassage* that Conroy captured the "pungency" of "the world of labor" more successfully than did any of his more celebrated contemporaries. It is Conroy's Defoelike veracity that makes *The Disinherited,* despite its technical flaws, so solid and convincing and gives it an honored place in the annals of the Great Depression.

DANIEL AARON

Warsaw, Poland
December, 1962

PART ONE

MONKEY NEST CAMP

THE MONKEY NEST COAL MINE TIPPLE STOOD twenty years; its dirt dump grew from a diminutive hillock among the scrub oaks to the height of a young mountain. Stubborn shrubs, wiry grasses, and persistent dewberries struggled for a roothold on it, but the leprous soapstone resists all vegetable growth, even in decay. Cold and white like the belly of some deep-sea monster incongruously cast out of the depths, the dump dominated Monkey Nest camp like an Old World cathedral towering over peasants' huts. To begin with, Mr. Stacpoole, the owner, had christened the mine the Eagle, but the miners had decided otherwise. Somebody had dubbed it the Monkey Nest, and so it remained—so it is yet in the memory of those who recall it or its history.

I first saw the Monkey Nest shaft when it was only head high to Old Man Vaughan. Father led me to the brink and I peered over fearsomely, clinging to his legs. Old Vaughan caught me under the armpits and swung me down; then he threatened to keep me there indefinitely, but I knew better. I was used to the miners' joshing. Three taciturn Italians were slicing the tough white clay with keen tile spades and throwing it clear of the edge, grunting "hah!" at each spadeful. Mike Riordan, the peg-leg sailor, was in the pit, and so was Lionel Stafford. Stafford

9

was ruefully peeling blisters off his white hands. He said something to Mike about the iniquity of a world which forced a man with a bachelor's degree to toil at such arduous and menial labor. Mike couldn't spade with his peg, and if he bore down too hard on it, it sank into the earth. So he shoveled the crumbs from the Italians' and Stafford's spades. He pinched me playfully, and then gazed nonchalantly in another quarter.

"Looky here, Larry," said Vaughan. "A dad-blamed crawdad's hole and a crawpappy hisself at the bottom of it. I've follered that scoundrel from the grassroots and here's the bottom o' his hole finally. You know, when I've been diggin' a ditch or somethin', lots o' times I strike a crawdad's hole, and wonder just how far it runs in the ground. But I never *did* see the *bottom* o' one before, did you?"

The crawfish, a small lobster-like creature, angered and bewildered at this rude violation of his retreat, waved furious and menacing pincers. Vaughan was delighted, having realized a long-cherished ambition; and I was tickled, too, because I had often wondered just how far a crawfish burrowed into the soil. I have felt that thrill of accomplishment only a few times since.

The shaft bored past the clay, past the blue hardpan, blasted through the rock and into the coal. The Monkey Nest's tipple rose; its hoisting engine vibrated the heaps of slag and soapstone, oftentimes starting miniature avalanches down the dump. Cages shot up and down the shaft like office-building elevators. A mine tipple is like a gallows, especially if you chance to see its black timbers etched against a setting sun; and the cage dangles from the cathead like a hangman's rope. I have thought whimsically when a miner's head has appeared out of the shaft, apparently supported by the cable only, that his tongue should protrude and his legs kick spasmodically.

My brother Dan went to work in the mine when he was only twelve. There were nine children at home, and Father had more than he could do to feed us. It was against the law for a boy under sixteen to work in the pit unless he was with his father. But even with his father, the boy miner's cheeks blanch just the same; his shoulders stoop, apparently trying to fold in front of him like an angel's wings; and the hollow asthmatic cough begins before he is twenty—if he dodges rocks that long.

Father was despondent every time he was forced to take one of the boys to the mine. He wanted us all to get an education, but measles, whooping cough, scarlet fever and diphtheria assailed us. Most of the time we had no shoes, no pants with seats in them. When I was nine, I had been to school only a few weeks, but I could read rapidly and cipher passably.

On the morning of one of my periodic returns to school, I crept down the stairs. Mother bustled about filling dinner pails with water and food. Father and my brothers were putting on their dank, sweaty clothes. They stank from the foul, sulphurous air of the underground world. They lifted their shoes morosely, turned them upside down, and tapped on the soles. Pebbles rattled on the floor. Father rubbed his stiff sox. They had been muddy the night before. Now ascending motes rubbed from the sox were illuminated in a shaft of morning sunlight and they gleamed with iridescent hues. Father had talked about such things when he was younger, but he was a tired man now and getting to be an old man. He puffed when he bent over to lace the rawhide thongs in his shoes. You cannot use cloth shoe laces in a mine, for the acidulous slush and mud rot them away. My brothers' faces were sad, their limbs moved sluggishly. Mother had to shake and shake the boys to arouse them from their heavy sleep, and they yawned and knuckled their eyes even after they had eaten breakfast and set out for the tipple.

"Come here, son," Father said to me as I peered around the balustrade. "You're starting to school again. This time I want you to keep going. Don't mind if they laugh at your clothes. I want you to study hard; I don't want you to be a coal miner like me."

"I want to be like you," I answered, coming closer. "You went to school and got a good education, but you're a coal miner."

"It's different with me," he parried harshly. It always angered him to remind him that he was an educated man. "I'm in a deep ravine with no path to the heights again. I must follow my rut to the end. But your life is just beginning; so is Tim's. Maybe Dan and the other boys can rise from the mine again, but it's doubtful as that story about the fellow in Palestine arising from the tomb. The mine is a tomb and once the earth gets over you, it's hard to hump up and cast it off. It crushes them all in the end. So you want to study hard and maybe I can send you off to college. Maybe you can be a lawyer or a doctor."

Expert miners thump the roof inquiringly with a pick handle before they venture into their "rooms" of a morning. They learn the meaning of a whole octave of sounds indicating the solidity or lack of solidity in the ceiling, but pot rocks slip out as though they were well greased. They give no warning rattle. And bell rocks spring like panthers, leaving a smooth cup-like cavity. Always the rocks hang overhead like the fabled Damoclean sword, except that the sword was not too wide to allow some chance of jumping from beneath it.

When the cage delivered him up to the world of sun and daylight, Dan walked a quarter-mile bowed double before he could straighten his cramped spine. Evenings he lay on his back in the yard, staring at the stars. But

12

he wasn't wondering where the Great Dipper or the Pleiades were located or whether there were people on Mars, as we used to do together. He never said a word, but only chewed the end of a timothy stalk. At nine o'clock, the very latest, he limped into the house to bed, and when I came in from playing, he snored loudly with his mouth hanging wide open. I never snored that way till ten years later, when I shoveled gravel all day long on the highway gang.

II

Our house wasn't a camp house. It had a neatly painted porch, and was a story and a half high. A barbed wire fence surrounded it and kept cows out of the yard. Below it the camp houses extended in a rough semicircle at the foot of the hill. At the extreme end of the semicircle perched Liam Ryan's Barroom, a favorite haunt of the miners.

The hillside was our commons, and on it we played wild horse, leap-frog, cowboy and Indian. Diamond Dick rode valorously to rescue his sweetheart Nell from scalping at the hands of the redskins just in the nick of time; while Handsome Harry, the old sarpint of Siiskiyou, proclaimed to the world that he was an extremely pisen rattler possessing sixteen rattles and a button; moreover, he was not a bit averse to biting viciously if he were provoked sufficiently.

The farmer boys were our natural enemies, and because of our communal life we easily triumphed in every combat. The isolated farm houses prevented any kind of defense organization, so we ambushed the rustics singly and collectively. Smarting under the implication—and, alas, the conviction—of social inferiority, we battled with extraordinary ferocity, fashioning spears out of horse weeds that grew rank in the creek bottoms, and charging the fleeing hinds with all the fervor of King Arthur in the lists at Camelot. We raided their school-house and even hunted the teacher far away through the brush, stuffing the chimney with rags and overturning the privy, which backed up to and squatted over a crick.

The older boys carried on the tradition, roaming the woods like satyrs, leaning against tree trunks and pumping doleful accordions, or sitting on fallen logs tootling merry flutes. They shot craps in the forest, and to the dour farmer youths they were mad and unholy. But the faunish farm girls giggled behind the buck bushes and squealed with mingled terror and delight when the miners chased them home. If one were imaginative enough one might fancy goat hooves and jaunty horns as the miners pursued their quarry through the second growth of oak saplings. Once a hired hand caught my brother Dick in a wild cherry tree where he had climbed after the fruit, and pelted him with Osage orange hedge-apples, as large as a small grapefruit and as hard as a cocoanut.

Ben Haskin was the most prosperous farmer thereabout, and he was the particular target of our wrath. Ben's cows gave down their milk in foaming abundance; his hens were never sluggards. His sprayed and pruned trees bore the most luscious fruits, and his fields were the envy of his neighbors. Ben's ruddy face wore a contemptuous look as he drove his sleek horses by the camp. We pelted him with mud balls and howled insults after him. He shook his store-bought buggy whip at us, the veins in his forehead bulging. Most of the farmers used hickory switches for whips, so Ben's buggy whip infuriated us. We considered it an effete gesture. He sure thinks he's smart, he'll get too big for his britches, we said bitterly.

I often lay like an Indian in ambush watching Ben and his family moving or working about the farm. Ben had wrested part of his farm from the woods and the woods wanted back the land. The oaks flung their acorns into the clearing and they rooted tenaciously there. The quick-growing sumac and buck brush pushed into the field and kept Ben and his hired hand humping with mattock and axe. I watched from behind the boles of the larger trees and amused myself by throwing rocks at the men whenever they turned their backs.

Bonny Fern Haskin was Ben's only child. I despised her because she had everything that my sister Madge lacked. Bonny Fern's meticulously curled flaxen hair was bound with gaudy ribbons, her dresses were starched and immaculate. She wore shoes and stockings the year round. Madge had to stay inside in the bitterest weather to keep her feet from freezing. At other times she had to brave the frosts barefooted, and her soles were tough as whitleather.

Bonny Fern followed Ben and the hired man as they grubbed away at the tough sprouts. Whack! They struck at a young sapling; it was crushed to the ground, rebounding with only its bark bruised to slap them in the face. Ben swore fluently when Bonny Fern was not about, but now he merely exclaimed, "Wouldn't that cork you?" or something equally euphemistic.

"It's a good thing you ain't like them triflin' coal diggers," Bonny Fern piped sagely. "If you was, the saplin's 'd grow all over the place. All they do is lay around on the grass and let the jimson weeds and burdocks take the place. All they can raise is snotty-nosed younguns."

She had heard her mother saying this, and Ben laughed at the exact imitation of his wife's sour homily. But it infuriated me. I found a hefty sandstone and hurled it with true aim. It struck Bonny Fern in the temple and she sank down with a moan. Overwhelmed with terror and remorse I bounded away. I could hear Ben and the hired hand shouting angrily and beating the brush in search for me. I reached home out of breath and hid in the upstairs closet. I reflected over the advisability of pulling out for the Wild West and becoming an outlaw. I cocked my ears for the footsteps of the police, but they didn't come.

Within a day or so I was lurking around the clearing again. As I watched Bonny Fern I grew conscious of how pretty she was. Her cornsilk hair was so shiny; she kept so clean and never fingered her nose as my sister did. I hunted on shady hillsides till I found an exquisite ladyslipper. I carried it gingerly to avoid bruising the fragile blossom or snapping the slender stem. I watched Ben and the hired hand go to the farther end of the clearing and then approached the spot where Bonny Fern was playing alone.

"Who are you?" she challenged.

"I'm Larry Donovan. I brang you this flower. I thought maybe you'd like it. You don't see 'em every day. I hunted and hunted; they're hard as the devil to find."

"Oooh!" she squealed. "You swore! You're a dirty-mouthed little boy. Go wash your mouth out with soap!"

"I didn't aim to," I said contritely. "I didn't know that was a cuss-word. Everybody in the camp says that, even my pappy and Mr. Stafford, and they got college education."

"A camp kid," she shrieked, starting back as from a leper. "My daddy won't let me play with camp trash! You get off our farm, you camp trash!"

Ben had heard the racket, and he bounded across the field, not heeding the sprouts and buck brush lashing his legs.

"Haul out o' here, you young shitepoke," he bellowed. "And don't let me ketch any o' you camp kids hangin' 'round my land. Somebody like to 've murdered Bonny

Fern day before yestiddy, and dollars to doughnuts it was one o' you hoodlums."

He fired clods at me as I retreated hastily into the woods. The clods were soft; they burst on tree trunks and showered me with dirt, but the hurt sank deep and intensified as I ran. Safe in the forest fastness, I sank down upon a rock to ease the stitch in my side.

III

Father came from Montreal. He wore a long and curly chestnut mane like that of a *fin de siècle* matinee idol and a most romantic mustache. Somehow he was always the Man from Mars among the miners. But he did not flaunt his superior education as Lionel Stafford did. You could catch Father muttering strange words to himself. He often sat stark still on the doorstep, thinking for hours.

It didn't take him long to win leadership of the miners' local union—or rather he had it thrust on him. When he spoke in lodge he used a deep rolling voice so much different from his ordinary tone that we called it his "meeting" voice. It was years before anybody discovered that he had been a priest in Canada, and it came out accidentally. He never liked to talk about *that*. At intervals, newspapers came from Canada, but they were printed in French. Certain items would be marked heavily in blue pencil. Father would sit and read them, then he would crumple the paper in his clenched fist and stare stonily across the fields.

Madge and I were exploring his desk and found a faded velvet jewel-box containing a rosary and a crucifix. I took them to Father to ask what they were.

"Beads! Nothing but beads!" he said harshly, "and this is a bit of gold, nothing else."

Then he spoke more kindly: "But your grandmother

gave them to me long ago. Put them back where you got them."

Lionel Stafford was a man of mystery, too. Some grotesque whim of Fate had deposited him in Monkey Nest camp. He was a tall, aristocratic man with a blond walrus mustache and watery blue eyes. Though he lived in the shadow of the tipple, he feared the underground and could never be persuaded to venture inside the mine, much less to work in it. Stafford liked to wear clean white shirts and pressed seersucker suits, but his wife was an indolent woman, deserting her washtub and boiler at the communal spring to wander around gossiping at the other fires. Consequently, an air of crumpled and injured but unquenched dignity hovered about Stafford. He cut tough water oaks for mine props and hewed railroad ties, he was not above hoeing corn, but work in the mine he would not. He said he hated the dirt that always smudged a miner's face; he said he wanted to die on top of the ground, not with tons of earth and rock around him and over him.

His son Paul was like him. Paul was a neurotic child and morbidly afraid of the dark. We Monkey Nest urchins found this out. We tied him to a tree till after twilight and the whip-poor-wills were whistling lonesomely. Paul's screams frightened us, and we had to release him. I hid in the brush as he was coming from school, and as he passed by I sprang out, flinging a sugar sack over his head. "You're a miner under a cave-in. A rock's on you, you're a goner!" I shouted, pinning him to the ground. He howled with terror and clawed wildly at the sack. His mother said that when he was an infant he couldn't stand anything over his face. If the blanket happened to get over his face, he'd go into spasms.

I would have liked him better, but he got to walking home with Bonny Fern. They walked along sedately, plucking flowers or admiring butterflies. I tried to goad him into a wrestling match.

"You leave him alone, you smart aleck," Bonny Fern scolded. "He knows how to be a gentleman. He's the only boy from the camp that tries to be a gentleman."

Lionel Stafford spent a great deal of his time and most of the little money he got hold of in Ryan's Bar. Fragrant odors emanated from the barroom, and I loved to hang around. I had heard tantalizing reports of the gaudy vice that was believed to flourish within. There were painted women from the town. I could hear their shrill laughter, and caught snatches of smutty songs the meaning of which I could only guess. Mike Riordan lurched into the bar gloomily, but came out singing chanteys. When Stafford came out, a smile hovered under his drooping mustache and he was mumbling poetry.

Evening. In the West a star beginning to burn brightly. Stafford is within the saloon and Mrs. Stafford is looking for him. She does not hesitate at the sacred portals—I envy her temerity—but pushes aside the swinging doors and strides coldly within.

"Here you are, you triflin' hound," she screams reproachfully. "Why, you're lower 'n cow dirt! Why, you . . . you . . . you! Squanderin' bread an' meat money fer rotgut. Layin' around and lettin' the flies blow yer pratt when you ought to be providin' fer yer family."

"My good woman!" . . . Stafford is striving to preserve his modulated and dignified tone . . . "My good woman! God give you sense! God give you sense!"

He comes out wearily and walks slowly to his hovel, his head bowed, his long, delicate hands clasped behind him.

This happened not once, but many times. Then Mrs. Stafford began to swell. I had noticed this happen to other women, but Mrs. Stafford seemed to bulge larger. Some

19

of the older boys said she was in the family way, that she was knocked up, but I didn't know what that meant. Mike Riordan said she had swallowed a pumpkin whole, and this seemed more plausible to me, for she had an enormous gash in her face. When she was good and mad at Stafford her pendulous lower lip was flecked with froth.

Mrs. Stafford sat lathering on her front doorstep on a sweltering July day. She stirred the sultry air with a frayed palmleaf fan marked "Compliments of Eagle Coal Co." and told Paul and me that she would melt and run down in her shoes. Maggie Ryals came along to retail some gossip she had heard. Mrs. Stafford could not travel around as nimbly as formerly, so she was keenly appreciative.

"Do you know," Maggie whispered hoarsely, not realizing that Paul and I, squatting near and playing mumblypeg, could hear. We cocked our ears but went on tossing the knife with assumed diffidence. "Do you know, that Liam Ryan orta be rode outa town on a rail. He's gone an' hired a chippy from Bess Arnold's whorehouse, and she's gonna dance stripped on the table. He's chargin' the men a dollar a head t' see. Brother Zeke owned up to it, tried t' borry a dollar from *me*, the low-down pup!"

Mrs. Stafford struggled to her feet. Her stomach pouched down like a watermelon in a tow sack. She trembled with rage, and the hairs on her upper lip were shedding sweat beads.

"Lionel's in there," she gritted. "Oh, I hope ever' last one of 'em goes blind! I pray the good Lord to blast out their eyes!"

She waddled rapidly toward the saloon, but midway she toppled over and began an eerie screaming. Maggie hastened after her.

"Oh, I ortn't ever told 'er!" she moaned. "Run away, little boys! Run home, Larry, and take Paul with you! Oh, help! Won't somebody help?"

20

We ran only as far as a dense clump of buck brush. We dived within and lay watching. A bunch of women surrounded Mrs. Stafford as she writhed on the sward, and their milling around shut off our view half the time. But what we saw sickened and frightened me. I never believed in storks after that. In the excitement, I had forgotten about the chippy who was going to dance naked on the table. I had intended to investigate that.

IV

We were starved for print. Our schoolbooks were worn threadbare, and this was before the paper Trust began educating the masses with *Western Tales* and *Love Confessions*. I have never overcome the habit of stooping down to capture every vagrant circular or stray newspaper that I encounter abroad. It is atavism from Monkey Nest days.

Then Rodney Millbank began delivering the Indianapolis *News* every morning. This was before rural free delivery had begun functioning. Rodney made a whistle of hickory bark when the sap was running, and shrilled like a postman as the paper thudded against the weatherboarding. We pounced on the *News* with shrieks of delight and devoured it from the front page to the last editorial, even the advertisements. I recall a favorite comic strip labelled "The Terrors of the Tiny Tads" in which the unfortunate principals were constantly harassed by hyphenated beasts such as the camelephant and the panthermine. Abe Martin sat on his sagging barbed wire and expectorated the bon mots that continued for twenty-five years until death silenced him. I shall always be grateful to the Indianapolis *News*. Wherever it may be or whatever it has grown to, it was to me a window and a door. Lionel Stafford came up the hill to read the *News* each evening. He and Father talked, but Father was not very friendly with him.

Such a transaction as buying a ton of coal would have seemed incredible to us. We bagged it in gunny sacks from the tipple, shifting the load continually in an endeavor to ease our smarting backs with a flat-surfaced chunk. We sank puffing to the sward half way home, and the surrounding terrain detached itself from the general landscape as though under a microscope. Maybe a busy tumble-bug patiently trundling his malodorous pellet, or a tribe of ants bearing a dead grasshopper. One had only to smash down with a stick or stone to feel like God loosing an earthquake or a tidal wave. We halted by a decayed log and placed our mouths against the ground, chanting: "Doodle, up! Doodle, up! Doodle, up!" If we waited long enough a small black bug would squirm energetically out of the loam, and we were always sure that the doodlebug came in obedience to our command, though tardy. It was a childhood legend.

Huge lumps of coal bounded down the chutes, and into flat cars, side by side. A screen divided the rough from the fine, coal dust fouling the air like a thunder cloud. We spat black for hours. Often chunks rebounded to the ground, and these were our legitimate prey. My brother Tim stood back and watched, warning us when the top men were about to dump; but he frequently became negligent or mischievous and we darted from between the cars under a shrapnel of fine and a heavy artillery of larger lumps.

The hoisting engine was a perpetual marvel to us. Its steel cable wound around a glistening drum, and had cut grooves in it. The cable extended through a hole in the wall and across the cathead of the tipple. The engineer was proud of his job, and handled the levers like a pilot of the

Cannon Ball Express, never deigning a glance toward the boys peering through the doorway. Behind his shack an exhaust coughed softly out of a rusty pipe from which condensed steam trickled in rust-yellow drops. Tim said if you held your hand over the end of the pipe, the boiler would blow up. When the spiffy engineer took notice of us long enough to chase us away, Tim hinted darkly that he would encompass the ruin of the whole shebang even if, like Samson, he brought down the fragments about his own ears. But he always relented before actual perpetration of the deed.

One day as we stood silently admiring the hoist, a miraculous contraption clattered down the slag road leading to the main highway. A revolving chain like that of a bicycle whirled over sprockets at the side, and its one-lunged motor coughed cacophonously. The proud possessor of this marvel, none other than the mine owner, Edward Stacpoole, leaped to the ground and extended a hand to his wife, who had been holding on grimly as the vehicle jounced along. As the lady descended, I caught a glimpse of an elaborately frilled garter, the first I had ever seen. Coal miners' wives and daughters held up their stockings with rags tied just tight enough to support the weight without stopping the circulation.

My sister Madge had a fashion of rotating her tongue madly in a small circle when she was excited, and she approached this curious object with her tongue agitated like a snake's. A Little Lord Fauntleroy of eight had descended, and now darted from behind his mother and pushed Madge into a mud puddle, jeering meanwhile:

"Coal miner's brat! Coal miner's brat! Catch and eat a rat, eat lean and eat fat!"

Tim was standing close to the exhaust pipe, and darted behind the building. I was sure he would carry out his threat to blow the works to kingdom come, and awaited

23

the explosion apprehensively. Mr. Stacpoole had disappeared in the engine-room, and Mrs. Stacpoole, attracted by Madge's wails, looked back, mildly reproving:

"Oh, Elvin! You *shouldn't* do that! Tell the little girl you're sorry. You hear mother? Tell her you're sorry, like a little gentleman!"

Madge was crying bitterly and smudging her already grimy face with muddy fists. Tim reappeared with both hands full of the greasy slush and filth that accumulates around all steam engines. Plop! Horrific and odoriferous gooey splattered over Elvin's straw hat and matted his golden curls. Splash! The second fistful completed the wreckage by polluting his lace collar and oozing down his virginal blouse. It was the nativity of a bit of "business" which has since made Hollywood rich.

Tim fled, whooping derisively: "Now go home and wash *your* black face, smart aleck." I helped Madge to her feet and we cut and ran, but not as the vanquished decamp; for we felt that whatever glory hovered over the ghastly field was ours.

V

Mother was frying salt pork when Jimmy Kerns came to tell her about Dan. You have to parboil it to get the salt out, and roll it in flour before even a strong stomach can hold it down, but it was cheap. That's the reason we ate it. Mother was tossing the white puckered slices into the skillet when Jimmy knocked.

"Aha! Mrs. Donovan, hard at it, I see," he blurted out with a feeble attempt at jocosity. It was a full hour before the quitting whistle should blow. Jimmy's beady eyes flew about the room, and Mother couldn't catch and hold them.

"Tell me, Jimmy! Is it Tom?" she cried, grasping both

lapels. Miners' wives and mothers sense bad news intuitively.

"Why, Missus Donovan, no! I . . . I just . . . y' see. . . ."

"Then it's Dan! It must be Danny! I dreamed of black, cold water last night."

She sank to a chair, her eyes dry and aching. She never knew the relief of tears. Four miners carried Dan in on a stretcher and eased him on to the couch; but when they had to pull the stretcher from under him, blood gushed from his mouth. He breathed in short jerks, his eyelids fluttering. Mother knelt beside him and held his hand; the palms were just beginning to callous. He was fourteen, but since he went into the mine at twelve his time had been mostly divided between the pit and his bed.

Paul Stafford was in the yard, and he ran screaming down the hill toward home. "Shut up, you fool," I called after him angrily. The sight of blood sickened him, and he told me afterward that he'd wake up hollering in the night and imagine the bed clothes were rocks burying him. This would arouse the new baby, who was always cross, and Paul's mother would whale the stuffing out of him.

"Where does it hurt you most, Danny?" Mother asked, stroking his face.

He couldn't get the answer out, and in the night I sprang out of bed when Mike Crumley's wife began keening piercingly and our collie howled mournfully and melodiously, as they are said to do always when there is death in the house. Dan had drawn the sheet off his feet in a final agony, and his toes stood apart like the fingers of a hand. A hemorrhage had finished him. Tim took his place in the mine, for he was already twelve and over and strong for his age.

Father was blue again. He wanted to take Tim out of the mine soon, but he never did.

"Are you studying hard at school?" he asked me earnestly, holding my face between his hands. His face looked so old and wrinkled and grief-stricken that I was ashamed that I had not studied harder.

"Yes, sir, I am," I replied emphatically, resolving to apply myself diligently to my lessons hereafter.

"Oh, I wish nobody had to work in the mines!" cried Mother. "I hope we can take Tim out, and I wish your father could get another job. I'll never let you go in the mines, Larry. I won't let the mines have all my boys!"

She caught me and kissed me passionately. I didn't want to work in the mines. I wanted to be a railroad engineer or a policeman.

Everybody wondered why Father worked in the mines. Everybody agreed that he was a funny man. For one thing, his best friend was a Frenchman and a Catholic. There were not many Catholics in the neighborhood and less Frenchmen. The sons of these miners readily joined the Ku Klux Klan when the fiery cross was burned years later. People said that Frenchy Barbour ate cats and snakes, and that he prayed to the Virgin Mary to make his shots roll out another ton of coal. His shack was so close to the dump that soapstone and empty powder kegs had rolled right into his front yard.

Every Sunday he walked seven miles to the Catholic church in town, and on the way back he stopped at our house. Father waited for him on the back door step, a big slab of rough stone. The earth around the back door was black and sour because Mother poured dish water there. Frenchy appears around the corner, smirking and twirling his waxed mustache. His blue serge suit is gray with dust, and his cuffs a little soiled where his wrists have sweated.

Coal dust will come out no matter how many times you wash.

"*Bon jour,* Monsieur Tom," chirrups Frenchy blithely, "how goes it everyt'ing?"

"Hullo, Marcel!" says Father. "Squat down and tell me something."

Frenchy jerks a perfumed handkerchief from his pocket, dusts off the step, hitches up his trousers to save the crease, and sits down. They talk, gouging in the ground with twigs blown off the maple tree in the back yard and tracing geometrical designs in the walk. They laugh uproariously and argue heatedly. Frenchy stalks off home in a huff.

Frenchy comes into Father's room at noon and gives him a little home-made wine out of the water deck in his dinner pail. He sits with his back against a prop, his legs extended stiffly before him, and draws pictures on soapstone with the smoke of his lard-oil lamp. Often they converse in French, and this makes the other miners sore because they fancy they are being discussed in a derogatory manner.

I had to see the French section of Quebec, with voluble citizens gesticulating on the street corners, before I realized that Frenchy had supplied something in Father's life that phlegmatic and practical miners could never give.

Madge and I waited for Father at the pit-head. As the haughty engineer shuttled cages up and down, we speculated as to which would contain Father and our brothers. The lard-oil torches appeared first, gleaming like smoky stars, then a coal-blackened face, then the torso with a dinner pail under its arm, and the full body was resurrected from the depths.

We had been warned about going too close to the open shaft, so we contented ourselves with standing back and watching. We were a little early when they brought Frenchy Barbour screaming off the cage, but so far away that we saw him first only when John O'Toole stumbled with his corner of the stretcher, draining the blood that had collected in the sagging middle. Frenchy almost rolled off, and the other miners gave John a mean look for his awkwardness. They laid Frenchy on the engine-room floor. He was panting like a rabbit. There was no telephone, but one of the miners rode like Paul Revere for the doctor. Frenchy swept the faces around him with a glance.

"Tom Donovan! Tom Donovan! Where is he?" he whimpered.

Father shouldered his way through the knot of men and knelt by his friend's side.

"Marcel! Marcel! Here I am!" he called out.

Frenchy gripped Father's arm till white spots blossomed on his finger nails.

"Tom, *mon cher ami!* I die! I am dying—finished, I know. No priest, *sacre Dieu,* no priest here!"

"Now! Now! Marcel, you know what I told you about superstition. Don't you worry any. I thought you said. . . ."

"Yes! Yes! I know, but it seems different now. Afraid? Yes, I *am* afraid! Soon it will be too late to be afraid."

He was going fast, gasping like a fish on a sunny bank. He chewed the ends of his mustache.

"Marcel!" Father spoke again. "You remember what I told you about the monastery?"

"Ah, yes! O Mother of God! But quickly."

He began to mumble feverishly: *"Confiteor Deo omnipotente . . . beatae Mariae semper Virgini. . . ."*

Father's "meeting" voice sounded clear and sonorous. I heard some of the words years afterward and remembered most of them. *"Dominus vobiscum et cum spiritu tuo . . . in nomine Patris . . . et Filii . . . et Spiritus Sancti. . . ."*

Frenchy was about gone, but he heard and it seemed to do him good. His hand dropped across his chest before he had finished the cross. When his face set, I absurdly noticed that his lower lip fell in a snarling grimace, exposing squirrel-like teeth stained at the roots by tobacco. Father faced the astonished miners with a challenging look. I was grown before I read Balzac's story of how Bianchon marvelled at Desplein's inexplicable devotions. I comprehended then a little of the affection Father must have had for the volatile little Frenchman.

"Well," remarked Lionel Stafford when he came up the hill to read the Indianapolis *News*, "I am not sorry that I resolved never to go in the mine. Paul will never if I can help it. It's bad enough to be buried in the dirt after you're dead, leave alone being buried alive."

Father said nothing. He sat gazing sadly into space. Mrs. Stafford howled up the hill that the baby was having another spasm. The baby was rickety and Mrs. Stafford was afraid it wouldn't be bright.

VI

There were no conversational amenities at a miner's table. We ate seriously and wolfishly, scorning sprightly banter. But we halted momentarily when Father vouchsafed:

"Looks like another strike the first of the month. We'll have to live on blackberries and sowbelly for a while."

Mother scoured the woods for the wild sweet blackberries, canning them against the days of the famine, but it always settled down to an endurance contest. I told her that the blackberries were bending down the vines in the woods near Ben's farm. When we got there, there were no blackberries and very few vines. I looked anxiously for Bonny Fern, but caught only a flash of her hair ribbon among the chicken coops near the house. Mother scolded me for leading her on a wild goose chase.

The mine-owners depended upon the miners' starving into submission; the miners upon the owners' cupidity dictating that it was cheaper to capitulate than to maintain the luxury of armed guards and inefficient workers who would themselves eventually organize. But hunger was esteemed by the operators as an effective gentling influence, and the miners knew they had better tighten their belts.

The first days of the strike were gay and exciting. Enthusiastic meetings, brave resolutions. Wagonettes loaded with strike-breakers appeared, guarded by detectives with menacing rifles. Each morning and evening the camp's population lined the road and the scabs had to run a gauntlet of taunts and epithets, and on occasion an impulsive striker threw a stone and the guards clicked their rifles ominously.

"Scab! Scab! Scab!" shouted the men.

"Scab! Scab! Scab!" the women shrieked, shaking their fists.

"Scab! Scab! Scab!" howled the children with lusty hate.

"Scab! Scab! O, you bloody mother-killin' bastards, O, you lowdown sons of bitches! You're lower than whale dung, and that lays right on the bottom o' the sea!" yelled Mike Riordan, his peg leg beating the earth like a drum stick.

Toddlers wabbled from the camp houses and piped "Scab! Scab!"

They drew it in with their mothers' milk. Even little Willy Stafford stiffened with rage when the scabs passed by. Mrs. Stafford shouted vigorously, but Mr. Stafford's lips barely moved. He was never agitated by the emotional currents that stirred the miners out of their habitual sodden lethargy.

The wagonettes hurried by, the drivers whipping up the horses; and the scabs kept their eyes on the ruts ahead, but flushed purple and scarlet even under the coal-dust.

Mother counted the ebbing cans of blackberries and began slicing the last flitch of bacon. Father sat about moodily, and my brothers lay in the sunny yard with their hats over faces, for want of something better to do. Mr. Stacpoole sent word that he wanted to see Father in his office in town, and I went along. Father took a flour sack, because he thought he might possibly get credit at some of the grocery stores. Miners used flour sacks and gunny sacks for shopping bags.

Mr. Stacpoole's lady clerk was a dazzling creature. She penned letters on elaborate letterheads bearing a more or less fanciful representation of the Monkey Nest, only it was always called the Eagle in this place. She wrote in a delicate Spencerian hand and her balloon sleeves drifted gently to and fro like miniature dirigibles. I thought they must have been blown up by a bicycle pump. Her heavy bust bulged above a waspish waist, but she was a baby doll in those days. The pen scratched and spluttered when it hit a flaw in the paper, and Mr. Stacpoole looked up.

"Oh, Donovan, I'm glad to see you here. I reckon you fellows know by now that the Eagle can run without you just the same. But I ain't no hand to hold grudges—believe in live and let live. I'll have to let the wage cut stand, of course, because I've contracted all my coal out on that basis, but I'll take all the old men back, and I just been thinking if you wouldn't make a dandy pit boss. . . . That's a fine boy you got there, and I'll bet he's a big help to you right now. . . . Miss Lotter has wrote out a contract, and if you'll just step around here by the desk. . . ."

"Yes, he *is* a fine boy, and this long trip *for nothing* has tuckered him out. We must be home by dark, and I got some groceries to pack, too." There was only mild reproof in Father's voice, but Mr. Stacpoole was champing his cigar venomously.

Phelps, the grocer, who had known our family for a long time, was sorry, but the strike had run him pretty close, too. The wholesalers were crowding him for their money.

So we went home with an empty sack. Mother was watching for us, shading her eyes so that she could see us far away across the field. She saw that we were not carrying anything, and when we reached home I could hear her sobbing quietly in the pantry. The shelves in there were almost bare; she had almost scraped the corners out of the flour bin.

Storms had a good chance at our house, but Father loved a tempest. He liked to stand in the back door and let the wind whistle through his hair. He liked to hear "heaven's artillery crash," as he called it, and he thrilled to the lightning's swift zigzag. He often seemed to resemble Ajax defying the Jovian thunderbolts as he declaimed:

"Thy spirit, Independence, let me share.
    Lord of the lion heart and eagle eye,
  Along thy steps I follow, bosom bare,
    Nor heed the storm that howls along the sky."

We thought that sounded grand, and we often repeated it ourselves.

Wind worried our house till its ancient timbers snapped like rifle shots. Rats milled through the attic, stampeding like wild horses when it stormed. Supple catalpas flayed the warped cedar shingles like a mule driver's lash. You notice a storm more at night, too, I guess. Anyway, we didn't hear the man knocking for a while.

When Father opened the door, he stepped quickly inside, shivering. Rain drops dribbled down his pit clothes on to the floor, and bubbles squirted out of his soggy shoes. Father stood aghast and undecided; the door swung to and fro, sucked by the wind. Mother was trying to shield the kerosene lamp with her body.

"I'm workin' at the Monkey Nest," the intruder chattered, his teeth clicking like castanets. "I must have went to sleep in my room, and nobody missed me. I found the shaft and climbed up the buntings. I don't know the way to town, and if you'll show me. . . ."

Before he finished, Father emerged from his trance and plugged him a resounding smack on the jaw. For a minute he lay with his feet in the door and his body outside. Then he scrambled to his feet and sloshed off into the night before Father could wrench his shotgun from its antlers above the door.

"You scab! You damned scab!" he roared, the shotgun booming and a red flash momentarily lighting the doorway, for the wind had extinguished the coal-oil flame when Mother had whirled to see what was happening. The room was in darkness and the air was pungent with powder fumes. Mother groped for the lamp and dropped the chimney with a sharp exclamation when it burned her fingers. She ignited the wick with a trembling hand.

Madge tumbled out of bed and hurried down the stairs. Tim and I were goggle-eyed. Father grasped each of us by an arm, crying passionately:

"Boys! Boys! Listen to me! If you must be one, be a thief, a murderer, anything, but don't ever be a scab! You hear me? Don't ever be a scab!"

"We won't never, pappy," we promised solemnly.

33

My father was not an unkindly man. On such a night his enemy's dog, though it had bitten a hunk out of his leg and the seat out of his pants, might have stood beside his fire.

But not a scab.

The Monkey Nest never gave Tim a chance to stray from his vow, because he cushioned the fall of a bell rock before he was sixteen. But I have never forgotten that night or the promise exacted.

The strike came to an end somehow. Reminiscing about it, it is hard to say definitely just how it did end or whether it was won or lost. Somehow the miners seemed to lose the individual strike, but steadily to progress along the far-flung battle line of their goal. The history of the miners' union of that period is punctuated with strikes. Each faction battled doggedly, but had to surrender something finally.

When the time came to dig Tim's grave it was raining and the ground was treacherous with Spring thaw. The clay kept slipping as the men dug and they had to pause frequently to clean off their spades with a discarded table knife. The sides crumbled so that Dan's coffin projected into the new-made grave. The years in the gumbo had started the planks to rotting. Somebody got the idea of masking the coffin with canvas so that Mother couldn't see it. I had been told that in the casket a man's hair and beard keeps on growing just the same, that his toenails and fingernails do not die. I wondered about this. Familiarity may breed a large contempt for death; but this morbid curiosity about it is also a typical characteristic of the mid-Western mind.

The unctuous preacher hurried a little with his palaver: ". . . And the dead were judged out of those things which were written in the books, according to their works.

"And the sea gave up the dead which were in it; and

death and hell delivered up the dead which were in them; and they were judged according to their works.

". . . And whosover was not found written in the book of life was cast into the lake of fire."

VII

Miners occasionally escaped from Monkey Nest camp to the outer world, but Father never did. His face became speckled more and more with blue lumps of coal under the skin. His shoulders stooped and his breathing was tortured by asthma. He worked alone in his room. Most of the older men had partners; the younger men didn't like to team up with an oldster. Many of the men of Father's age had their sons working with them. Father was growing deaf and Mother was afraid that he couldn't hear the rocks that were about to slip down. A miner must have keen ears, but mostly he depends upon some inner intuition to warn him of impending danger. Often, without conscious volition, he leaps suddenly out of harm's way just as a rock crashes down where he sat. So Father told Mother not to fret. He sang a song: "I'm Old, but I'm Awfully Tough." But his voice was less jolly than it had been.

Though I was nearing the age at which all my brothers —now side by side beneath the gumbo in Sugar Creek graveyard—had entered the pit, Father declared that he would never allow me to work in the Monkey Nest or any other mine.

"There are other jobs," he said. "You just make up your mind that you'll study hard and grow up to be a doctor or a somebody, not a coal digger."

I was not unwilling to forswear the calling, for I knew that the camp children were pariahs everywhere they went. No self-respecting farmer would allow his offspring to attend our school; we were segregated in a dilapidated frame structure which looked as though it had never known paint. In the winter we had to wrap our feet with gunny sacks and leave them on in school. Our hands were often too numb to hold a pencil. The farmer kids and their parents snubbed us on the road and chased us off their land.

Bonny Fern walked by the camp with her eyes set rigidly in front of her, her yellow curls swinging majestically. Willy Stafford watched for her each night, and she unbended to smile at him. He grinned at her with imbecilic affability. Everybody thought Willy was not bright; his eyes were at times dull and glazed and again flamed with an insane luster. He had had fits since he was a baby. When the fits came on he rolled on the ground with horrible throaty sounds, he became rigid as death and his lips turned blue. Foam fell from his protruding tongue.

The other boys teased Paul about his brother, singing:

> "Had a little boy,
> Didn't have much sense,
> Bought him a fiddle
> For fifteen cents.
> Only tune that he could play
> Was 'Ta ra! Ta ra! Boom de ay!'"

This pleased me; I remembered that Bonny Fern had called Paul the only gentleman in the camp. But when I saw that Paul was hurt and when I knew that he worried so much about his half-wit brother Willy, I made the boys stop singing. I was big for my age.

We began trading with a German butcher named Koch, and I often made the trip to town to fetch the meat. I walked warily, feeling as insecure as a foreign spy within a hostile land. Most of the camp boys who ventured within the territory of the "town dudes" were chased clear of the city limits.

At the tail end of one of the periodic strikes, Koch's genial manner waned. He began hinting so strongly about the size of his unpaid bill, that I dreaded to face him.

The floor of Koch's butcher shop was covered with a thick layer of sawdust which felt cool to my bare feet after the burning pavement outside. There were barrels of piccalilli and sauerkraut with mosquito netting over them to keep .the flies out. When Koch came staggering out of his immense ice-box with a quarter of beef and threw it down on the block, the flies rallied. They settled on his hairy arms and on the meat. He slashed at an insistent bluebottle with a cleaver. "Want to blow skippers in the meat, Schweinehund?" he cried angrily.

Koch waited on everybody else before he turned to me.

"I want a five cent soup bone," I said timidly.

Koch picked up a blue-knuckled bone and sniffed it. He always sold the best meat to cash customers, and the next best to good paying credit customers. Whatever was left went to those like us, who had run up a big bill during the strike.

"You papa's gone back to work, ain't he? Ain't the strike at the Monkey Nest settled?" Koch inquired as he wrapped up the bone.

"Yes, sir, he has gone back to work."

Koch knew as well as everybody else that the strike was over. But I knew what he was really driving at.

"Well, you tell him to come in and see me Saturday night. Don't forget it, now, will you?"

"No, sir, I sure won't. I'll tell him the very first thing."

There were eleven saloons in Marlton. I hung around, and when the swinging doors parted to admit or eject a patron, my eyes flew curiously into the interior. In the Frisco Bar I caught sight of an enormous painting of a nude woman reclining on a couch. The artist was of the circus billboard school, but the lady's heavy breasts and opulent hips excited me strangely. I yearned for the time when I would be able to push casually through the doors and look at my leisure.

Mike Riordan plunged head first out of the bar-room and fell swearing at my feet. He was soon on his feet again, weaving perilously on his peg leg.

"Come out, ye cowards," yelled Mike to somebody within the saloon. "Come out here and ye'll last about as long as a fart in a whirlwind."

Then he spied me. He lurched over to me and put his arms affectionately about my shoulders. His breath was fragrant.

"I told 'em, didn't I, me boy?" he greeted me. "Well, I've been t'rowed outen better dumps than that."

Anger had deserted him. He sang hilariously as he accompanied me home. He could walk along briskly on the pavement, his peg clicking merrily, but when we reached the muddy lane to Monkey Nest camp, Mike couldn't travel so fast. It was getting dusk. I hurried on and left him struggling through the gumbo. Now and then he paused and kicked the clay off his peg.

Father looked worried when I told him what Koch had said.

"It's hard to get the bills paid up between strikes," he said despondently.

Fred Dodson, who owned the house we lived in, drove down the lane and hitched his horse to a fence-post. He greeted our fawning collie with such excessive geniality that Father was immediately struck with misgiving.

"Hullo, Tom," said Fred. "Y'all well?"

He tweaked a timothy stalk from beside the door step and began chewing it; at the same time wooling the collie's head and repeating: "Good ol' boy! Good ol' boy!"

"Very well," Father answered. "How's all your folks, Fred?"

"Tol'able, jist tol'able! Nothin' to brag on. Leona's been doctorin' all Winter, but she don't seem t' git 'er stren'th back like she'd oughter."

This was before operations were so fashionable. At that time professional invalids took a melancholy pride in their ability to remain bedfast for amazing periods.

"Leona's sick spell cost me a mint. I jist been tryin' t' c'lect in a few bills here and there, and thought maybe— bein' as you're workin' agin—you might be able t' let me have a little on the rent."

"You've been mighty obliging to me, Fred, and I appreciate it," said Father slowly. "I haven't drawn a pay yet, but when I do, you'll get something. Just now, it's a question of paying as much as I can in as many places as I can with devilish little to do it with."

"I knowed it! I knowed it!" exclaimed Fred heartily. "I was tellin' Leona this mornin' that you was one man I c'd bank on. Well, y' all come over some day an' spend the day."

After Fred left, Father sat for a long time on the back door step. He drew caricatures on the packed earth of the walk with a twig, and the next morning we saw that he had also been writing down figures and adding them up.

Now that the Monkey Nest was running again, Madge and I waited for Father at the pit-head. The miners who passed us often stopped to give us something out of their lunch pails. An apple or an orange was all right, but a sandwich, pie or cake was always soggy and tainted with a sulphurous taste. Not many of the miners could afford bananas or oranges, and if they could they were apt to eat them themselves. We always accepted the gifts with polite thanks, but as soon as the donor was out of sight we gave

39

the food to our collie. He usually buried it somewhere near, growling fiercely at anything that came close, but we never saw him dig up any of his cached provisions.

Mike Riordan came lurching along on his peg leg. Mike had told us that a shark had bitten his leg off while he was diving for pearls in the South Seas. He unstrapped his peg when he was working at the face of the coal; he'd sink down on his knee and the stump of the other leg and pick tirelessly all day long. There were few miners who could load as many cars as he. When the weather was bad, he'd say the lost leg was itching and then he'd scratch in the air about where the missing toes should be. Mike never failed to grab up my sister and carry her off under his arm.

"I've got a cellar full o' fat rats, and they're gettin' hungry," he growled ferociously. "I'll t'row ye in wid me rats!"

I howled in spurious fright, and Sister bellowed: "Please, please, Mister Riordan, I'll be good!" At the same time, with cool calculation, she was aiming kicks at Mike's legs. He carried her for a few yards, and then set her down. He stood chuckling as she ran back; the zest of the joke was never diluted for him.

Mike's arms were covered with tattooing. There were stars and anchors and serpents, but the most fascinating piece showed a naked woman. When there was nobody but boys or men about, Mike would move the muscles of his arms in a way to make the woman's hips wriggle. As accompaniment, he hummed an air he had picked up on the Streets of Cairo at the World's Fair, and on occasion he would sing these words to the tune:

> "Oh, what a funny feelin'!
> Stepped on a banana peelin';
> Heels flew up and hit the ceilin'."

When we told Mother about this, she was angry and said we must not look when Mike did such things. She waited for him one night and gave him a good talking-to. He said he was sorry, and after that he'd make the woman dance only when there were no small boys around.

As we waited at the pit-head, Ben Haskins drove up with a load of mine props in his wagon. Lionel Stafford had cut them, and he and Paul were riding on top of the pile to help unload them. As the wagon turned a corner, the props rolled and pinched Paul and his father. They rose to their feet with startled exclamations.

"Look out, them props 'll take a piece outen yer butt," laughed Ben.

"Now you git daown, Mister Stafford an' you an' Paul c'n pile 'em in a tidy pile right nigh the shaft so's they'll be handy fer the cager t' send below."

Stafford and Paul exchanged disturbed glances. They climbed down from the wagon, but edged away from the open shaft.

"Come awn! Come awn!" called Ben impatiently. "I gotta do the milkin' an' gether in the eggs yit t'day."

"I'd rather not stand near the open shaft," Stafford confessed shamefacedly. "I'm afraid of the underground and so is Paul. I have heard of cases where persons have become obsessed by an insane desire to leap into such a pit."

"Heifer dust!" snorted Ben. "Stand back! Next time put britches on yer ol' lady and send her. I'll bet a man a purty that she wouldn't be afraid."

He leaped down without touching the wheels, lost his balance and stumbled against me. He glared at me insolently.

"Why don't you keep outen the way, kid?" he snarled.

"Why don't you look where you're going, clodhopper?"

I retorted calmly. I considered him an invader here. On his own farm, I would have wilted before his wrath.

Stafford and Paul moved off dejectedly toward the camp. Ben called after them in a conciliatory tone but they did not heed.

Cages began rising and falling in the shaft. The shaft was divided by a partition in the center into two compartments. When one cage was ascending, the other was going down. A pair of wiry, vicious pit burros came up. They were battered and raw in many places where the drivers had beaten them or singed them with torches to accelerate their speed. They were galled from the friction of trace chains and their eyes had a cloudy look about them. Day in and day out they pulled strings of cars along narrow gauge tracks in the depths of the pit, and when they came to the surface they were blind, even on a day when the sun was not shining. They stumbled uncertainly about their lot near the dump or stood humped and disconsolate until it was time to take them below again.

They were brought up only on rare occasions, and for what reason we could never determine. Perhaps the Humane Society was enforcing a law that the mules must spend a certain amount of time above the ground, just as city social workers insist that tubercular sweatshop hands shall have a two-day vacation in the fresh country air every year. The burros squealed and kicked one another as swarms of flies gnawed at their raw flesh; they bared their teeth and bit desperately when shuddering their hides failed to displace their tormentors. The pasture lot was covered with soapstone and burning slag; nothing green ever sprang up in it. Even the hardy white oak scrub was blasted when the acrid soapstone spread about its roots.

When Father came up, he first emptied the brackish water out of his dinner pail, then he smudged out his lard-oil torch against the tipple. I grabbed his dinner pail. It always reeked with the sulphurous stench of the mine, which clings to clothing, hair and skin as well. We trotted along beside Father, one carrying the pail and clinging to an arm, the other grasping the other arm.

"Did we get any mail today?" Father inquired anxiously.

"Only some papers from Montreal," I answered.

"No letter?"

"No, no letter at all."

Father ordinarily told us all that had happened in the mine during the day, but since Koch had sent his message and Dodson had stopped at the house to hint for the back rent, he hadn't had much to say. Miners' asthma—which no one who works underground for any length of time escapes—was beginning to plague him more and more. He wheezed painfully before we were half way home. The air was heavy, and he was forced to sit down to blow for a spell.

Coal haulers drove their creaking wagons past our house. In muddy weather portions of the road were sheeted with roily water and teamsters who had not been that way for a time descended from their wagons and plumbed the holes with a shovel handle or the butt of a whip. They had to double teams to pull through the worst chug holes and even then the wagons might sink to the hubs, and the spokes splinter under the weight.

The horses lathered and steamed, fluttering their nostrils. They became unruly, and see-sawed back and forth instead of pulling steadily and in unison. Then the cursing drivers set their shoulders against the endgates and shouted themselves hoarse as they added their own strength to that of the horses. With hickory poles for levers, they pried the wheels out of deep holes and poked the clay from between the spokes.

Father had always helped the teamsters, but the last few weeks he hadn't noticed them. Most of the time he'd been sitting beneath the catalpa tree in the front yard, leaning his chair against the trunk, his head slumped upon his breast.

"Hey, are you crippled?" yelled a driver at him that evening. Father arose with a start and climbed over the barb-wire fence and put his shoulder to the wheel.

I heard Father and Mother talking in the kitchen after I had gone to bed.

"Larry would have had a chance there," Father said. "In Montreal he would have been able to go to school. I never asked them for anything before; now that they've snubbed me, I never shall again."

I knew that he was talking about the letter from Montreal which he had been expecting. I had gone through the grades at the rural school, but Father had not yet found any way to send me to town.

VIII

One morning my Aunt Jessie came to take me to the home of a miner who had been crushed by a fall of rock in the Monkey Nest. It was thought that the sight of a dead man might serve to counteract my excess of youthful spirits, for in those days joy was invariably associated with the Devil, and a lugubrious manner and countenance were esteemed as hallmarks of sanctity. Though I had no desire to see the dead man, I was not a bit averse to the trip thither, for the day promised to be glorious. The wild plum thickets along the lane were carpeting the ground beneath with their petals. As we cut through a clover field, bees trafficked busily in the blossoms underfoot, and I trod warily with my bare feet, for I had once been stung on the ankle by a bumblebee.

Aunt Jessie was a pretty girl with full red lips and a rope of wavy chestnut hair, but she kept it twisted in a tight knot. She was a good Christian girl and never went to dances. Sometimes she asked me questions about whether boys talked dirty about the girls around me.

"Did you ever hear Rollie Weems say anything about me?" she asked as we struck across the fields.

"Well, yes, I did," I admitted, "but I don't dare tell you, or you'd tell Mother and have her whip me."

"Oh, no, I wouldn't!" she assured me eagerly. "No matter what it was, I want to know. Go on and tell me and I'll do you a favor some time."

"Well," I said boldly. "He was talking to a bunch of fellows down by the saloon. He said you was the dandiest baby doll this side of the Mississippi, and that he'd give forty acres and a team of mules to get in your britches."

"Ooh!" she squeaked indignantly, but her eyes sparkled. "Would you allow anybody to talk about your aunt that way? You ought to have slapped him square in the mouth!"

"I didn't know he meant any harm," I countered hypocritically. "I didn't know what he meant by that, anyway."

I was lying, and I suspected that Aunt Jessie knew it. The collie scared up a quail and it ran limping and fluttering away with the dog barking excitedly after it. Then I knew that the bird's nest was near; and that as soon as the dog had been decoyed far enough away, the quail would rise up and fly back. I found the nest burrowed in the ground, and it was full of eggs. For a moment Aunt Jessie was smiling as she knelt to look, but the realization of her grim mission brought her back to her feet, and she pressed resolutely on, telling me to hurry.

We waded knee deep in lush grass on which the dew had dried only at the top; we passed through a meadow infested with tickle grass and it worked up my pants leg and set my aunt to scratching, too. She pinned her skirt beneath her arms, but her petticoat was soon drenched and stained green. When we came to a fence, she looked cautiously in all directions to see if anybody were about, then she knelt and crawled under as I held up the bottom strand. Her stays were laced so tight that her face reddened every time she stooped over.

The dead man's hovel was jammed with sorrowful relatives and curious neighbors. Rollie Weems was standing in the yard among some men who were talking solemnly in undertones. Rollie's face brightened when he saw us.

"How do, Jessie!" he cried, doffing his hat.

"How do, *Mister Weems!*" she returned icily, sweeping past him into the house. But she turned to the window and looked back.

As we entered the front room, the dazzling sunlight was instantly blotted out and with it my exuberance. For a moment I could see nothing but a dim, shrouded figure reclining upon one of the folding biers that undertakers used. One of the relatives who seemed to be a sort of master of ceremonies came forward and with a dramatic gesture ripped the sheet off the corpse. There he lay like a trussed blue fowl, his feet protruding from beneath a cheap cotton shroud. His scarred hands were folded across his chest; coal dust still blackening his nails and showing between his toes. His lips were glued in a hideous grin. I wailed in fright and attempted to retreat to the outdoors, but my aunt was not to be diverted from her purpose and what she considered her Christian duty.

"Touch his face!" she cried sternly.

She seized my hand and planted it on the dead man's forehead. Revulsion overwhelmed me—I snatched my hand away as though the dead flesh were burning instead of icy. I grew faint and felt as though I must retch.

For days the dead man's face appeared before me every time I closed my eyes. I awoke in the night a-sweat with terror, fancying my hand was still on his brow and that the curious paralysis which often affects one in dreams would not allow me to withdraw it. There was a mouse between the walls in the room where I slept and I could hear his sharp teeth nibbling, nibbling, and bits of plaster and lath falling. My imagination transformed the mouse into a dead man scratching with long finger nails at the lid of his coffin. I recalled grewsome anecdotes of people buried alive and how, when they were unearthed later, it was found that they had turned over on their faces in the casket, fighting for breath, and had wrenched handsful of hair from their heads.

"If ever you hear that ornery Rollie Weems say anything more about me, you let me know," Aunt Jessie told me as we trudged home from the dead man's house.

That night I heard Mother and Father talking in the kitchen.

"It's all I can do, and I must do it," Father said. "I could tend the garden in the morning, go to work at noon and dig till four, then fire the shots. Four dollars extra on the day will soon pay up our debts and leave enough over to send Larry to school in town. The way it is now, we're like the frog in the well. Every time he jumped up one foot, he slipped back two. We might figure ourselves to Hell, but never to the top of the ground."

Mother protested that shot firing was a single man's job, and that nobody ever lasted long at it. Shot firers were paid a premium rate for an hour or two of work after the other men had finished. When a man accepted the job it was considered that his days were numbered—that the Angel of Death had already checked his name on the waiting list.

But Father was obdurate. After a great deal of indecision, he had found what appeared to be a way out. He said he would be very careful; moreover, Mike Riordan would be his partner, and Mike was an old hand who had fired shots unscathed in the days when miners still used sulphur squibs. The squibs were like Fourth of July nigger-chasers. When a match was touched to one end, the squib began to fizz and back up. They were placed in small copper tubes tamped in drill holes containing a charge of powder. One end of the tube extended into a paper cartridge filled with powder; the other projected from the drill hole, and into this end of the tube the squib was placed and lighted. Then the shot firer had to heel it pretty lively to dodge the flying chunks of coal, for it didn't take the squib long to reach the powder.

Presently the slower safety fuse was invented. Miners were compelled by law to leave four feet of this fuse protruding from the drill hole, and it burned slowly, allowing the firer ample time to leave the room. This did not eliminate accidents, however. Shots frequently blew through into adjoining rooms; rocks were loosened and fell; there were dust explosions.

The miners fashioned their powder cartridges from newspapers by rolling a sheet tightly about a section of smooth pipe. Then the edges were glued with laundry soap and the cigarette-like cylinder crimped at one end and filled with coarse grained blasting powder. Sometimes when a heavy charge was required, several of these cartridges were pushed with the tamping rod to the back end of the drill hole, the last cartridge having a fuse end tucked into it. Several cartridges filled with drill dust were then tamped in around the fuse, the end of the fuse was split so the shot firers could light it readily, and the shot was ready.

Mike lived alone in one of the camp-houses clustering at the foot of the hill upon which our slightly more pretentious house stood. None of the girls thereabout would have anything to do with him, for it was said that he had the evil eye and had been talking to the Devil in his shanty at night. Also, the girls didn't like the idea of a one-legged beau, and Mike was past middle age. The girls jeered at him and called him "Peggy." If a child fell suddenly and unaccountably ill or a man was hurt in the mine, Mike's evil eye was blamed.

We frequently went to visit him in the evening after he came home from work. If there were any rats in his cellar, they must have had webbed feet, for the place was always full of foul smelling water. We crept down the rotting steps at the side of the house and watched the mosquito larvae wriggling about in the water, and there was a frog that perched on a floating shingle and became so tame that he would not dive off with a splash, but sit and watch us solemnly, his whitish underthroat throbbing like a beating heart. Mosquitoes in dense clouds swarmed about Mike's shack; he burned rags to keep them away. The company doctor was always wondering why Mike did not die of malaria, living, as he did, over a pool of stagnant water. Mike always replied that one born to be hanged would never perish otherwise.

He never mentioned his rats or tried to scare us when we went to see him. He would descend the cellar steps, roll up his sleeves, grope about in the black water, and fish out a bottle of beer. Before the Fourth of July or a Miners' Union picnic, he would have a keg of beer floating in the cellar. I didn't like the beer at first, but after a while I begged Mike for more than he would give me. After he had drunk three or four bottles, he would begin to curse the English and to extol the military and cultural glories of Erin. Presently, in a more jocular mood, he'd dance a hornpipe as best he could, his peg sinking in the earth when he stamped too vigorously. He stumbled and fell,

49

but scrambled up merrily, laughing and jigging away fit to kill. He explained that age was stiffening his joints, and that he'd have to catch some fishing worms and put them in a bottle to melt in the sun. He said that all the circus acrobats used fishing worm oil to lubricate their joints.

At first, Mike sang a merry ditty such as:

"In Ireland they have buttermilk ninety days old.
The maggots and wiggletails get very bold.
It would put any man in the greatest surprise
To see them turn up their great goggle eyes.

But as dusk thickened and lamps began to twinkle in window panes, he grew mellow and shifted to reminiscences of his old Irish mother and the peat bogs of Erin and the River Shannon. His tongue thickened and his words blurred. He mumbled a sentimental ballad which all the miners knew, and we joined in the chorus:

"Down in the coal mines underneath the ground,
Where a gleam of sunshine never can be found;
Digging dusky diamonds all the seasons round,
Down in the coal mines underneath the ground."

For us Mike held the irresistible attraction of the devilish and verboten. How he could spin glamorous tales of far horizons! He told us how to induce a monkey to throw down cocoanuts by thumbing one's nose at him, of savages whose lips had been artificially distended to form duck-like bills, of deserted jewel-studded temples reclaimed by the jungle and forgotten by man.

Willy Stafford came up and rubbed against Mike like an affectionate dog. Mike was Willy's best friend, and protected him against abuse from adults and children alike by threatening to exercise his occult powers against anybody who molested him.

"Ye'd best scoot home, Willy, me boy," Mike advised

50

him. "You come back tomorry night and Mike'll cut yer hair. You're gettin' shaggy as a wolf."

Willy moved off in the twilight, gurgling thoughtfully.

We sat entranced, listening to Mike's tales till the stars began blossoming, and his voice became more incoherent and drowsy, fading as thin as a worn-out phonograph record. His head dropped forward and the rising moon silvered his hair. It became so still that we could hear a cricket chirping beneath the house. A snore told us that the story telling was ended for that night.

Father made so much firing shots that he soon had all the bills paid up, and he talked about sending me to school in town. Getting a large sum for back rent pleased Fred Dodson, and he put up some screens to the doors. Screens were almost unheard of on miners' houses at that time; they were considered luxuries for the rich only. Flies usually buzzed around the table as though they owned the place, and one of the family had to stand guard at mealtime, slowly waving a leafy wand of alder or buck brush over the victuals. But the flies soon got used to this and settled tenaciously on everything that tempted their appetites.

Father was paying Koch every Saturday night, and he brought home a striped bag full of hard stick candy as a treat. It was a gala event and we always waited up far past our habitual bedtime. The candy was vile, unpalatable stuff, no doubt, but we relished it keenly, licking a stick with the air of a connoisseur sampling a rare vintage, and then laying it aside for future consideration. Sugar was a precious item in our diet, and in lean times sorghum might be used for sweetening coffee. At other times both the coffee and the sorghum were lacking.

Father arose at six and labored diligently in the garden till noon. He was proud of the garden. He fought potato bugs and cut worms and slashed weeds. When the ground was dry, he scanned every floating cloud before he descended into the mine at noon and hoped that it might be raining pitchforks when he came up again. Weather never intruded in the mine—the miners left the upper world behind for the period they were below.

The shot firers calculated their route so as to avoid the powder fumes and smoke which the powerful fans drove along the entries. They left the mine by climbing up an airshaft ascending from the end of the main entry leading from the shaft bottom. Father and Mike ran from room to room, touching their lamps to the fuses and pausing a moment until the end hissed and sparkled to be sure that it was really lighted. They shouted "Fire in the hole!" to one another as they lighted each shot. The steel cap on Mike's peg knocked fire from the rails and sometimes he struck a soft place and sank to the stub of his leg, where he had the vacant pants leg folded as a pad. The stub was tender on the end, and when Mike struck it on a rock he'd swear luridly. Some of the men were afraid to curse while in the mine, but Mike never was.

The air shaft had a shed above it with a door which was always sucked tightly shut by the inrush of air. We laid our ears to the cracks between the rough planks and listened to the dull booming of the exploding shots. They vibrated the earth. Then we could hear the sharp click of Mike's peg as he and Father neared the top of the spiral stairs, though the incessant roaring of the air current inside drowned most sounds. Sometimes we contrived, by exerting our combined strength, to pry open the door. We peered fearfully within, clinging to the jamb. The boarded walls sweated icy globules of sulphurous water, and flabby white toadstools reared from crevices. When we sighted the glare of the lard-oil lamps or heard Mike's peg hitting the steps, we withdrew and shut the door, for we had been ordered never to venture inside the shed.

One night we waited at the air shaft a long time but nobody came up. We heard a few shots going off, and then nothing. We pried open the door and I descended cautiously a step or two, but the steps were treacherous with slime and the roaring darkness of the nether regions terrified me. As I retreated, the whistle at the tipple began blowing. It never paused—its level piercing blast echoing among the hills. We knew something was amiss and set out for the shaft. Before we arrived the whistle had ceased blowing.

At the pit-head a group of men and women had gathered. Mike was lying near the engine-house on a folded stretcher, his face covered with blood and his peg leg shattered. Mother was standing silently near. She was afraid to ask any questions, but she was hoping that somebody would tell her something. Six or seven miners' wives surrounded her and led her back home, for the rescue party below had signalled to the engineer to hoist. They had arranged beforehand to blow three blasts if it were better for Mother not to see. Mother walked along quietly. She had inherited the stoicism of a long line of miners; fainting and hysterics are practically unknown among the Spartan women of the mining camps.

Father was found crumpled under a huge lump of coal with another chunk imbedded in his side, but he was still alive. His right eye was gone. The rescuers could tell that a shot had blown from the adjoining room. The intervening wall had been too thin. But it was after Mike was able to talk coherently that the full story was learned.

Mike had come to a wet hole in his rounds—a hole drilled but not loaded with powder or tamped. Whenever a miner drilled a hole into which he thought might seep enough dampness to prevent the powder from igniting, he prepared the cartridges and fuse and laid them near the hole, leaving a sign indicating that the shot firer was ex-

53

pected to load and tamp the shot and fire it instantly while the powder was still dry. It took five minutes or more to prepare the shot, and Father came in to help Mike. As Mike lit the shot and turned to go, he stepped in a soggy spot and his peg plunged down in it. Father helped him to his feet, but he had sprained his ankle and could not walk. Behind them, the ignited fuse was hissing and burning toward the powder. However, only the loose end outside the hole was as yet burning, and Father cut it off close to the coal. But as he prepared to help Mike outside, the wall of the room leaped toward them with a terrific detonation. Ordinarily, the shot in the next room would not have harmed them, but the shot must have had too much powder in it or it might have been drilled at the wrong angle. The wall between was too thin to withstand the blast.

The lamps were blown out. Mike said he felt flying chips of coal stinging his face like needles, but, luckily, the only large lump that struck him was the one which knocked his peg leg off. He heard Father calling for help, but he could not see him. When he tried to stand, he remembered his sprained ankle. He found that half of his peg was blown away. So he groped on all fours to where Father lay beneath the coal and tried to lift it off him, but he couldn't budge it. He felt around and found a stout mine prop, but even with it he could not move the lump.

Father by this time was silent, and Mike thought he must surely be dead. He followed a rail to the main entry, and his keen sense of direction enabled him to crawl toward the shaft. He could not find his lamp, and a match would not burn in the strong draft. Mike was bleeding badly, and he knew that he must hurry, for the powder fumes were making him dizzy. He held his head close to the ground and pressed doggedly on, rocks and lumps of coal lacerating his palms and knee and the stub of his leg. Red and blue spots were blooming before his eyes when he saw a faint beam of descending light. He knew that he had reached the shaft. He was able to pull the signal cord before he collapsed, and the rescuers who came swarming at the whistle's screeching found him unconscious with the cord clasped tightly in his hand.

An incessant procession of visitors invaded our house, and relatives we had not seen for years appeared to take charge of everything. "What's the use of havin' kinfolks if they can't he'p you in a time like this?" they'd say. Meals were served continuously, and the pallets of self-invited guests littered the floors. Madge and I roamed about disconsolately, for Mother had taken to her bed and nobody seemed to pay any attention to us—we seemed aliens in the house.

"You all has certainly got my sympathy, Jessie," said Rollie Weems soberly to Aunt Jessie, who flew about the house constantly.

"Thank you, Rollie, thank you!" said Aunt Jessie, forgetting to call him Mister Weems. "I certainly need every bit of it; and if it wasn't for just *havin'* to hold up, I ought to be in bed right now."

I walked up and down the rows of potatoes in the garden, and noticed that weeds were pushing up here and there and the bugs were coming back. I picked a few off and mashed them between a thumb and finger, but I remembered that that would raise a blister. The bugs were called blister beetles. Some of the farmers who came on horses turned them loose in the yard and before long they were ranging in the garden and cropping the potato tops and pea vines. The ground was pock-marked with hoof prints and tender tomato plants were being trampled.

Father had been proud of the garden, and I wanted to go into the room where he lay and tell him about it. I wanted to tell him, too, that I knew he had taken the shot firer job in order to send me to school, though I had never said anything about it before. But the nurse wouldn't let me in. Through the door of his room, I could hear him puffing louder than he ever had with the miners' asthma. I grew discouraged about the garden, for nobody seemed to take any interest in it any more. Cutworms were clipping off the cabbage plants. I went along the rows, and where a plant had wilted down, I probed in the earth and pulled up the roots with the slaty slug curled about them. I squashed the marauder with savage satisfaction.

The third day after the accident, I became obsessed with the notion that my own sin had been responsible for what had happened. So I built a tabernacle of gunny sacks and poles behind the shed and fashioned an altar from a wooden box. On it I sprinkled "holy water" from the rain barrel under the eaves and burned candles left over from a Christmas tree. I slashed my wrist with broken glass and daubed a bloody cross on the altar. I had an inchoate idea of appeasing an angry God with prayer and sacrifice. But nothing did any good. On the fourth day, Father tried to raise himself in bed, but stiffened out. His hands clenched on the counterpane and could scarcely be pried loose.

He lay on a bier in the front parlor for two days, and during this time hundreds filed past, paused, looked at his face, and passed out the front door. Lionel Stafford and Paul hurried past, averting their eyes, as though they were rushing through a disagreeable duty. Their faces were pale as that of the corpse. Even Ben Haskin and Bonny Fern came. Mike Riordan had come every day on crutches asking to see Father, and each time he was refused he swore horribly and went away, vowing never to return. All the women thought that he should not be allowed to come even after Father was dead.

Mike's face was speckled with blue lumps of coal under

the skin; he would carry them till he died. The miners had taken up a collection to buy him a cork leg. He told us that the leg looked good, all right, and bent at the knee just like a genuine one, but he didn't like it—it didn't feel natural. Besides, he had to wear two shoes. He said that before that he had just waited in the shoe-store till a man with the other leg off came in and they got their heads together and bought only one pair of shoes, each paying half the price and each taking one shoe. We didn't know whether to believe this or not. Mike's new leg creaked like a leather wallet or new harness as he walked.

Inside the parlor, relatives and neighbors were gathered —most of them women. They greeted Mike with frigid silence, remembering his indecent language of the last few days. He might be tolerated as a painful act of humanitarianism, but never welcomed. He appeared to sniff the hostility in the atmosphere and halted in the middle of the room, balancing himself with difficulty on his sore ankle and unfamiliar cork leg. He braced himself as though facing a gale at sea or the roll of a shifting deck. Then he hobbled awkwardly to the casket.

"Goodbye, Tom! Goodbye, you poor old son of a bitch!" he said steadily. Then he turned to his horrified audience. "Goodbye, you sluts! I hope you all miscarry!"

On the day of the funeral somebody was electrified to hear a rapid gasping noise apparently issuing from the coffin. In those days death was considered as assured if a mirror remained unclouded when placed before the lips, and it was said that a pin hole in the flesh of a dead person would not close up again. By these tests, Father was dead. Everybody was rooted to the spot by amazement, when our collie emerged from the curtains hung around the bier. The day was warm, and he had been lying beneath the coffin, panting.

I stood directly in front of the coffin while the funeral

was being preached, and I could see Father's nose above the edge. The undertaker had a folding organ and the organist from the Methodist Church knew how to make it quaver in a way to make everybody cry. The Methodist choir sang "Jesus, Lover of My Soul." The preacher was thought to be very eloquent, but many were disappointed because he did not choose the verse about "greater love hath no man, than this; that he lay down his life for a friend." Of course, Father had not really laid down his life for Mike, at least not intentionally—I felt that he had laid it down for me—but that was a dramatic, soul-stirring text and the disgruntled auditors recalled many strong sermons that had been preached from it. The preacher could have caused a lot more tears to be shed if he had used it.

The stifling scent of hothouse flowers filled the room. The wreaths were banked about the casket; waxy, unearthly petals floated down. Each wreath had a card bearing the name of the donor inscribed with flourishing letters, and tied with ribbon. I heard two or three people say that they would rather have the flowers while they were alive and could enjoy them. They said it with the air of one voicing a trenchant apothegm for the first time.

The yard was full of carriages hired from the livery stable. The only time the miners used a livery rig was for a funeral or maybe when one of the young bucks got drunk and wanted to cut a dash. The hearse was shiny black with folded curtains carved on the sides. Somebody said that the undertaker didn't know his business, for the hearse should have been grey for a man as old as Father. White for a child, black for the young and middle aged, grey for the old.

But the carriages soon filled and the hearse pulled out of the yard with the horses stepping high and easy. Mike was leaning on the fence across the way, his crutches propped against a post. We were in the coach reserved for relatives, just behind the hearse. As we passed, Mike's hand was raised as though in salute. His sleeves were rolled up, and the naked woman tattooed on his arm was plainly visible. I thought everybody must be noticing him, but the other occupants of the coach were sitting and sobbing or burying red noses in handkerchiefs. Mother's nose showed red through her heavy black veil.

At first I thought that Mike was making the woman dance, but I decided it was the heat waves shimmering between, for Mike looked solemn and as I turned to watch him a little longer, I saw that tears were running down his face, or he might have been sweating. The driver of the hearse slapped the horses' backs with the lines and clucked loudly. As we went around a bend in the road I looked back through the diamond-shaped pane in the back of the coach and saw the carriages stretching out of sight. I thought that the funeral procession must be a mile long, or maybe even longer.

Ben Haskin was plowing corn in a field adjoining the graveyard. Bonny Fern was with him, and as we dismounted from the coach, she eyed us with pert curiosity but with no sympathy. Tears started to my eyes as I envisioned myself lying in the casket, and Bonny Fern's heart wrung with belated penitence.

IX

After Father's funeral, our house slowly quieted. For days, I had fallen asleep with the chatter of sympathetic friends and relatives still going on, but after a few nights I began to awaken when the house was so silent I could hear the clock ticking at the foot of the stairs, unless the rats in the garret were making too much racket. I had never minded the rats before, for they had been there since I could remember, but now the fear of them harried me night and day. I dreamed that my bed was an island lashed by waves of blue noses and cold, naked tails. When the wind was high, the house swayed drunkenly and its timbers groaned like a human in pain. The darkness teemed with fearsome shapes—miners moaning beneath cave-ins, graves yawning at midnight to disgorge the undead, and vampires ranging abroad to slake their grisly thirsts.

"There's nothing to be afraid of in the dark," Mother reassured me. She threw wide the door and revealed the black curtain of outdoors. But I was unconvinced. The kerosene lamp flickered in a draft, and Mother shut the door quickly and bolted it. Cane had been planted in the field across the road and it had grown until the blades rustled incessantly, even when the wind was not stirring. It sounded like somebody whispering stealthily. My sister slept placidly, and it irked me that she should be so unconcerned.

The nearest houses were the camp houses at the foot of the hill, and before Father had died Mother had often said that anybody could eat us up hide and hair before help arrived from the camp. The miners came home dog-tired, gulped down their suppers, and almost immediately fell into a deathlike sleep. It was said that on the Judgment Day Gabriel would not be able to arouse them with his trumpet; he'd have to go around shaking shoulders. But Mother never mentioned anything like that any more. She kept telling us that the camp houses were too close for anybody to molest us.

We heard a hesitant rapping one night, and when Mother opened the door a huge Negro staggered in and plopped heavily on a chair. He had evidently been badly beaten. One eye was closed. The other glistened chalky white. His lips were battered. Mother stood stock still, but I could see her trembling.

" 'Scuse me! 'Scuse me! 'Scuse me, Missus, fo' my bad

manners!" he burst out. "Some white folks like to 've killed me and th'owed me in a coal car. I tumbled out at the crossin' up heah. I been askin' all the farmers fo' a drink, but they set their dogs on me. I'm so hongry an' thirsty, I cain't hardly stan' it. But doan be a-skeered o' me, Missus, I wouldn' hurt you none. I ain't no bad nigger, jes' a po' boy long ways from home. From Alabama. Tha's wheah I come from, Alabam."

"Why did the men beat you?" Mother inquired, trying to appear calm.

"Dogged ef I know, Missus! I never did fin' out. They jes' beat me up an' called me a scab, and tol' me not to come back no mo'."

"Oh, you were scabbing!" Mother said accusingly. "You were taking another man's job. You should expect to get beaten up for that."

I was afraid this would incense our guest, but he appeared to be astonished. The eye which was still open widened.

"Shoot me fo' a black buzzard ef I knew I was doin' any hahm," he exclaimed earnestly. "White boss man come up to me in Mobile an' ast me how I'd lak t' wuk on a job in Missoury. I ain't never wukked in this country befo' an' I thought I'd try it. They shipped me to a little town up the line heah named Sevier, and the fust night I left the bunk house t' look aroun' a little, them white folks jumped on me an' beat me up. They tho'wed me in that air coal car, and heah I am. But I certainly didn't aim t' do nobody no dirt."

The Negro ate and drank gratefully, and departed with fervent vows never to be inveigled into such a situation again. I had always regarded a scab as a sub-human beast endowed with an inherent vileness. I had never before regarded a scab as a puppet manipulated by those who stood to gain the most, but who never braved the wrath of the strikers. I could not hate the Negro with his doggy, pleading eyes, his humble, ingratiating smile.

Mother bolted the door a little more carefully, and let down all the windows, though the heat was stifling. The house was like a furnace. We all slept in the same room now, Mother and Madge on one bed, and I on another. I was afraid of the empty rooms upstairs. In the night I awakened sweating and heard a swish-swish as Mother plied a palm leaf fan over my sister's face. Then she turned to me, and I felt the stale air circulating and cooling— though almost imperceptibly. In the morning Mother looked worn out, blue shadows underscoring her eyes.

Though we had never lived luxuriously, we found that we could live on a great deal less than we had before. The miners and their wives brought small gifts for a time, but after a few weeks these ceased. Aunt Jessie brought a batch of home-baked light bread.

"Where's Rollie Weems?" she asked me. "I haven't seen him around the camp for a long time."

"Why!" I answered, surprised. "Haven't you heard? He's pulled out for the Indian Nation. He left two weeks ago."

"What for?" Her voice was low and troubled.

"Mike Riordan said he had knocked up Mattie Perkins, but I believe that's a lie. I saw her the other day, and she didn't look like anybody had hurt her. I don't believe that Rollie would hit a woman. I don't believe he would knock Mattie on the head." I maliciously feigned innocence, but when I saw Aunt Jessie's face screwing up, I was sorry. She turned her head to hide her face.

One day a group of church workers came to see us. They sat decorously in the front room, their inquisitive eyes ferreting into every crevice.

"We have come," announced a lady with a heroic bust, "to make some arrangement for the adoption of the children and for your own support and welfare. We know you are having a hard time, and we wouldn't be Christians if we didn't help you. We have been told that the children haven't enough to eat and wear, and we have talked the whole thing over. Mr. Ryerson" (indicating an angular old fellow with mutton-chop whiskers) "will take the boy, and I'll take the girl. It'll be several years before she's big enough to earn her salt, but the boy is big enough right now to work in the fields. Jethro Haines' wife has been bedfast for several years, and we have found a place for you there, doing the housework and taking care of her."

Mother's face clouded. She nervously laced and unlaced her fingers.

"You folks are mighty kind," she said, "but I don't like to break up my home. I'm going to try to raise the children the best I can. If I can't do it, then I'll have to make other plans."

The committee members made it plain that they considered themselves bitten by that keenest tooth—ingratitude. They arose collectively and stiffly, and visibly washed their hands of us, saying they were sorry that we would not allow them to help us.

Mother took my face between her hands and looked at me so earnestly I felt uncomfortable. I turned my head away.

"You've got to be a man now," she said solemnly. "You're the only man I've got left. These people will never offer to help us again."

Though I wasn't sure what being a man involved, I readily promised to be one henceforth. I was eager to run outdoors, for I heard some of the camp children on the hillside playground chanting:

63

> "Bushel o' wheat,
> Bushel o' rye;
> All not ready
> Holler 'I'."

I knew that a game of hide and seek was in progress, and I ran to join in. Before I reached the base where the boy who was "it" was hiding his eyes against a tree trunk, he gave his final warning before he began the search:

> "Bushel o' oats,
> Bushel o' clover;
> All ain't hid
> Can't hide over."

The next morning Mother said we must go to the communal spring to wash clothes. The spring was within the semicircle of camp-houses. Even when drought parched all the fields thereabout, the cold, clear water gurgled from a fissure in the rocks and trickled down a ravine, around which lush grass and vegetation flourished. Here the miners' wives did their washing. It saved carrying the water home, moreover there were always people coming and going so that the spot was a social center. All of the miners' wives did their own washing, but some of the men were bachelors or widowers and had to hire their washing done.

Mother went to the spring every day. She was taking in washings not only from miners but from Koch, the butcher.

My sister and I considered the excursions to the spring quite a lark. Mother humped all day over the steaming tub, but we had only to gather firewood, help carry water, and dump suds into the creek. Crawfishes had bored their shafts in the damp earth, erecting at the mouth of them a mound of the slatish clay that lay below the stratum of gumbo. Mason wasps came for mud with which to fashion their multi-celled homes. So many came that we thought this must be the only muddy spot within miles. The wasps alighted at the rivulet's brim and buzzed earnestly, as though they were gossiping with one another.

Mother's hands were always puckered and grey while she was washing, but when they dried for a while at night, her palms were red and shiny. The wrinkles never smoothed out. Her ordinarily pale face became flushed as with a perpetual fever. Her head was enveloped in a cloud of steam all day. The washboard kept her waist frayed, and the front of her dress was always moist with soapy spray. She bobbed up and down, up and down, as tirelessly and as mechanically as an automaton on a peanut roaster, pausing only long enough to hang out a batch of clothes or to stir those in the boiler with a stick.

The iron boiler was propped up on flat stones, and my sister and I carried firewood to keep up the blaze under it. The ground was covered with brittle branches the wind had torn off the oak trees. Mother always cautioned us not to burn wood with ants in it. She said that anything which lives also feels. If we thrust a stick in the fire and saw ants swarming out of it, we quickly withdrew it and rubbed it in the dirt to extinguish it.

Mother had to be most careful with Mrs. Koch's clothes. She had garments the like of which we had never seen before. Mr. Koch's shirt bosoms were resplendently pleated, and each pleat had to be ironed separately. If the starch was a little lumpy or the clothes not immaculately white, Mrs. Koch complained volubly.

Mother had to iron at night, heating the heavy sad irons on a coal stove which sent a withering, sirroco-like blast coursing through the house. Long after Madge and I were abed I could hear the monotonous rhythm of the irons sliding back and forth across the scorched and padded board. Sometimes, in desperation, Mother threw open the door, but the cheep of a night bird or a roving gust rustling the cane sent her scurrying to lock everything tight. I stole to the middle door and watched her standing with arm moving as inexorably as a piston. She pushed her greying hair back from her eyes with her suds-wrinkled hand. Sometimes her eyes were closed as she ironed. Blinding sweat dripped from the tip of her nose and from her chin.

Years afterward I was working with an extra gang on a track job. It was so hot that the rails were said to stretch a foot a day. The ballast heated like live coals; the rails ahead warped and writhed in the heat rays. One of the bullies holding a spike with a pair of tongs while another started it in the tie with a maul toppled forward sunstruck and the long point of the maul crashed through his skull as though it were an eggshell. In morose silence we propelled the hand car back to the bunk cars. We all felt woozy and sick as we sat down to supper. The cook brought in a stew and when we whiffed the steam off it, we all felt our stomachs rolling. It stank like something dead a long time. One fellow found two flies in his dish. He sprang to his feet and flung the mess full in the cook's face, howling like a wolf. Instantly we were electrified with unreasoning rage. The cook leaped from the car and bounded down the track with all of us after him in full cry. We hurled rocks after him and hunted him clear to the city limits of a small town.

As we ran past a house surrounded by a baize-green lawn a fine looking lady came hurrying out. There was a small boy in a bathing suit lolling under one of those revolving sprinklers that are used to water well-kept plots. The lady hugged the wet boy to her and told him she wouldn't let the bad men hurt him. We were a hard looking lot, unshaven and ferocious. Still, we wanted to tell the mother that the sun had made us a little dippy, but we wouldn't hurt the kid for the world. Her haughty manner struck us dumb, and we didn't say a word. The anger which had buoyed us like the momentary exultation of whisky died out, and we felt only sick and shaken and ashamed. The cook disappeared around a corner, and we all trudged back to the cars to get our clothes.

So when they spread the goo on Mother's Day, I don't get any lump in my throat. It seems that it was all designed for mothers like that boy's mother. What could you say to a coal camp mother ironing away at midnight on someone else's clothes? I never found one of those Western Union canned greetings that fitted my mother—I never saw one that I could send her in remembrance of the nights she sweated over the irons or the days she spent bent over the steaming wash tub.

X

The rural mail carrier left a bulky package one morning. This was such an unusual event that we were afire with curiosity as Mother clipped the strings. The package contained three books: "Robin Hood and his Merry Men," "Lays of Ancient Rome," and "Curlyhead and his Neighbours." They were from our father's sister in Montreal. Her husband sent a formal letter inquiring if we were in need of anything, and hoping we would like the books. Mother had Madge and me to write a polite note of thanks and she assured our aunt that we were doing very well. We never heard from them again.

Robin Hood entranced me for a while. I prowled through the buck brush and white oaks searching for a stout yew tree for a bow, or a sturdy ash for a quarter-staff. The greenwood resounded with blasts from a cow-horn as I summoned my merry rogues, the rachitic spawn of Monkey Nest miners.

Then Macaulay's orotund passages captured me. They rolled so melodiously out of one's mouth. The "great Lord of Luna", in the guise of a one-gallused urchin, "fell at my deadly stroke, As falls on Mount Alvernus A thunder-smitten oak." We neglected even our small part of the work connected with the washing, and often wandered far away through the underbrush to the mound we had christened "The rock Tarpeian Where the wan burghers spy A line of blazing villages Red in the midnight sky." Imagination magnified the thin spiral of smoke from the fire under the wash boiler into a mighty conflagration. Mother never called us, but conscience frequently spurred us back to the spring, just as the murderer is said to return to the scene of his crime. We would find Mother heaping sticks on the greying embers or breaking fagots under her feet. The smoke stung our eyes, but we were soon away again. Mother stood all day with the muggy vapors of the tub curling about her.

In the character of Horatius, I valiantly defended the log foot bridge across the creek against the combined assault of all the Monkey Nest boys. I modeled a "molten image" of Horatius out of an agglutinous lump of gumbo and baked it to a turn in the fire beneath the boiler. I raked it out with a stick and let it cool for a moment. When I picked it up to admire my handiwork, I realized that I had not allowed it to cool long enough. It scorched my fingers and I let it plop into the boiler full of clothes. It sank to the bottom and the water quickly assumed an amber tint. Stricken with dismay, I retreated into the brush, but remorse dragged me back. Mother was fishing the clothes out of the boiler with a stick. All of the garments were stained a hideous saffron; Horatius was a semi-dissolved gob. Mother must have been sure of my guilt, for she had seen me molding the image.

"These are Mrs. Koch's clothes," she said more dejectedly than angrily. "I'm afraid that stain will *never* come out, and she's *so* particular."

I quaked inwardly at the prospect of facing Mrs. Koch's fishy blue eyes, steeling with resentment, her double chin congealing into lines of disapproval. Mother divined my thoughts.

"I'll take them back myself. You're only a lad, and I don't want to see your spirit crushed too soon. There's little enough fun for a lad in a coal camp."

She scrubbed vigorously, but the saffron cast would not entirely fade out. She ironed till midnight and the next morning set out with the bundle. When she came back, her eyes were red and swollen. I was afraid to ask her what Mrs. Koch had said, and she did not tell me. I delivered several more washings before Koch deducted anything from the bill. Koch was allowing Mother to wash clothes to help pay our bill. It kept getting bigger. Koch assumed a reproachful air as he handed me the slip showing "total amount due." It seemed that we ate faster than the Koch family dirtied clothes.

Mike Riordan had not been seen since Father's funeral, but that evening I saw a light in his shack. It was thought that he had been in Kansas City on one of his periodic sprees. I went down the hill to talk to him. He said that some leprecauns had carried him away, tying him in a hollow tree. He had a peg leg again in place of the cork leg the miners had bought him. We found out later that he had pawned the cork leg in Kansas City when his money began to run short. He said he liked the peg better, anyhow, as he could use it for a potato masher or to punch holes in doughnuts.

When I told Mike about the ruined clothes and the grocery bill at Koch's, he sat sucking his pipe thoughtfully. He rattled the stem against his teeth. I told him

69

about the Negro scab who had been ignorant of any wrongdoing.

"I thought all the scabs were just born that way," I said. "Why don't the union men talk to the scabs and make them see that they are just being used for tools by the operators?"

Mike was not so sure about that. He grunted dubiously. He said he had seen many a scab in his day, and he had found that the most efficacious way of getting them to see the error of their ways was to massage their craniums with a pick handle. But he supposed somebody as guileless as Willy Stafford might be innocently misled into strike-breaking.

A few nights after Mike came back we heard somebody walking around the house. Mother whispered for us to be still, and we listened for a long time without moving. Then Mother grasped the stove poker and tiptoed to the door, opening it cautiously an inch at a time. A large wooden box was resting on the sill, and we found it was full of groceries.

One of the boys in the camp had been lending me his paper-backed novels, and I was well acquainted with the theory and practice of such eminent criminologists as Nick Carter, Old Sleuth, and King Brady. If I could have found some cigar ashes, I'd have considered the mysterious visitor as good as caught, but all I could find were some circular imprints in the hard earth of the pathway. Then I thought of Mike's peg leg.

"Somebody left a big box of groceries at our house last night," I told Mike. "Who do you suppose it could be?"

"Leprecauns, like as not," he answered gravely. "The little buggers like to do a good turn now and then to make up for some of their divilment."

"I believe it was you," I charged boldly. "I found some holes that looked like your peg had made them."

I was surprised when he flew off the handle and told me if I mentioned anything of the kind to Mother he'd skin me alive. So I kept mum, and the groceries appeared on the doorstep regularly.

I realized now that the grandiose plans for making me an educated man had gone on the rocks, and I did not care much. Yet I knew that Father had wished it more than anything else and Mother was mad enough to dream about it over the wash tub. She wanted me to find a job in town to work for my board while I went to school, but this was hard to do. Meanwhile, the miners struck again.

This time Mr. Stacpoole declared that he was tired of their foolishness and would run his business to suit himself.

"I'll make them bullies draw in their horns; I'll have 'em crawlin' back to eat out of my hand," he boasted.

He imported a gang of strikebreakers and some city plug-uglies for guards. Eviction notices were served on all the strikers living in camp-houses, and tents were stretched near the pit-head. Here the strikebreakers and guards ate and slept, but they soon fell to grumbling at their rough fare. The superintendent came to see Mother about cooking for them, and letting them eat in our house.

"I could get plenty others to do it," he said, with the manner of one determined to do a good deed, let it cost him what it might, "but I got to studyin' about you bein' a widder woman and I made up my mind to he'p you. They're all decent, well-behaved boys from Christian homes and I won't stand fer no bla'guardin' around the kids. No use of you breakin' your back over the wash tub no more."

"You'd better get somebody else to feed the scabs," Mother said quietly, but with such finality that he knew it was no use to argue further. He seemed very much disappointed, for our house was the only one of any size within easy reach of the mine.

A day or so later Fred Dodson came down to the spring where Mother was washing. He stood clipping clover blossoms with his buggy whip, and after a bit he blurted out:

"Mr. Lorton told me he'd made you a proposition about feedin' some of the miners. . . ."

"Yes, he did. I refused it."

"Well, I reckon you know your own business, but a person's gotta do lotsa things in this life they don't wanta. You gotta look out fer number one. He says the house is the only one around here big enough t' feed the miners in. He offered me double rent for it, but if you was t' change your mind and decide t' feed 'em, the rent wouldn't cost you a penny more'n it does now. He'd make up the balance hisself. So's your rent wouldn't be no more, but I'd get twicet as much as—ahem!—I'm supposed to. I think he made a purty fair proposition. I sh'd think cookin' would be easier and better payin' than takin' in washin'."

"I can move," Mother said resolutely.

"Pshaw, no!" Dodson deprecated. "I wouldn't have you do nothin' like that fer a forty-acre farm. But I'm a poor man; my crops burned up this year and I don't see how I'll feed my stock through the Winter. I jist thought if you wanted to take up the proposition, we'd jist wipe off that four months back rent you owe me off the slate. But I don't want t' face the Judgment Bar knowin' I was the cause o' bringin' sorrow to a poor widder woman. You jist think it over in a cool way; nobody wants t' be a bullyraggin' you."

After Dodson left, Mother said we must look for another house. I was almost thirteen then and getting rather large. Mother could no longer find washings, but I had determined to earn my own money. I had been reading some of the Alger stories of boys making their way in the world, and I was eager to make a start.

Rollie Weems had not gone to the Indian Nation after all. He came back to the camp with a new suit on and said he had a good job in the railroad shops in town. He told me I could get a job as an apprentice, and after I had served my time, I'd have a trade at good wages. I'd never have to work in the mines then. Rollie said that had been a false alarm about Mattie Perkins, and it was a load off his chest.

After I had delivered Koch's wash the next day I meandered into the railroad yards. It was a fearsome region, with engines snorting and darting here and there, cars banging and moving about on every hand. I had been expressly admonished against such ventures, but this time I excused myself on the grounds that I was on business. The tracks spread out like an immense spider-web, and I was kept looking in all directions for engines. Trainmen ordered me out of the yards, some in fatherly, others in vitriolic tones, but I kept on doggedly, stepping high and gingerly over the switch frogs. I had heard of a man who had been caught in such a trap and lost both his legs when a locomotive bore down on him. After dodging about for some time and becoming more and more confused, I came to a section of the yards where men were tearing down and repairing box cars. The ground was littered with nail studded planks, and a sharp stab in my foot reminded me that I was barefooted.

An impish, freckled boy of about fifteen came along with a greasy stool, a long iron hook, and a pail. He planted the stool before a box car truck, sat down, and began pulling the lubricating waste known to railroaders as "dope" out of a journal box. I stood behind him and coughed sharply. He turned about, and I was scandalized to see that he was chewing tobacco.

"Hello, kid," he grinned.

"Hello, goat!" I retorted insolently. This was considered a crushing reply to the salutation frowned upon by the well-bred.

"What 're you lookin' for?" he pursued genially.

"For the general foreman," I announced importantly. "I want a job."

He doubled with exaggerated mirth.

"You go to the tool room and ast 'em fer a left hand monkey wrench. I gotta take the nut offen one o' these box bolts. Then I'll show you the foreman."

"G'wan!" I jeered. "I ain't as green as I look. Don't try to feed me that."

"I see you ain't to be fooled," he said with feigned astonishment. "That's the foreman comin' down the line there."

"That man with greasy overalls? He looks just like a common working man to me."

"Jist dresses that way t' be comfortable. Besides, he c'n slip up on loafers easier when he dresses same 's anybody else. G'wan and ast 'im. He hired about a hundred this morning."

The man appeared bewildered when I accosted him, but he grinned when he saw the frolicsome dope puller howling with glee. He explained to me that my informant was joshing me. When I turned to reproach the dope puller, he had vanished behind the box car. The laborer told me where to find the general foreman. I caught him rushing out of his cubby hole of an office with a handful of papers. He almost fell over me.

"Are you hiring anybody today?" I inquired, manfully, drawing myself to my full height.

He paused long enough to eye me scornfully.

"Hell, no! We ain't hirin' no *men*, let alone kids! You ain't got all your teeth yet, have you? Better go home and get some titty. Get outa here 'fore I spit in yer eye and drown you! *Skiddo, 23!*"

Fear buoyed my feet till I reached the yard limits, then humiliation overwhelmed me. Gusty sobs shook me. I dreaded more and more being a man, but I also knew that retreat I could not. As I turned into the Monkey Nest lane, I saw Rollie Weems and Aunt Jessie strolling along close together. When I told Rollie what had happened he said you had to pull some strings first to get the job. He said he would fix it up for me with the master mechanic.

I came through the woods adjoining Ben Haskin's clearing, and sat down for a while near the edge of the field to see if I could catch a glimpse of Bonny Fern. While I was sitting there a tough looking fellow appeared, walking from the direction in which the Monkey Nest lay. Though the scabs still lived in their quarters near the pit, I felt that this was one of them, and I resolved to awaken his conscience and set him on the right path, as Mother had done with the Negro.

"Hello, buster," he greeted me, speaking out of the corner of his mouth. "Do you live far about here?"

"Yes. Do you?"

"That's for me to know and you to find out. But turn about is fair play. Sure! I'm cooped up at the Monkey Nest and if I have to stay there much longer, I'll be daffy for true. We're all getting pretty horny, for one thing. Old Man Stacpoole promised to bring some women out from town, but he claims he can't get any to risk it with such a bunch. Show me one that even has got to walk with a cane, just so she's got one tooth left in her head. . . ."

"Don't you know that you oughn't to work at the Monkey Nest?" I broke out reprovingly. "You're taking other men's jobs. Maybe you didn't know that. You ought to go back and tell the scabs to go back where they came from. They're working men just the same as. . . ."

"What's it to you?" he cut in savagely. "Don't try to preach to me. I've had my job taken when I came out on strike, and now it's my turn."

He strode over to me and grasped me by the throat. I tried to tear away.

"Don't go blabbing you saw me here, either," he commanded. "You fan your butt away from here and don't let any grass grow under your feet."

He slapped me smartly across the face to speed me on my way. I ran a short distance, but crept back to the edge of the clearing. Then I saw Bonny Fern moving among the trees at the farther edge. I was electrified to see the scab peeping from behind a tree bole. Bonny Fern was a big girl now, and she was beginning to look like a woman. Her breasts were as big as oranges and stretched proudly against her tight sweater. She was wailing in a lugubrious tone:

"There's just three things in this world I wish for,
'Tis my coffin, grave and shroud.
But when I'm dead please come and see me;
Kiss the girl whose heart you broke."

I tried to tell myself that she had me in mind. The scab edged from behind the tree. I selected a stout hickory cudgel from the fallen limbs near my feet. My knees were trembling and my heart thumping so against my ribs that I was sure it could be heard both by the scab and Bonny Fern. A kaleidoscopic sequence of events flashed in my mind: The scab lying with bloody, bashed-in skull. Bonny Fern in a semi-faint, her arms flung about my neck. Ben shaking hands with me and thanking me again and again. "You saved her from a fate worse than death, my boy."

The scab emerged from the trees and Bonny Fern halted in her tracks with a sharp cry. "Now! Now!" I thought, but stir I could not. A terrible weight anchored my feet as effectively as if they had rooted and thrust radicles deep in the earth.

"Hello, honey!" The scab's face was lighted with a desperate hunger that I was just beginning to comprehend. "Hello, honey! I won't hurt you. Come and sit down with me."

Bonny Fern began to scream.

"Don't do that, honey! Please don't! Look!" He pulled a roll of bills from his pocket. "I'll give you five dollars! Ten dollars! Hush! Hush! Oh, for the love of God, hush!" He was slobbering at the mouth; his eyes rolled pleadingly.

"You'd better get away from here! You'd better hurry, too, or my papa'll kill you!" yelled Bonny Fern, turning to run.

The scab's face twisted up as though he had bitten in a green persimmon. He wheeled about and made off through the brush, sobbing like a cow bawling. Bonny Fern stood watching his flight with amazement. I had ventured out into the clearing, and she saw me for the first time.

"Oh," she said suspiciously, "what do you want here?"

"Nothing," I answered, regretting that I had shown myself. I was eager to hide.

"Come here," she called imperiously. "I want to talk to you."

At any other time I would have felt encouraged, but I was overwhelmed with shame. Confronted by a crisis, I had failed miserably. I was half way home before I realized that Bonny Fern's voice had sounded rather friendly.

The next evening Rollie told me everything was fixed

up with the master mechanic, but he couldn't be expected to buy a pig in a poke. He wanted to look me over first to see that I was sound in body and reasonably sound in mind.

Mother and I walked through the echoing halls of the division office building till we came to the master mechanic's door. Mother slicked down my hair and straightened my necktie.

"Don't be afraid to speak right up to him," she whispered sepulchrally.

There were several girls sitting at tables inside the outer office. We stood within the railing and waited. Mother's hands gripped the rail. She looked tired, and I wished that somebody would ask her to sit down. I had thought until a moment ago that her Sunday dress was rather stylish, but when I saw the natty garb of the clerks, I realized that she was dressed pretty shabbily and old-fashioned. I could tell that she knew it, too. One of the girls was tapping away at a typewriter. Writing machines were no longer a novelty, but I had never heard of one in Monkey Nest camp.

The girls chattered and frisked about as spry as chipmunks. Though they undoubtedly saw us, they ignored us completely, as though to impress us with the fact that the ponderous wheels of the railroad must revolve inexorably, and our petty concerns could wait. Mother shifted from one foot to the other. I knew that her feet must be blistered from the long walk. At last one of the girls looked me directly in the eye and asked me what she could do for me. I thought I would have a hemorrhage. My hair seemed to bush up like a Hottentot's, and my feet loomed monstrously in their unfamiliar shoes. My heart hammered furiously, a lump arose in my throat, and I was struck with consternation to find that I could not utter a sound.

Mother answered for me, and we were soon ushered into the private lair of the great man himself. I sat by a window watching some garrulous English sparrows quarrelling on the ground below. Mother had to nudge me frequently when the master mechanic directed a question at me. I answered in a subdued tone, and wished I were almost anywhere else.

"You want to watch that boy," the master mechanic advised Mother. "Looks to me like he's coming down with a fever. His color ain't natural."

"Don't you feel well, son?" he asked me. "Do you feel strong enough to work?"

I told him that I did, and Mother explained that I was just bashful and always got red when I talked to strangers. I did not particularly relish the prospect of spending my days in the shops. The clanging of locomotive bells, the couplers crashing as cars banged together, the hoarse shouts of the workers drifted in the window like a bad dream.

My heart sank when the master mechanic announced with the air of a sovereign bestowing a knighthood that he would put me to work as an apprentice in the car department. Then he launched into a story of his own courageous ascension from nadir to zenith. He had once been a water boy for an extra gang working on the section. He did not need to tell us what he was now, for the aura of consequence hovered about him. He had had no Aladdin's lamp to rub, he said, no genii to do his bidding. He had fought every step of the way. He intimated that I might ascend to the same dizzy heights ultimately if I attended to business and made a good and faithful hand.

"Do you smoke or drink, lad?" he asked, rolling a fat black cigar in the corner of his mouth.

"No, sir, I don't," I replied virtuously.

"That's the boy!" he applauded. "You'll find a bunch of rough boys here—bad eggs—but you want to stay clear of them. You want to go to Sunday School every Sunday and mind your mother. I always did."

My wages would be eighty cents a day, and we made arrangements for my lodging with a relative until Mother could find a house in town. Dodson was looking more reproachful every day; he palpably considered himself a martyr for allowing us to stay in the house for which he had been offered double rent. Moreover, all of our friends were clearing out of the camp, and strikebreakers moving in. Mike Riordan was one of the last to go, and when he left, the baskets of groceries appeared no more upon our doorstep. Though Lionel Stafford had never worked in the mine, he considered himself among the dispossessed, and moved into town. It was no use trying to teach Willy anything, but Paul was bright enough.

When we reached home after the interview with the master mechanic, Mother set to patching my clothes. After they were all collected, the bundle wasn't very large. I dallied about all day, somewhat reluctant to start out. I ran to the clearing and gazed earnestly toward Haskin's. But nobody was stirring around the place. I wondered if Bonny Fern would even know we had moved; I wondered what it was she had wanted to tell me. I was conscious of breaking loose from moorings—I knew that something epochal was happening to me, and I shrank from the dark ahead. It was past dusk when I kissed Mother and my sister goodbye. The kerosene lamp had already been lighted, and through the unshaded window I saw that Mother had gathered Madge on her lap. I thought this was ridiculous, for she was nine years old and her legs dangled on the floor. Mother was singing to her a lullaby that had put all of us to sleep time and again:

"Bobby Shafto's gone to sea,
Silver buckles on his knee;

He'll come back and marry me,
Bonny Bobby Shafto.

"Bobby Shafto's fat and fair,
    Combing down his yellow hair;
He's my love forevermore,
    Bonny Bobby Shafto."

It struck me that Mother might still be afraid to stay
in the old house with its creaking timbers, the rats stamping in the garret, and the memories of her dead. When I
stepped into the lane, the ripening cane blades rustled
harshly. The night became peopled with eyes and tongues
—became vocal and spying. I began to whistle, but the
sound startled me. I kept clear of the cane field, fearing
something unnamed that might be hiding in the mysterious depths between the rows. I could have saved a
mile by cutting through, but I preferred to walk down
the middle of the lane. I was glad that my feet made no
sound in the velvety dust. The lights from the town stained
the sky. Monkey Nest camp retreated into the dark. There
were few lights in the windows now. Some of the strikers
had been stealing back at night to stone them out.

XI

My life had been dominated by the Monkey Nest. We
had set our clock by its whistle. When it was silent, we
were hungry and anxious to know when it would open
again. When it hummed with activity, there was the fear
of the rocks, the faces tired as death beneath the grime.
Miners' wives clutch at their hearts when there's an un-
expected knocking at the door. So when I left the camp,
I felt that Father would have been glad, had he known.
He wanted passionately to keep me out of the mines, and
I was going away.

Though the Monkey Nest was getting old as mines go, it lived a few years after it retreated in my mind to the status of a memory. Years crowded in on the Monkey Nest. A mine dies young in the sparse croppings of Missouri; twenty years is a hoary old age. But the Monkey Nest left monuments to its memory in many cemeteries, particularly Sugar Creek graveyard, where the pine headboards bristle among wild blackberry vines and rampant tiger lilies that long ago burst the borders of prim beds and sent their progeny adventuring across the mounds. Frenchy Barbour's grave caved in before he had been buried many years, for his coffin was cheap and not made to withstand much weight. Sand and gumbo must fill his skull and stain his squirrel-teeth browner than tobacco did. Father and my three brothers are side by side.

Worked-out mines marked only by a hummock of vegetation-defying soapstone or a rusty boiler tilted on one end, its flue holes resembling a great Swiss cheese, hedged the Monkey Nest in. Tunnels that radiated in all directions from the shaft were always breaking into abandoned works. Deadly black damp and water seeped in. Incombustible sulphur gleamed in the coal like gold, and the dwindling veins faded until a man was forced to crawl on his belly like a snake to pick out the sparse coal.

Then the tipple fell in a whirlwind, and the stiff legs stuck ludicrously in the air like those of an overturned wooden horse. Time has had its way with the Monkey Nest. In its quiet grottos crumbling rails and phosphorescent ties are sinking in pallid slime, while flabby fungi cling to the rotting timbers. Bats scream and fight. A venturesome boy climbed down the shaft, but fled in terror when he was covered from head to foot with pulsing, furry bodies before he could travel twenty feet into the main entry. It was lucky for him at that, because the black damp knocks you out without warning. A lamp flame will not live in it.

To keep cows from falling in the open shaft, it was decided to fill it. The assorted urchins of a superannuated miner volunteered to perform this incredible feat, more stupendous than any storied Herculean labor. In casting about for a comparative peg on which to hang their undertaking, I must mention the persistent Mr. Beers of the poem, who, amidst his neighbor's jeers, has been resolutely digging in his garden, with China as a goal, for forty-seven years. Think also of that prodigious rock in Svithjod land, a hundred miles high and a hundred miles wide. To it every thousand years comes a canary bird to whet its dainty beak. When that Gargantuan boulder shall have been worn to the level of the plain, preachers are fond of saying, it will be only breakfast time in Hell.

But the boys rigged up a coaster wagon that had been discarded by some more fortunate child, and began wheeling soapstone and slag to fill the gaping void. At first a faint splash was the only evidence of their toil, but within six months they could see bottom by throwing down a kerosene-soaked and ignited cattail. It took them a year to complete the job, but they were paid twenty-five dollars in cash, not in trade out of a company store.

So the Monkey Nest's mouth is stopped with dust, but in its time it had its pound of flesh. Yes, I figure it had its tons of flesh, all told, if laid side by side in Sugar Creek graveyard.

PART TWO

BULL MARKET

I WAS THROUGH WITH THE FORMALITY OF "HIRING in" and stood waiting beside the freight yard office to see what they would do with me. I was wondering what the work would be like. Car knockers hurried by with their tool boxes. Lumber hustlers appeared with piles of siding boards on their padded shoulders, and others rolled car wheels. One man carried a "wheel stick," a stout oak stick with a notch in its side. It looked like one of a pair of stilts. When the wheel needed to be turned, the stick man thrust the notch beneath the journal, elevating that end of the wheel in the air. Then the hustlers pushed on the other end and swung it about. It terrified me to think that I would soon be expected to do such things.

"Hello, kid, lookin' fer the foreman agin?"

It was the frolicsome dope puller, Ed Warden.

"Yes, I am, but no matter who you tell me he is, I won't believe you," I answered in an injured tone.

"I ain't givin' you no bull this time," he said earnestly. "That's the labor gang foreman, Fritz Heinemann. He'll come git you d'rectly." Ed indicated a bearded, elderly man with an enormous knot on his back. The knot was sharp on the top and appeared to be almost punching through his overall jacket.

"How'd he get that hump on his back?" I had heard

87

that humpbacks were somehow associated with luck, but I couldn't recall just how.

"Why, he was in the army—in the War between France and Germany—and he was a greenhorn; couldn't never git the commands straight. They give him the order to shoulder arms, and he got flustrated and shouldered his fanny. He ain't never been able to get it back down ag'in."

This enraged me. I thought he was taking advantage of my rural innocence again, but I later learned that the joke was a stock one in the freight yards repertoire.

"Don't look like you'd been caught suckin' eggs," advised Rollie Weems, seeing me. "Ain't nothin' to be afeared of. Listen! Next time you see your Aunt Jessie, tell 'er that was nothin' but a lie about me an' Mattie Perkins. Jist some skunk wanted t' bust us up. I think a heap o' Jessie. She can put her shoes under my bed any night, or she can hang her bloomers on my bed post any time she wants to."

Just then Fritz called my name. He told me that no car apprentices were being put on, and that I must work in the laboring gang, cleaning up the rubbish and planks torn from cars by repair men.

I learned that monotony often galls more than labor. The laborers had devised a system of apparently innocent whistles to apprise one another of Fritz's exact location, and it kept him busy searching the yards for idlers.

The car repairers were all busy men. They worked piece work, and had to shake old brown to make anything. Consequently, they ripped off boards and threw cracked castings without much concern as to where they might light. After my head had been peeled a few times, I learned to watch the piece workers and to dodge when they flung anything.

The hours limped along with the speed of a rheumatic

turtle. I devised sun dials in the narrow aisles between the box cars, computed the time by the shadows of buildings. I listened eagerly for every school bell and factory whistle and asked what time it was so much that the men told me they were wearing their pockets out pulling out their watches. Some of them advised me sourly: "the whistle blows for poor folks."

Each day became an ordeal to be dreaded, the quitting whistle a signal for rejoicing. There were ponderous broken castings and journal brasses to be wheeled to the scrap dock, rotten sills removed from the box cars to be carted away. I crawled to bed with my muscles numb and awoke, seemingly after only a few minutes in bed, with them aching like a sore tooth.

"Larry! Larry!" Mother called me for the tenth time. "It's past six, son. Rollie went by a while ago and you'll not have time to swallow your breakfast."

I lie in bed remembering my awakenings in the old house in Monkey Nest camp. I had galled under the strictures of the country school, which I had attended irregularly at best. Now, half-awake, I recall the drowsy Autumn afternoons when I could sit for an hour idly watching the squirrels frisking about in the shagbark hickory trees outside. The squirrels scolded vivaciously as they sent nut hulls rattling down through the leaves and branches. Gaudy butterflies winged languidly through the open windows, fluttered about the room, and escaped through the opposite side. Long white strands of milkweed silk and spiderwebs mounted high in the blue sky, and the smell of ripening apples and of goldenrod was everywhere, indoors and out.

"Yes, ma'am, I'm coming," I called at length, rolling out of bed.

I ate my breakfast morosely. Outside I could hear the heavy brogans of the shopmen on the cindered walk. I kissed Mother and grabbed my cap; I swung into the stream of men tramping toward the shops. Dad Lyons, a skinny machinist, was my companion each morning.

"Good morning, Mr. Lyons," I said.

"Good mornin', Larry. Well, a little chilly this mornin'. We'll be having frost one o' these mornin's."

"Yes, about time for it, Mr. Lyons."

At the corner of Oak and Sixth Ed Warden joined me as he did each morning. I fell behind to talk to him. He had told me how he escaped from the orphans' home of a great fraternal order, how he had a room of his own —he could even slip girls in when the landlady was out or became careless. She was deaf as a post, too.

I tingled all over to hear this.

"Do you like the women?" Ed asked slyly.

A divine ecstasy mingled with terror flooded me, and my face flushed hotly. "Oh, a little. Not much." Diffidently, as though girls were no novelty to me, and I couldn't afford to bother my head about them.

My wages were low, but Mother somehow managed to send Madge to school and to save enough to pay my tuition at a night school.

"You can go to the night school and get an education that way," she said. "Lincoln had only a burning log to study by and not many books, but now his name will never be forgotten. Don't you get in with that pool room bunch like Ed Warden, son. You know what your father wanted you to be: a lawyer or a doctor."

This prospect fortified my resolution when the night school's teacher droned away till his voice became a lullaby, and the figures on the blackboard squirmed like anguished worms. My tortured eyes narrowed to slits, my head banged on the desk and I awakened with a start, stiffening to attention. Outside the windows of the night school, couples strolled through a small park, arm in arm. Inside the grubbing students humped over their books. I rubbed my eyes and stared determinedly at the page.

This was the way of escape, I knew. When I saw the broken, apathetic old men about the shops, I told myself that I would study all night, if need be, to save myself from such a fate. The work-dulled old men a few years from the grave, stamped with resignation and defeat. I saw their bleary, leaden eyes before me, their humped backs and gnarled hands which groped for tools even when at rest. After the old men were discharged as unfit for further service at the shops, they sat forlornly on skimpy front porches warming their meagre bodies in the sun, waiting for death.

So when Ed urged me to take a night off to meet Wilma, I told him I couldn't spare the time from school.

"You can play hooky one night, surely," Ed urged. "Wilma said she could tell her Ma she was spendin' the night with Gertrude. C'mon! You can have the room all t' yourself. Are you game? Wilma's a baby doll, built like a brick outhouse. What about it, kid? What about Friday? Don't try t' lie t' me! You only go t' school on Mondays, Wednesdays, and Thursdays, anyways."

"What's the good of it? I go to the library on Friday night and read. Like as not Wilma's as ugly as a mud fence besides." I wanted to convince him that I was a blasé connoisseur of womanflesh.

"I know. You're skeered. You ain't never had none yet. I thought you was gettin' big enough t' have hair on yer belly."

My manhood was on trial. And the adventure for its own sake lured me.

"All right. I'll be there, but don't tell anybody. I don't want any stink started."

On the appointed night I walked slowly to the rendezvous. I glanced furtively behind me to ascertain whether anybody was spying on me. I felt deliciously wicked. When I passed a policeman and he scrutinized me closely, I thought that some occult power had enabled him to pierce my mask of innocence. As I passed an alley, a rawboned nag hitched to an evil-smelling spring wagon emerged from the shadows. Perched on the seat, Lionel Stafford scrupulously avoided recognizing me openly. He had grown a full beard since he had taken to cleaning outhouses and hauling garbage after nightfall. Clop! Clop! The horse was a little stringhalted and when it trotted its bowels grumbled loudly; the wagon's wheels were dished, causing it to lurch crazily. The Bachelor of Arts hunched over his noisome load. He had a hard time keeping Paul in school, but, like my father, Lionel Stafford wanted his son to be a Somebody, not a coal digger nor even a railroad man.

Ed's room held only a bed, a chair and a bureau with a mirror mottled by black spots where the silvering had peeled off the back.

"I'll fetch 'er," Ed told me with a knowing grin. "The landlady's off t' prayer meetin'. Before you let Wilma out, though, you wanta peek out and see that the coast's clear. If the landlady happens t' ketch 'er . . . *good night!*"

I sat nervously on the edge of the bed, staring at the door knob. I heard stealthy footsteps on the stairs. Now and then a board creaked and I winced involuntarily. The knob turned; Wilma's smirking face hove into sight.

Wilma was a full-blown girl of fifteen. Her mouth was a scarlet gash; an apple-shaped dab of rouge decked each cheek and an aura of cheap perfume enshrouded her like a fog. She looked to me like the chippies who used to infest Liam Ryan's saloon and dance naked on the table.

"Hello, kid. Lonesome?" Simpering, she sat down beside me. The sagging mattress threw her heavily against me. She did not draw away again; her eyelids fluttered coquettishly. I was disappointed and ill at ease. "Get busy! Get busy!" I mentally prodded myself. "Ed said she'd go the limit." I thrust a tentative arm about her and pinched her lightly upon the breast. She shrank away coyly and tittered: "You tickle! You're perty brash with the girls, ain't you? Ed told me that's all you think about."

A screen banged below. We both sprang to our feet. "What's that?" Wilma whispered hoarsely, but she didn't seem very much frightened. "Sit still!" I shushed masterfully. "I'll see how the land lays."

I peered out, stole down the stairs and opened the front door. Nobody was in sight, but I re-entered the room in stealthy haste.

"The old lady!" I hissed. "You got to get out of here some way!" I tried to feign agitation.

"Ain't she a little deef?" Wilma giggled in a rather loud tone. She grasped my hand and pulled; her dress creeping up to her thighs. "Lay down and lay low till she goes t' bed. Ain't no use to go off half-cocked."

"Too risky!" I declined hoarsely. "The springs might screek!"

"How they gonna screek if you lay still like I said. Wouldn't you lay still?" she demanded playfully, her foot whirling upward in a kick, permitting breath-taking revelations.

A warm and terrible voluptuousness instantly charged the atmosphere of the room; a boarish rush of blood pounded in my head. A more irresistible compulsion than Wilma's hot hand overwhelmed me. Madness, awful and delightful —the sweet hell of illicit pleasure tasted for the first time.

A half hour later. Why, Wilma's ugly and coarse, I thought resentfully. Her legs are thick and meaty; her body a gross lump. She'll think she's got strings on me. Ed's to blame for this. The landlady *will* be back, sure enough, before long. A shout ascended from the street, shattered in dissonance against the walls, re-echoed portentously like a trumpet blast.

"War! United States Declares War!" the newsboys shrilled, happy over the harvest of nickels they were reaping.

Everybody had been half-expecting it, but the European war had never been anything but a far-off spectacle to me before. It had been a matter of headlines—something big and dramatic, but somehow remote, too.

"War! United States Declares War!"

Wilma sat up and began to arrange her clothes. I hated her then. All of the heroic stories of the papers came back to me: The women of Russia fighting in the trenches, carrying a bottle of cyanide inscribed with the motto, "Death before dishonor!" Joan of Arc appearing to lead the French troops. The Russian Czar, depicted in an English journal, holding his sword aloft and crying to his reluctant troops, "Who follows me for Holy Russia's sake?"

"War! United States Declares War!"

"When we gonna get together again, sweetheart?" Wilma's honeyed voice jangled in my ear. I turned on her savagely. She became the embodiment of lust; the synthesis of evil. Women were fighting and dying in the trenches while this shallow girl lay unmoved by the tremendous news vibrating in the streets.

"Don't you hear what they say?" I shouted. "War! All

94

of us will have to go to fight for our country. Some of us won't come back!"

"You needn't holler that way," she reproved. "The old lady will hear you sure enough if you cut loose like that again."

"Did you say something, Ed?" the landlady called from the foot of the stairs.

"No!" I replied, imitating Ed's voice as best I could. *"War! United States declares War!* Getcha poipa heah! All abawt ut!"

The streets were alive. Waves of people rushed from the houses, buying papers, talking excitedly, cursing the Germans.

Mother was vociferous against the war from the start. People hinted that it was because of her German blood. I told her that people were talking about it, and we might have our house painted yellow.

"You'd better stop talking that way," I warned. "People won't say anything about you when I'm around, but they talk about Mr. Stafford. He's against the war—tries to get fellows not to enlist. He says he'll kill Paul himself before he'll let him go."

"I'd rather see you in Sugar Creek graveyard than in the army."

"Everybody is sore at him about it. People are getting so they won't even let him clean out their backhouses. Say they'll get a 100% American."

I was big for my age. Bigger than some of the fellows who left the shops and came back swaggering in uniforms. These guys cut quite a dash; the girls hung around them and paid no attention to boys still in civilian clothes. The recruiting officers held meetings on the streets, and swell-looking peaches would hug and kiss anybody who'd step up to enlist. Even Wilma was always busy with a soldier boy. It made one feel out of things. I met Bonny Fern in the five and dime store and she nodded curtly. I sensed condemnation in her manner.

Rollie Weems had been meeting Aunt Jessie regularly at our house. "I'm gonna enlist, Larry," he told me one night. There was an argumentative inflection in his voice, and he was looking not at me, but at Aunt Jessie. She was sniffling, and had tears in her eyes the size of hazel nuts.

"You'd better not," she said darkly. A look of secret understanding flashed between them. From her: desperate entreaty. From Rollie: sullen determination.

Rollie and Aunt Jessie were married the day before he left. People were beginning to gossip about her just as they had about Mattie Perkins. They said that Rollie wouldn't go with a girl very long unless he had his way with her.

Ed had tried to enlist twice, but each time he was turned down as underweight. We wandered disconsolately about the streets, reflecting bitterly that we had been born a little too late; we should have been a couple or three years older. Sometimes we met Paul Stafford, but he didn't like to talk about the war. He was as cowardly as he had been in Monkey Nest Camp.

"Oh, I think it'll soon be over," he said nervously. "Papa says it won't last much longer. I hope it doesn't."

Ed spat in disgust. Paul was becoming more and more scholarly looking—more like a sissy. It was said that he was the brightest boy in high school.

"I don't believe in fightin', either," said Ed, "but when them Germans get t' cuttin' off little children's hands, they ain't men—they're animals. You gotta fight snakes like snakes."

Paul hurried on. Mr. Stafford had put him up to his crazy notions, Ed said, and everybody knew that he had bats in his belfry. Then I remembered what Mother thought about the war, but she was only a woman and didn't understand things—she'd have to be excused because of her sex.

"Look!" exclaimed Ed. "A street meeting! Wonder what it is. They don't usually have Liberty Bond meetings this late."

As we drew closer, we saw a slightly bald, stoutish man haranguing a group of railroad workers. Across the street Lionel Stafford had reined up his horse and sat on his garbage wagon listening. When the wind shifted a little, someone on the fringes of the crowd shouted angrily for him to take his stinking load away. He gave no evidence of hearing.

"Comrades! Workers!" cried the speaker as we halted to listen. "The war mongers have been *asking* you to fight for Morgan and Rockefeller, now they're going to *make* you! The selective draft will take care of that. But you can stop it! You *must* stop it! They'll put a gun in your hands and tell you to shoot a German worker, but if you come out on a strike for a living wage, they'll use the same gun to murder you. They can't fight a war without working men for cannon fodder. German workers don't want to fight any more than you do. Stop the troop trains! Don't repair cars and engines to haul American boys to the shambles! Down with Capitalism! Down with war! When you've smashed the head of the capitalistic rattle-snake, there'll be no more war. . . ."

He paused and wiped his round, steaming face. He must be an agitator, I thought, but he didn't look like the newspaper pictures of them. The crowd muttered and shuffled restlessly.

"Kill the yellow sabotagin' rat!" a small man suddenly screamed, springing forward and dealing the unsuspecting speaker a resounding blow which staggered him but did not down him. Anguished incredulity suffused his features as he strove to stanch his blood-spouting nose.

The mob closed in. When the press cleared for a minute, we saw that both the agitator's eyes were closed and he was reeling blindly, groping with his hands. He sank to his knees. A railroader wearing a number twelve shoe spiked with hobs kicked his behind lustily and sent him sprawling on his face. A pool of blood trickled from beneath him. He was still crying, "Comrades! Workers!" more in amazement than in anger.

Lionel Stafford pushed his way through the crowd. Some of the men said later that they could smell him before they saw him, for he wielded his odoriferous shovel and the effluvia of his vocation hovered about him. He fought his way to the side of the prostrate agitator and straddled him, brandishing the shovel. His scraggly beard bristled and defiance glinted in his eyes.

"Go away and leave him alone!" he yelled. "I'll smash in the skull of any man that touches him again. He's telling you the truth. You'll find out. . . ."

Somebody in the rear of the crowd flung a long iron bolt. It caught Stafford on the temple; he crumpled up and slumped down across the agitator.

"Tar and feather the pair of 'em. Ride 'em on a rail! Kill the yella bastards! Get the pro-German sons of bitches!"

"There's old man Stafford's wagon. Full, too. Say, why not roll both of 'em in it? . . ."

The crowd acquiesced with a mounting roar of approval. They lifted the two limp bodies and bore them to the wagon. The agitator's mouth was a black well out of which blood was bubbling. One of his teeth clinked on the sidewalk as they lifted him; one eyeball lay out on his cheek. The men of the mob uttered guttural snarls, and some of them spat and slobbered in an ecstasy of excite-

98

ment and wrath. Eyes and teeth were gleaming brutishly. I turned my head and burst into tears.

"What's the matter, baby?" Ed scoffed. He was not taking any part, but I could see no sympathy in his face. "Ain't they got it comin' to 'em? You can't be chicken-hearted in a war. Them Germans don't have no mercy. When they capture Allied soldiers they torture 'em t' death, cut off their penises and stuff 'em in their mouths."

But I could not stifle the sobs that wracked me. They tore off the canvas masking Stafford's load. "One! Two! Three!" somebody sang merrily as four huskies pitched Stafford in the mass; they lifted the agitator and began swinging and counting. I turned and ran, blinded by tears.

"More fun than a barrel o' monkeys," old man Lyons told me next morning as I joined him on the cindered walk, en route to work.

"Stafford's old lady wouldn't let 'im come in the house. Said he'd stink a dog offen a gut wagon. Made 'im lay out in the shed. The gang daubed his shack with yaller paint and it skeered that kid Paul till he dirtied his britches. Willy, the half-witted one, he had a spasm. The boys quit paintin' when they found out he was havin' an extry hard fit. He like to 've died."

Lionel Stafford lay sick for a week in the shed, the agitator tossing in delirium beside him. Paul went to school no more. Mrs. Stafford packed up their shabby belongings and told Paul to give the spring wagon a good scrubbing. One night Lionel Stafford, A. B., his family and worldly possessions pulled unobtrusively out of town. He was never seen in that section of the country again.

I decided that everything about the war was cruel. Behind the Liberty Loan posters, I saw the agitator's bloody, tragic face. I would retreat into myself, shut out the world, and study—get ready for my chance. When influenza swept through the town, I was untouched. The crazy idea that I was a Man of Destiny set on earth to accomplish some momentous task obsessed me. Mother became ill with the influenza, then Madge. Still I did not break out of myself and my stupendous dream.

Aunt Jessie could not come to nurse Mother and Madge, for her baby had just been born. Rollie had only been gone seven months, and he and Aunt Jessie had been married only a day when he left. Aunt Jessie said that she had fallen down the steps and this had caused the baby to be born early. Yes, sniffed the neighbors, funny it's always the *first* baby that's born ahead of time.

Mother began to regain her strength, but Madge wasted away. I recalled then with regret that I had not seen her much since we came to town. She was always away at school, or I was at work or night school. In Monkey Nest Camp we had been together all the time.

She died. This time it was raining when we set out to Sugar Creek graveyard. Rain chapped our faces, yellow rills trickled down on the casket, and the gravediggers started to filling the grave at once. Petals were beaten from the flowers on the wreaths. The preacher stood beneath an umbrella and now and then a drop filtered through onto his Bible. He shook it off impatiently. There were a lot of raw, yellow mounds in the graveyard. Under most of them lay soldiers who had been stricken with the influenza in the training camps. They were miners' boys who had dodged the cave-ins and the loose rocks.

II

There were not many young fellows left in the railroad shops. Ed tried repeatedly to get in the army, and at last he succeeded. After Ed left for the training camp, I signed up to work on one of the cantonments. Railroad men were being given furloughs because of the shortage of help. The pay was good, and around home the epithet "slacker" was being cast freely at anybody who was old enough or not too old to be in uniform.

The train pulled up and left us standing on a wind-swept field. We had our tool boxes with us and we stood them on end to use for seats until the trucks came for us. The smell of pine, paint, disinfectant and smoke could be whiffed from afar. Thousands were coming and going along the dusty roads to the cantonments.

After the truck had taken us to the cantonment on which we were to work, we stood about all day before we saw the foreman.

"Just wait here, sport. I'll give you a job directly," he told me the next morning as he hurried by. I stood in the same spot or loitered nearby for five days. The time-keeper checked me up each day, but said he had nothing to do with the assignment of work. My time was going on, so I did not worry. I confided my situation to a wizened, toothless man of about fifty who daily tended a burning rubbish pile outside the window in which I reclined.

"Don't fret yer mind," he grinned, his gums flashing so red that his mouth appeared to be filled with blood. "The contractors do this work on the cost-plus basis, a certain per cent fer profit. The more cost, the more profit. Lookut these hyar pine blocks. They're sawed offen bran' new scantlin's. Keeps a man busy sawin' 'em up, another fetchin' 'em in a barrer, me a burnin' 'em. Good lumber ruint. That kind o' work goes on here alla time. Lotsa cost thatta way; lotsa profit."

The breeze whipped acrid pine smoke in his eyes. He stumbled blindly to the opposite side, and sat down placidly upon a nail keg. He lit a cigarette. Then the smoke shifted, and he had to move again.

"Hardest work I have is keepin' outa the smoke," he grumbled. "They say smoke follers beauty." He yawned indolently. "Hooray! Hooray! Hooray fer the cost-plus!" he whooped enthusiastically.

"I ain't too old t' like a little o' that other," he pursued after a bit. "And Gawd knows you oughta be able t' give the gals a treat. I know damned well I was at your age. I know a good place if you wanta go with me t' night. Creoles and Frenchies. Trouble is, the dad-blamed sojers keep the gals busy as a nigger at election most o' the time. Anybody with a unyform allers gits bred fust. N'Awleans Bessie's so patriotic she's got "Fer Soldiers and Sailors Only" tattooed on 'er belly. But shake three bones at 'er and she's rarin' t' go even if you ain't got no unyform."

The whores were not permitted to stray near the cantonments, but they flourished in the town nearby. Their addresses were printed on cards and circulated extensively.

The cribhouses were always jammed. The Madame stood at the foot of the stairs consulting her wrist watch. "Time's up, buddy!" she called inexorably after a customer had been upstairs fifteen minutes. There was always a bunch waiting.

> "The clap is bad,
>   Syph is worse.
>   Watch your step,
>   Safety first!"

warned a latrine poet. Tin signs advertising certain efficacious remedies were tacked on the walls. There were copies of a booklet purporting to be a directory of the Twin Cities, giving names of streets, principal public buildings, parks, monuments and theatres. But the significant part of it was the section dealing with the ravages of venereal diseases. I could imagine myself possessing many of the symptoms gruesomely described by Dr. Bardell (all consultations either in person or by mail held sacredly confidential), the altruistic publisher of the booklet, whose only desire was to save indiscreet young men from a "living hell on earth."

The maggots of agonized uncertainty wriggled inside my skull. But my wizened mentor, the fire tender, had told me that all danger was past nine days after exposure. When that period had gone, I solemnly resolved to lead a chaste and exemplary life thereafter, just as I had oft before. I told the fire tender that for all of me New Orleans Bessie thereafter could abide strictly by the motto inscribed on her belly.

The work on the cantonment was easy. Everybody who knew the business end of a saw was classified as a carpenter, and loafing was not only tolerated, but actually encouraged.

Eventually, the job was finished. I returned to the railroad shops. There were only girls at the night school then, or older people trying to get an education late in life.

I wondered why Ed never wrote to me. One day I encountered Bonny Fern on the street and she planted herself in front of me, smiling brightly. I was astounded; I could feel my face heating.

"I get letters from a friend of yours," she said amiably. "Ed Warden. He got my name from Lester Garber. He sure writes interesting letters."

"Yes, he's a friend of mine, but I never hear from him."

"That's funny! He writes me most every two or three days," she giggled. "What sort of a lookin' fellow is he?"

"Oh, a kind of a . . . a . . . a—well, a pretty good-looking fellow, I suppose," I said lamely. "Did you hear that the Staffords have left town?"

"Yes. We're goin' to, too. Papa's goin' to pull up stakes and move to Detroit. He's got a cousin that's makin' good in an automobile factory there. He's made up his mind that farmin' is too hard work for the money in it."

The war was still like a troubled dream crying into an asleep ear. To me the exploits of the American troops seemed as unreal as the storied feats of King Arthur's knights. One day the locomotive bells began clanging, the whistles blowing. The war was over, we were told. We swarmed into the streets to celebrate. I found myself running beside old man Lyons. He was wheezing badly, but trying to keep up with the others.

"Well, Mr. Lyons, it looks like it's over," I had to shout to make myself heard above the din.

"Yes, Larry. Them yellow-bellied Huns found out they wasn't fighting women and children when the Sammies tore into 'em! LOOK OUT!"

He dragged me out of harm's way as an automobile turned the corner on two wheels, dragging behind it a stuffed effigy of the Kaiser. A German helmet, relic of a Liberty Loan drive, was affixed to the effigy's head, and it clanged as the bounding figure struck the bricks. Pistols were fired incessantly. Jubilant whoops resounded. Joyous patriots belabored the image of the Kaiser with clubs, pelted it with over-ripe fruit, and finally poured kerosene over it and set fire to it. Dignified business men snake danced with grimy laborers about the bonfire. An exuberant drunk, full of beer and seeking relief, expressed his contempt for the Kaiser and all his works by extinguishing the fire in a manner which would have insured his arrest on any other occasion, but nobody had the heart to rebuke him.

That was a great day for Liberty, and the best part of it was to think that all our friends who were still alive— such as Ed Warden and Rollie Weems—would soon be coming back. Aunt Jessie was always grieving because the baby had never set eyes on its daddy. She said Rollie would be tickled because everybody said that the baby was the spitting image of him.

The soldiers came back a few at a time. Rollie Weems was first. He was full of stories about amorous French girls. He said the French government was a whole lot more broadminded than ours, because they furnished whores for their troops, while the Americans had to rustle out and find them the best way they could. It was never difficult, though. He warned me not to say anything to Aunt Jessie about this. He had brought back a package of French postal cards that took my breath away. He couldn't keep them in the house, for he feared that Aunt Jessie might find them and burn them. He hid the pack under a pile of shingles in the coal shed, and when friends came he'd take them out back and give them an eye full.

It was hard to get all the soldiers placed in jobs again, but Ed was lucky enough to get back on at the shops. He would say little about the war. He had been wounded in the leg by a bit of shrapnel and limped slightly. He liked better than anything else to sit in the small park at the end of Main Street, watching the fountain playing and the people walking idly about. When an automobile backfired, he nearly jumped out of his skin. He sat with a cigarette between his fingers till the fire crept up and burned him. Sometimes he would oblige a bunch of small boys and roll up his pants leg to show a livid welt on his calf.

One night as we sat on the bench in the park, a small boy marched up briskly, clicked his heels together, and saluted smartly. He was wearing one of the military uniforms which were still popular.

"When I get big, I'm gonna be a sojer like you," the boy piped. "I'm gonna crost the big, big ocean and kill me some Germans."

Ed seemed to go off his nut. He grabbed the kid and shook him till his cap fell off and he began blubbering with fright.

"Don't talk like that, you little fool," hollered Ed. "That's the way I was when I got into it. The next time they have a war, they can kill me, they can burn out my eyes with red hot stove pokers, but they'll never get me in the goddamned army!"

Then he shook himself as though sloughing off a spell, picked up the boy's cap and set it on his head. He fished in his pockets. As soon as Ed released him, the kid made tracks away from there. Ed sent a dime spinning after him, and the boy, hearing it clink on the pavement, stopped long enough to grab it. Then he retreated at a more leisurely gait toward an ice cream cart.

Ed sat smoking for about an hour, then flipped his snipe into the fountain. It died out with a slight hiss, and only the splashing of the water and Ed breathing a little heavily could be heard for a moment or so. He hadn't been gassed very badly, but sometimes he made a queer noise in his throat like a hen clucking. After a while he stood up and yawned wearily, stretching his arms above his head.

"Believe I'll hit the hay," he said. He started to move off, but halted as something struck his mind.

"I wrote to a girl," he said. "Lives out near Monkey Nest Camp. Name o' Bonny Fern Haskin, and I think she wrote me you know 'er."

"Yes, I know her. They're going to Detroit. I think they've got everything packed now."

"Then I've gotta work fast. She wants me t' come out and see 'er some night. What sort of a looker is she?"

"She's pretty as a picture, I think."

"I'll go out and look 'er over."

"Listen, she's a good girl. Don't try any rough stuff."

"Nobody's gonna force 'er. Ain't she past the age of

consent? Soldiers learn a lot about women, kid. You've got a lot to learn about 'em and their ways. They all fall fer the right kind of blarney."

III

Ed and I had attained sufficient stature, weight and experience to qualify as car repairers. When we started working on a box car, I'd always slide open the door and vault inside to explore. Usually there were newspapers from out of the way places littering the floors, and I squatted down to pore over them, unmindful of Ed's sarcastic banter as he opened our tool boxes and set to work with wrecking bar or hammer. I was intoxicated at the sight of print, just as I had been in Monkey Nest Camp. It was always an adventure to come across a newspaper from some hitherto unheard of town in Maine or Oregon.

Box cars are great travelers. One leaving its home road may not come home for years. They come back powdered with the alkali of Arizona sidings and with desert sand sifted into the crevices in the floors and between the timbers. Sometimes the fierce sun of Mexico has drawn bubbles of resin out of their sides, and often they've been in the north of Canada where snow plows must go ahead to cleave a pathway through the drifts, where the wooden sills of the old timers snap with the cold and the wheels whine and crunch over sleety rails.

The walls of the cars were decorated with signatures of hoboes, messages or greetings from them, obscene verses, and crudely executed lewd drawings. Advertisements for certain hospitable establishments, composed by grateful patrons, were chalked up, such as: "Mable La Rue, 1395 Blank St., Frisco. French and Spanish girls: $2.00. Chinks and Japs: $1.00." The sad-eyed boes, shivering in their pallets of mouldy straw, remembered the soft bodies of the whores and marked a testimonial on the box car walls.

"Oklahoma Dude, New York Bound—1-16-22." was the calling card a fast rambler had penciled, while another admonished whom it might concern: "Mean bull at Mouldon, Kas. Unload outside west yds, take dirt road to east yds."

Almost every car displayed the limerick about the old nigger in Guinea whose casual lover soon discovered that she was dead and obviously had been dead for some time. Another wayfarer complained:

> "Of all the poets beneath the skies,
> A box car poet I most despise."

Another observed caustically:

> "One would think, from the amount of wit,
> That Shakespeare's ghost had been here to sit."

Refrigerator cars often exhaled the fragrance of oranges when we swung open the heavy, insulated doors, but sometimes the cold air that rushed out was rank with the stench of packing house meat or putrid with the odor of decayed vegetables.

Once we found a bum in a freezer car. When Ed opened the door, the bum tumbled right out on him and knocked him flat. He had been leaning against the door, almost unconscious. He was so cold he couldn't talk for a few minutes, but stood batting his eyes and shivering. When his tongue thawed out he started exclaiming: "Holy Jesus! Holy Jesus!" over and over, his voice gradually strengthening. He said he had crawled in the freezer somewhere in Indiana and while he was asleep some shack had evidently banged the door shut on him. He didn't know how long ago it had been, for it was dark all the time in there and he had slept some. He had kicked the toes out of his shoes and clawed his finger nails to the quick but he had been unable to loosen even a splinter from the smooth tongue-and-groove lining. The insulated walls and doors were so thick nobody could hear him. He said he was hungry enough to eat a dead skunk, tail and all. Ed and I gave him fifty cents and he stumbled across the rails to the yard office beanery. Ed said he bet he wouldn't order ice cream.

The railroad company had been very complacent about loafing while the carriers were under federal management. As at the cantonments, the government footed the bills; but things were different now. "Get to work, the war's over," we were constantly reminded.

"Hey, Herman! Why the hell you eatin' me up blood raw all the time?" Ed demanded of our foreman one day after a particularly vitriolic bawling out. "You usta be my pal, I thought, but now you buck an' r'ar like a wild mustang with a cockleburr under his tail. What's chewin' on you?"

Herman plunged two fingers in his package of cigar scraps and withdraw a prodigious gob, holding it poised before his mouth as he answered: "By Jupiter, Ed, I *gotta* make you walk about a little. The Master Mechanic says we gotta put the fear o' God in your souls. He says durin' the war you guys got to thinkin' your sweat didn't stink. You wanted t' work in silk shirts an' kid gloves. You had the company in a tight crack then, but now they gonna have their way a little while."

Herman popped the tobacco in his cheek, his jaws moving rhythmically.

"Not me, I didn't," grumbled Ed. "I was wallerin' in guts an' blood Over There, afeared t' raise my head count o' I might get it blowed off. Then I had a hell of a time gettin' this job back after they got done cheerin' and throwin' confetti at me."

"This is a foreign car you're *supposed* to be workin' on!" barked Herman, chewing angrily. "While you stand there belly-achin', the company's payin' a dollar a day demurrage. So humpty diddy, an' do your jawin' of a night."

The chairman of the union's grievance committee came by.

"It's strike," he reported grimly, squatting down and peering at us as we lay on our backs beneath the car hammering at a draw-bar. "If we took the ten per cent cut, next time it'd be twenty. So tomorrow mornin' we pull the pin."

We had taken a strike ballot the week before. The strike was scheduled to begin at ten-thirty the next morning, but all through the morning rumors flew about that it would be called off and a settlement made. Excitement ran through the shop yards like a prairie grass fire; and men huddled in groups among the box cars. The old-timers were afraid the apprentices didn't take it seriously enough.

"This is no picnic," grey-headed machinists warned, shaking their heads. "I remember in '94 ———"

10:30!

Planers in the wood-mill whined and died, while from his post in the sawdust car the sacker leaped, followed by a shower of fragrant resiny shavings. As a gesture of rebellion, he ripped the dingy "NO SMOKING" sign from its post and trampled it underfoot. The roaring oil forges coughed, paled to purple and black. Soot flakes drifted in the sudden silence. Lathes ceased grinding out the spiral steel chips. Blacksmiths untied their leather aprons, and instead of hanging them in a locker they folded them up neatly to be carried home. Car knockers and coach carpenters came stooped under tool boxes that were leaving the yards for the first time. Care had gone into the tool boxes—a great deal of sighting down poplar boards to find a straight edge, and diligent work with jack-planes and emery paper. Now they were leaving the yards and they never came back.

An air of jubilation hovered around the strikers. An abundance of horse-play and good natured jostling. They ganged around the time keeper who was grabbing time slips thrust at him from all quarters.

"So long, cocky," Rollie Weems said confidently, "we'll see you in about a week." But his voice seemed to challenge an insidious doubt that already reared its head. "We'll be back! We'll be back!" cried the strikers, as though arguing against a silent but resourceful adversary.

The great shops lay helpless, but telegraph wires were humming. The strikers had defied the authority of a Government Arbitration Board. This was treason! In a hundred little towns bugles were blowing assembly and pale clerks and ruddy farmers awkwardly shouldered arms. And idlers passing the time away around the bulletin boards of employment agencies were startled to see shirt-sleeved clerks scribbling furiously:

"MEN WANTED! Railroad workers. No experience required. Machinists, Boilermakers, Electricians, Blacksmiths, Carmen. All Crafts. To replace men striking against decision of U. S. Arbitration Board. No trouble. Ample protection. Highest pay and bonus. High grade commissary and food prepared by Pullman chefs. . . ."

Within a few days an army of strike breakers had been recruited. Professional strike breakers who would take a job at no other time, out of work men desperate enough to clutch the thirty pieces of silver, foreigners not entirely understanding what they were about. The railroads handled them in special coaches, they were shuttled across the continent, regaled with delicacies, liquor and women. Often they were a little bewildered when they climbed down from the coach between serried ranks of guardsmen, and found angry-appearing men regarding them balefully from beyond the yards. The strike breakers marched to the shops in military formation, herded by the militiamen.

"Them's not the ones that'll do the work, Larry," said the veteran, Old Man Lyons, to me. "They're jist fer the show, jist t' scare us into givin' in. They 'low we'll starve out afore long. If we stick with 'em, we're bound t' win."

The pickets worked in shifts, and my first one was the "graveyard" shift from midnight till eight in the morning. Nothing much happened the first few nights. The militiamen paced monotonously up and down the tracks. Sometimes they sang. If any of us moved toward the tracks they called out sharply: "Halt! Who goes there?" A boy and a girl came chattering down the track. A guardsman halted them, ordering them off the railroad right of way.

"Aw, g'wan!" jeered the maiden. "Who are you, anyways? General Pershing? Where did you get that Boy Scout suit and that air rifle? Don't let it go off in your hand. We don't want to carry off a box car."

The pair calmly resumed their way, and the guardsman was baffled. He didn't know what to do. The pickets howled with mirth, and the deserted yards echoed derisively.

Then we lay in the shadow of a coal shed that flanked the road and talked softly. The night deepened and dew wet the trampled weeds and grass under us. Freights rumbled around the curve, spotlighting us in a blinding glare. Then guardsmen and pickets eyed one another curiously, marveling at the barrier between them. Normally, they should have been ganged together in one bunch; talking of baseball, weather, crops, and the favors of women.

A roving bum swung from an oil tank and attempted to merge with the protective coloration of the darkness, but we apprehended him.

"Hey, Buddy, where you going?"

"Jeez! I'm wantin' t' go t' Fort Wayne! Is they another war? I see sojers ever'where. Parsons—Topeka—Kansas City. . . ."

"Naw! A strike! Say, you ain't aiming to work in the railroad shops, are you?"

"Christ, no! I never fell in love with work, and I'm damned sure I ain't cravin' t' take any man's job."

Pickets escorted the wayfarer to the other end of town and shipped him East on the first drag.

About 2 A. M. a farmer boy came plodding down the road. His bare feet stirred up dust clouds. His pinching Sunday shoes were slung across his shoulder, the strings tied together. He shied skittishly when we spoke to him, but he declared positively:

"Ya dang right I come t' git a job in them shops. I seen the ads and the proposition looks good t' me. Criminentlies, I'm tard o' ol' farm work—this kin an' cain't system."

"Kin and cain't?"

"Yeh! Go t' work as soon's y' kin an' work till y' cain't. Stand back, stranger; my mind's done made up!"

He made only a few steps toward the tracks before we bore him to the ground. He kicked lustily and squalled bloody murder, while the militiamen dashed up and down the track excitedly. So far, their orders were merely to stay on railroad property and to disregard everything else. The rube edged stubbornly toward sanctuary, but we swarmed around him and swept him back.

"Looka here, friend," counselled Rollie Weems, "if you wanta dodge trouble, jist ankle back the way you come."

His spirit crushed, the seeker struck a smart trot down the highway, hastened by a hail of cinders.

"We might as well be home poundin' our ears, Larry, for all the good we're doin'," Ed said cynically, rolling onto his back and staring at the stars. "It's all a snide, kid. Like the war. They had us all steamed up about that, too. Them shops is gonna run without us. They hold the loaded dice—the marked cards. We'll never wear 'em out in God's world."

"You talk like a crêpe-hanger a'ready," broke in Rollie Weems, darkly. "If we was all like you the strike would be lost, sure enough."

"My father was a union man. The coal miners won strikes lots of times," I retorted warmly. Ed's weary cynicism about everything nettled me.

"Maybe so! Maybe so!" conceded Ed, scratching at grass chiggers.

I had never before realized how stubborn was the faith of Rollie Weems in the union. A federal injunction forbade meetings of all kinds. The picket lines were repeatedly shattered by the guardsmen; and soon almost all the strike leaders were exiled or arrested. The shops began to fill with men really anxious to work. The great wheels revolved slowly at first, but with steadily increasing tempo and smoother rhythm. Some of the union men who were not blacklisted because of strike activities stealthily bargained for their old jobs. Landlords were getting insistent, grocers were petulant, strike funds dwindled and disappeared. There was talk of treachery and misappropriation of the funds by union leaders. Neither Rollie nor I would believe these accusations, but Ed did. His aspersions about the strike leaders enraged us.

The strike breakers, at first housed in barracks on the railroad premises, ventured cautiously about the town.

Their nonchalance grew. They imported families from far and near, and they were protected by every device of law. To speak disrespectfully to or of a strike breaker was to invite a sentence of six months or more.

Rollie was talking to a bum who had just been kicked off a Red Ball.

"Aw, yer only wastin' yer time, buddy," carped the bo. "Youse fellers 'll be damned glad t' git yer jobs back, if ya can. Git wise t' yaself! Yer head union men has sold ya out. Ain't no use fightin', pal, ain't no use fightin' the moneyed man. He can hire yer brother or yer father to jab a bayonet in yer rump. He can buy off yer strike leaders, and that's what's happened now. Stay in with him, that's all, an' get all you can. Stay in with him. It pays in the long run."

Rollie seized the bo and shook him till his shirt pulled out of his pants and fluttered like a flag.

"God damn your soul! Don't tell *me* I'll break a strike! Don't try t' tell me that, you bastard!"

"God A'mighty, cull," gasped the bum. "Take it easy, fer cripes sakes! I didn't say *you* would! They's workers in them shops now. I jist said *workers* would. Laborin' man ag'in laborin' man. They know how t' keep 'em divided, that's all."

Rollie turned the bum loose, but he never would believe the strike was lost, or that the strike leaders were not doing their best.

"Wait till the snow flies," he said when wild geese, bearing north, honked overhead. "They gotta give in! They won't be able to fire them moguls so's they'll pull a heavy drag in cold weather with leaky boilers and rusty flues. They can't run cars with flat wheels and burnt-out journal boxes when the rails is covered with sleet and slick as hell. They *got* to give in! Ain't they gotta give in, Larry?"

He was sitting in our kitchen, and as he spoke he

pounded the table with his fist. Rollie's curly hair was greying a little, and lines like spider webs radiated from the corners of his eyes.

"Sure," I agreed, "they got to give in finally. They're just bull-headed, I guess." But I was feeling doubtful about it. The strikers were leaving town; the scabs becoming bolder.

"Ed went to Detroit along with Ben Haskin and his family," I remarked.

"He *can* go," Rollie said darkly. "He's single. But a man with a wife and a mess o' younguns can't traipse off so easy. Larry, lad, don't never marry, you hear me? A single man has got a chancet. When I was single nobody never said 'boo' t' me but what I'd up and blow the job." Then he began singing in what he intended to be a humorous voice:

"When I was single, O then, O then,
When I was single, O then,
When I was single, my money did jingle;
I wish I was single again, again,
And I wish I was single again."

"I'm going to tell Aunt Jessie that," I warned lightly.

"Go ahead," he said, gloom clouding his face once more. "Poor woman, she can't help it, I guess, but it sure has got t' be a habit for her to have younguns. I look fer 'em t' start comin' in litters next. Listen, if you do happen t' git married—though you'd best take a fool's advice and not—and your wife can't have any younguns, jist borry my old britches and hang on the foot o' the bed. First crack out o' the box, you'll get twins. Maybe it's jist me. I'm too much of a man. Look at Mattie Perkins. . . ."

"I thought you told me that was a lie about Mattie Perkins."

"So I did! So I did! Well, no harm in ownin' up to it

now. She *was* knocked up, all right, but I took 'er to the old Injun yarb doctor clost to Hell's Tater Patch, where all them Irish woodcutters live. He fixed 'er up. Damn my eyes, I'd certainly give a man a purty that would tell me what kind o' yarbs that Injun used! He's dead and gone now."

When blizzards swept down from the North, Rollie came ploughing through the drifts to our house, his eyes shining. "It won't be long now!" he cried. But the trains kept rolling.

Rumors drifted in from the East. Separate agreements were being signed on any possible terms. The strikers talked bitterly of a sell-out by the union officials, who were urging the members of their organizations to return to work—if they could get back.

"HEGIRA OF THE SHOPMEN CONTINUES" headlined the local newspaper. Since then I have seen my former comrades in many places. One trekked to Oklahoma and became a respectable realtor and Rotarian, bleating loudly the virtues of "Service." One killed a man in a harvest field quarrel out Kansas way and sat on the hot chair and sizzled for his sins. Another was in the crowd when Wild Bill Shatov drove the last spike in the Turksib and cheers roared from a thousand bronzed throats and bands were blaring "The Internationale." Rounding windy corners in distant cities, I have collided with shopmen, grasped their hands, crying: "Well! Well!" striving to capture in a net of words the memories resurrected by the sight of a well-remembered face.

Rollie got to sitting on his front porch because the picket line was abandoned and he couldn't stir out of the yard without bumping into a scab. They wouldn't avert their eyes as they had at first, but faced him squarely. Then his hands itched to be at their throats, and virulent words squirted through his teeth, no matter how tight he clenched them. Rollie could whittle a wooden chain out of a single pine board, and he must have carved a hundred for his kids. The world of a man who's always worked with his hands brittles to ash after weeks of idleness extend into months and most of his friends are gone, God knows where, and he sits staring at the softened callouses on his palms.

Rollie's oldest girl had started to school in the Fall. She came home crying.

"I got to set with a scaly," she blubbered. "I told teacher you said I mustn't, but she said it didn't make no difference. Most of the kids in our room is scalies now."

"Like hell you do!" shouted Rollie. "No kid o' mine will set with a scab's youngun."

So he took her out of school. He worked on the highways, but often he glanced up from his shoveling to see a scab rolling by in a sleek automobile and regarding him with either pity or contempt. He hurled his shovel through the windshield of a scab's car, and spent ten days in jail for it. He hired out to a plumber, but quit when they sent him to repair a toilet bowl that wouldn't flush and he found out that a scab lived in that house. A scab moved in next door, and Rollie dared not protest because his own rent was six months in arrears. The children next door peered wistfully over the line fence, and Rollie caught them talking to his youngsters several times.

(You remember how the rats inundated Hamelin in that old tale—how they worked in every garbage pail like squirming maggots. Waving forests of cold, naked tails. Not a cheese in that town without the scars of sharp teeth, not a corner but projected a whiskered blue nose. Night-floors rang with scratching, scurrying claws; and, rising asweat with terror, you felt hairy bodies writhing under your bare feet. Close your eyes to blot them out, and— dear Christ!—pale, pink eyes gimleted through your lids.

The city stank with them, and—go where you would—there was no escape and they closed you in on every hand.)

"I hate to see you creditin' them snakes, Barney," Rollie said to his old friend, the butcher.

"Well, Rollie, I got t' live same's anybody else. The packin' houses expect their money ever' Saturday regular. Them guys pay me regular and they buy heavy—fancy cuts, too. Though I won't say I love 'em, their coin does help me to carry along a few of my old pals that's hard up at present."

This crowning ignominy was a knockout blow. So the scabs were feeding him! His own bill with Barney was so large he felt ashamed to ask for soup bones and dry salt belly—the very cheapest meat in stock. In spite of most rigid economy the sums mounted and unpaid slips made an unsightly protuberance in Barney's credit file. They bulked ominously when Barney flipped the steel leaves.

It didn't help any when the kids next door tantalized his own with ice cream cones. "Why don't your daddy ever buy you none?" they inquired with assumed innocence and hidden malice. His wife's stifled sobbing thundered in his ears like an accusation of guilt—a sense of utter failure weighted him down.

Rollie told me all of this one evening. He sat staring at his feet for several moments. Then he burst out:

"Larry, I want t' talk to you, man t' man. I want you t' help me. You know how I got this strike in my bean. Jesus, I gotta get my hands on somethin' solid 'r I'll go plumb cuckoo. I can't fight a box car 'r tear up a rail, 'r dynamite a bridge. Now I got a line on the cornfield canary that took my job on the wheel press. He still lives in the country and he rides a hoss t' work. He works till after dark every night, and he's gotta get off his hoss t' open a gap on the four mile lane. I'm gonna meet him out

there and tangle horns with him. I want you t' go along—
jist fer company. I don't want you t' raise a finger—jist
set in the Ford."

"I don't like your idea, Rollie," I demurred. "You know
what the law says about rough stuff. . . . The injunction. . . ."

"I know! I know! But I'm not gonna hurt him serious.
Jist fist and skull and the best man win. It's dark as pitch
out there, and he can't tell us from Adam's off ox. I ain't
asked you fer a favor in a long time. They's mighty few
in this burg I *could* ask a favor. Say! Will you go?"

"Most likely he packs a gun," I objected uneasily.

"Naw! They did at first but they quit all that long
ago."

"Yes!" I answered at length, "yes, I'll go with you just
to keep you out of trouble if I can."

IV

Frogs chorused in a bullrush swamp beside the four mile
lane, and a whip-poor-will whistled weirdly. Rollie and I
sat in the Ford and waited. Rollie was reminiscing aloud;
he was in the round house again. Engines, breathing regularly, pant for the rails of the main line. Flanges of engine
wheels clang like gongs as the men whirl them out of the
press and send them spinning. A finger caught between
two flanges would be nipped off sharply, and sometimes
the whole hand may go. Rollie fondled a stub on his own
hand. Workers hurry here and there with their smoky
torches, the smoke ascending to blackened rafters where
chittering sparrows nest and foul everything beneath.

"I jist got t' thinkin' of the ol' boys and the ol' times,
Larry," Rollie mused, more to himself and to the darkness
than to me. "They're mostly all gone—scattered to the
four corners of the earth—and they'll never be rounded

up ag'in till Gabriel blows his horn and the graves give up their dead. I don't make new friends so fast. If I could git outa here like Ed, maybe I could git a fresh holt. But there's Jessie and the kids. Workin' man ain't got no use with a wife, then when he needs to, he c'n pull up stakes and tear out som'eres."

I secretly thought that I would not be a working man long. I had finished the course at the night school and had started on a correspondence course. But I didn't want to humiliate Rollie and remind him of his own failure by mentioning this.

"You still got a chancet," Rollie said, as though divining my thoughts. "You got an education. But you better be sure that you're on Easy Street before you tie up with 'ary wife, lad. You gotta get outa this burg. Go to Detroit where Ed is. Betcha he's sparkin' that Haskin gal, Bonny Fern, right now. She's got so she's got a butt on her like a Clydesdale mare—a shape like you write home about. Now in my younger days. . . ."

Just then the scab rode up quietly and dismounted before we knew he was there. His horse blew through its nostrils and stamped. The noise disturbed Rollie's homily, and he jumped out of the car.

"Hey!" he called. "I want a word with you."

"What do you want? Money? You're S. O. L. if you do," said the scab. His voice sounded unsteady and troubled.

"It's not money I want, but satisfaction," announced Rollie, coming closer, stumbling a little over the uneven ground. "You gotta fight me."

"Why should I fight you? I don't even know who you are!" The man was genuinely astonished.

"You're a scab, that's why! My kids is barefoot and ragged, and my wife is ashamed t' go down town because the likes of you can deck yer women out in silks and satins. Put up yer dukes, scaly!"

"O come off! It's been a year since the strike. The shops are running full blast now and the strike is over. Your head union men say so. They're talking of organizing us into the union."

"As long as I live the strike is never over!" shouted Rollie. "Put up yer dukes!" He was near enough to make a pass at the man. The blow landed and barbed wire creaked as the scab staggered against it.

"Come on, I got plenty more," invited Rollie, dancing and shadow boxing.

I was climbing out of the car when I heard four shots in rapid succession and a bullet zinged past me. Another shattered the windshield. By the time I reached the gap the scab had climbed on his horse and made off. The hoofbeats grew faint.

"Did he get you, Rollie? I was afraid of this. . . . I told you. . . ."

"Nix! A bum shot!" answered Rollie, but in a queer strained voice. We walked back to the car and Rollie climbed in.

"Get my hat, will you, Larry?" he said thickly, spitting and holding his hand over his face. "I feel tuckered out."

While I was groping over the ground, Rollie kicked the starter and the Ford moved up the road.

"Hey, where you going? Why are you leaving me?" I yelled.

I overtook the car before Rollie had up much speed and landed on the running board. Rollie let go of the wheel with his right hand and caught me a jab in the jaw. As I turned loose the dashlight illumined Rollie's face for an instant. Blood was dribbling from his chin and gushing from his nose.

"Hightail it away from here, you fool!" gurgled Rollie.

"Git home and never tell anybody you seen me t'night. If you do, I'll ha'nt you—I'll git even with you even if I have to do it through a weejee board!"

I followed the car till my breath gave out and a stitch in my side doubled me up on the ground. The ruby tail light faded down the road, leaving me alone with the bull-frogs and the whip-poor-wills. I ran to town as fast as I could, and before the Alamo Pool Hall I saw the shattered Ford, but Rollie was gone. Some of the excited pool room loafers re-created the scene for me.

The boys in the Alamo heard a crash and a street light burst through the window, knocking a Granger Twist display galley-west. Splintered glass showered over the youth eagerly scanning the baseball scores chalked on a black-board. Fragments plinked in the sticky pink depths of a yum-yum sundae being consumed by a pimpled pool player at the soda fountain.

"Well, fer cryin' out loud!" he exploded indignantly. He strode outside and stood leaning on his cue, blinking at the Ford invading the sidewalk. At the base of the broken-off post, severed wires had shorted and were spitting blue. Rollie lay crumpled under the steering wheel. A crowd was gathering.

"Stewed to the gills!" said the pool player. "Honest to Christ, with drivers lappin' up this canned heat, and Jamaica ginger, and ill-natured alcohol, a man ain't safe nowheres, not even in bed with his woman."

He returned to his yum-yum, grumbling and pondering over the iniquities of the world.

It was another who came from the other direction that saw the crimson stain flooding the running board and overflowing to the sidewalk. A man drilled twice through the lungs bleeds like a stuck hog.

The strike had finally ended.

I walked past the house several times before I turned in at the gate to tell Aunt Jessie. She padded to the door and let me in sleepily. When I looked at her and remembered how pretty she was in Monkey Nest Camp, I couldn't hold back the tears. Her chestnut hair was stringy and her stomach hung down in a pouch beneath her kimono. One heavy breast protruded, and it was webbed with blue veins. In the bedroom the children started whimpering. Fully aroused now, Aunt Jessie ran to my side and grasped me by the shoulders. Realization and anguish dawned simultaneously on her face.

Rollie had had some insurance as a member of the union, but when I wrote to headquarters, I was informed that since his dues had not been kept up, the insurance was no longer in force. Rollie had paid dues for years; his family was destitute. I reminded the District President of the union of this in a letter which was never answered.

Then I resolved to go to the city myself and to see about it. While I was there, I'd look for a job. Mother had to go back to washing, and Aunt Jessie was helping her. Mother was not as young as she'd been in Monkey Nest Camp.

I waited in the cool ante-room of the District President's office for two days. The first day his secretary told me he was playing golf with a railway Master Mechanic. The second day he rushed by me and entered a conference with several well-dressed gentlemen who had sauntered in and walked boldly into the private office. When the conference was over, the secretary told me that office hours were over for that day, but I could come back the next day.

The morning of the third day I was admitted to the private office. The District President sat sternly behind a vast expanse of mahogany desk. I recalled the stories I had heard during the strike—stories of this official's gallivanting around with railroad executives while union men were being beaten and shot on the picket line.

The District President's cool, slightly contemptuous manner beat back the things I had come to say. I stammered out a few sentences; he frigidly reminded me that non-payment of dues invalidated the insurance. There was nothing he could do. He was sorry, but he had a great deal of work to do.

The Union to me had meant fighting on the picket line, hating scabs, tightening one's belt and starving if need be. I could not transform this suave gentleman to the electric atmosphere of strike meetings and picket lines. I couldn't imagine him in the crowd when the militiamen rushed us with drawn bayonets and drove us from the observation posts we had established near the right of way.

I walked quietly from the building, but anger was surging within.

The din of the streets bewildered me and I wandered about aimlessly for a bit. I wanted to get a job, but didn't know how to go about it to get one. I remembered Mother and Aunt Jessie bobbing over the wash tub.

"City and Country Jobs. Stanowski's American Employment Agency" read a sign outside a low, dingy building about which a gang of rough looking men clustered.

A vulpine featured clerk came out and scribbled:

"5 men for steel mill. Must be husky."

"That's me!" I said, unconsciously speaking aloud.

"That's a job for a horse. Besides, they ain't no union," spoke up a grizzled veteran beside me.

"I don't care," I retorted, starting inside.

"You'll get a bellyfull of it," called the old timer, moving down the street.

125

V

When I reached the steel mill the next morning, a motley assembly was waiting for the employment office to open. Two Danish lumberjacks with gaudy mackinaws, a sprinkling of such nondescripts as are always hanging about such places, half fearful and half hopeful that they'll be hired. But the one I noticed closely was a red-faced old fellow who was particularly conspicuous. You wouldn't be likely to remember him long if you saw him on a front porch smoking in the twilight or reading a newspaper by lamplight, but sitting on the stiff scarred benches of the employment office, he seemed incongruous and ludicrous. There are thousands—maybe millions—like him, but they never fail to excite mirth, and pity, too. Verifying Emerson's axiom that an object removed from its habitual environment at once becomes humorous, he was a comical figure. Deliberate and labored optimism sat upon his rotund countenance, but other emotions broke through. He was pretty old to be in such a place; a steel mill is not an old folk's home. He simulated savoir faire by drumming on the bench with short, hairy fingers tipped by broken and worn nails.

Presently a swarthy Sicilian padded out of the janitor's closet. His professional interest centered upon the square wooden boxes filled with sawdust; he seemed on the point of bursting into tears. The two lumberjacks sprawled upon the bench, spraying the cuspidors with commingled snus and tobacco juice. Theirs was the abandon of the logging camp, and they were not a whit impressed by the poignant reproach in the janitor's eyes. The heir of the Romans retreated into his den and reappeared with a handful of Application for Employment blanks, one of which he handed to each sitter, at the same time uttering, "Fill out," with such mechanical precision that one felt he had practiced diligently upon the phrase, probably the only English he found essential.

To some of the applicants, filling the blank was a more formidable task than locating the Holy Grail or cleansing the Augean Stables. Knees arose as writing desks and subdued requests for the loan of a pencil were heard. A reverent hush fell upon the gathering. Even the devil-may-care lumberjacks set to work with furrowed brows, yearning for the comparatively easy job of breaking a log jam or felling a forest giant.

"Maybe you could help me a little," I heard a hesitant voice at my elbow. It was the old fellow. Spectacles rode his nose and the sweat of concentration coursed down his cheeks—bedewed his bald head. He had dragged forth from beneath the bench a papier maché suit case, battered and gnawed at the corners as though rats had chewed it. Traveling by freight does that, for when boarding the train you have to throw your luggage any place you can. No obliging porter assists you; and when the bulls have chased you out of the yard limits, the drag may be going like a bat out of hell by the time it reaches the place you have to nag it.

Inside the suitcase, I could see some articles of clothing, a packet of assorted needles, a Bible, an open spectacle case surmounting the heap. After NAME he had filled in: "Robert Lee Grady." A few other spaces were occupied, such as DATE OF BIRTH: "October 18, 1870," and PLACE OF BIRTH: "Prairie Home, Ohio."

"It says here: 'Give complete details of all former positions, date of and reasons for leaving same.' That would take a dozen cards the size o' this, 'cause I ca'late I had two hundred jobs all told, and sence the War it's kep' me jumpin' from here to yander and back ag'in t' keep in one. Reckon I'm a jack of all trades and master of none."

"Oh, put anything," broke in a beady-eyed man standing near. "It doesn't matter. No one will pay any attention to it, anyway. Just put down you're a retired pretzel bender or your trade is plain and fancy hemstitching," he counselled flippantly. It was apparent that Grady's concern seemed ridiculous to this hardened job seeker.

"But I never *did* do anything like that," Grady objected seriously. "Reckon *them's* two jobs I never did have."

By that time the janitor had opened the inner office. We filed in and stood hopefully before the employment manager, who sat behind his desk and fondly believed that he was psycho-analyzing us through and through. We endeavored to express, as individual histrionic talents might allow, supplication, an almost unrestrainable eagerness to have at some heavy stint, a cheerful and trusting air, and withal a soupçon of humility to make the mixture slab and good. Our scrutinizer beetled his brows and read us like an open tabloid. Suddenly he pointed at a pleasantly simpering Swede, who—sensing disaster—started violently. His ruddy complexion deepened to scarlet as he shifted uneasily from foot to foot, pushing the snus higher under his pursed upper lip.

"You! Your name is Olaf Peterson, isn't it? Don't lie to me! And when you were laid off last October you walked off in the middle of the afternoon when you had already drawn your check with full pay for the day. Also, you said 'To hell with the job.' You can't expect to work *here* any more. Thought you'd slip up on me, eh? Thought I'd forget that mug!"

"Listen, boss . . . my brudder . . . looks yust like me . . ." protested the Swede feebly, casting about for some plausible explanation, but without hope. It was no use; the inquisitor dismissed him with a wave of the hand and turned to Grady, who was still scribbling furiously in an attempt to get his application properly filled out.

"How old a man are you, dad?"

128

"Thirty-nine!"

"Thirty-nine! Come! Come! You were thirty-nine when Sullivan fought Jake Kilrain. I want your age, dad, not your chest measure. Where's your hair gone at thirty-nine?"

"I wore it off on the bedstead," countered Grady, with a weak attempt at jocosity. This was a reply he had picked up somewhere; and, finding it a good one with which to jolly hiring bosses, pulled it off frequently.

"Ha, a joker, are you? Your head looks like a skating rink for flies!" The employment manager's face split with a grin. This was a cue for the other job seekers to break forth into discreet guffawing, none too ostentatiously, however.

"Honest to goodness!" implored Grady, longing for Clarence Darrow's tongue. "I had the scarlet fever and my hair fell out in big handsful. But I'm stout as a bull, a better man than two-thirds of these young high school squirts that ain't neither willing or able t' do a day's work. A man at my age is jist in the prime of life."

"Nothing today, dad. I'm sorry, but this work is dangerous. A man has to be spry, and it takes a young man to stand the gaff."

But as Grady's painfully erect shoulders wilted like a pricked balloon, the employment manager seemed to reconsider. The milk of human kindness was softening the iron resolution of this man of steel.

"Wait! I think I *will* use you some place, after all. Not so easy for a man of your age to get a job these days, I guess. Is it, dad?"

"You bet it's not so easy! Much obliged t' you, sir, and you won't never be sorry fer yer kindness. I'm gonna make you a hand you won't need t' be ashamed of."

Then the momentary weakness crystallized into customary efficiency. Once more the masterful man of business faced us; now the gossamer cobwebs of whimsy stiffened into realistic steel cables. He selected several more applicants with strict regard for utility, docility, and—least important—intelligence. Then he shooed the chaff from the Presence.

A grim office boy, resolutely champing gum as though it were an unavoidable part of his daily routine, conducted us through the plant, dropping off a man here and there.

"This is Solinsky," he announced, handing the gang foreman a slip. "Foller me, please, men."

Then we pursued our devious way among the girders and angle irons lying on trestles and rollers. A huge overhead crane cruised back and forth. It extended the full width of the shop, and dangled immense beams and entire bridge spans. At its approach, some watcher shouted "Headache!" whereupon everybody bowed down like pious Moslems genuflecting toward Mecca. At intervals the crane travelled to the extreme end of the building, which opened up as two great doors. Mill hands gathered around these massive portals and pushed like medieval serfs throwing wide the gates of a feudal castle. The crane proceeded outside and deposited its burden upon a railroad flat car.

Grady trotted along in the rear of the party, continually stumbling over some obstacle, his eyes glued apprehensively aloft. He did not rely upon the strident Klaxon to warn him, nor yet the cry of "Headache!"

"He had me in a tight jam about that age business," Grady confided to me as I fell a few paces behind, "but a little girl in a labor agency in Pontiac, Michigan, give me a tip about that.

"'Listen, dad,' she says, 'get wise on that age deal. Never be a day over thirty-nine. You can get by at that.' So that's what I've been tryin' t' do, but I don't think nobody believes me. Ol' Marster been good t' me, that's all, and I'm lucky t' be here."

"Dis is Grady," sang out the office boy, stopping before a gang of men bolting together a bridge span. "Foller me, please, men!"

The gang foreman handed Grady a wrench. "Get on to tightening them nuts, dad," he ordered.

As we moved away I heard the foreman disgustedly: "Playin' hookey from the old folk's home. Plenty of young men cryin' to be hired, and I have to draw him!"

Grady fumbled awkwardly with the wrench. In attempting to screw on a nut he crossed the threads and could move it neither on nor off. By this time he was thoroughly flustered. He dropped his wrench; and, stooping to retrieve it, balanced himself by grasping the span. It was freshly painted a vivid red, and when he let go, his hand appeared to be filled with blood. The foreman, who had been regarding him with mingled despair and contempt, now bellowed: "Hey, you! Keep ya hands offen the fresh paint, will ya?"

I paused to watch a moment. Grady, sweat streaming down his face and already damping his chest and underarm, wiped his forehead and set a bloody mark across his brow. The paint stung his eyes. He swiped his hands across the seat of his pants as the crane came hurtling a ten-ton beam.

"Look out, dad! Headache!" yelled the foreman. The beam end grazed Grady as he ducked just in time. The top of his head looked like an ostrich egg dropped in a sparrow's nest.

I was the last to be placed. The office boy led me out of the building into blinding sunlight. As he stopped to light a cigarette, forbidden on the inside, a terrific shrill screaming intruded upon my ear drums, a piercing racket that ascended to the thin, high edge of sound. The office boy, puffing like a locomotive, zig-zagged among piles of channels and girders and plunged into a small corrugated tin building. I followed and beheld the steel saw. A fellow with cotton-stuffed ears clung to a wheel like that of a ship and directed the whirling saw against a twelve-inch channel, sitting before it on a bench equipped with rollers. An aureole of sparks attended the saw's revolutions, while a smiling Italian, protected from the searing chips by a wooden shield, stood before the saw carriage, jockeying the channel along with a pinch bar, halting it for sawing at certain marked lengths.

My conductor tapped the saw's steersman upon the shoulder, nodded at me, hung my slip on a nail, and headed for the office. When the channel was finally reduced to shorter lengths, the saw was shut off. Silence weighed oppressively.

The man at the saw's wheel, whose name was Romeo, was really the foreman, I discovered.

"No goddam Bohunk, anyway," he observed with evident satisfaction. "Boy, you picked yourself a mankiller for a job. Average life of a steel saw man is six months. If the noise don't drive you goofy, a pile of steel'll topple over on you, or a dumb crane man lower a girder across your neck."

This greeting was not exactly encouraging, but I was not surprised or disturbed. I had learned at the railroad shops that to fill a new man with misgiving is considered great sport. It is the same impulse that impels schoolboys to persecute a newcomer. The saw, in repose, was nothing more than a flat circular disk, hacked by a cold chisel on the sawing edge.

"Tomorrow I queet," the Italian confided. "Deesa job no gude sonama beech. No gude *here*!" He pointed to his cotton-filled ears. "I ketchem dandy job wid Guiseppe Fiorella. Wait! I show you." He vanished behind the saw.

"You take 'er now," invited Romeo. "All you got to do is bear down hard on the wheel." I grasped the wheel as he threw the switch and the low whining increased in volume. The Italian reappeared bearing a thermos bottle which he uncorked and handed to me. "Guiseppe's!" he said flashing his big white teeth.

I saluted the donor with a grandiloquent flourish and repeated the toast usually considered appropriate for such occasions:

> "First to my lips,
> Then to my gums.
> Look out, guts,
> Here she comes."

The fiery liquor sent me reeling against the wall.

"Knocked the filling out of my teeth," I gurgled, but proved I was game by taking another snort.

"What a man! What a man!" exclaimed Romeo in feigned admiration.

When the saw struck its mark a tremor assailed me, and I winced as the sharp, grating noise probed at the nerves in my teeth. Romeo wagged his head sympathetically and withdrew to cool off. Exhilarated by Guiseppe's hooch, I piloted the saw with superfluous squinting at the mark and widely flourishing elbows. I boasted to the Italian that I could run the saw better than the man who made it. He grinned like an amiable gargoyle, not hearing. The words never seemed to leave my lips; the saw's din pushed them back down my throat. When the last length was sawed and the saw stopped, I called loudly for more steel.

Romeo had returned and was sitting on an empty rivet keg, writing in a time book he had pulled from his hip pocket.

"Where did you work last, buddy?" he asked.

"On the railroad. I've been out on strike."

"Oh, you mean you *quit* your job. That's what it

amounts to. All a union's good for is to graft off of workin' stiffs."

I said nothing. I was thinking of the District President ensconced behind his shiny desk, but I also remembered the strikes in Monkey Nest Camp.

"We got a different kind of union here, a company union," pursued Romeo. "There's insurance if you get hurt or if you get killed. If you feel like you've been done wrong, there's a grievance committee—old man Baxter—that'll go and straighten it out with the super."

"Tie that bull outside! That's the kind of stuff that makes the grass grow green," broke in a tousled, impudent looking giant, thrusting his head in the door.

"Pull your freight out of here, bolshevik!" said Romeo angrily. "Your job ain't none too safe, Lipkin! They're gettin' tired of your gripin'. If you listen to that belly-acher, kid, you'll be in grief up to your neck all the time."

"Baxter!" snorted the giant derisively. "He jumps like a cat shot in the tail with a bootjack every time the super looks cross-eyed at him. Don't be ashamed of strikin', lad. It's better to strike and lose like a man than to kiss the bosses' fat rumps to hold a job."

Just then an inside foreman came in, leading Grady by the hand. A blood-stained bandage encircled his head and he staggered woozily.

"Set down on a keg, dad, and try to pull yaself to-gether," said the foreman. Then he beckoned Romeo out-side.

"Come along," said Romeo to me, "we got to measure some stuff."

"For the love of Christ, Romeo," began the foreman, out of Grady's hearing. "Can't you use that old stiff out in the yard here? He just got knocked flatter 'n a pan-cake by the crane. Can't hear none too good, but that won't matter out here. He'll get killed inside before he works a day."

"A man needs to be pretty active out here, too, pilin' steel and all," remonstrated Romeo. "Remember what happened to old Joe Vash."

But when Romeo learned it was either the yard or the gate for Grady, he relented.

"O. K.! O. K.! I'll give him a whirl at it, but I know damned well he'll be a nuisance. Pasquale will be quittin' tomorrow. Whenever I see an old gent like that buckin' up against it I think of my own old man."

"Do you know a cheap boarding place?" I asked Romeo. I had slept in a 50-cent hotel the night before.

"No, I don't," he said, absent-mindedly, jotting down figures in his note-book. "Oh, yes, I do!" he continued. "There's a fellow named Nat Moore, lives over in the Low Ground and works at the rubber heel plant. He used to work here, but got let out. I seen him on the street the other day and he said that he wanted a boarder if I knew of any of the steel men that wanted a place to stay."

The Low Ground was a marshy plot which originally had been dubbed Sunset Meadows. The magnificent public school of the promotion folders had dwindled to a one-room brick structure, and the luxurious villas, fair with velvet lawns and clipped hedges, were actually displaced by the austere fruit of mine and factory—row on row of unpainted hovels, cast in identical and eye-outraging molds.

"Nat Moore? Yeh, he lives close t' here, neighbor, but I'll hafta go along and *show* ya the place," replied a citizen of whom I inquired the way. "These here danged houses are as like as two peas in the same pod. They say one feller come home the other night, went in the wrong house, got in bed with another man's wife, thinkin' he was at home with his own wife. At least that's what he said when the woman's husband cotched him. Got by with it, too." He paused before one of the cottages. "This is the place," he said, and moved away.

"Just a minute! Just a minute!" I heard a feminine voice cry impatiently as I knocked. I could hear scurrying around within, the moving about of furniture. Then a faded but still rather pretty woman opened the door. She was dressed in a kimono and seemed to have trouble keeping it pulled together in front.

"I was told you wanted a boarder," I stammered. Her intense scrutiny disconcerted me.

"We had been thinkin' of it," she replied. "Won't you step inside?"

The room was a combined bed room and sitting room. The chairs were arranged decorously and a pile of cheap magazines rested on the library table. She had evidently been scurrying about to straighten up the room. Draped on the foot of the bed was a pair of pink rayon step-ins.

"Please excuse the mess this room is in," she said, walking slowly over and picking up the step-ins. She folded them neatly and deposited them in a bureau drawer. I fidgeted inwardly.

"Mr. Moore ain't in," she continued, smiling brightly. "But I know it'll be satisfactory with him. We really oughtn't to take in any boarders. I'm not very strong. I got falling of the womb."

I was relieved when Nat Moore came in. He was a nondescript chap of forty or so, one of those inconspicuous, punctiliously pleasant fellows that Nature seems to turn out in such profusion that it is impossible to remember one for long or to differentiate them.

"Nat, this is a young gentleman that would like to board with us. I declare, I don't believe I caught your name," laughed Mrs. Moore.

"Larry Donovan."

"We'll just call you Larry," she said vivaciously. "We want you to be just like home folks here, don't we, Nat?"

"You bet! I swear, Lena, you look all perked up tonight, honey. Are you feelin' better?"

"I feel some better," Lena whined in a changed, petulant voice. Her animated face clouded, settled into discontented lines.

VI

"I got the funniest nickname you ever heard," Grady said to me a few days after we began. "Bet you could never guess it. Bun!"

"Bun?"

"Yeh! When I was just a little tike my mother usta pull up my little underskirt and say: 'I'm gonna take a bite of that purty bun.' Then she'd blow on my stummick like this." He selected a clean spot on his arm and bluttered loudly with his lips, like a horse fluttering its nostrils. "She called my little stummick my *bun*, and people found it out and kept the name up just to joner me mostly. So I was called Bun Grady after I was a man grown."

Grady soon learned to perform the duties of the absconding Pasquale with reasonable aplomb, but piling steel in the yard was ever a fearful ordeal. He approached each experience with trepidation, heaved a sigh of thanksgiving when it was over.

An overhead crane lowers the beam to the edge of the pile and poises it there while a man on each end catches on with a bar slotted at the tip. Then the crane lowers the cable to release the hook, the full weight of the beam falling upon the two bars. The trick is to flip the beam quickly upon the pile, both men letting go at the same instant. On the first Grady was a little too slow; the bar caught him amidships, hurling him heels over appetite. He lay stunned a moment, then rose doggedly. His overalls were torn at the knee and cinders stuck in the flesh like raisins in a plum pudding."

"Too confounded tough to kill," Bun wheezed in a rasping voice.

Romeo's constant admonition was: "If you could see the shape old Joe Vash's in, you'd be more careful. I expect you *will* see him before many days; he's due out of the hospital this week."

Joe Vash walked on two crutches. A pile of steel had careened on him and two crane men had put in an extra shift hoisting the beams off him. One leg was gone to the thigh, the foot on the other one appeared to be traveling north when Joe was headed west. For weeks he hobbled after us, croaking warnings and prophecies of doom like a dyspeptic raven. Than himself no more cautious mortal ever existed, yet look at the shape of him now, he gloomed. A pile of beams, apparently as solid as Gibraltar, might, in sooth, be nothing more than a deadfall balanced on a hair trigger and ready to come tumbling down, according to Joe. He was willing—nay eager—to point out the exact spot of his burial. Handing Grady his crutches to hold, he eased himself to the ground and indicated a dark stain on the wooden pilings.

"Dassa da blude," he said lugubriously, "an' a bone she stoock right out tru my overall leg four eenches. New overalls! An' she poonch beeg hole tru."

Grady did not relish Joe's grisly anecdotes. His misgivings grew daily. Romeo, a practical joker, soon learned that if he would rock a pile of beams and holler "Watch out!" Grady would cut and run like a scared rabbit. Joe had an extensive repertoire. A favorite tale was one often recounted to vivify his warnings that the saw itself, if speeded overmuch, would suddenly burst asunder, mowing down everybody in the immediate vicinity. Jagged holes torn in the sides of the shed were pointed to as evidence of this propensity. An unfortunate saw helper, Joe related, standing in the identical spot where Grady always stood before the saw, having survived unharmed for three months, considered himself possessed of a charmed life. But the saw decided to disintegrate, and a flying fragment neatly decapitated the erstwhile favored of the gods, his head rolling among the scraps hewed from the beams. The body, with uncanny sagacity, started toward the first aid station, but—possibly recalling that the loss of its head was a fatal handicap—halted after a few steps and crumpled in a heap, spouting at the neck like a geyser.

Vash turned to Romeo for confirmation of these heroic episodes, and I never knew him to demur. Rather, he occasionally essayed modest attempts at embellishment. Lacking Joe's lurid imagination and graphic descriptive powers, he nevertheless aided and abetted the cause by standing off from the shed and bombarding it with scraps when the saw was in motion. Having failed in his pleas for a reduction of the saw's speed, Grady was already in a receptive mood, and immediately surmised that the saw had exploded. Flinging his bar in the air with a yell that transcended the saw's clamor, he bolted for safety, only to return sheepishly when he spied Romeo doubled with mirth.

"I like a little funnin'," he said, "but I can't see much fun in that kind of carryin' on. S'posin' I had a weak heart. S'posin' I was to keel over dead, how'd he feel about his skylarkin'? I guess when Ol' Marster aims fer me t' go, though, he'll call me home to glory, so they's no use t' worry my head about it. What *is* to be *will* be."

Then in a quavering tenor:

"God will take care of me
Through every day;
O'er all the way . . .
He will . . . take . . . care . . . o-o-f . . . me-e-e . . . ."

Nat Moore came home with the piercing smell of the rubber plant in his clothes.

"Did you have any of yer sinkin' spells today, honey?" he asked hanging his hat on a nail.

"I ain't had any sinkin' spells for a month, and you know it, Nat Moore," she snapped peevishly, her cheeks flushing.

"You needn't snap my head off," Nat retorted. "I'm goin' out on the back porch t' smoke before supper. Call me when it's ready."

I followed him outside. We sat on the porch steps, Nat smoking thoughtfully, making little sucking sounds in his pipe stem.

"Wimmen is queer," he mused. "She was about t' die till the last week 'r so, but she seems to 've perked up considerable. First time I see'd 'er pitcher I thought she was danged perty. It's funny how I got acquainted with her. It was in a newspaper ad fer Dr. Bradley's Indian Root Female Complaint Remedy. She said she'd took four bottles and it had cured 'er and she felt so thankful she wanted t' tell the hull world about it. Give her address, too. I got t' writin' to 'er and finally went t' see 'er. But that female complaint come back on 'er. We ain't never had no kids. . . ."

"I heard you!" Lena blazed from the back door. "Ain't my fault we ain't got younguns, you little fizzle! If you was a real man. . . ."

"Pshaw! Honey, I never meant no harm," Nat soothed.

"Come to supper; it's ready. Come, Larry! Don't you

put no stock in what that windjammer tells you. He jist talks to hear his head rattle."

During the meal she glared at Nat. He ate noisily and with gusto. He didn't seem much disturbed. In the night I heard them arguing in their bedroom, which adjoined mine. The walls were thin.

I took a short cut through the yards one night on my way home, and as I passed the saw house I heard a terrible commotion inside. Heart-rending groans alternated with supplications to Ol' Marster. Investigation with a flashlight I carried revealed Grady reclining upon a pallet of burlap bags behind the saw. There was quite a space back there, and it was dry and dark. He had been saving room rent by sneaking back of the saw and bunking there.

"I'm dyin'," Grady wept. "The ol' jug has gone to the well fer water the last time!"

I was young, and the romance of this situation at once appealed to me. The midnight hour, the homeless wanderer far from his native heath and kindred. I knelt beside the prostrate man and held his head.

"Listen, Grady," I said solemnly, "If you got any word you want sent to your kin folks, I'll take it to them. Any message! If they're in the world, I'll hunt them up and I'll never rest till I find them!"

"Only a few distant kin folks at Prairie Home, Ohio, that I know of," Grady answered, getting the words out with difficulty. "They wouldn't be interested. What you should ought t' do is fetch a doctor." Evidently he was not convinced that he was indeed dying.

I ran after a doctor. The starlight was dim, and I barked my shins frequently. The doctor came somewhat reluctantly and suspiciously to the incongruous spot.

"What kind of monkey business are you up to, young man?" he growled. "You better step high, wide and handsome with me. I'm armed, and besides I never carry any valuables or cash on my person."

"Nothing but indigestion," he pronounced after a hasty examination of Grady. "What have you been eating, and what are you doing in such a place? You're too old a man to be camping out like a Boy Scout."

I was vaguely disappointed that it was nothing worse, and I felt foolish.

"Doctor, I been pretty hard up and grabbin' a cold snack at the grocery stores. I done it before. And I save money by sleepin' here. It ain't so bad here," said Grady, breathing more easily. "How much do I owe you, doctor?"

"Two dollars," answered the doctor, writing a prescription by the flashlight. "Get yourself a bed and go to eating some decently prepared food or your intestines will twist up into a double bow knot."

Grady paid him with two one-dollar bills, each divided into four sweat-stained squares where they'd been folded in his pocket. He lay breathing heavily as the doctor departed.

"I'll keel over in one o' these spells, Larry," he said. "I'm gettin' purty old to be knocked around from pillar t' post and nobody t' take care o' me. A man needs a woman t' watch out fer 'im. I gotta sew on buttons, patch my clothes. I tell you it ain't no picnic fer a man o' my age."

"My aunt's husband said a working man should never get married," I countered. "He got shot and left three kids for my aunt to support. He said that as long as a man was single he didn't have to take any slack off anybody; he could pull up and leave."

"Well, I don't know," Grady returned miserably, rubbing his hairy belly. "They's two ways o' lookin' at it, I guess. The best thing is not t' be a workin' man at all.

You get you a white collar job. You use big words like you had an education."

"That's what I'm going to do," I answered complacently. "I'm studying every night so I won't have to be a steel worker all my life."

Grady persisted in maintaining his lair behind the saw till the night watchman caught him.

"I was makin' my rounds," the night watchman told me, "an' dogged if I didn't hear the all-firedest hullabaloo in the saw house. Somebody was prayin' like thunder. There was ol' man Grady wrapped up in gunny sacks snug as a bug in a rug an' talkin' in his sleep. I fetched him a good kick on the behind and hollers: 'Get up an' pay fer ya bed!' an' he jumped up blinkin' an rubbin' his eyes. I hadda laugh at the sight of 'im in his ol' baggy patched underwear, saggin' at the seat and the knees. I felt a little sorry fer 'im, too, but it woulda been my job if the high mucky-mucks had knowed he was there. I hadda ol' father myself one time, so I tol' him t' finish out his beauty sleep, but not t' let me ketch him there again."

"I found a dandy place t' stay," Grady said to me during the day. "The Rescue Mission. Beds as clean as a new pin. Listen! Fer twenty-five cents I get meat, vegetables, a piece of pie, and all the bread and butter I can hold." He was jubilant for days; even unloading an unusually difficult car of steel could not quench his exuberance. He felt like stout Cortez when with eagle eyes he gazed on the Pacific. He considered, perhaps correctly, that beds and meals were matters of paramount importance and his discovery of the peerless Rescue Mission was an epochal event.

I envied him the meals, for Lena was a wretched cook. Nat often grumbled that she could not boil water without scorching it. Potatoes were served with a brown crust burned on the bottom where they had stuck to the pan; her biscuits were sad and soggy.

"You get lots of letters from women," Lena greeted me archly on the steps. "I bet you're a lady's man."

"That's from Mother or Aunt Jessie, I guess," I replied, taking the letter from her. She grinned coquettishly. Her teeth were getting bad.

"No, it's not, it's from Dee-troit. You got a sweetie in Dee-troit?"

I ripped the envelope open hastily, and saw that the letter was from Ed. Lena was peering over my shoulder.

"Dear Larry," read the letter. "This is a great place to live. Lots to see and good money, too. Bonny Fern and I went across to Windsor the other night. It's in Canada and you can get real beer or whisky there, also a drink you don't hear of much in the United States, at least not back home: ale. Bonny Fern wouldn't drink, but I got tight and like to have not got on the ferry. She sends regards. Wish you was here, old pal. Your friend, Ed. P. S. Bonny Fern will address the letter because I'm such a rotten scribe."

"Just from a friend of mine," I said casually. So, Bonny Fern is getting wild just like all the rest, I thought. Well, a fellow like Ed, who would show them a good time and raise the dickens was the kind the girls liked.

"Who is Bonny Fern?" asked Lena, who had contrived to read all the letter. "She ought to watch her reputation and not go chasing around with drunks. First thing you know people will talk about her and say she's putting it out."

"She's a girl we knew back home," I said stiffly. Lena's persistent veering around to give a sexual flavor to everything annoyed me. Her eyes were hollow and burned in their sockets.

"No use to wait on Nat," Lena said, setting the table.

"He went on the night shift today, working from four till twelve. So you and I will have to keep house alone tonight."

"I intended to go to the movies," I broke in hastily. Lena's steady gaze made me feel uneasy.

"I'm kind of 'fraid here," she said. "A big nigger broke in Mrs. Ricker's house and tried to force her about a year ago. Mr. Ricker won't let her stay alone any more, but Nat wouldn't care who forced me. It wouldn't mean anything to him one way or the other."

After the show, I walked about the streets till past eleven. As I softly entered my room, Lena called:

"Is that you, Larry? I been scared. I had a sinkin' spell a while ago."

"Yes, it's me," I answered shortly. I was tired of hearing about the sinking spells and falling of the womb. The door between the two rooms was open and I could discern Lena's dim bulk in the bed.

"Would you mind giving me a dose of that medicine in the blue bottle on the dresser?" she asked. "I feel so shaky I don't like to get up."

I carried her the bottle and a spoon.

"Snap on the light so I can see," she said.

She sat up and thrust a bare leg sidewise from beneath the sheets as she poured out a spoonful of the medicine. Her breasts strained tight against her night gown. She must have been pretty as a girl, I thought.

"Thanks! Thanks!" she breathed, patting at my arm. "What makes you always look the other way when I talk to you, Larry? What has Nat been telling you about me? I heard him talking about that female complaint business, about me having my picture in that ad. I did do that, but it was mostly for fun. There wasn't nothing wrong with me *then*. I want you to know. . . ."

"About time for Nat to come home," I interrupted. I wanted to get away.

"Yes," she snapped bitterly. "He'll come home with the rubber stink around him. This bed stinks like rubber and like him. Then he'll snore like a hog and keep me awake the rest of the night, unless he happens to feel like loving a little."

She flopped angrily in the bed, disarranging the covers, the night gown taut about her hips. I retreated into my room, closing the door behind me. Pretty soon Nat came in, and I heard Lena jawing with him. I was soon asleep.

"Leave the old gent stay on, Romeo," urged Lipkin, the giant who had interrupted Romeo's eulogy of the company union. "I'll soon be gettin' the sack, anyhow. I feel uneasy, 'cause I've kept this job longer than I ever kept any other."

"I've tried to tell him a dozen times today," Romeo said. "I would have told him a while ago if he hadn't looked just like my dad from the back. I thought what if somebody was givin' *my* dad the sack in the dead of winter."

"Just like Lady MacBeth when she fell down on the job of knifing Duncan," I said.

Romeo had orders to lay one man off, and he had decided that it must be Grady.

"It's a good thing you're stout as a bull, bolshevik," he said to Lipkin. "Nobody enjoys your company or your rag-chewin'. But you do know how to flip them beams. No, one man must go and it must be Grady. He's getting worse. Seems like the cold weather has gummed up his joints. It's dangerous enough to handle steel in warm weather."

"I'll go," I offered.

146

"Nix! I couldn't keep *him* anyway if you did. Aw, Christ! He'll find some place to hole up for the Winter. He can stay at the Rescue Mission. They keep a whole raft of bums that never pay a red."

"Hey, go inside the mill at noon and get yourself washed whiter than the snow," yelled Lipkin derisively, raising his voice so that Grady, standing two hundred feet away, could hear. "One-round McKay, the ex-pugilist evangelist 'll show us the road to salvation."

Grady fixed him with a reproachful stare. Lipkin's blasphemy never failed to horrify him.

One-Round McKay had erected an altar in the shop and held forth during the noon hour. Grady was a devoted disciple, circulating among the men with a hat to catch the few coins. One-Round staged a furious bout with "Kid" Satan in pantomime, and naturally forced him to kiss the canvas, but only after a tough go and a pretty exhibition of shadow boxing.

One-Round's sermon on "Mother" was the pièce-de-résistance. This required musical accompaniment, and a folding organ had been lugged to the spot. The auditors soon learned that One-Round had been a pretty tough egg in his day, and he dwelt on his ill-spent past with a singular gusto. An unscrupulous seducer of virgins and a bibber who not only looked upon the wine when it was red but also consumed incalculable quantities of it, he was saved by a nocturnal spiritual visitation of his sainted mother. After exhorting his listeners to cease from their wandering and going astray, he signalled to the waiting musician, who had been listlessly gazing at the toe of his shoe and picking his nose. The organist swooped down on the keys as One-Round inhaled a deep breath and sang:

"Take me back to the scenes of my chi-i-i-ldh-o-o-d,
When I'd whistle and pla-a-y

147

Round the old home each da-a-y
And Mothah—Gawd bless her—was ne-e-ear."

The boys were a little more liberal when Grady made his second go-round with the hat. "In the memory of your mother, alive or dead," beseeched One-Round, "Give freely to the work of Christ."

"I ain't ashamed o' cryin'," Grady said as we trudged back to work. "Any man that's got a heart in him would cry at a sermon like that. I seen tears in more than one eye. Lots o' these hard-boiled fellers ain't as hard-hearted as they try t' make out. Lipkin looked like he was about ready t' blubber."

"Like hell I did!" scoffed Lipkin, "I got weak eyes, maybe. That kind of baloney never moves anything but my bowels. I remember my old lady, yes. She had a hump on her back like a camel from bendin' over the tub; she was old at thirty. My wife's gettin' the same. But crap like that ain't gonna help her."

Grady mused over the saw half the afternoon. Once or twice I had to walk over and touch him to get him to shift the beam to a new sawing mark.

Romeo fidgeted around as the afternoon advanced. He hesitated to break the news to Grady. But when the sun slanted among the piles, he hurried up with two checks, blurted out his story to Grady with his eyes fixed on the ground. Grady pretended to be glad.

"Never felt jist right about this place," he said. "I'm leavin' it with sound bones, not like ol' Joe Vash. I'm not frettin'. Ol' Marster has seen me through so far. Not a sparrow falleth but He knows it."

I observed that He would have done better by the sparrow if He had prevented its falling in the first place. Grady was aghast, but he told me to look him up some time at the Rescue Mission.

148

Lena's aunt had come to stay with her a while. Nat had insisted upon it, though Lena had protested she did not need anybody.

"He's jealous, that's all," she whispered fiercely to me when her Aunt Lily had stepped outside for a moment. "He's afraid somebody might try to fool with me while he's gone."

But she was really ill. Her cheekbones protruded, her full lips were turning blue. Her cushioned hips were slackening beneath her dress.

I walked downtown, glad to get out of the house. The odor of medicine and the indefinable stench of illness and the sickroom hovered about it.

Sidewalk eddies were collecting around a gospel band grouped in a semicircle next to the curb. An adenoidal mission worker who had to be chary with the vehemence of her gestures lest she burst her dress farther underarm, stepped forward, clasping pudgy hands together, heavy breasts heaving.

"Brothers and sisters . . . friends!" she called out. "To-night—God willing—we aim to march to the New Hope Mission on the East Side. But first Brother Grady wants to testify what the Lord has done for him."

Grady detached himself from the semicircle and advanced to her side. "I jist wanta say—praise Him!—that He has washed all my sins away in the precious blood of Jesus, hallelujah! He has guided my footsteps in the paths of righteousness for His name's sake. Sinners in the sound of my voice, trust in Him. He'll take care of you."

The procession swung into the stream of traffic. The trumpeter tried a few soft notes on his battered instrument, then flung a high clear call to the encircling towers. Grady strapped the bass drum to his back and fell in. Voices caught up and carried the air:

"Like a mighty army
Moves the church of God
Brothers, we are treading
Where the saints have trod."

I saw him again at Christmas time, standing on a cold
corner tinkling a bell and stamping his feet. His nose was
running, and he wiped it on the back of his fur mitten.
I knew him in spite of his false whiskers. It was only fake
fur on his robe; you could read the Lord's prayer through
the sleazy stuff he was dressed in. He was shivering and
his beard was not snow white and jolly but dirty grey
and mangy looking.

"Hello, Santy," I cried gaily, "bring me a steel saw."
I tossed a coin in the pot he was begging people to keep
boiling and it tinkled lonesomely beneath the chicken wire
top.

"How are you?" he said, shuffling his feet faster.

"It's bolshevik Lipkin again," Romeo said the next day.
"Hear him roar. Let's go in and see what's goin' on."

We ran inside the mill, and saw almost the entire force
gathered about the bulletin board hard by the time clock.
Lipkin, his face livid with rage, was shaking his fist at
Baxter, a small mousey fellow whose nose twitched nervously like a rabbit's.

"You low-down double-crossin' coward," Lipkin bellowed. "We pay dues for you to represent us, hah? We got
to *pay* you to help bugger us! Fifteen per cent cut! Why,
holy Jumpin' Jesus, we oughta have a twenty-five per
cent *raise*."

"It saved a lot of us from the street, Lipkin," argued
Baxter feebly. "By takin' this cut, we keep a lot of men
workin'. Don't you go to raisin' a stink."

Lipkin leaped at him, his great arms flailing. Somebody

hollered for the guards, while Baxter retreated into the office. Lipkin ripped the notice of the wage cut from the bulletin board and ground it beneath his feet. He snatched a rivet from a keg nearby and sent it crashing through the face of the time clock. The men stood dumbfounded at this affront to the regulator of their lives.

"Tick away my life, will you, God damn you?" Lipkin howled. "Another job gone to hell! Oh, I try to keep still but something inside me pushes the words out of my lips. Another job gone, and already it's 'too old' when I try to grin like a kid in employment agencies. I'll cut my boys' throats and stuff them in a sewer before I'll let them live like I have!"

A guard ran in and struck him a cruel blow with a hardwood stick. Lipkin sank to his knees but came up fighting. Something sang in my blood, and I sprang to his side.

"Leave him be!" I shouted. "Don't hit him again."

The guard wheeled and struck me a numbing blow on the shoulder, my entire right side seemed paralyzed. Four or five other guards had arrived and seized us. Lipkin's rage had slacked; his face was ashen, but his eyes still blazed like coals.

"Outside with both of them," ordered the employment manager, coming to the door of his office. "You see what comes from associating with bolsheviks, young fellow."

"Well, you *quit* another job, Larry, like you did on the railroad," Romeo sang out maliciously.

"The two-man strike! The two-man bolshevik strike!" jeered the men, dividing into a lane as the guards hustled us out.

"You worms! You lice!" shouted Lipkin, flaring up anew. "Take your maggoty bone and gnaw it, it's more than you deserve. Lick the hand that socks you in the puss and be grateful!"

We walked along, kicking at the grimy snow. Lipkin felt ruefully of the goose egg on his head.

We parted at a street corner. He shook my hand.

"You got the stuff, lad. Now I got to go home and tell the old lady. That's the hardest part. She don't understand what comes over me and makes me speak whether I want or not. This has happened before. We was just gettin' our debts paid up from the last time."

I wondered what Mother and Aunt Jessie would think, too. Since I had been sending them almost half my wages, they had been able to live without doing washings. But I did not worry. There were plenty of other jobs, maybe a white collar job. I had finished one correspondence course and was on another. When I finished it, I would be an expert accountant. The school's prospectus had assured me that employers would bid avidly for my services then. There would be a cozy bungalow. I'd sit smoking my pipe, a baby or two at my knee, wife leaning lovingly over my shoulder. I'd be looking proudly at my bank book. "Just think, dear," I would say, "two years ago we didn't know where the next meal was coming from. But like Lincoln, I prepared myself with home study. Today the superintendent called me into his office. 'Donovan,' he said, 'we've been keeping tabs on you. The Pasadena branch needs a manager. If you want the job, it's yours.' " The face peering affectionately over my shoulder was always that of Bonny Fern.

VII

Lena's aunt had gone home again, and Lena was up and about. But her hip bones punched against her dress and her arms were skinny. She moved about preparing my supper, but now and then she'd sink down panting upon a chair. I told her about the trouble at the steel mill.

"I guess I'll pull out for Detroit," I said.

"Oh, no!" she objected quickly. "Don't do that. Aunt Lily's boys are in Detroit and they don't work half the time. Nat says they need hands at the rubber plant. Don't you get like the cow that thinks the grass in the next pasture is greener. You'll never get ahead that way."

I promised to see Nat about the job. Since I started the course in accounting, I had been staying home nights. About nine o'clock I heard Lena calling from her bedroom. I opened the intervening door.

"Larry, do you mind leaving the door open? I like to see your light and know you're there. It makes me feel less lonesome," she said.

"Sure," I replied briefly, not without misgiving. I left the door open a crack.

After a bit she called faintly for her medicine. When I fetched it, she grasped my hand. Her fingers burned as they tightened about my own.

"Don't be afraid I'll poison you," she said huskily. "Sit by me for a while. Listen, do you think I've got to looking like a scarecrow?"

"No," I answered, sitting gingerly on the edge of a chair.

"Has Nat ever told you how he goes to other women?"

"No."

"He has me. Even nigger whores. He says I'm no good any more."

"Maybe he's just trying to make you jealous."

"No, he means it. Don't you think a woman's got the same right as a man?"

"I suppose so," I answered, gently loosing her fingers. She turned her back and burst into tears as I returned to my own room.

"I know what you're thinking," she screamed. "You're

going to get you a new boarding place just because I'm sick. I've done the best I could."

"It would be less trouble for you," I answered.

"Don't go, Larry! Please don't," she begged. "I won't ever bother you again like I did just now. You don't know what it is to have to live with a man you hate like a rattlesnake. Say you won't leave. I'm going to try to cook better and keep the house neater. I just got a new cook book with a lot of dandy recipes in it."

"All right," I answered, closing the middle door tighter.

I was still awake when Nat came in. I heard Lena talking to him and presently he called:

"Hey, Larry, you awake?"

"Yes."

"You want a job at the rubber heel plant?"

"Yes, if I can get it."

"You kin. Feller up and quit today. I'll take you down in the morning and hire you in. We're gonna start at five o'clock in the evenin' and work clean through till morning after this."

"All right, Nat. Thanks!"

Nat knew what he was talking about. At the rubber plant I was stripped and examined minutely, particularly my lungs. I learned afterward that the dust soon clogged up strong lungs, but weak ones wouldn't stand it even for a short while.

Shortly before five o'clock I arrived at the plant, armed with my work slip. Sunset bathed the squat building, which seemed to burrow into the hillside to hide its grey ugliness from the world. "Rubber Heel Plant" was the legend inscribed upon its sparrow-fouled façade. It was almost time for the day shift to knock off, and some of the men were already leaving. They paused outside the door and lighted pipes or cigarettes. A piercing odor emanated from their clothing. The heavy revolving door swished regularly as though the building were panting stertorously.

The air inside was thick enough to cut with a knife. The door opened upon a small platform lighted by a single dusty bulb, and several feet below lay the floor of the mill. A stair that was more like a ladder descended. I could hear heavy machinery rumbling and belts whirring in the darkness, but at the moment the mill was unlit. A time clock ticked placidly and when it gave a sharper click I knew the ribbons had shifted for the hour. It was five o'clock or very near it. Nat came in and punched his card.

"Woulda walked down here with you, but Lena had another of her sinkin' spells," he apologized. "Didn't want a leave her till the last minute."

His face was haggard, his eyes sunken and shadowed. A brisk fellow with a foxy profile came in. He wore the bright, sly look of the inveterate joker. After punching his card, he regarded it earnestly for a full minute before he filed it in the IN rack.

"Hello, Rip," he greeted Nat, "you got them dreamy eyes ag'in tonight, I see."

He climbed nimbly down the ladder.

"What makes him call you Rip?" I asked.

"Oh, that's a nickname he gives me. He gives everybody one. 'Count o' me goin' t' sleep on the job sometimes. I git so *stinkin'* sleepy long in the early mornin'. The work itself is bad enough, and on top o' that the fumes eat a body's eyes out. But it's the night work that gets you. A man wasn't *made* t' work at night. Night was made t' sleep in. Listen! You watch that feller, Jasper Collins, that jist spoke t' me. He'd rather play pranks than eat when he's hongry. Jist a natural born fool."

Still grumbling, Nat edged down the stairs. I followed him, advancing an exploring foot ahead cautiously. As I reached the floor, a siren shrilled somewhere and instantly the room sprang into light. I stood irresolute, looking for the foreman. Men were trundling trucks here and there. Neon tubes palpitated with blue light, and the cylindrical mills caught and reflected their glow. Somebody catapulted against me and almost threw me off my feet. It was Jasper Collins, and I was a little alarmed to see that he carried a huge knife.

" 'Scuse me, buddy!" he gasped. "Gotta slice some o' this shoddy."

A pile of reclaimed rubber lay near by, and he began to hack at it lackadaisically, but his eyes were riveted aloft. Then I heard the ting! ting! of the time clock and the shuffling feet of the heel-trimming girls coming down the stairs from the second story. They punched their cards and passed out on to the street, chattering in subdued tones that increased perceptibly in volume the moment they crossed the threshold. The rays of the setting sun pierced through their sleazy print dresses, silhouetting vividly the contours of their bodies.

"Oh, mama!" gurgled the ecstatic watcher. "Too much t' see here! Man oughta have a million eyes, like a fly!"

To express his enthusiasm, he sliced energetically at the shoddy. The sun soon went out of sight beyond the horizon's rim and the stream of girls dwindled to a trickle of stragglers. Finally a Negro scrub-woman clumped down the stairs. As she lit her corncob pipe, the match was a tiny flambeau which fantastically lighted her cheeks, concaved by sucking on the stem, and her pursed blue lips. There was no voluptuous interest here, and Jasper turned away.

"Here comes Bonyparts, the boss," he told me as he left, "only you'd best call him Mr. Erton till you get better acquainted."

A misshapen cherub-faced man padded up and stood

interrogatively. I produced my work slip. His lips moved as he read it half aloud.

"Okay, lad," he wheezed asthmatically. "You get to tearin' that smoke sheet apart over there by the mixers till I find a place for you."

Equipped with a small hook like that of a longshoreman, I tackled the bale of smoke sheet, or raw gum rubber. It was composed of several continuous sheets jammed together, and when I pressed it down with my knee, it squeaked crisply like a head of cabbage. Within an hour I had succeeded in tearing off half a dozen small strips. I could see Jasper and a cadaverous elderly chap weighing and compounding batches of material for the millers. They used more gum rubber in one batch than I was likely to tear loose all night. I was a little perturbed and rolled the bale over and over, seeking a more vulnerable spot. My hands blistered and the blisters burst open. Jasper had been watching me and he divined my anxiety.

"That's only a spare time job," he reassured me. "You ain't supposed t' get much done. You oughta take it more easy. Wait a minute."

He brought two lumbermen's cant-hooks and fastened one on the side of the bale. I hooked mine into the opposite side and we both pulled. The layers ripped off like slabs of bacon, but sometimes Jasper had to cut off a connecting fold with his knife. The sheets all had the words: "Straits Settlements" stamped upon them.

"This stuff comes a long way," I observed.

"Yes, from Africa," said Jasper.

"No, from near India," I contradicted.

But he was obdurate, and would not accept the evidence of the stamp that branded the sheets. It was just a trademark, he said. I pointed to the flimsy wooden boxes which had encased the bales. "Via Singapore. Stow away from boiler on shipboard," and a number of Chinese characters were stenciled on them. As we halved one bale a circular object dropped out and clinked on the floor. It was an ancient copper coin. I thought it must be Chinese, for one side depicted a dragon evidently attempting to swallow its tail. Any trivial diversion was enough to rally a group of men. They stood about and speculated as to the origin of the coin. I scratched away the green canker, looking for a date.

"Let me see it, please," broke in a slight dark fellow who had been standing near.

I handed it to him.

"It is a coin of the Chinese Empire," he pronounced unhesitatingly, "but the exact value I cannot determine."

I was astonished at his meticulously chosen speech, his crisp accent which sounded so strange among the slurred syllables of the others.

"I had quite a collection of coins several years ago," he continued, "and there were several Chinese coins among them." He hurried away through the door leading to the press room.

"Aw, he's only puttin' on!" muttered Jasper. "Don't know no more about it than anybody else. Say! He was in the German Army during the war. Said he was a coward when he went, but got brave and deserted. He'd make a dog laugh tellin' how he et turnips and slept in haystacks. I think he's a little goofy. Soon as Bonyparts goes t' sleep —like he does ever' night—I'll take you in the press room and have him tell about it. Hah! I see that Hearne has twisted up with his cramps ag'in. By doggies, he makes me tard always chewin' the rag and makin' out like he's sick."

Hearne was Jasper's partner. He had improvised a couch of empty jute bags upon a truck, and now lay curled in a semicircle, his arms clasped about his stomach. Now and then he vented a gruesome moan; again, possibly to prove he was game but physically unable to stand the gaff, he would rise to his feet, totter a moment, and then double up like a jack-knife. He winced as though he might be the brave Spartan boy, stoically trying to conceal the evidence of a voracious fox chewing at his vitals. Jasper exuded scant sympathy, but sulkily prepared to weigh and mix the ingredients. Hearne had memorized the formula, and to save time he called out the proportions to Jasper:

"Stearic acid, eighteen ounces. . . . Shoddy, twenty pounds. . . . Gum, five pounds. . . . Paraffin, sixteen ounces. . . . Don't forget the zinc oxide. Watch your scales!"

Jasper squinted at the weights and balanced the scales as carefully as an apothecary apportioning some potent physic. Hearne saw that I had abandoned my battle with the rubber. He arose, and this time stood his ground, beckoning to me.

"It's the dust. All these chemicals simply clog up and eat a man's lungs away," he began. He picked up a stubby broom and used the handle as a pointer, indicating a blackboard used to tally the number of batches. It also bore a crude drawing palpably designed to represent the inner mechanism of a human being.

"The lungs there—" he pointed out two balloon-shaped figures on the chart—"you see, they gradually fill with dust. Once the dust gets in, it never in Christ's world comes out again. It settles to the bottom like this. . . ." He whited a generous segment of each lung. "So the pores of the respiratory organs close up gradually. Right now I'm breathing out of one lung only. Soon . . . only a matter of time. But what does life amount to when all is said and done? A walking shadow—a poor player who struts his little hour upon the stage . . . a tale told by an idiot . . . full of sound and fury, signifying nothing." His tongue stumbled over the last words as if he were doubtful of them—as if he were reading with difficulty from a book printed with characters almost effaced by time.

"You look surprised," he said. "I haven't always worked at this menial labor. I was for years on the boards with Fowler's Mammoth All-Star Minstrels, and I've done nearly every Shakesperean rôle in the repertoire. How I came here is a long story. Listen, lad! Let me give you a little advice about liquor and women. . . ."

I waited expectantly, confident of hearing some juicy revelations. But, warned by some mysterious intuition, I glanced furtively over my shoulder and saw Bonyparts approaching. I fell to wrestling with the bale, while Hearne, miraculously invigorated, pushed Jasper aside and began to agitate the scale balances diligently. He remarked to Jasper in an affectedly casual but very loud voice that they certainly had plenty to do and would have to shake a leg the remainder of the night. Jasper, momentarily dumbfounded at the inexplicable usurpation of his job, soon discovered the cause, and, with marvelous presence of mind, leaped at a pile of shoddy and threw it about aimlessly. Bonyparts stood blinking and exploring his nostrils with a pudgy forefinger; then he padded out of sight around the mills. The amenities observed, Hearne collapsed upon his couch and burst into fresh lamentations.

"You can get a wienie from the lunch girl, if you're hungry," Jasper told me, "or coffee to keep you awake through the Graveyard Shift from twelve till morning. Sleepy time ain't here yet. She gets in around about 8:30 or 8:35. She oughta be here now; it's 8:36. She never *was* this late before."

He seemed disturbed, and trotted to the door leading to the press room several times. The girl's tardiness was something unusual, and thus a matter of grave concern. In this drab place the men's thoughts fumbled and pawed over any slight deviation from monotony. The lunch girl was a welcome diversion. Jasper hurried to help her as she trundled her cart down the slight incline leading from the press room. Her high heels clacked briskly as she ground them into the concrete as a brake. Jasper piloted the cart on to the mill room floor.

"Come and get it while it's hot!" he shouted.

The men scampered up, their eyes exploring the lunch girl from sole to crown. She was an exotic flower in this murky air, where grey was the only color that endured. Red heels and black ones soon were submerged beneath the dusty pall that eternally swirled in the air and kept settling, settling. The grey walls sweated the most where the building was buried in the hillside, and from the broken wires that had held the forms together when the concrete was poured, the walls suppurated a pallid liquid like ichor from a sore that would not heal. The lunch girl's crisp white frock seemed almost virginal by contrast, though it was spotted here and there by mustard and chili sauce and was a little greasy and sweaty at the neck. The men mumbled their orders, swiping their oily hands across the seats of their pants. They gobbled the sandwiches noisily, squirting mustard and weinie juice from the corners of their mouths. The girl eyed me with cool insolence.

"What's *your* dish?" she demanded haughtily.

"A weinie," I stammered.

Somehow it seemed indecent for her to be here. She speared a weinie and it hissed slightly as the fork tines punctured its skin. She deposited it on a bun and smeared it with mustard.

"Ten cents!" she chirped archly, and her right eye screwed itself into a broad wink.

I trembled somewhat as I handed her the coin, but I was inwardly triumphant. I was still young enough to

161

retreat from such bold overtures. Her hips waggled provokingly as she went pushing her cart and smirking over her shoulder.

"With that curly hair, ain't it a shame you drink?" she giggled.

The men were snickering at me, and a muffled drum beat rhythmically in the back of my head. My temples pounded. I knew that I, too, would watch for her every night. Tedium enveloped us again. Sleep was an enemy to fight, not a friend to comfort us.

"Bonyparts always takes a nap this part of the night," said Jasper, "so let's us go in and see Hans, that German feller."

We walked up the incline and pushed open a heavy metal door. A withering blast of steamy, rubber-scented air singed our hair.

"Hotter 'n the hubs o' Hell!" cried Jasper. "When I think I got a tough titty fer a job, I come in here and right away I get t' thinkin' I got a snap."

Men stripped to the waist were tending the steam presses which melt the raw biscuit-shaped heel into the cured one. Their skins were flushed as with fever, their lips parched. Sweat blinded their red-rimmed eyes, but they were too busy to wipe it away. They jiggled tiny washers, inserted to keep the nails from pulling through the brittle rubber, on to pegs set in the cavities of heavy steel molds. Heat-puffed fingers fumbled the washers. Then raw heels were imposed upon the pegs, and the molds were closed and shoved into the press. As fast as a new mold was elevated to the steam chamber, a cured batch was ready. Hastily drawing on asbestos gloves, the pressmen pried open the sizzling molds and tore out the heels.

Hans was not at a press, but sitting on a stock pan, holding his head in his hands. He told Jasper he had got a ringing in his head and stopped sweating, and that his eyes blurred so he couldn't see the molds. So he had sat down to blow for a spell. To stop sweating is dangerous.

"Say, Hans," began Jasper, "wasn't you in the German Army? Tell this new man about it."

"Yes," replied Hans, seemingly little inclined to talk.

"But you never did shoot no Americans, did you?" pursued Jasper.

"I never shot anybody. I was a follower of Karl Liebknecht and he was opposed to the imperialist war. But I was called out in the *Landwehr* and I lost my courage and went."

Jasper winked knowingly at me; he appeared to be consumed by inward mirth. The droll fellow had *lost* his courage and *joined* the army!

"Well, I woulda thought you'd'a lost it if you *hadn't* went," marvelled Jasper. It was plain that Hans both baffled and amused him, and that his efforts to classify him as a definite specimen, motivated by familiar understandable impulses, always resulted in added confusion.

"I went because I was afraid," insisted Hans, sullenly, "but my courage returned and I threw my rifle down and ran away. I hid in the daytime in haystacks and traveled nights. I ate turnips from the fields and stoned wild birds. Once I snared a field mouse and ate him raw. But I reached the Swiss border and there I stayed till the Revolution."

"It looks like you could of done more good by stayin' right with the army if you wasn't a-skeered," Jasper commented. "If you was fer the Allies, couldn't you of strafed the Germans from their own side?"

"I wasn't for the Allies," Hans returned.

"But didn't you fight ag'in the Gov'ment?" inquired Jasper.

"After the Revolution I returned and fought with Liebknecht's Spartacides. But after he was shot, I lost

163

heart and left the country—came here to America to live with relatives."

We saw the press room foreman approaching and retreated toward our own department, but not with the precipitate haste which would have betrayed our unauthorized presence in the press room. The boss eyed us suspiciously, so we carelessly masked our badges with our hands to conceal our identity. The boss glowered at Hans, who returned to his press and began filling a mold. Then, having restored order, he folded his arms majestically across his chest, and backed against a window, scouring the room for other idlers. An impish idea popped into Jasper's head.

"We'll slip around outside, and I'll make him get away from that window," he said.

Outside, he groped on the ground for a sharp stick with which to prod the foreman. But before he found one, a fearful howl arose in the press room and light from the now unobstructed window streamed out upon us. Hans' eyes had blurred once too often, for he hung dangling by one arm from the press. He had forgotten to take his hand off a mold that was ascending into the steam chamber. When they carried him past the window his eyes were closed and we could see that his right hand was flopping horribly, the fingers crushed into a pulp of blood and bone.

Jasper and I returned to the mill room; the joker was subdued and morose.

"Bonyparts said you should he'p me on the mill," Nat announced, handing me a short blunt knife. "Don't know what he's got ag'in you t' wish a job like this on you."

The rubber mills are two huge, hollow steel cylinders which revolve so that the materials are caught between them and fused into the amalgam from which the raw heels are cut. But before the mass adheres to the cylinder and the powders are assimilated by the rubber, paraffin and stearic acid, the stuff drops to the pan beneath and must be constantly shoveled above. A prismatic cloud from the many-hued powders harries nostrils and eyes. The mixture cracks terrifically. When the rubber begins to stick, the short knife is used to slice it away and keep it feeding through till all of it has been thoroughly blended. The supreme test for the miller is to slice the rubber off the mill in a constantly widening strip with one hand and to roll it into a "jelly roll" with the other. The miller who can roll a huge jelly roll of half a mill full is considered expert.

"It's like tryin' t' pat yer head and rub yer stummick at the same time," sympathized Nat. "Took *me* a coon's age t' git on to it. Both hands allers wanta do the same thing at oncet."

Truckers roll the jelly rolls to a calender, where they are flattened, cut into even strips, and cooled for the cutters who blank out the raw heels.

Nat taught me the song which all the millers sang:

> "O jelly roll! jelly roll!
> Jelly on my mind.
> You jazzed my poor ol' gran'pa
> And my poor ol' gran'ma blind!"

The glistening mill reflected my body with all the ludicrous distortions of an amusement park mirror. I grimaced, squatted, and thrust my head near. Instantly I was metamorphosed into a snarling ogre with a monstrous head and toothpick legs. I drew my head back, thrust out my chest, and rose to my full height. I became a pin head with a massive bust.

"Don't you be watchin' that mill," Nat warned, " 'cause it'll charm you same as a snake charms a bird. Put crazy idees in yer head, 'specially during the Graveyard Shift.

If ever you let a loose end of a strip wrop 'round yer wrist, up you go between the rolls, and goodbye hand, arm, and maybe head."

As the rubber heated, its penetrating stench increased in pungency and brought tears to our eyes. Nat knuckled his eye-sockets and staggered to the water fountain. He directed a stream of cold water directly against his eyeballs. I saw him look at the clock, which was visible from the fountain but hidden from the mill.

"What time's it getting to be?" I asked. This question would be asked many times during the Graveyard Shift.

"Eleven o'clock," responded Nat, dejectedly.

"Might as well be no time at all," I commented. This was a stock phrase which everybody used to save the effort of thought.

"You oughta wash yer eyes out," Nat told me. "It helps better'n anything a man can do. The time passes faster if you don't even look at the clock. I made up my mind I wouldn't look toward it, but it draws my eyes same's molasses does a fly. Always think maybe it's later than what I think it is."

At midnight we ate a cold lunch. Lena had wrapped up some bacon sandwiches for us, but I had forgotten to suspend mine from a string and rats had chewed them. A thick-skinned orange had discouraged them and I ate it. Each man drank a quart of milk, for it was esteemed as an antidote for the rubber poison. Nat champed his jaws furiously. He had only a few teeth left.

"Gotta do *some* maneuverin' t' git my grub t' where I can grind it with these snags," he volunteered, opening his mouth and pointing within. Even the orange tasted of rubber; I seemed to swallow liquid rubber along with the milk.

When everybody had finished lunch, a few minutes

remained before work time. Hearne sprang to his feet and pulled two pairs of rattle bones from his pocket. He began to clatter them softly, holding them deftly between his fingers. Jasper whispered to me that the bones had to be made from the ribs of a young beef.

"Watch how spry the old staller is," Jasper muttered to me. "Watch how he can jig. That's what makes me think he ain't as sick as he makes out."

Hearne faced us with a low, sweeping bow, rattling the bones, furiously.

"Gentlemen, be seated!" he cried.

He carried on both sides of a dialogue between Mr. Tambo and Mr. Bones. He started with a slow weaving motion above the waist. Then he stepped it lively, slinging his feet as though his ankles were hinged or made of rubber. He sang:

> "Elephant walk a rope,
>   Flooie! Flooie!
> Elephant walk a rope,
>   Flooie! Anna, John.

> "Elephant walk a rope
>   All slicked up with grease and soap.
> Wasn't that a fine walk,
>   Flooie! Anna, John?"

As Nat and I descended the slope toward the Low Ground, dawn was cracking the sky. Nat took off his hat and let the wind blow through his hair.

"Let some of the stink blow off," he said. "It sticks to you closer'n a brother and you get t' tastin' it in yer coffee."

He halted before a cottage exactly like his own, and

167

for a moment I thought he had mistaken the place. But the yard was neat; prim curtains were hung at the windows. It lacked the slatternly appearance of his own abode. Nat fidgeted uneasily.

"You can go on, Larry," he said. "I stop here of a morning sometimes to get a cup o' coffee. Widder lady name o' Emma Hallem. I git tard o' Lena's slop," he added defensively.

But before I had traveled far he overtook me.

"Don't say nothin' to Lena," he said contritely. "I oughtn't t' do 'er that way. I ain't a gonna stop there no more."

We walked along in the dim light. Day men were hurrying along the streets on the way to work; the smell of frying meat and boiling coffee filled the air.

"I hope Lena has felt good enough t' cook our breakfast," Nat said as he opened the kitchen door.

But the table was still littered with supper dishes, caked with stale victuals. Egg shells crunched underfoot. Nat found three fried pork chops in the skillet; in the night the grease around them had whitened. Nat worried his nose to and fro with the back of his hand and looked troubled. He shook the coffee pot and heard a splashing inside.

"Maybe we could make out with this coffee het up and the pork chops warmed over," he suggested timidly. "I hate like the mischief t' wake Lena up when she's restin' easy."

The coffee was stale and bitter and the pork chops had absorbed a lot of the grease and were a little rancid near the bone. The spoons were all dirty, but Nat rinsed a couple at the sink faucet. I felt my way into my room. I wasn't surprised to find the bed as disordered as I had left it. I pulled the blankets around me and curled up.

168

I awoke to hear children singing in the street. I arose yawning and my jawbone cracked painfully; my head throbbed dully. When I ran up the shade, the bright sun blinded me. I had it in mind to chase the children away, but I paused. They were forlorn tatterdemalions with stringy hair and spindly legs. One, clothed simply in a grimy diaper, sat on the curb fingering its protuberant stomach. Solemnly, as though performing a religious duty, they joined hands and hopped about grotesquely in a circle. Their feet seemed several sizes too big for their legs. Their reedy voices piped:

> "Green gravel, green gravel,
>   The grass is so green;
>   All over Creation
>   'Tis a sight to be seen."

I lowered the shade and felt for a glass of water on the bureau. It was brackish, and my teeth caught something. I spat the drowned fly against the wall. The cold was making them fall from the ceiling. My head pulsed so strongly that it seemed to contract and expand. No more sleep. Neither did I feel like studying on the correspondence course. I had planned to devote part of the day to that.

I raised the shade high enough to admit light, but sufficiently low to keep out the sun's glare. A mudwasp's queer metallic buzz sounded from a ceiling corner; and I watched it while it made many trips through the window after fresh mud to build its cells. I thought of the mudwasps about the communal spring in Monkey Nest Camp, Mother's wash boiler propped on the flat stones, the smoke of the fire ascending to the tree tops, Mother's tired grey face, flushed a little from the steam. Well, she had kept me out of the mines at least. When I finished the course, it would be easier.

169

The voices of the children climbed to higher pitch:

"Dear mother, dear mother,
Your true love is dead.
He sent you a letter
To hold up your head."

"Make them go 'way, hon," Lena whined to Nat in the next room. "They give me the creeps singin' about bein' dead."

VIII

Hans was rid of the press, because he couldn't handle it any more with his fingerless hand. The thumb remained. He had to be given work of some kind, so they put him to sorting damaged heels. He was not very popular with the others, for he never laughed at the one kind of joke— the sexual. In the chill morning hours when Bonyparts was safely asleep, the thoughts of the men turned to clean, white beds in darkened rooms. Always there was a woman between the sheets.

So anyone who learned a new smutty story was quick to retail it. Ribald poetry was carried about and exhibited until the sheets, creased and grimed, fell into separate squares. The magazines emblazoning beauty unadorned, intended solely for artists and pure-minded lovers of art, were gloated over eagerly. But just as an ancient and sated rake who had exhausted the conventional delights resorts to more novel means of indulgence, so the demand for more reality spurred on the rubber hands. Jasper somehow came into contact with a French dealer who boasted that he "fulfilled every ardent desire." Jasper was hailed nightly with: "What have you got that's dirty tonight?"

Jasper couldn't get Hans interested in the photographs, and this infuriated him. He made the German's life as miserable as he could by using him as the butt of his banal practical jokes. A favorite was:

"Glad t' see yer *back*!" striking him heartily on the back.

"I believe I *nose* you!" tweaking his nose.

"Bin two *years* since I seen you!" pulling his ears.

Hans grinned foolishly and went his way. Jasper caught him in the shower bath and reached beneath the partition with a rough warehouse broom, jabbing viciously. Hans came slipping and snorting out of the booth.

"So you want to be an accountant," Hans said to me one night. "In America students think of making money, not of preparing for a fuller intellectual life. The majority of them are bound to be disappointed. I hope you won't be one."

"What kind of intellectual life is there here?" I asked. "I want to get into a better environment."

"You like the photos, eh?" he asked shrewdly. "You like the lascivious photos better than you do Corot?"

It was the truth. The photos haunted me. Shut my eyes, and I could see the voluptuous models—their organs and dimensions—floating like white, unhealthy flowers before me.

"Listen!" Hans almost shouted. "We fought on the barricades. Men—and women, too—dying for the Revolution! Do you wonder these dull apes turn my stomach? Don't think you'll escape them if you get a better job. The higher-ups love the photos even better than these fellows. Find something to take hold of beside the ambition to rise about this factory. If you keep the French postcard mind, you'll not be much better off. You'll find Jasper Collinses everywhere."

This sounded like moralizing, but I knew Hans was not a religious man.

"You can make that lunch girl easy as fallin' off a log," Jasper told me later in the evening. "All you need is a good line. Put it up to 'er strong. They all want to be coaxed but they like to be bullied, too. Try t' date 'er up t'night."

I did ask her to go walking with me the next day. We walked about the streets and in the bare park, went to an afternoon movie. She chattered about trivial things such as: "And he sez: 'Who's yer friend?' 'That's fer me t' know and you t' find out!' I sez." She debated as to which was the most juicy brand of gum, and always had a wad in her mouth. She voiced positive opinions as to the relative pulchritude of the movie stars, male and female.

One afternoon we ascended the steep bluff to Lovers' Leap. Legend had it that an Indian brave and his sweetheart, whom he had been forbidden to marry, leaped hand in hand from this eminence. We peered over the brink at the tree tops far below. She shuddered and clung tightly to me. I felt encouraged and flung my arm about her.

Across the river, the sun and clouds were checkering the land—here a patch of bright sunlight, there a swath darkened beneath the shadow of a cloud. The sun was going down. I recited Arthur Davidson Ficke's:

"I am in love with high, far-seeing places
   That look on plains half-sunlight and half-storm,
In love with hours when from the circling faces
   Veils pass, and laughing fellowship grows warm."

"Gee! That's keen!" she whispered softly, ceasing to chew gum. "Now say me the one about "old ships like swans asleep, Beyond the village which men still call Tyre."

172

We walked slowly down the winding road to the base of the cliff. Dense brush lined each side. Here was my opportunity, I thought. Jasper had said that a bold frontal attack never failed.

"Let's go into the brush," I said roughly, seizing her hand.

"What for?" she cried, startled.

"You know."

I dragged at her arm. Then she came at me like a cat and ripped my face with her nails. She struck me a stinging blow across the face, kicking simultaneously at my shins. I let go of her hands.

"So that's the game?" she gritted.

My respect for Jasper as a tactician diminished. The girl walked rapidly down the hill, leaving me running my fingers over the scratches on my face. Why, she painted as much as Wilma and almost as much as New Orleans Bessie! She had winked at me several times and had wiggled her hips at me. I ran and overtook her. She was sobbing loudly.

"Don't cry," I begged. "Forget about it. I didn't mean any harm."

"I thought you was different," she gulped. "I liked you talkin' that poetry and not feelin' and pinchin' all the time like the rest, but you was just after the same thing as the others."

"What made you wink at me?" I demanded.

"Oh, I don't know! Fellers won't pay no attention to a girl that don't look like she's got some pep. If you wanta get a steady you gotta show 'em some encouragement. But they all want the same thing."

I walked beside her in a quandary. She sniffed and dabbed at her eyes with a handkerchief. When I asked her if I could come and see her again she said she never

173

wanted to set eyes on me again. After that I hid when the lunch cart came through the mill.

The next day after my rebuff, I met Jasper in front of the post-office.

"Say!" I began indignantly. "You got me in trouble. . . ."

"I'm in trouble, too—plenty!" he interrupted, plucking nervously at my sleeve. "Look what I got! A letter from the gov'ment!"

"Dear Sir," read the letter, "We are holding at this office a letter addressed to you from a foreign country. It is suspected of containing matter prohibited in the mails. Please call at Window 15 and consult with Mr. Barton regarding the disposition of this mail."

"Go in with me," begged Jasper, licking his dry lips. "This is serious."

Jasper rapped at Window 15 and after a moment Mr. Barton popped his head out.

"Something I can do for you?" He was a stern, official-looking chap, and his tone was a challenge. Jasper quailed.

"It was about a foreign letter addressed to Jasper Collins," he stammered. "That's me, I reckon, but I-I-I don't know nobody in no foreign country. Guess somebody's aimin' t' play a joke on me."

Mr. Barton's lips congealed in a straight line. He disappeared for a trice and returned with a square envelope with a mangled side revealing the gaudy, flimsy inner lining used for foreign letters. Mr. Barton withdrew a half dozen postcards and spread them fanwise before Jasper's agonized gaze. In this chaste atmosphere the monstrous things seemed infinitely more obscene.

"This letter burst open in the mails," Mr. Barton announced primly. "Such—ahem!—objects are not allowed in the mails, and the penalty is extremely severe. The buyer, as you may be aware, is equally responsible with the seller."

"I don't know nothing about 'em," Jasper contended doggedly. Rivulets of sweat trickled down his furrowed brow.

"Very well, then. I assume you do not wish to claim them."

Mr. Barton slipped the cards back in the envelope and thrust it into the inside pocket of a coat that hung near.

"Usually a fictitious address is attached to such communications," he said. "If, in the interests of justice, you wish to give me the *correct* address, I can assure you that the information will be respected as confidential and that no trouble will come to you because of it."

"I told you the Lord's truth, mister," protested Jasper. "I don't know nothing about it."

"Good day, then," snapped Mr. Barton, slamming the window of his cubby hole pretty hard.

"No more o' that fer me!" breathed Jasper fervently.

We were passing the Rescue Mission and I thought of Grady. I went inside to ask about him. The mission worker had on a new frock which had not yet burst under the arm.

"Grady? Grady?" she reflected, cudgelling her brains and whistling thoughtfully through her nose. "That's quite an ordinary name, and we *do* have so *many* here. Let me think! Yes! I remember him. An oldish man, quite bald, red face—medium weight. He was here until a week or so ago, but Mrs. Lanning of the United Charities cut down on our appropriation. We had to trim expenses, and Brother Grady volunteered to leave. Said he was going to Cleveland, if I'm not mistaken."

I was a little late, and hurried home to dress for work. Nat had already gone.

"There's a letter for you, Larry," called Lena weakly

from the other room, hearing me moving about. "It's from Dee-troit. Why don't you let me read it?" She was unable to get up.

"All right," I called.

"Dear Larry," read the letter. "This is the life, kid. I got another raise. This is the time to get a job in the auto factories. Don't stick there at low wages. Tell all your friends to come if they want. Have to just scribble this. Bonny Fern and I are going to a dance at the Dreamland Gardens. Wish you was here. Ha! Ha! Your pal, Ed."

I carried the letter to Lena.

"Read it," I said. "I must go."

"Are you going to Dee-troit?" she asked.

"Maybe so."

"I wish you wouldn't before I die. I'll die soon. I've give up all my bad thoughts. I had bad thoughts about you ever since I seen you but I've made my peace with God and I'm ready to go when he calls me."

"You won't die," I said.

"Yes, I will. Nat's the cause of it, too. He caught a bad disease somewhere at his chippy-chasing, and he give it to me. He got cured, but I couldn't never be cured. That's what made me so mad when he told you I had female complaint like I claimed Dr. Bradley's Indian Root Remedy cured me of. I never did have female complaint in them days; I was full of ginger when I was a girl and always up to some devilment. That's why I wrote and told 'em that their remedy had cured me and sent my picture to show how healthy it had made me. But I hadn't never even been sick then. But I've forgive Nat all the trouble he brought me—how he brought me to my grave. A person had ought to go to her grave with a heart full of love for everybody."

I was tired of hearing Lena's intimate revelations, and

I secretly resolved to move at the first opportunity, perhaps the next day.

"Nat's hired a woman to come and do the housework," continued Lena. "A widow lady, a Mrs. Emma Hallem. Do you suppose he's thick with her?"

I rushed off and did not answer. Clouds had been gathering all day, and now rain came down in sheets. In the Spring the Low Ground was always flooded, and more than once the Deer Creek dam, which had been built in order to reclaim the real estate development at first grandiosely dubbed Sunset Meadows from a marsh, had broken and inundated everything in the valley.

It rained for five days without ceasing, and on the fifth day Lena died. I had moved the day before to higher ground. People were moving their goods in trucks, wagons and on wheelbarrows, but Nat stayed. That night the Deer Creek dam burst and flooded the valley again. Many houses went floating down the swollen stream.

Nat remembered that Lena had always wanted the funeral preached at the house, and so the preacher was rowed over. It was all so queer that the Sunday papers got hold of it, and there was a picture in the rotogravure section of Lena lying quietly in her coffin in the bottom of the skiff, and the preacher raising his hand as though in benediction. The bereaved husband stood sorrowfully by. In the background Nat pointed out Mrs. Hallem and her two children. Mrs. Hallem's full motherly bosom belied her vinegary hatchet face. Nat bought twenty-five copies of the paper and gave one to each of us.

Hearne didn't show up one night, and we learned that the doctor had ordered him West—that he had t.b. After that the sprightly Jasper was a changed man.

"It'll get me, too," he gloomed, "but a man might as

well be dead with t.b. as starved to death. No chance to get any other job."

"Oh, yes, there is," I contradicted, "and at double the wages we're getting here, too," I told him of Ed's letter.

"You write and ask that guy if he's certain sure we can git a job. By doggies, I ain't tied here. I can pull up stakes."

"So can I if there's more money in it," broke in Nat, who had perked up since Lena died and Mrs. Hallem was keeping house for him.

"I'll stay here till they kick me out, I guess," said Hans, gazing ruefully at his mutilated hand. "I'll have to stay in the place that crippled me or I'm out of luck. When they want to get rid of me here they'll do it fast enough."

"Gee, I'd hate to stay here the rest of my life," I burst out impulsively, without thinking.

"You all may see the day you'll be begging for a job like this. Read Marx," said Hans quietly. "Marx charted the course of civilization almost a hundred years ago."

"The Good Book will tell you about all these things," put in Nat. "It predicted the horseless carriages, the ships flying in air, everything. Don't have to go past the Word o' God to know what's what and what will be."

"Bah!" snorted Hans.

"Marx! Marx! Tellin' us t' read Marx! What's a workin' man know about Marx? How many workin' men ever heard of such a feller? A measly, puny man tryin' to figger out God's plan!" He cackled derisively. "Read the Word o' God! That's all a workin' man needs t' know."

"Your brains will never tell you what Marx taught, no," conceded Hans contemptuously, "but in the course of time your belly will tell you. It may all work out the same in the end."

I had never read Marx, but I intended to do so. Hans had given me a lot of advice about reading, and I respected his judgment. However, it was a long time before I got around to reading Marx.

Hans was quick to note Jasper's serious mind. The comedian had been transformed into a morose pessimist. Because he wanted revenge or because he was sorry for him and wanted to cheer him up, Hans essayed to take Jasper's place as the joker of the mill. He always used Jasper as his subject. He constructed a slapstick of two thick boards with a chip between. Every time he caught Jasper stooping over, he thwacked him resoundingly. It didn't hurt much, but it made a fearful detonation.

Nat began having his hair cut every week and using bay rum to take the rubber stink out of it. He was always the first to meet the lunch girl. He found Jasper leaning against a post and snoring peacefully.

"Wake up, Rip Van Winkle!" he shouted joyously. "Snap out of it! Git the sleepy look outen them there dreamy eyes!"

Then he scratched the back of his ear with the tip of his knife.

"Say, Jasper," he said, looking a little embarrassed, "You know them pictures you usta have. . . ."

"I don't know nothing about 'em," Jasper interrupted sadly. "You'll hafta ask Mr. Barton down t' the post-office."

When the lunch cart made the rounds that night, I showed myself for the first time since the trip to Lovers' Leap.

"Hello, Helen," I said.

"Oh, hello," she said casually. Her fingers tightened on the handles of the cart till the knuckles showed white.

"I'm going to Detroit, Helen."

"Well, what of it? Do you expect me t' take down my hair and have a good cry? Good luck to you, kid."

"You're not sore now?"

179

"Why, no! Why should I be?"

"Will you write to me, Helen? Will you let me take you to the movies before I go?"

"No! I went up the Lovers' Leap with another fresh guy. I'm tired o' fightin', so this time I goes in the bushes. See?"

When she moved away her hips did not waggle as they had the first time I saw her. She walked stiffly as a wooden soldier might.

Sure, we could get jobs; what a foolish question, Ed answered to my letter. Come ahead, as many as wanted to. Jasper was ready. He was growing cadaverous, either from worry or from the dust ravaging his lungs. Nat had married Emma Hallem, but he intended to go with us, sending for Emma later.

"I don't care if people do talk about me marryin' so soon," Nat said. "Lena—God rest her poor soul!—wasn't never a real wife t' me. I never hear any moans about falling wombs now, and everything around the house is kept as bright as a new tin pan. It sure makes a world o' difference!"

I had not quite finished the accountancy course, but thought I'd do so as soon as I reached Detroit and settled down. I had managed to send Mother and Aunt Jessie enough money to keep them for several months. I felt free. We decided to travel by freight to save expenses.

IX

"We must nag it before it gets to going very fast," I said. "Let's get that empty box car!"

I jumped in without difficulty and so did Jasper, but Nat hung on the threshold, his hands clawing desperately at the floor, his legs threshing outside. Jasper and I each grasped an arm and tugged.

"Don't stick your legs so far out, brother," admonished a bland voice. Its flashily dressed owner came into sight from the end of the car. "You'll get them knocked off. All together now, men! Allay oop!"

We hauled Nat inside. He lay panting and blinking his eyes.

Box car traveling makes most men garrulous. We soon learned that our fellow passenger was a carnival barker who had been stranded when the show went on the rocks out in Kansas. He was beating it back to Detroit to start anew. The barker preserved his natty appearance even in one of those sleazy suits which flap outside the shops of cheap clothiers. Through all the vicissitudes of the journey he had miraculously contrived to keep his trousers creased to knife-edge sharpness. He enlivened us with stories of what we might expect in the automobile city—then a magnetic moon drawing the tides of men from all sections of the nation.

I kept sliding the door open and peering out into the twilight. As the door opened, the clatter and roar of the train ascended to higher pitch. The coolness gathered first in the low places—rushed into my face. Across the fields the hills purpled slowly, the low sun gilding their crests briefly now and then. I was breaking loose again, as I had when I left Monkey Nest Camp for the railroad shops, as I had when I went to the city to see about Rollie's insurance.

"When hills take on the noble lines of death," I said to myself aloud, slow tears, not of grief, welling in my eyes. I thought of Helen and the walks we had taken in the afternoons. I heard Jasper giggling lewdly as the barker told about the "strippers" in the burlesque shows who disrobe piece by piece when persuaded by persistent applause.

I felt resentful toward Jasper. Against the darkening hills Hans' dark, earnest face flashed; Lena's sallow face just before she died; Bonny Fern as I knew her last, peering from between her yellow curls; Mother at the washtub; Rollie with blood dribbling from his chin. I understood then why Hans despised Jasper so.

"What you crying for, bub?" the barker said curiously at my elbow. He peered closely into my face. The light was fading fast now.

"Nothing," I answered, ashamed.

"Guess you hate to leave home. I know how it is. Maybe got a sweetheart. I heard you reciting that sonnet of Ficke's. I like that, too. You wouldn't think I was a college graduate, would you? Well, I am, *magna cum laude*, too. It's the old story:

> 'A pretty lass
> And a whisky glass
> Made a blooming ass
> Of me.' "

The lonesomeness surged up in my heart and I told him of my ambitions.

"Forget it about making a success by grubbing, kid!" he said. "There ain't any more Alger heroes now. It's the front you put on, doing the other fellow before he does you. All right to get the education, yes; but learn how to use it. The other fellow's just wanting the chance to gig you. Beat him to it, that's all. You'll find out I know what I'm talking about."

Every time the train halted, we slid the door shut and huddled silently in a far corner. We could hear car inspectors shouting along the string of cars; lifting the lids of journal boxes and slamming them down, tapping at the wheels, and testing the air brakes.

At one stop the door was flung back, and a flashlight's

182

beam flitted about the walls. We flattened ourselves against the end of the car and tried to quit breathing. Then a burly dick wearing a cowboy hat vaulted into the car and whipped out a pistol from a holster which he wore beneath his arm. We instinctively raised our hands above our heads.

"Come *awn*! Come *awn*!" blustered the dick. "What ya ridin' on?"

He was hinting for a cash bribe in return for the favor of letting us ride unmolested. But we knew we could catch another freight soon, and money was more valuable than time.

"We're all broke, chief," volunteered the barker in his most honeyed voice. "Just working boys trying to get to Detroit and find an honest day's work."

"The highways ain't crowded, are they? Ya got sore feet? Hadda nag a Red Ball, didn't ya, so's t' git me eat up blood raw? I was gonna be easy on ya, but, by Jesus, they's some o' you crummy bastards don't appreciate it when a man aims t' treat ya white. D'ya know what a hobo gits in this state? Sixty days on the highways, makin' little ones outen big ones! Now you bums unload out o' there! Hit the dirt! I aim t' take ya all t' the cooler."

We climbed dejectedly down and stumbled along the right of way in the wake of the dick, gravel rolling under our feet. The barker kept lagging behind, trying to engage the dick in conversation, but he sternly ordered him to walk ahead. Suddenly the barker crumpled up on the ground, began moaning and nursing his ankle. As the dick came up and leaned over him, the barker sprang up like a jack-in-the-box and sent the dick's pistol spinning with one blow, staggering him with another.

"Run like hell!" shouted the barker, diving into the dense alder bushes fringing the right of way. We plunged after him, following him by the sound of his crashing progress, until our sides stitched with pain. We could hear

183

the dick howling and cursing. After a while he recovered
his revolver and began firing in our direction. When the
bullets whined dangerously close, we retreated farther into
the brush. We felt comparatively safe, for the alders were
thick, we were far afield, and the dick did not dare to
stray far away from the train. Presently we heard the
train getting under way, the melancholy toot of the whistle grew faint, and only frogs croaking and mosquitoes
humming spitefully disturbed the solitude. The barker
reminded us that his nimble wit had saved us all from
disaster, and we were not disposed to argue with him.

"If you can learn to think just a second faster than
the other guy, young fellow," he said to me, "you're just
as good as wearing diamonds right now. If you can't, all
the education this side of hell will never make you anything but a slave to somebody else who can think a little
faster than you."

We returned to the track, and sat down on the rail to
await another freight. A water tank loomed across the
way and we could hear the soft "drip, drip, drip," of drops
from the spout into the chat beneath. The barker recited
for us a monologue he'd learned on the stage. The refrain
of it was: "You'll always find that money is your best
friend after all."

"D'ya suppose he's a real play actor?" whispered Nat,
slapping at the mosquitoes nipping at his ankles.

Now and then a passenger train shot by, carrying in its
wake a mighty rush of air which momentarily flattened
out the weeds along the ends of the ties. We shrank into
the bushes and gazed into the glittering, fleeing world
within the coaches. It hung suspended for a moment like a
flash on the moving picture screen, then hurtled away
forever, leaving the night blacker. The rails ticked for a
moment and then lay silent. A dining car with suave
colored waiters in attendance and complacent swells wield-

ing silver cutlery and dabbing at their mouths with linen napkins reminded us that we had not eaten since noon, twelve hours before.

"I wonder what Emma's doin'?" mused Nat, yawning.

"Well, brother, I guess you're like the fellow that wanted to find his wife when he saw her next just the way she was when he left her. Is that right?"

"Sure," said Nat, suspiciously. "Why not?"

"That's what this guy said, but another one says: 'Be damned if I do. I just give 'er a hell of a good lovin' before I left, and I'd sure hate to find 'er in that condition when I get back!' Think it over, brother, think it over! Naturally, a man going on a long journey such as this would want to. . . .'"

"I don't see much fun in that," Nat grumbled testily. "Don't like to hear such bla'guardin' about a good Christian woman like my woman. . . ."

"Oh, no harm intended, no reflections cast, my dear man," assured the barker, hooking his thumbs in his vest and teetering on his heels. "Just a little fun, sport and amusement. The more you see, the less you know. Gentlemen, the hand is quicker than the eye . . . ! She'll shake it up for you; she'll make you like it. Look down deep in the well, gentlemen, and see naughty Fatima do the dance of the seven veils. . . ."

A whistle sounded far down the track. A dog at a nearby farmhouse roused and set up a furious barking. Soon the engine could be heard laboring up a grade and then the headlights rose over the horizon like a sun. Their glare sent us into the bushes out of sight.

When the train stopped, we peeked cautiously out. No dick was in sight, but there were no empty cars. The barker and Nat climbed to the top of a box car and stretched out on the running board, but Jasper and I preferred to stand on the coupling blocks between two cars, for the air off the lakes blew chilly after midnight. The barker warned us that we were in danger of becoming drowsy and falling beneath the wheels. We stood facing one another with a foot on each block clinging to brake shafts and grab irons. The drawbars extended or withdrew like a turtle's neck shooting in and out from beneath its shell. We were careful not to set foot on them, for we knew that more than one uninvited passenger of the railroads had had his foot crushed off in that manner.

The monotonous rush and roar, the rhythmic clicking of the wheels on the rail joints, lulled me. I found my eyes closing when a quick jerk of my head aroused me. Then I grasped the brake shaft like a vise. But everything persistently faded, and I suddenly felt a sharp blow across my stomach. I found myself sprawled across the drawbars with my feet dangling on one side and my head and arms on the other. Jasper was holding onto me grimly to keep me from slipping beneath the wheels, where I would have been ground into hamburger meat. We climbed shakily to the tops and lay watching the crimson glare from the firedoor against the low flying smoke as the fireman opened it up to shovel in more coal. Cinders pelted us, and the wind had not cooled some of them. They stuck and burned.

The train roared and rattled on; the whistle shrieked demoniacally. In the weak morning light we could see spider-webs of tracks branching away like opening fans, then factories checked into blue squares by neon lights. We swung off the freight at an outer depot and mingled with the thousands of workers hurrying to their jobs or standing on corners waiting for buses or street cars. They rarely spoke; most of them gazing morosely and steadily before them. The street cars clanged, the trolley wires sputtered blue overhead. Some of the men were walking, planting one foot ahead of the other heavily, their eyes leaden and swollen. Some of them yawned and spat in the gutter. The address Ed had given us was on the other side of town. The barker gave us a lot of benevolent advice before we parted with him. He told us we'd more than likely see him again.

Ben lived in a district of outmoded wooden residences formerly occupied by the aristocracy of the 90's. Some of the houses had skimpy yards, decorated with rusty iron deer and trash-littered and dry fountains, in front; others were flush with the sidewalk. Widening the once narrow thoroughfare had cut off the yards. Brick shops were arising among the decaying wooden houses; the wreckers were busy. Dingy signs advertising "Sleeping Rooms" and "Furnished Rooms for Light Housekeeping" appeared in the windows of most of the ancient structures.

Bonny Fern opened the door. She had rounded out; her curly hair was bobbed. She was prettier than Helen, the lunch girl, I thought, but in a colder way.

"Oh, hello," she said casually. "Ed'll be tickled to see you. He's expecting you. Come in and bring your friends." Her speech was short and crisp, the kind of utterance that always makes the Southerner or Westerner think the city dweller of the East is out of humor.

Ben and Ed were both working at Premiers Motors, she said. She was going to Detroit University. She asked about everybody back home in an off-hand way. Jasper and Nat fidgeted uneasily, and after a bit Jasper whispered hoarsely that they'd go outside to look around a little, find a place to room. After a few minutes of commonplace conversation, Bonny Fern said she had some work she must get at, and I could just make myself at home. There were magazines—love and western story pulps, I noticed—and the radio if I cared to turn it on. I was glad to be alone, for I could think of nothing to say to her. Her bold and steady stare disturbed me. It was the city life, I thought; she had not looked that way back home. I thought she was careless about the way she crossed her legs without bothering how her skirts were disarranged, and she had on too much rouge. Each cheek was decorated with a spot as round and vivid as a winesap apple. After a while, I went down the street and found Jasper and Nat. I stayed with them in the room they had rented until almost time for Ed and Ben to come home.

"Well, you got here, kid," said Ed when he came in. His tone was quite as diffident as Bonny Fern's but his eyes shone with pleasure. Bonny Fern seemed to liven up now. She began to chatter gaily. Ben was bald, his wind- and sun-reddened face had faded to a sort of greasy grey and his jowls hung limply on his face. He sat down heavily and turned on the radio so strong that Bonny Fern walked over and snapped it off. Ben looked at her resentfully and muttered something about the modern generation having no respect for grey hairs.

"We're goin' to a show," said Ed after supper. "Wanta go along?"

I almost let the bromide about "two's company, three's a crowd" slip out, but caught it in time.

"No, not tonight. I've got to go down to Jasper's and Nat's room. They rented a room down the street."

"We've got room for you here," broke in Mrs. Haskin. She was prematurely aged, as all farm and working class women become. "So you come back here. I wish we had room for the other two fellows, but we haven't."

"What about the job?" I said to Ed. "The job's what we came after."

"Oh, you won't have no trouble gettin' a job," laughed Ed. "They ain't hirin' anybody in the enamel department where I work, but they will be soon. You c'n git a job most anywheres. They jump outen the factories and drag 'em in offen the streets. Brother of a feller in my department is a foreman out at Badger Motor Co. He says they'll hire a slew of machine runners today and tomorrow."

"What kind of a machine would I be expected to run?" I asked.

"Don't let that worry you. You never see the guy that hires you again. Only thing, don't say you're a tool and die maker. Can't fool 'em on them trades. But on most other work, they got to break a new man in, anyway. They got the machines so anybody with a weak mind and strong back can run 'em."

Jasper, Nat and I stood in a snake-like queue before the Badger Motor Co. the next morning. We could see that a few men were being hired up ahead, but more were being turned away. The job seekers were speculating as to what factors determined the hiring clerk's choice. He stalked up and down the line, sweeping each applicant from head to foot with a contemptuous scrutiny. It was said by some of the men that he chose every tenth man arbitrarily; others contended that he was partial to blue eyes and golden hair. The line shuffled along. The fifth man ahead of me was rejected when he called himself a machine runner. "Drill press," sang out another, who was hired. So, when I halted before the hiring clerk I cried: "Drill press," confidently.

"*You* look like a drill press hand, you apple knocker!" he jeered. Nevertheless, he caught hold of my shoulder and shoved me headlong through a door into a room where thirty or forty other fortunate ones were huddled, conversing in awed undertones. Presently, Nat, grinning triumphantly, catapulted to my side.

We were stripped, weighed, marched and countermarched to various officials. Doctors probed in our mouths, made us skip and run, bend over, cough, asked some of us when we last had a bath. In the final winnowing, half the candidates were rejected. The survivors were issued badges which would be our open sesame to the gates the next morning when we could file in through the envious alleys of the jobless. Nat and I were among the elect, but Jasper had not even made it to the front office. He had made the mistake of sticking to the "machine runner" story or the hiring clerk did not like his looks. It was all a gamble anyhow.

Nat returned to the room to write Emma of his good fortune while Jasper continued to look for jobs. I sauntered down town and sat on a bench in Grand Circus Park. Because it was useless to look for work after nine o'clock, the park was always crowded with job seekers who would look again tomorrow. A man had time to apply to only two or three places a day. I was amazed to hear many of the men declaring they could not find work, though they had sought it diligently and everywhere. I learned that the automobile industry enjoyed a period of feverish activity during January, February, March and April. Possibly it held up during May, but was almost sure to decline precipitately in June and July and to remain at low ebb until the next January. I began to consider myself lucky in getting a job so soon.

A stocky oldish man occupied the next bench. He had his head turned, but the back of it looked familiar. A naked dome arising from a grizzly fringe of hair. I walked around and peered into his face. As I had thought, it was Bun Grady. He was reading a newspaper fished out of one of the waste cans. He dropped it and began picking and biting callouses off his palms. I stood watching him silently; he did not notice me. He drew a huge clasp knife out of his pocket and pared his thick finger nails. The sunlight glinted on his hairy, muscular arms as he flexed his biceps and stared at them ruefully.

190

"Hello, Mr. Grady," I said after a moment.

"Oh, hello!" He gazed at me dully for a full minute, then he recognized me. "Jist tryin' t' place ya. You've filled out; got t' be more of a man. Didja lose your job at the steel mill?"

"Yeh, got fired! Had another job since. What have you been doing?"

"Oh, I get a job diggin' ditches or cleanin' streets, sometimes at pearl divin', ever so often. But in the factories they don't want a man that's been weaned. It's all speed like a foot race. They got to have wet nurses in some of the factories to change didies and give titty to some of the kids they hire. What they gonna do with us old bucks? Guess they'll get so they'll shoot a man when he gets a certain age or throw him in the river with an anvil round his neck."

"You'll get a job here. But it may take time. Let me lend you ten dollars till you find something."

"I'd hate t' have you do that. Are you positive sure you c'n spare it?" Then without waiting for me to answer: "Yes, I *will* borry it, Larry, and many thanks t' you, lad! With that ten dollars I c'n live at the Helping Hand Mission fer a long time. You oughta come around sometime. Reminds me of the Rescue Mission. Ol' Marster sent you here, son. He ain't deserted me yet. I'll get me a job and pay it back. A man c'n jist have *so much* bad luck, and then his luck's bound t' change."

He walked briskly away, his shoulders erect. He was humming a hymn. I never saw him again or heard of him, but now and then one sees an item in the papers about some oldish man found beside the railroad tracks. Perhaps a battered suitcase will be found a little piece down the right of way, or a package of assorted needles or a Bible may be discovered among the ties. One of these might be Bun Grady.

The bums in the park stretched out on the benches and spread newspapers over their faces to keep out the sun and flies. Cops came along at intervals and aroused the sleepers by hammering on their shoe soles with sticks. Panhandlers infested the locality, but they had to keep a wary eye on the police. They delivered their importunities in a low, hurried voice and hastened away at the least suggestion of annoyance.

Powdered, perfumed and rouged men strolled among the benches and occasionally accosted a bum, offering to take him on a party or buy a bottle. They addressed one another as "Agnes," "Gertrude," or some other feminine name. Often the bums chased the perverts in real or simulated anger, threatening to murder them, less frequently their blandishments were successful.

"Say, friend, you look like a working man to me," I heard an oily familiar voice saying close at hand. I turned about and saw the barker talking to a man who was obviously a factory hand on holiday.

"I got a $75.00 pay waiting for me out at Flint," the barker continued, "but I'm damned near dead-broke. Got hi-jacked in a joint out in Hamtramck. I just lack two-bits of having enough carfare to get home. If you'll lend me the quarter, I'll send you a dollar by mail. First time I ever had to do this. I've been walking up and down here trying to screw up courage to ask somebody."

The man gave him a quarter, and the barker thanked him fervently, promising to mail a dollar the next day. He carefully set down his benefactor's address in a note book. I saw him accost at least a dozen men within two hours, and only two or three refused him.

"Sure, it's a fake," the barker confessed when I confronted him. "I haven't got any pay at Flint or anywhere else. But I only take a small amount from each one, and it makes them feel at least a quarter's worth better for doing a good deed. I'm not physically strong enough to hold down a job in a factory. Besides," he burst out passionately, "those factories'll drive you cuckoo! You have to dash around like a blind dog in a meat shop or a turpentined cat! I *know*! Try to get a job slinging hash, or pearl diving, pimping or capping, but steer clear of the factories."

I watched the methods of the panhandlers after that. Some of them asked for as little as two cents, claiming they had pay or assistance waiting for them and needed only that infinitesimal sum to buy a stamp. Asking for a smaller amount meant a smaller percentage of refusals, and most of them could probably eke out at least a slender existence at their trade.

X

Just as Ed had predicted, I didn't go to work on a drill press, but "on the line," screwing on a section beneath coupe doors. The bodies moved along on a chain conveyor; the men hopped on, performed their tasks, and jumped off to catch the next body. Each man had a definite task to accomplish—screw on this bolt, tack on that section of upholstering. When I first looked at the chain, I thought its progress was very slow. But the men were chasing about, sweating and cursing, working furiously for a moment, then flying to the next task. Some of them never rose. They sat on low wheeled seats and propelled themselves along with their legs, their heads thrust beneath the bodies, their hands flying like a weaver's shuttle. Somebody was always dropping something in their faces, but they could not stop.

I fumbled with screws and let the screw-driver slip out of my nervous fingers, where it caught in the chain, causing it to buck violently. The other men entreated me to get out of the way so they could do their stints. The floor was littered with tacks lost from the mouth of an agitated Italian boy who frequently clapped a magnetized hammer to his lips. It came away with a tack sticking to it.

"Whatcha how fast I do thees! Justa watch, Bill! Justa like lightning!" he pleaded, pushing me aside. He unrolled the cloth along the roof bows and tacked it as it unrolled. I watched him, open-mouthed. One of the men told me that the boy's stomach was full of tacks, and that he was going to be cut open soon.

In spite of all my efforts, I fell steadily behind and at last the boss stopped the chain. I had not worked there long enough to comprehend the enormity of my offense, but the horrified glare of the men imparted some realization of it.

At noon the chain halted twenty minutes for lunch. The men dropped down soddenly and ripped open newspaper wrapped packages. They looked for a bench or empty truck on which to lie flat while eating. Some of them dozed fitfully. The chain would soon be moving again, and every moment of respite was dear. Nat found me just a minute before time to go to work.

"Got me on the putty glazin' job," he told me. "Sure kept me hoppin' about, but it pays eight dollars a day! Think o' that! I'm gonna send fer Emma and the kids."

"You all got lead in the seat of your pants," the foreman jested as he stood watch in hand, ready to punch the starting button. "You got the dropsy and heart failure. You drop down soon's the line quits and your heart fails you when you have to get up."

Just before quitting time, the men were animated by a current of exuberance. They discussed plans for the evening, inquired the time of day every few minutes.

"Soon be *that* time," one of the men said to me late in the afternoon as he waited while I struggled with the screws and screwdriver. The ends of my fingers were sore and bleeding.

"First thing I do when I get home," pursued the man, his eyes half closed. "I take a good wash, then I read the sport page and look at Barney Google to see what kind of devilment he's into. Then I eat me a good supper and go over to Herman's in Hamtramck and put a few cold steins under my belt. Sometimes I go to the Avenue burlesque when they got a good hot show on."

As we trooped down the stairs, our feet resounding like the tread of a routed army, the men chatted gaily and some of the younger bucks played leapfrog. The grey steps would look different in the cold wan light of morning.

Ed and I walked down to Cadillac Square after supper. I told him that I had about finished the accountancy course. He laughed.

"Forget about it, kid," he said. "You got to have a pull to get anywhere in the white-collar jobs. They start you in at lower than factory wages and keep you there till you dry up and blow away. Stay in the factory work. You'll soon get used to it."

"Will I have to work in a factory all my life?" I asked. "What can I build up to in a factory?"

"You might get t' be a foreman. That pays higher than most white collar jobs you'd likely wait years for. I know you got ambitious ideas, kid, but it'll only be an accident if you ever get out of your class. You might as well make up your mind you're a workin' stiff and that you'll stay one unless lightning happens t' strike you—some kind of luck that hits only one out of a million workin' men. You'll work a while, maybe raise a mess of kids, get too old t' work in the factories and hafta sponge offen your kids the rest of your life. It's in the cards, kid. You might as well get used to it and enjoy yourself as much as you can."

I had an uneasy feeling that he was right about this. I did know many clerks who had grubbed for years without getting anywhere. There had been several college men working in the rubber heel plant, and they were not college boys out for a lark, but men who should have been securely moored in their destined position in life.

We came to a dark narrow street where a swart young man with bushy hair was haranguing a small knot of idlers. A Salvation Army band blared farther down the street, and a magician arrayed in a fantastic costume decorated with figures of black cats stood on an improvised platform attached to the back of a large automobile. He was performing miracles with the license numbers of passing cars, the ages of his spectators and any other casual figures anyone might want to give him. He reminded his hearers that they, too, could be just as nimble with figures if they'd read his marvelous little book on mathematics, costing only fifty cents. He sold a lot of them.

"That radical ain't got much chance," Ed said. "Give a worker a full gut and he's satisfied, even if you kick him in the butt every day. He oughta get in some kind of graft like that feller sellin' the books."

A little farther down the street the barker stood before a hallway, intoning like a muezzin calling the faithful to prayer: "Big crap game upstairs, gents! Big game upstairs! Walk right up; this is your lucky day."

The policeman on the corner ignored him, crossing to the other side of the street and pretending not to see him. The barker said to me sotto voce, from the corner of his mouth: "Stay away from here, boy. They'll take you to a cleaning."

I was so slow at the body job that I was transferred to a department where I had to touch up the small unpainted spot left by air bubbles at the top of fenders as they passed through the enamel tanks. After I painted the spots, I had to grab the fenders off the conveyor and pile them on a padded truck. I soused the brush in the paint can, dabbed rapidly, set the paint can and brush down, and wrestled with the fender. Sometimes the hook caught and I was dragged several feet before I could disentangle it. The paint ran off the brush and down my arm as I raised it. My gloves were always sticky, and if I touched the finished fender with them, they left a marred spot. In my hurry I scratched many of the fenders. Sweat stung my eyes and my nose itched incessantly, but when I thoughtlessly brushed my face, the paint smeared it and burned all the more. I was told that the conveyor ran twice as fast as it had the year before and that 25 men did twice as much work as 250 had done in 1921, before the conveyor system was perfected.

"You can't beat that merry-go-round," one of the old hands complained mournfully as he watched my frantic efforts to keep up. "Might as well try to fight a buzz saw, pardner. Before they started the conveyor system a man had some chancet. Now you jist gotta stand and take yer punishment or git out."

Days and weeks flowed along and a year passed. We were glad to leave the factory at night and spent a great deal of the night and all our holidays trying to forget it.

Nat was well satisfied. He expected to be a straw-boss soon. He had bought a lot in Rosewood Manor, a new real estate development only a half mile or so from the end of the bus line. He was living in a garage on the back of his lot, but he intended to build a fine brick veneer home as soon as he could afford it. Just then it kept both him and Emma scratching to pay the sixty dollars a month payments on the lot and the garage. Then they had to pay four dollars a week to have the children cared for. They had paid a stiff price for the lot—one which would have astounded the farmer who had owned the cow pasture from which the subdivision had been laid out. But the city was pushing nearer year after year. The stock market was booming. The ants like Nat who were preparing for the future derided and pitied the irresponsible grasshoppers like Ed and me who spent our money as fast as we earned it.

I had half-heartedly tried several times to find a white-collar job, but when I saw men who had spent years at clerical work pouring into the factories because of the higher wages, I decided to stick where I was. Mother and Aunt Jessie could live very well on what I was able to send them; I had the rest with which to find surcease from the endless procession of auto bodies on the belt that moved through my waking hours unless I sought respite in excitement. And excitement for the automobile workers usually meant one or both of two things: liquor and women. If I resolved to stay at home and improve my mind by reading, the letters squirmed before my eyes. I'd fall asleep and awake hours later, stiff and sore.

After quitting or getting fired from several other jobs, Jasper landed in the same department with me. Our conversation was always broken by the exigencies of our work, and it sometimes required all of an afternoon to discuss something which might have been disposed of in five minutes had we not been interrupted.

"Boy, I met up with a hot baby!" Jasper exulted, just as I had to go chasing a fender about to escape down the conveyor.

"Did you?" I asked when I returned.

"Yes, name of Bessie. She's got a movement like an Elgin watch." He dashed off with a truck full of fenders and returned five minutes later.

"Bessie? I knew a girl by that name during the War. See if she's got 'For Soldiers and Sailors Only' tattooed on her stomach." I went chasing another fender. While I was gone Jasper filled his truck and went off with it.

"I never noticed, but I'll find out," he said when he returned. He was gone six minutes this time. He had rushed into the toilet for a minute.

Thus we whiled away the hours.

We walked out of the plant under the surveillance of the plant guards. They were supposed to examine each lunch pail to see whether the owner was carrying anything home with him. But the guards were usually old men worn out in the service of the company, and they grew negligent. For weeks they would pass the lunch pails through with only a casual glance and without asking to see the inside of them. Most of the guards stationed at the gate were mutilated in some way or other—one had lost an arm, another the fingers of a hand, while another had had a cheek bashed in and grinning teeth showed through. The old men dozed in their padded chairs. Then, too, the homing workers surged past the gates so tempestuously that it was impossible to look everybody over closely.

Jasper stepped along with studied nonchalance; he greeted the guards with loud cordiality. Just as he passed through the gates, his toe caught on a high brick and he stumbled, throwing his lunch pail ahead of him. It burst open. Bolts, nuts, and a light bulb rolled out. The guards aroused and ran forward as Jasper, glowering behind him, shouted indignantly: "Who throwed that at me? Wanta knock a man's head off?"

But his ruse was unsuccessful. The guards confiscated the plunder, made a note of Jasper's badge number, and told him to report at the payoff window in the morning at 10. He walked away rapidly, swinging his battered pail savagely.

Neither Ed nor I saw much of Bonny Fern any more.

She stayed in her room at night and her mother said she was always having to write a theme or something of the kind. For me she had never fully emerged as a creature clothed with flesh. I was still the rebuffed urchin of Monkey Nest Camp. Ed complained that her college education was giving her the big head.

XI

"It was her, all right," Jasper insisted. "Helen, the lunch girl at the rubber heel plant. I seen her on Woodward Avenue, but she didn't wanta talk much. She ast me where you was, though. She wouldn't tell me where she lived."

My pulses pounded. "You show me where you saw her," I said.

"All right, I will, but you'll hafta go right now. I jist got on at the Chevrolet Gear and Axle Plant and I've got a hell of a long ways t' go t' git there."

He left me on a corner.

"I've seen her here twicet in the last week," he said as he swung aboard a street car. "Likely she comes by here every day."

I waited for two hours, but she never came. The second day I saw her.

"Hello, Helen!" I said.

She paused and averted her eyes.

"You've made a mistake. I don't know you."

"Oh, yes you do. Where are you living?"

"I tell you, you've made a mistake. Let me be."

"Hey, masher," called a cop who happened to be sauntering by. "You can't get by with that kind of stuff here. D'ya want me to run ya in?"

"I guess he just made a mistake. Don't arrest him," Helen pleaded. The cop ordered me down the street and Helen boarded a street car.

The third and fourth days she did not show up, so I gave it up for a while. Weeks and months passed and one day I saw her on Cass Avenue. This time I followed her and saw her enter a hot dog joint in a cheap business section. I took down the number and resolved to come back again. I could see that she had not stopped at the counter but had gone on to the rear of the place. So she must be working there, I thought.

Nat came each day during our lunch period and sat with me. I learned that he was having a tough time trying to pay for the lot and garage-dwelling in Rosewood Manor; and he and Emma were getting impatient for the brick veneer house they had promised themselves.

"They tell me they's a world of money in home brew," Nat remarked. "Yeast, malt, sugar, bottle caps and all don't amount to more 'n a cent a bottle and you c'n git twenty-five easy as pie. Do you think they's any harm in good healthy beer? Even Christ turned the waters into wine."

Then a few days later: "Seen Jasper the other day. He was out t' the house. He said I orta set a batch o' home brew every week and I'd soon have that brick veneer."

"Well, why don't you?"

"By doggies, b'lieve I *will*! I'll talk it over with Emma. She's a God-fearin' woman, and I am a man, but lotsa Christians drink."

When I reached home that evening, I was surprised to find Bonny Fern in the sitting room. She said hello, and continued reading a magazine with a striking cartoon in black and white on the cover.

"What's that, a new comic magazine?" I asked.

"It's not so comic," she replied handing it to me with a smile. When she looked me in the eyes as she did then, I could feel my face flushing. "It's *The New Proletariat*. Ever see it before?"

I told her I never had. She left me reading the magazine and I read it till ten o'clock without getting sleepy.

"What did you think of *The New Proletariat*?" Bonny Fern asked me the next evening.

"It's great!" I said.

"You should get interested in something like that. You need something to take hold of to help you cut out that boozing. It'd be more economical, too. How'd you like to go down to the soap-box corner tonight? They're always selling such things down there."

"Will you go with me?"

"Sure, why not?"

"It seems like a rough sort of place."

She laughed. "They're not rough. Sometimes the police get rough if they block the sidewalk and push you around a bit. But I shan't mind."

On the way back from the street meeting, Bonny Fern swung on my arm.

"You're thinking about it, I see. That's good. My sociology prof. talked to me about all that. He says that what the radicals say is true in theory, but that they're laboring under a delusion in believing that the actual proletariat takes any interest whatever in its self-appointed leaders and saviors. It's a game, Larry, a kind of escape from reality. You'll find comfort in it if you can make yourself believe that workers are brave and intelligent as those soap-box orators do. I half believe it myself. Professor Dane says that every American worker thinks that some day he'll be a capitalist himself, and thus he is just as zealous in defense of the system as the millionaire. The Europeans are different; once an aristocrat, always an aristocrat there. And a European worker doesn't kid himself about his chances of getting to be a plutocrat as the American worker does. . . ."

"If it's all a delusion why bother with it?" I broke in. "Might as well entertain yourself with crossword puzzles."

"Everybody believes in even greater delusions. Some believe in God. Remember how many innocents swallowed the 'War to End War.' And as long as you believe it, you'll be happy."

I enjoyed this arguing with Bonny Fern. I exulted to think that we had found a common ground of interest. She was prettier than ever when her eyes revealed more than a casual concern in what I had to say. When we reached home I told her that I thought I'd walk around a bit, since it was still early and I was not sleepy.

"Out to Hamtramck to drown Marx in suds!" she laughed.

"No, not tonight," I protested. But I had not told her what I really intended to do. I was going to look for Helen at the hot dog joint. I found the place easily. Several men were coming out, and another came up, entered and walked through the front room to the rear.

"Give me a hot dog and a bottle of pop," I said to the fat, elderly woman behind the counter. She wore a brilliantly flowered kimona instead of an apron. Her thick lips cracked in a grin that displayed almost a full set of gold teeth.

"Does a girl named Helen Baker work here?" I asked as she waddled toward a steel plate set over a gas jet which was not lit.

"Sure! D'ya wanta see Helen? Think she's busy right now. You've been here before, then. I've bragged on myself that I never forgit a face, but I can't place yourn."

"No, I've never been here before. Where's the hot dog?"

She came back with a weinie, flipping it between her fingers.

"This good ol' rubber weinie is the only one we've got in stock, and it might hang in yer teeth. We bought it from a magic trick store, but it does to fool snoopers with. The Civic Morality League watches things purty closet sometimes. D'ya want me t' call all the girls out so's you c'n take yer pick, or will it be Helen?"

Then the realization of the kind of place it was socked me like a heavy fist. I might have known it the minute I came in. I was pretty much of a greenhorn, I guess. All this time I had remembered Helen and secretly hoped that I'd make everything right with her. All that was gross about the memory of her had been shed away since I had walked with her down Lovers' Leap the last time. I wanted more than anything else to get away from the fat Madame's leering scrutiny and into the air. An unsteady drunk wabbled from the back of the place, and made several jabbing attempts to insert a nickel in the slot of a mechanical piano standing in the corner. At last he succeeded, and began to caper nimbly but precariously as the piano and a phonograph attached ground out:

"She's got great big diamond rings.
She knows her onions."

"I want to see her again!" It reverberated insistently in my head to the rhythm of the music. "I must see her again." (. . . "She's got lots of other things. She knows her vegetables.") "I want to see her again!" But I wanted something to give me courage—perhaps lend me a subtle tongue.

"Wait a minute! Have you got any shut-eye here? Give me a pint," I said. I drank the pint in a few gulps. It was raw and vile and I sputtered and coughed. The woman laughed shrilly.

"There comes Helen's company now. Go right back to

Room 14," she said as a beefy fellow lumbered from the rear.

The back of the building was divided into a number of cells by plasterboard partitions. Inside each cell were an iron bedstead and a small dressing table. Women in kimonas lolled on the beds or sat on the edge, swinging their bare legs. Some of the doors were closed.

"Hello, Helen," I said, pausing before the open door of Cell 14. She started violently and pulled her kimona closely about her. Her cigarette dropped from between her fingers and burned a hole in the coverlet.

"You're drunk!" she said.

"Sure."

"You never used to drink."

"Lots of people get to doing things they didn't always do. Like you. . . ."

"Go away and leave me alone," she begged, beginning to cry.

"I've got money."

"There's other girls here."

"How would you like to have me say you a little poetry, then. You used to like that. Here's one by John McClure:

> 'I shall steal upon her
>   Where she sits so white,
> Creep-mouse, creep-mouse,
>   In the twilight.' "

I couldn't remember the rest. The whisky was potent stuff.

"That's pretty," she said, without raising her head. "Why did you come here, Larry?"

"Why, what does everybody come in here for?" I recoiled from the words as soon as I had spoken them.

"I couldn't help wishing I'd see you again, but not here."

"Why are you here, then? I followed you and I thought you were—working here."

"You did? Oh, I'm glad! You just wanted to see me for myself, didn't you?" Her shadowed eyes, brimming with tears, begged me.

"Tell her! Tell her how much you've thought about her all the time," was one of the warring impulses that gained ascendancy tenaciously. The whisky muddled me all the more. I just stood weaving on my feet as though I stood on rubber legs.

"Why are you here, I asked you?" I repeated at length.

"I didn't mean what I told you when you told me goodbye in the rubber plant. I was still sore at you, I guess, but I thought sure you'd write to me if you really cared anything about me even if I did tell you not to. There's something about me that makes me say smart-alecky things when I can't get out what I'd like to say. Like the time I first saw you and winked at you and tried to attract your attention. When I didn't hear from you I got reckless, got into trouble, and the guy left me and pulled out for Chicago. Before I could find a doctor that would do anything for me, I had to quit work. I come here to Detroit thinking maybe I'd see you, but I didn't want you to see me—not here, anyways."

"Gee, Helen! Gee!" I muttered stupidly. I sat down beside her and drew her to me. Her kimono fell away, baring her breasts. My arm tightened about her instinctively, and I could feel her soft body stiffening. She broke away.

"No! Please, Larry!" she sobbed. "Not you—not that! Sit down and let me comb the tangles out of your hair like I used to up on Lovers' Leap."

It broke through my fuddled consciousness that I could not have her then as I could have once. I could not have her by paying her two dollars. Jesus! Everything was scrambled and I couldn't see any way back for us. I felt her fingers in my hair and with the touch the sense of irrevocable loss stabbed me more deeply. I must be hard-boiled. No, I must think things out when I was sober.

"How would you like to take a walk with me?" I wanted to get her out of there. I thought the cold air might blow the cobwebs out of my head.

"Oh, I can't! Oh, I can't leave here!" she sobbed.

"I'll pay you for your time at the regular rate. How many dollars do you usually take in in an hour?" I said brutally, and instantly regretted my words. I wanted to tell her I was sorry, but I didn't.

"Go away! Leave me alone!" she screamed loudly. I could hear excited voices outside.

"Helen's friend's gettin' rough," I heard the Madame say. "Rex, oh Rex! Give 'im the bum's rush! Raus mitt 'im!"

"It's no use, you can't unsnarl it! First it was Jasper that was to blame, but now it's you that's pulled a boner," a demon urged in my ear. "Show the cockeyed world you don't give a damn! Show 'em all they can't get the best of you! Smash! Make a cleaning here! You'll feel better if you smash something!"

"To hell with this joint! I'll wreck this joint," I shouted, kicking a hole through the plasterboard partition. I swung at my own image in the mirror of the dressing table and blood spurted from my fist as the glass jangled on the floor. A hubbub arose.

"The damned fool! He'll have the cops closin' us down. They told us they'd do that little thing—divvy or no divvy—if there was any hell around here. Put the quietus on him, Rex!" the Madame howled.

"Oh, Larry, watch!" I heard Helen cry. "Don't hurt him, Rex! Don't hit him! He'll leave! He'll go!"

I wheeled about, but too late. Rex loomed before me

and something crashed on my head. I awoke in the alley at dawn. Somebody had neatly tied up my mangled hand.

I wasn't able to work the next day, but I walked down to the soap-box corner in the evening. Bonny Fern would not go. She knew that I had been drunk and in a scrap. Ed walked down with me but decided to go on to a burlesque.

Weeks passed in this manner. Ben moved from the rooming house district to a small house farther out. He had always felt cramped in the rooming house, and he often spoke longingly of his farm near Monkey Nest Camp. He had tried to keep up the taxes on it, but they were two years in arrears. The tenant had not paid any rent for a year. Ben was idle a great deal, for men of his age were always the first to catch it in a layoff. From June to January he worked little.

Kentucky hill billies have a mountain or a thousand acres of blue grass for a backyard sometimes. In Glasgow, Ky., I remember the Negroes raking dead leaves in streets wide as a city block. The white pickets enclosed lawns bigger than The Hub Department Store. So the desperate Ishmaels like Ben, transported to the city, flee as soon as possible from the tortures of dismal "Furnished for light housekeeping" rooms. Cribbed, cabined and confined in a diminutive "living room" and a microscopic kitchenette, the walls press on their minds. Decaying relics of a pristine gentility, the rooming houses are unsanitary, dark, and fetid. When you stumble up the sudden stairs and snap on an unshaded bulb, a million cockroaches scamper for the shelter of a dank and rusty sink. The wall paper is damp and bilious with liver-spots. The children have no place to play.

Up and coming second hand furniture dealers are quick to capitalize the rural immigrant's yearning for deliverance. Outmoded furniture can be varnished, puttied, and repaired—and advertised cunningly: "Three room outfit for $125.00—Four room outfit for $175.00—$15 down—Easy monthly payments—Don't stay cooped in furnished rooms." A few payments cover the initial cost, and the stuff can always be repossessed, ·revarnished, and resold.

"Say, Larry," Nat said to me the day after we moved to the suburbs. "I got a little home brew out there at the house. I don't make a business of it, but I aim t' make it clean and charge a fair price. So if any of your friends wants a drink of good healthy beer, they'll know where t' find it."

"Sure, I'll go with you, kid," Ed said to me after supper. "You need a little rest from that heavyweight stuff you've been readin'. Some day you'll learn it don't amount to a hill o' beans. Workers is made t' be gouged; bosses is made t' gouge 'em. It's the law of Nature, kid. Ain't nothing so small but what it lives off something else. They tell me that even fleas has got littler fleas eatin' on 'em, and so on down the line."

Ed and I stepped off the bus at twilight and walked a mile down a dusty road to Rosewood Manor. Two grandiose brick columns supporting a gilded arch marked the entrance, and multi-colored pennants fluttered along the graded earth streets. Weeds were blotting out some of the avenues—Delmar Vista Boulevard was two faint tracks in a growth of wiry grass that stabbed at our ankles like knives. There were iron lamp posts, each bearing a cluster of white globes like ghostly blossoms, at the street corners, but they were unlighted. The electric power lines had not yet been extended that far.

Only one of the lot purchasers had built a house—the others were living in garages at the rear. The garages were of the ready-cut variety. They were identical, and—as in

Sunset Meadows where Nat and Lena had lived—a man a little fuddled would have had difficulty in finding his own home among its many counterparts. Here and there a bit of shrubbery or a rose trellis attested the owner's revolt against regimentation. Some of the inhabitants stood in their doorways, leaning against the jambs and peering out at the spots where their houses would stand after the lean years of sacrifice had borne fruit. The hovels were comically small—nagging tongues of women and the petulant howls of babies resounded from several of them. Office grubs and factory hands stood with their backs toward the cubicles called homes and raised their faces to the wide sky, breathing gratefully of the deep spaces studded with stars. No doubt they were thinking of the day when Delmar Vista Boulevard would be a credit to its impressive name.

Nat had divided his garage home into two diminutive cells. The "front room" was furnished with a tapestried living room suite and a small library table. One had to scoot sidewise to pass between the table and the davenport. Emma tried to temper her acidulous smile, but was only partially successful. She apologized for the way things were cramped up, and said we'd have to come out when they built the brick veneer. Nat and she could not agree as to the floor plan of the proposed house. Each of them produced a plan and solicited our opinions of them. We agreed with both as decorously as we could, and wondered about the beer.

After a while Nat furtively drew the shades and produced two quart bottles of home brew, dripping from the tub of cold water in which they had been immersed. The children had been put to bed in the other room. The beer was sour and doughy-tasting, and there was such a thick scum of yeast on the bottoms of the bottles that we had to pour carefully to keep from stirring it up. Nat said he put potatoes in the malt to give it more kick, but it tasted as though the potatoes had been rotten.

Emma hovered about, anxious to please. She had stood on her feet all day long in a department store, and Nat kept telling her to sit down, for goodness sake, and let him take care of everything. She took off her shoes and rubbed her feet. Nat ran and fetched a clothes pin to clamp on his nose, saying he knew there was something dead in the house. We knew that Nat was conscientiously trying to be funny, so we laughed uproariously. Emma begged us not to laugh so loudly, for some of the neighbors were terribly snoopy and would enjoy nothing better than to turn somebody in for bootlegging.

Nat drank one bottle, but Emma kept looking at him so hard that he declined thereafter, even when Ed offered to set 'em up for the crowd.

"He can't stand it," Emma explained darkly. "He makes a fool of himself. I don't mind to see a person drink if they don't make a fool of theirselves."

About ten o'clock somebody rapped thunderously on the door, the impact seeming to shake the flimsy walls. Emma started to grabbing bottles and hollering: "In a minute! Just a minute!"

Nat opened the door a crack and inquired who was there. His voice quavered nervously. Jasper lurched through inside, dragging a simpering flat-faced, frizzle-haired woman behind him.

"Had a hell of a time findin' your joint, Nat," shouted Jasper. "You oughta have a sign out. Like to 've walked the legs offen Bessie."

He lowered himself onto the davenport and extended his feet, shoving the table a foot and overturning some glasses and bottles with yeasty sediment in them. Emma came running with a towel. She was finicky about her furniture. Bessie sat up as stiff as though she had a ramrod down her spine, but now and then she lost her grip and weaved to and fro. She bared doggish fangs in a mirthless laugh.

"I didn't expect you tonight, Jasper," Nat stammered.

"No matter! I'm spittin' cotton and so's Bessie. Bellies to the bar!" Jasper whooped. "See what the boys in the back room 'll have!"

Jasper had already had a few bottles, but only enough to tease him. Nat fetched two pints, and Jasper exulted volubly over the way they popped and smoked when they were opened. He called for salt.

"Beer," he announced with the manner of a lecturer, "beer is a food. Some people like more salt in their food than others. . . ."

He salted the beer till it hissed and slushed over on the table. Emma stalked over grimly to wipe up the froth. After a while Bessie elevated her feet to the table, her skirts falling back past her thighs, and asked Jasper for a cigarette. She lighted it with some difficulty. Emma stiffened with disapproval.

"Hey, Larry," Jasper called, winking at me. "She's not the same gal you knowed during the war."

"So I see," I answered.

"Beer's not intoxicating," Bessie mumbled. She swished the beer in her glass around and around, squinting at it and smiling crookedly.

I was getting so that I was afraid to rise. Vapors seemed to curl about everything, and I was often startled to see Bessie's face appear like a movie close-up before the end of my nose. The rest of her body was nebulous, giving her the appearance of a Cheshire cat. Voices alternately boomed and ebbed to the drowsy hum of summer bees.

"Rough-house Rosie!" Jasper exclaimed at Emma as she carried in more beer. "How 'll you trade women, Nat?

Little change o' pasture, y'know. . . ." Emma evaded his groping hands, and her brow grew darker.

"She ain't much of a hand fer jokin'," Nat observed with a piteous grin.

"I seen Helen ag'in," Jasper told me. "She ast about you. How'd she know you was in that scrap and. . . ."

"You get them drunks and that chippy outa here," Emma's wrathful voice cut in from the other room. "I don't care if we do need the money to build the house. The very idea! Why, my old mother would turn over in her grave if she knowed about these carryin's on. What about these little innocent children layin' here, listenin' to all this bla'guardin'? It's a sin and a shame, and I won't stand it."

"Helen! Helen!" donged in my ear like a knell. "She asked about me!"

Then something impelled me to down the yeasty dregs left in the bottles. "He's drinkin' the yeast! He'll puke like a dog!" I numbly heard somebody say. I grinned insanely as Ed wrested a bottle from me. Bessie's hyena laugh pealed, but I could not see her. Jasper neighed like an amorous stud-horse, and Nat snickered weakly.

"I'm through! I'm a respectable woman! This is a respectable house!" Emma shouted, appearing with a broom. Nat interposed, extending deprecating palms, but Emma thrust him aside and stood with arms akimbo, as implacable as the angels set at the gates of Eden as executors of God's relentless scorn.

We all arose with elaborate dignity and paid our scores, walking gingerly to the door. I stepped into the black void outside and pitched on my face in the cindered walk. Ed tried to help me to my feet and sprawled across me. Bessie tittered by. I felt a flood of sour beer against my teeth and in a minute I felt better.

I found myself before the counterfeit hot dog joint

213

where I had raised the rumpus, but the place was dark and a "For Rent" sign was in the window. My stomach burned and my head ached.

I wandered to a small square with a few benches scattered around it. Workers were pouring into the armchair joints, clattering of dishes and shouting of orders resounded. The smell of food sickened me. Soon street cars began to clang past, glum workers hanging on straps and staring gloomily out of the windows. In the restaurants they hastily gulped down their cheap breakfasts, handing greasy meal tickets to be punched. An ineffable sadness overwhelmed me, and maudlin tears coursed down my cheeks. Yesterday's newspapers, yellowed by the sun and fouled with grime and sputum, fluttered around the square. Bold, black headlines stabbed at my bleary eyes: "Wealthy Realtor's Love Letters Read in Crowded Courtroom." "Poverty will be Abolished, Says Hoover." "Stocks in Meteoric Rise; Permanent Plateau Reached."

A fresh-faced boy came along, shouting "Poipa! Poipa!" lustily. He carried a bundle of morning editions, smelling of the press.

"Come here, bub! Come here!" I urged, my heart yearning toward him. He seemed somehow to represent the antithesis of our sordid bacchanal of the night before. "How many papers you got left?" I asked the newsboy.

He backed away suspiciously, thinking I was a queer. But the morning editions died soon and would be corpses on his hands; already the presses were grinding out others to replace them. The newsboy paused and scratched his right ankle with the nail of his left big toe.

"Fifteen, Cap!" he answered. "Jeez! I ain't havin' no luck this morning."

I handed him a dollar bill, and he grasped one end cautiously, still afraid I might grab him.

"T'anks, Cap! You're the real McCoy!" he cried, saluting like a soldier.

All that day I saw his shining face.

Bonny Fern was in the living room when I came in.

"Drunk again," she said scornfully.

"Yes! The giggle soup makes me feel for a while as though I had accomplished all I used to plan for myself when I was ambitious. Tell your professor here's another biological specimen to pin on a board like a butterfly. They'd better draw on their rubber gloves, though. They classify us so nicely, define our impulses, explain our behavior. They squint at our sweat and blood in a test tube. Let them buck a conveyor once. It's not a game. They'll find that out. And there's something gathering in the factories that will break some day like a storm!"

"The professor said the trouble with the half-educated is that they cannot weigh things impartially. They're invariably fanatical."

"I know I'm half-educated," I returned bitterly, "but some things you never know till you live them."

"Oh, I'm sorry I said that," she broke in contritely. "Only you should remember that most workers *are* perfectly content."

The nemesis of old age pursued Ben just as it had Bun Grady. He never lasted long any place, and after he tried all the factories, he decided to go some place for a fresh start. He hadn't paid for the reclaimed furniture, but he could let it go back.

Within a year and a half I held a dozen jobs for short periods. I hired in as a millwright, but I balked when I was ordered to climb up a slim and wabbly ladder to oil some madly whirling pulleys among a maze of moving belts. The floor was viscous with grease. I had mounted a few rungs hesitatingly when I felt the foot of the ladder slipping. I jumped down, handed the oil can to the exasperated boss, and escaped to the sunlight outside. For various reasons, I fled from other jobs.

But I never really escaped by quitting and changing jobs. All the factories had the same conveyors, the same scientific methods for extracting the last ounce of energy. The same neon tubes pulsing with blue fire and the same automatons toiling frantically beneath the ghastly rays that etched dark shadows under their eyes and blackened their lips to resemble those of a cadaver.

After Ben and his family moved to Toledo, Ed and I soon tired of boarding houses. Ben was lucky enough to find a job at the Inland automobile factory, and when we came down on the trolley to visit him one Sunday he told us he could get us on, too. We told him to go ahead. Ben had bought another houseful of reclaimed furniture, and he hoped he could hold onto it this time since Bonny Fern had found a job in an office.

PART THREE

THE HARD WINTER

*A*UTUMN WAS SHARPENING THE AIR AND THE Jackson street crowd had thinned out. The Market had just crashed to the cellar, leaving a sick and empty feeling in the stomachs of cockroach capitalists, rolling in unaccustomed wealth and firm in the conviction that a perpetual saturnalia was written in America's destiny. Now they were scurrying to cover, perishing beneath the wreckage or jumping from eighteenth story windows. Titanic earthquakes rocked the marble fronts of the street; shattering lightnings played about hitherto impregnable heads. It was the end of an epoch to some, the stormy sunset of the Hoover Prosperity. To us it meant nothing—yet. The manipulations of the bulls and bears, wedged between the screaming headlines of the front pages and the antics of Mutt and Jeff, ordinarily escape the attention of the working stiff. Ed was not perturbed by the soap-boxer's prophecy of the wrath to come.

That battle-scarred veteran of many panics had been shouting "Wolf! Wolf!" too often. Ten years, almost, since 1921, so long that the younger workers had forgotten it. But the oldsters remembered.

"The Money Power is clampin' down again," concluded the prophet. "I've seen it too often. Just as soon as some of you fellas get the wrinkles outen your bellies you forget. Before two weeks the Inland works will close down tight as a drum. My advice is to get out of town while you can. Ride a freight, thumb, walk—or crawl! But get out. Do like me. I'm goin' to California, if I can make it. I ain't so fast at naggin' a Red Ball as I usta be, but the bulls sometimes respecks my white beard—not often, though. Go to California, comrades, where you won't starve and freeze both—only starve. If you stay here you'll starve and freeze, too. This is gonna be a hard Winter like you've heard the old folks talk about. You'll tell your kids about it—if you live through it."

A hush fell on the street. Hambone, the mad Negro evangelist, ceased his lurid description of the hell-fire sizzling for this iniquitous generation; the militant atheist forgot the knotty problem of where Cain got his wife; the throbbing of the Salvation Army tom-tom died away, and tinkling tambourines jingled to silence. It seemed as if the prophet's upraised bony finger had written *mene, mene, mene, tekel, upharsin* across the dull brick wall opposite.

"Christ, they're always bellyachin', ain't they," reassured Ed. "What t'ell does the Stock Market have to do with us Inland hunkies? I ain't buyin' no General Motors Common or Willys-Overland Preferred, are you? Let's go over to Adolf's and lap up a few cold ones."

Adolf was a Russian who had been a brewer in the Old Country. He never seemed to understand why he couldn't, without violating the laws of the Refuge of the Oppressed, make beer for his family and his friends, just as he had under the Czar. He never learned concealment, so he was frequently hailed into court, fined, and sent home without comprehending what it was all about. His mild blue eyes lit up when he opened the door for us. I often visited him to talk about Russia. Soon the beer loosened his tongue and he spoke of his native village.

"I could see the tax collectors coming through the wheat. It was higher than their shoulders and heavy-headed. They were good men—it was the nobles that ground us down. My mother set out black bread, salt pork, vodka, hot pickles. One of them he geev me a kopek, called me Yellow Hair. A long time ago—long, long ago now—Say! You like black bread, salt pork, and hot pickles?"

Several steins had reduced us to the state in which anything seems good. Adolf produced an immense flitch of bacon, a jar of pickles, and a long flat loaf of bread, as heavy as lead.

"This pork," he said proudly. "I have heem two years already."

The pork had been embalmed by some occult process, but it was rancid, and repellant to an American palate. But the beer lent piquancy to it. We gulped down greasy morsels of pork, hunks of black bread. Tears streamed from our eyes as we mouthed the fiery hot pickles.

The furniture and corners of the room were hazy when an accordion began whining old folk songs. One in a minor key sounded like "The Prisoner's Song" and we wept into the beer.

"The Czar!" Adolf's voice broke through the fog like a trumpet. "He burns in Hell! I spit on him and his nobles! Their throats are all slit now; no more I raise my cap and step off the road in the mud when their coaches pass by!"

The plaintive accordion rose to a passionate crescendo, crashed into the stirring thunder of the Internationale. We cheered like mad, and fell into happy slumber.

But Adolf's face was dead when he bade us goodbye, and we were half-drunk and more than half-sick.

"Paper say it's goin' to be a hard Winter," he said as he closed the door.

Ed and I worked in the enamel department at the Inland, tending an enormous enamelling oven.

All day the smoking hot fenders slid down on a conveyor from the cavernous inferno of the drying chutes. The rheostats glowed in the dusk of the depths. It was stifling in the room, for the windows had to be tightly closed to exclude the possibility of a grain of dust marring the glistening finish. Automatically we grabbed each fender, deftly disengaged the hook, and transferred it to another conveyor leading to the assembly line. Merged with the rhythm of the machine, our thoughts flew here and there, seeking escape from the suffocation of the place. We taunted each other with reminiscences of Adolf's home brew.

"The cork pops like a shot-gun," tormented Ed, "and the smoke—how it flies!"

"The foam—it sticks to the top like ice cream; you have to cut it with a knife; and the golden bubbles spring up from the bottom of the glass!" I retaliated.

It was very hot in the room. We were galled at the knees and under the arms; the pungent scent of scorching paint was everywhere. We sweated abominably. We cursed each other, prohibition, and Hoover.

An enamel conveyor must glide along inexorably. It stops only for some serious reason. The withering heat wrinkles the surface of the fenders unless the steady progress is maintained; eventually the whole oven bursts into flame. Once when a fuse blew out I groped my way through the black smoke towards the open, collided with a wall, ran a hook in my eye. Next day the room was a mass of ashes and twisted steel.

When the oven conveyor stopped at 10:30 A.M. we

222

knew something was wrong. Behind the switchboard we found George, the foreman, throwing the heat switches one by one.

"What's the matter, George?"

"We're done for today, and for two weeks. The force is due for a big cut, too. Production off fifty per cent. You birds better wait till I notify you before you report for work again."

When Ben saw us coming home in the middle of the day, he knew that all was not well. We wondered to see him home, too. Only something momentous brings a worker home at midday. Ben smiled ruefully, his children grouped about him, open-mouthed at his anachronistic appearance. It was like having Christmas come on the Fourth of July.

"They pulled the number five trim line," he said. "By God, it seems like just when I get a fresh start, some furniture about paid for, settled down for a while—bang! Everything blows up. Well, Bonny Fern's still workin'. Maybe she can keep things going."

But Bonny Fern did not have a job long. The office where she worked reduced the force, and she was without a job. After a few days about the house she became peevish and I seldom talked to her. Sometimes her eyes were red from crying.

Ben had a fourth-hand flivver, and every morning Ed and I lay between the blankets listening to the matutinal rite of starting it. Sometimes it leaped to life with a belligerent roar, but more often it was recalcitrant, coughed sullenly, and subsided into stubborn silence. Then Ben jacked up the hind wheel and spun the crank till the fenders rattled like a skeleton on a tin roof. Every morning he chugged away looking for work. About noon he would return, fling his hat in a corner, sit down on the day-bed and stare at the wall.

"Men everywhere! 'NO HELP WANTED' is all you can see around the factories. Men on the street corners. Men at the factory gates. They turned the hose on 30,000 of them at Ford's in Detroit the other day."

A few times Ed and I went along, but not often. The lake winds cut like knife blades in the morning air, and we still had a few dollars left. We were waiting for something to break.

As the factories closed or cut their forces and hours, the exodus from the city increased in volume. We lived by the Chicago pike, and had nothing better to do than to watch the procession pass. Some in shiny new sedans, but more in asthmatic antiques, creaking under burdens of furniture, bedding, lares and penates, children, and even Kentucky hound dogs, their long ears flying like banners in the breeze. The children peered out brightly, merry over the prospect of the long trip south.

Not all in cars.

In a driving November rain a man passed the house pulling a heavily loaded coaster wagon and followed by a staggering woman, ineffectually striving to shield a blue-lipped baby from the cold and wet. Ben called them in, fed them, and dried their clothing. The husband had been laid off in Detroit and spent his last penny looking for work, and they were trying to make it home to La Follette, Tenn., still many a weary mile ahead.

I saw a middle-aged man seemingly petrified by the side of the highway. He stood like a statue, one arm extended toward the west. His face was set and hopeless like a stone mask. Begging a ride, he did so proudly; no energetic thumbing and appealing. A battered suitcase rested between his legs. Nobody heeded him. The cars whizzed along the grey concrete and the Winter dusk settled down. Trucks rumbled along disdainfully. A lithe speedster festooned with smart baggage purred by, and the boys inside were singing, sentimentally: "Highways are happy ways when they lead the way to home."

A gang of youths in a collegiate Ford, its dilapidation camouflaged by many a chalked wisecrack, spied the immobile figure, and brakes howled to a stop fifty feet away.

"Are you tired of walking?" inquired the lad at the wheel.

"Yes!" cried the man eagerly. He picked up the suitcase and ran briskly toward the car, his frayed overcoat whipping between his legs and hindering him.

"Then run a while!" retorted the comedian, quickly throwing the car into gear for a flying start. Laughter drifted back.

A single oath which seemed to plumb the nadir of despair broke from the man's lips. He walked steadily westward, as though drawn by a magnet.

A girl in a short red sweater came along; and as she passed the house she turned and looked like a cow struck by a train that I saw once. The dumb agony of her face startled me. I ran and told Ben's wife, who hailed the girl. She had walked from Detroit, where hard times curtailed the demand for hash slingers, and a bone felon on her finger aggravated her other woes. When she unwrapped a huge improvised bandage of rags we were horrified to see the bone protruding from the gangrenous flesh.

"I must get home to Muncie somehow," she said.

"Can't you get rides?" asked Mrs. Ben.

"Yes, but I know what they'd expect."

To me there was something sinister in this western migration. I told Ed we'd better get out while we could.

"Listen, kid," he reasoned, "all these hill billies clearin' out is pepper in our soup. They's *gotta* be some work goin' on—so much of it all the time. And us that's left can soon step out and get a job anywheres. Stick around!"

So I decided to stick around a while longer, but I did

go down to the employment agencies on Erie Street early one morning. The bunch of regular hangers-on was augmented by a throng of factory workers with clothes still snappy, there for the first time. Everyone stamped his feet and muttered in low tones.

The office didn't open till eight, and the waiting line grew until it filled the street and overflowed on the opposite sidewalk, where the Fort Dixon Museum displayed a depressing window full of stuffed and mangy pumas, faded parrots and other curios, including a ghastly wax figure, representing a small child clothed in the style of fifty years ago, seated stiffly in a chair. Time had rotted the fabrics, and tatters hung between rigid legs. The face had assumed the blue pallor of death, and the sunlight streaming through the pane had caved in the cheeks.

"Looks like it'd stink if you got close enough," mused a morbid observer. "Well, lots of us will look that way before Spring if times don't change."

Suddenly terror smote me like a cold wind.

Hundreds were gathered, and policemen were ineffectually trying to sardine them on the already crowded sidewalk. It was a futile task, but it gratified the sadistic impulse of the cops to shove and bawl.

Promptly at 8:15 a dapper clerk popped out of an inner office, opened the outer door, and leaped instantly and nimbly back behind the counter, thus narrowly escaping the press that immediately jammed the room.

I was swept along by the wave, but I never reached the door. A short, saturnine Jew beside me spat disgustedly, and began to worm his zig-zag and contested way to the fringes of the crowd. "The thundering herd!" he pronounced contemptuously. I followed him as the employment office began to disgorge the rejected job-seekers.

"It's no use," Ben said. "I gotta get out of here. The

226

landlord's give me notice, and they're gonna take this furniture back. The kids is out of shoes; the teacher writes a note they should have more nourishin' food. I'm goin' back to that little patch of white oak land. I usta make it easy there before I let Bonny Fern talk me into comin' t' the city. Now she's got her college education, what's she gonna do with it?"

"I can't help it if I can't find anything to do," Bonny Fern retorted resentfully. "There are lots of college boys and girls out of work—who have never found jobs."

"That's what education does," grumbled Ben; "makes 'em too nice t' handle a hoe or wash the dishes. We gotta get back to the simple life like our grandfathers."

"The farmers are not making anything," I said.

"Well, they can't make less than the city factory hand. I'll chancet it, anyhow. Lizzie's gonna take us back, if she holds together long enough. You and Ed better go along. Might hang on the fenders."

"No, I want to stay here. There's going to be something doing in the cities. Men won't starve quietly in the world's richest country."

Ed snorted derisively: "You've been listenin' to them soapboxers again. They'll have the squirrels in the park after you if you don't watch out."

"My sociology instructor said. . . ." began Bonny Fern.

"Heifer dust!" snapped Ben savagely. "Every time I hear of that danged college I feel like a man that has throwed good money in a deep well with no chancet of gittin' it back."

Bonny Fern began to cry. "I'll work it out on the farm," she sniffed. "I'll milk the cows, hoe corn, cut sprouts. I'll pay you back."

Ed and I could not bear to see Bonny Fern cry, and we didn't know how to comfort her, so we went outside and walked around the square.

227

When we came back to the house, we found a letter for Ben in the mail box and I took it inside, thinking it might divert his mind from his jeremiad about the value of a college education. Unluckily, it was the final ultimatum from the furniture dealer.

The second-hand dealer's notice to a delinquent customer is truly Chesterfieldian—to begin with. Merely a faint intimation that the usual tithe has been "overlooked," and "please remember we are ever at your service. Your credit is firmly established here. Just look over the stock and say, 'Charge it!'" Presently a subtle hint that while a payment is not entirely indispensable it would not be scorned. Then a rather bald invitation to come in and settle up. Finally, the address of "our legal representative" blooms in a corner of the letter, heavily framed in black.

Ben knew they meant business then. Three days later he pulled out of the yard. I found his wife sobbing softly in the kitchen, staring at the deserted furniture.

"I never wanted to come here in the first place," she said. "These high wages—they never last. Every time I get furniture I have to give it up and start over; we can't *never* settle down since the War—since we left the farm. This runnin' around—it's no way to bring up kids."

I found Bonny Fern in the back yard.

"Well, send me a picture of yourself milking the cows," I said lightly.

"I'll soon get used to that . . . but it'll be lonesome there. That's the worst with the farm. I wish you and Ed were going back, too."

"Thanks!" I said, secretly delighted. "You want somebody to argue with."

"It's better to argue than to yawn."

"You'll have a radio. You can get Amos and Andy on clear nights."

"That *would* be wonderful! But it takes money to buy

a radio, money to keep the batteries charged. Oh, yes, the farmer knows luxuries that his forefathers never dreamed about. . . . But how *can* we live without hearing Amos and Andy?"

"Now you're talking like the sociology prof," I laughed. "You can hear sociological discussions on the radio, too, providing it's the right kind of sociology. You can read, and improve your mind."

"By a coal oil lamp? Between milkings?"

Ben had the Ford loaded like a Christmas tree, and was honking impatiently. I held Bonny Fern's hand a long time and had a notion to try to kiss her.

Ben had a long and troublesome trip ahead; but, like a candidate for the chair, he was anxious to have at it—to end the suspense of waiting. Bedding and a few small articles of furniture—the baby's kiddie kar which he had refused to leave—bristled from the chassis.

"Do you think I can clear the trucks?" Ben asked.

Before they had travelled a hundred feet, a front tire gave out—not with a staccato pop but with a soft sigh of resignation, like a pious and confident Christian surrendering his contemptible life to Jehovah. Ben pulled to the side of the slab, unloaded the wife and kids, who stood about him forlornly, and dug his tools out of a mélange of odds and ends. Patiently he began to jack up the wheel.

"Better leave them tools out handy. You'll wear 'em out before you hit the Missouri line," was Ed's comforting farewell. Bonny Fern waved her handkerchief with assumed gaiety as we walked away, on our way to town.

II

We moved down town to room with Bill and eat at Jimmie's American Lunch. Bill was a retired barkeep and active bootlegger; while Jimmie was a moist and pachydermous Greek whose air of excessive joviality and all around *bonhomie* became boresome. We had less than twenty dollars apiece, and hunted work pretty regularly; but with the expectation of a chap trying to win a $250 limerick prize from *Liberty*. The competition was too fierce.

I was dining not elegantly but enjoyably upon lamb stew (twenty cents with bread and butter and coffee) when an emaciated guy blew in and leaned against the counter. A carload of Murads couldn't have given him the nonchalance he essayed.

"Salt? Pepper?" he grinned weakly as he timidly pushed the cellars toward me. He grimaced idiotically like a clown. Jimmie came puffing up.

"Somet'ing?"

"Why, friend, you got any scraps—just bread crumbs, stale loafs, left-overs, for a dog? Got a little dog travelin' with me. Do tricks! Wish you could see him! Just for a dog, friend . . . anything!"

"Naw! I ain't got notting. Is *that* all?"

"Why, yes . . . I guess—that's all!"

His eyes were misty like a water-spaniel's, but they blazed when he sniffed my stew on the way out.

"A dog! A dog!" Jimmie derided. "A new one, by damn! Bones for a dog!"

"That's all any of 'em ask," Ed commented sagely, trying to get a rise out of me. "Give 'em a bone with even a shred of meat on it, and they'll set up and beg, roll over and play dead, or jump in the coldest water t' fetch out sticks."

When I asked Jimmie for credit two weeks later, he engraved on my mind an inchoate image of himself in the rôle of Atlas nobly but totteringly upholding all the burdens of a populous city.

"Boys, I am *ver'* sorry," speaking over deprecating and

spread palms, "but business she been so rotten. I got plenty expenses, too. Hones', I don't see how I'll make it t'ru."

Al Satcher was feeding a thousand a day at his Athletic Club. Soup and stale bread from the bakeries, but better than nothing. The Athletic Club was thrown wide open, a huge banner inviting one and all to partake of free food and shelter. We had to crawl out early to get Al's free chow, and always found a long line waiting, stamping cold feet, grumbling, jesting with the acidulous and pertinent wit of the down-and-out.

"Thanksgiving's most here, and I'm thankful, praise God! Yes, I'm thankful," intoned a wag whose phonographic cadence told me that he had a good joke, but that the initial zest had been diluted by excessive repetition.

"What the hell are you thankful for?" marvelled Ed.

"Why, I'm thankful I ain't constipated!"

Here was a rendezvous for the professional panhandlers and dead beats; they actually were faring better than in more prosperous times. Free soup kitchens where one can pass by casually and get his sluff without *earning* it. That *is* grapes! Often you had to testify luridly to harrowing crimes of omission and commission, to don conspicuously the sackcloth of penitence, and wallow in the ashes of counterfeit remorse. Inquisitive policemen had a fashion of asking why you weren't working; worse still, they even whisked the seeker off to a free employment agency and sentenced him to a job at hard labor. Now it was possible to answer in the words of the Wobbly song book:

"How the hell can I work if there's no work to do?"

Not infrequently the professionals doubled. Immediately after being slopped, they attached themselves to the rear of the queue and came back for more.

"Wasn't you just fed?" The suspicious caterer paused, poising a ladle of steaming stew.

"Who? Me?" the grizzled bo disciplined his battered

231

phiz into what he conceived to be a mask of cherubic innocence. He assumed an air of aggrieved virtue and a wolfish look. "Jesus, buddy, I ain't et fer three days. I jist blowed in from K. C., lookin' fer work. Hungry! . . . Christ! My belly thinks my throat is cut." Thus, with his third helping, he rounded out a meal.

We slept on the hard concrete after Bill informed us that our room was urgently needed for a *paying* guest. With overcoats for pillows, we slept fitfully, always sensitive to groping hands exploring our pockets and bodies, sometimes for money—or tobacco. These places catch all kinds. In the night, the burden of thought breaks many a derelict's mind. They gibber, curse, pray and laugh immoderately, while the aroused invite the disturbers to die or go to sleep.

One night I heard someone singing in a cracked brogue:

"In Ireland they have buttermilk ninety days old.
    The maggots and wiggle-tails get very bold.
    It would put any man in the greatest surprise
    To see them turn up their great goggle eyes."

I crept near the voice.

"Mike! Mike Riordan, is that you?" I called out.

"Yes! Yes! I'm Mike Riordan!"

"Mike, do you remember Larry Donovan? Remember how you used to sing that song to Madge and me in Monkey Nest Camp?"

"Sure, I do!"

"Aw, nuts!" growled an awakened guest nearby. "Don't let that hophead feed you that bull. He's full of smoke. Ast him if he's Janet Gaynor; he'll own up that he is."

I felt over the singer's body till I found his legs. He had no peg.

"You're not Mike Riordan," I said.

"No! What difference does it make? I'm thirsty, lad.

I'm dry as a fish. My guts is on fire! Fetch me some water, for the love of Christ!"

"If you'd lay off that rotgut, you wouldn't be so thirsty. Must've salted your whisky," broke in another close by.

"Pipe down!" "Go to sleep!" "Talk about that tomorrow!" resounded through the room. I lay still, but did not go to sleep. The man who had been singing mumbled feverishly for a bit, but fell silent. In the morning I found that he didn't look very much like Mike Riordan. Moreover, he was dead. This was not so strange, for scarcely a night passed that some guest of the flophouse did not die.

In the night I lay thinking of Mother, of Bonny Fern, Hans, Helen, Jasper and Nat. Jasper and Nat had both been laid off, we learned from Jasper, who wrote us occasionally. Jasper was going West, and Nat was about to lose his home in Rosewood Manor. It had never progressed beyond the garage stage, anyhow. I was glad that Mother had plenty. She had saved several hundred dollars out of the sums I had sent her, and I knew that would be enough to tide her over till I could find another job.

The stirrings of the derelicts, their inarticulate moans and sighs, the pungent smell of disinfectant, sour sweat, and the horrible odor of unwashed and diseased humanity confined in a stuffy room—these beat upon me as I lay. The night became peopled with monstrous shapes, sights, sounds, smells. I was shouting without conscious volition, unable to hold my tongue.

Ed gripped my arm tightly, held my hand.

"Steady, Larry! Steady, boy! I'm here! I'm with you till the cows come home. We'll see it through, kid, you and me. Whatta ya say, buddy, you wouldn't lay down on me, would you?"

"Throw 'im out!" "Give 'im the bum's rush!" men called from the darkness about us. I calmed down. Soon the room was quiet save for the undertones that tore at my nerves more than the more strident noise that arose when somebody went off his nut.

Nothing impairs morale like the dissolution of a last pair of shoes. Maybe it starts with a little hole in the sole; and then the slush of pavements oozes in, gumming sox and balling between your toes. Concrete whets Woolworth sox like a file, and if you turn the heel on top and tear a pasteboard innersole, it won't help much. There are the tacks, too. You get to avoiding high places and curbstones because that jabs the point right into the quick. You walk mostly on the toe if the tack happens to be in the heel. Soon the tack has calloused a furrowed hole, and you don't notice it unless you strike something unusually high or solid, or forget and walk flat-footed. You pass a thousand shoe-shops where a tack might be bent down, but you can't pull off a shoe and ask to have *that* done—for nothing.

I worried about my pants. Every icy blast off the lake found the thin spots unerringly. I brooded about the disastrous consequences of a sudden breaking asunder. Often on rounding a corner I felt quickly and apprehensively behind me, convinced that the inevitable had occurred.

A Winter nose is no respector of persons—the lake wind puts them all to flowing. But the nose of Mrs. Van Arsdale, when she alights from her town car, is daintily stanched by a cobweb of cambric. The chauffeur may honk into a square of linen, very decorously. A bandana is *passé* to the *haut monde* but extremely efficient withal. But when you have got no job and no home, a rag must suffice till it's too dirty to pull on the street. Then the back of your blue-black hand. Embarrassment leaves off where desperation begins. You walk and stare in shop windows. A pink and white ham simmers in the Bandbox

Lunch. You suck up your guts as the sergeant used to tell you to do. A long time till Al dishes out the soup. Ye Cosy Radio Shoppe flings harmony for five blocks and a thunderous optimist yammers as from a barrel, bassly: "We are now in the dining room of the Commodore Perry Hotel. Lights! Good food! Music! Youth! Is Everybody Happy! The orchestra enters into the spirit of the occasion with that tuneful selection: 'Happy Days are Here Again.'"

Our concrete bed sores had begun to heal when we heard that the Lakes Milling Company would hire some huskies to hustle beet pulp. Silhouetted against the faint dawn, the plant loomed like a feudal castle, with many a turret catching the daybreak. Gaunt watchers lay in ambush along the hall leading to the employment office, sleeping with their hats crushed over their eyes. Burlap bedding had been filched from the mill. One fellow spat incessantly. The spit froze in white bubbles.

The applicants sprang to their feet, electrified, when the employment agent showed up. He shouldered his way through the ranks. "Need any men today?" flew around him from all sides. When he attempted to close his office door, I had already wedged my foot and wormed in. After shuffling some time-cards with a practiced pinochle technique, he snapped: "No jobs today," and fell to writing furiously in a huge ledger.

The seekers were flattening their noses against the glass partition, and some heard and withdrew, routed and outdone.

I waited stolidly. Finally he looked up again. "No jobs," he repeated mechanically, and then sized me up. I weighed two hundred pounds.

"Ever truck—heavy work—outside—only a few days— forty cents and ten hours?"

"Yes! I got a partner."

"Well, maybe him, but really, I shouldn't. Come on."

He picked up two time-cards and stepped out in the corridor. Stragglers lurked about, still hopeful of being chosen.

I beckoned to Ed. We were both husky.

"Aw, he's lookin' fer beef today!" griped the stones by the builder rejected.

At the end of labyrinthine passages and breath-taking stairs the employment manager halted and thrust our cards into a rack beside a clock that was to tick off many slow minutes for us. "Report to Al," he said, and fled.

We found Al at the end of a huge warehouse, surrounded by stacks and stacks of serried beet pulp, and a group of disciples. And he spake in parables, saying: "Christ! I didn't know they come that dumb; but actually this Polack hadn't never been in a sportin' house. . . . Laugh! I thought I'd die. . . ."

The snitch and the yes-man always find the foreman's most trivial pun howlingly funny. This job had gathered the disinherited from many a closed and crippled factory; and the cruel competition for bare existence made rats of them. They pecked eagerly for small favors like expectant sparrows following a well-fed horse.

Going on a new job makes a man fidgety. The first morning, anyway. The foreman eases his watch out now and then, and you wonder how long you have to wait, what you're going to do. The regulars eye newcomers with all the hostility of a cannibal tribe.

A long conveyor, built like a derrick, extended through a sliding door into a box car; and the other end tilted up to a dim nave, where sacks of pulp had been piled symmetrically. We quailed low, and prayed for and dreaded the zero hour.

"Stack monkeys up!" shouted the gang leader, bearded

like a mastiff. Part of the gang skinned rapidly up the slick conveyor onto the stack. We followed as best we could, awkwardly. The others rushed into the car and the conveyor began revolving rapidly. Soon the ears of sacks shot over the end of the whirling belt, and Red, the gang leader, caught the first one deftly, letting it fall on his back and his head.

"A good stack man can catch 'em any way," he said modestly, and we later learned that this was a stock phrase with him which he repeated incessantly and monotonously. His cap was worn out on top, a peculiar circumstance we had noted at once, caused by the manner in which he caught the bags of pulp. "By Jesus, the cap's gone and next the hair 'll go," he would say.

The conveyor could be elevated to any height and we soon found out that the stack monkeys tried a new man by having it raised so high that the impact of the falling bag would knock the neophyte down. I braced myself and grabbed behind me desperately at the hard round sack, dampened and almost petrified in some way by exposure. I staggered headlong for ten feet and managed to drop my burden just before I fell. Ed was not so lucky. He fell with the bag across him. The monkeys howled like their jungle brethren.

But we kept on. The piled bags were treacherous underfoot, rocked and sagged into sudden, ankle-twisting holes. The rotten jute burst, cascading the rough pulp down our backs. It cut our flesh like a knife. We had been using certain definite movements in the automobile factory. Now atrophied muscles were being recalled to use, aching protestingly. The monkeys watched us anxiously, hoping we would quit or give out. We clenched our teeth to keep from wincing when the sacks slithered down our raw and bleeding backs. We had jobs . . . jobs! . . . We had to remember that when the world seemed to   its haunches, waiting to rend us when we dropped. No more concrete bed-sores—a real bed with sheets! No more charity sluff—but ham and eggs and maybe a chicken dinner on Sundays.

We made it through. Two- and three-day weeks several times, but we made it through.

The sparrows bothered in the big shed. But I knew this one wasn't any sparrow the minute he flew over. I looked up. A pert robin was shivering and preening his feathers, jerking his tail.

"Spring is here, Ed," I rejoiced, "and we can say we've lived through one hard Winter. How many more do you suppose there'll be?"

"God knows! As many as the fatbellies want. They's no fight in lice like them guys workin' here. You know that."

"If they're pushed too far, they will. Besides, you can't judge all the workers by the bunch on a job like this. It catches the dregs."

"Yeh, like us," Ed reminded me.

The cars of beet pulp came in more slowly as Spring advanced. Often we came to work only to be sent home for a few days. One after another the stack monkeys were laid off. Everybody speculated as to the next to go.

"You two is buddies, I know," Al told Ed and me one morning, "so I'm gonna lay you off together. Only a few days more and we'll wind up our ball of yarn here till next Fall. You boys got so you can horse a sack as good's anybody, and if you ain't starved to death by next Fall, look me up again."

III

"Let's buy us a second-hand car and beat it out of here, kid. Let's go home," Ed urged. "If we shilly-shally around

238

here lookin' for jobs that simply ain't, we'll be flat again. We oughta went when Ben did. We won't go home like I always aimed to—with a roll big enough to gag a cow, but I ain't got much pride left in me after the Winter we been through."

"Let's stay a while. We can stand it if others do. They're stirring here, organizing block committees to resist evictions. They've moved furniture back into houses, fought off the police."

"Yeh, but the police always win out in the end," Ed retorted. "You watch. Remember the railroad strike. Soon as it got a little too hot, they had the troopers. You're like the old woman that spit in the sea and said: 'Every little bit helps.' Carryin' back a few sticks of furniture ain't gonna help us none."

"It helps as an emergency measure. Nobody advocates it as a cure for the cause of ——"

"Come on!" Ed grinned. "In another minute you'll be shootin' them fifty-cent words at me. Talk United States if you want me to get hep to what you're drivin' at. That's why them soap-boxers never get anywheres. Why don't they talk about beans and potatoes, lard and bacon instead of 'ideology,' 'agrarian crisis' and 'rationalization?' "

I continued to argue. He walked along with a good-humored but skeptical smile curling his lips. When we reached our rooming house, I found a letter from Bonny Fern. It read:

"Dear Larry: I promised your mother I wouldn't write you about her, but I'm going to do so, anyhow. You think she has money, Larry, but she hasn't. The bank here failed last Fall and she lost all she had. Dad helped her all he could, but we had a hard time making it through the Winter; had to borrow two hundred on the farm which must be paid back this Summer in some way. But if you have any money or can get any, send it to your Mother. She's living in one of the deserted camp houses in Monkey Nest Camp with your Aunt Jessie and the three children. The place leaks like a sieve and can't be fixed without buying material. Dad went over and did the best he could, but we couldn't afford to buy any nails or roofing. Since you're laid off again, you'd better come home. There's a pipe line going through a few miles from here, and you and Ed can get a job on that—if you don't get crushed in the stampede when they go to hiring."

"I'll have to go now," I said to Ed. "Mother's been writing me all the time as though she had plenty; she even asked me if I needed any money, and I had a notion to ask her for a ten once. Bonny Fern never mentioned it in her other letters, but I see the reason why. All right, let's go home."

"We'll get us a second-hand car and that'll be handy to run around in lookin' for work," Ed suggested. "You can get 'em cheap now. Let's look around."

After diligent search we at length located a most promising Chevrolet. The agent assured us that the car, like old wine, had improved with age, and it did run amazingly well while he was demonstrating it. But we had scarcely left the city limits behind before it began to develop disturbing symptoms. It heated badly, the radiator sprung a leak, and the porous tires seemed to pick up every tack or nail on the road. A sharp pebble penetrated them easily. Ed swore that the car had been pieced together with putty, and that it would soon disintegrate like the wonderful one-hoss shay. He could wish the affable dealer no worse fate than to place him in our shoes. Our small cash reserve was depleted by the purchase of small parts and by repair bills.

"Let's boot it through!" Ed shouted above the engine's

din. "Like the old man that was hurryin' t' paint his house before the paint give out."

Indiana was a blur of green fields and sudden filling stations set in tree-arched villages, white houses and careful picket fences. The tires began blowing out every hundred yards or so. We bought tire patch with our last quarter, and used it before we had proceeded fifty miles.

At last Ed said: "Christ! It's no use tryin' t' run on the rim without any gas and without money t' buy any; it's no use tryin' t' patch tubes that look like a crazy quilt already and as holey as a Swiss cheese. We simply gotta mooch, steal, get a job, or something, before we can go any fu'ther."

So we pushed the recalcitrant Chevrolet from the slab and hoofed back to a little place we had just passed through.

"Any work around here?" I asked a residenter dozing beside a greasing rack.

"Hell, no! I *never* did see things so tight. This place is dead as a doornail, stranger, and you'd better not stop here for work. Dozen men for every job—you can't buy a job—I ain't had a day sence. . . ."

We left him muttering. A fellow with an Illinois license drove up just as we repeated the question to the servant of Standard Oil (Indiana).

"I need a couple of experienced men—riveter and bucker-up," the motorist broke in, sizing us up. "I'm on a bridge job fifty miles west of here."

"Why, that's lucky!" I exclaimed. "I was born with an air hammer in my hand, and my partner is a bucker."

"Where did *you* ever handle a rivet hammer?" he challenged belligerently.

"I worked for the Pittsburgh-Detroit Steel." The saw's piercing din has not faded from my ears yet, but I had never been a riveter.

"Well, I'll give you a trial, anyway. Hop in."

"We got our own car down the road a piece," said Ed. "Trouble is we got no gas and our tires is flat. Could you pay us a coupla bucks or so in advance?"

"You're a fast worker," our employer grumbled. "But here. . . ." He peeled three one-dollar bills off a sizable roll and handed them to Ed. "You keep ahead of me, and don't try any monkeyshines. I'm on to you flivver tramps. If you try to fool me, I'll ketch you sure as God made little apples."

With gas and repatched tires we limped along and came to a high bridge etched like a Lozowick drawing against the sunset, spanning a muddy river. We slept jack-knifed in the car as usual, and in the morning reported stiffly for work.

"You've worked high, of course," the boss answered himself. "Don't get dizzy."

"Sure!"

I was lying. Height terrifies me; I'm a fellow who was born to have one leg on the ground all the time; but how we needed that job! Oh, how we needed it!

I lifted the pneumatic hammer, assuming an air of familiarity, and cautiously pressed the trigger. The plunger shot out and banged a laborer on the shin. He cursed me fervently.

"Hey! Be careful, you!" bawled the boss. "Is *that* the way you handle a hammer. Wanta break a leg for somebody?"

I learned to stand the hammer loosely on a plank and tap away like an energetic woodpecker beside my foot. Some men never get used to climbing; never learn to forget the ground and to remember not to look down. I'm one of them. The river spun like a pin-wheel with the bridge in the center, fields swung madly in a blur of color. I felt myself slipping, but my head cleared just in time.

242

I pulled the heavy hose and hammer along, scooted fearfully across the I-beams. The old hands were scornfully nonchalant, walked cat-like across narrow girders without holding or watching their feet.

Try it, if you think it's easy, you who have been thrilled by the shoot-the-chutes at Coney. Wind plays a high bridge like a harp; the structure sways to a weird rhythm. To nervous feet a hundred feet in the air, steel is like the glass mountain in the fairy tale.

From a platform far below a bored rivet heater tossed fiery rivets to Ed, who was supposed to catch them in a large cone with handle attached, but more often he missed and they fell hissing in the river, followed by a shower of sparks like the tail of a comet.

"Git a basket!" called the rivet heater sarcastically, and Ed was too dejected and scared to curse him.

"Not so hot, big boy!" I encouraged, but he finally caught one, only to find the holes out of alignment. It was necessary to punch them into line, and by that time the rivet had changed from red to purplish, and grey scales were flaking off. It's hard enough to buck a white-hot rivet but a beginner is out of luck trying to buck a half-cold one. It backed up, though Ed jammed the bucking bar against his chest and hung on bravely with elbows and knees. You can't hold a rivet hammer straight, I found. You must weave it in a circular fashion to make a good head. The vibration shook Ed like an ague; but still there was half an inch play and the head was a misshapen blob.

"That won't do," the foreman reproved, passing us on his way to the ground. "You got to have a snug fit and a perfect head to pass inspection. Get you a crack chisel and cut that out."

About an hour of this, and a stiff breeze rose off the river. My cap blew off, and instinctively I wheeled to grab it, slipped and fell. I clutched wildly but only tore off two finger nails to the quick as my hands slipped off the smooth steel. Nothing could stop me. It seemed as though the bottom had dropped out of my belly. But a girder caught me amidships and I hung limply balanced like a bag of bran, my breath forced out in an explosive yell. The pneumatic hammer had plunged to the end of its hose, snapped the coupling, and disappeared in the river. Among the rods and girders the hose writhed and hissed like an angry snake. Weakly I clung, and Ed, his face blanched, began to climb gingerly down toward the good old solid ground.

"Come down, you farmer! O, you awkward son-of-a-bitch!" the boss roared from below. One of the old hands helped me down.

"Steel men! Steel men, hah?" the boss sputtered. "A hammer gone! Get out of here! Don't *ever* say you can work high again, you dumb bastards . . . you . . . you . . . !" He choked and belabored the air with his arms.

Ed clipped him neatly on the chin and he went down like the Titanic. We left him sprawling on the bridge floor and started to run for the car. Nobody offered to follow us.

"He needn't worry!" I rasped painfully, my windpipe yet in a knot. My guts still hurt from that fall, and the blue ridge has never faded away altogether. "He needn't worry. Catch me off the ground working again!"

"Well," Ed cheered philosophically, "we got some gas and the tires may hold up a hundred miles more. He was so het up he forgot about the dough he advanced us, and I was afraid he'd make us work out the price of the hammer."

Nights were still cool, especially where the concrete highway swooped down into a small valley or skirted a lake or river. We could feel the chill air rushing against

244

the windshield and tempering the fever of the Chevrolet's laboring engine. On the upgrade the pistons pounded alarmingly. The car lunged spasmodically if we attempted to slow down. We knew that the spark plugs were badly fouled, but we were too weary to scrape away the carbon which accumulated so rapidly. Ed sat stolidly at the wheel with his right foot clamped on the accelerator, his left one hovering over the brake and clutch pedals. We knew our gas was running short, and—worse still—we were again without money. All our negotiable property had likewise evaporated. An involuntary interlude in our homeward journey seemed imminent.

Sleek limousines zipped by us, honking superciliously at our difficult progress. They passed by us in a flash, their non-skid tires whining as they gripped the slab, their ruddy tail lights gleaming but an instant before they were out of sight. Through the small sleeping towns we sped. After midnight most of the streets were deserted, but all-night filling stations blossomed jewel-like in the dark. The attendants sat reared back against the walls of their kiosks or appeared at their doors, yawning with arms stretched above their heads as our Chevrolet shattered the hush of the hours just before dawn.

In the open country we could hear dogs barking around farmhouses far afield when we shut off the rackety motor to coast down a hill.

The car began to sputter and we knew we couldn't go much farther. When the engine faltered on a rise, I instinctively leaned forward to help push.

"Give 'er all she's got!" I howled to Ed.

"If I tromp any harder, I'll run my leg through the floorboard," he assured me grimly.

We reached the crest of a hill none too soon, and saw the lights of a city winking across a river below us. The East was flushing rosily as we gravitated toward the bridge,

Ed having prudently turned off the ignition switch. In the sudden quiet we could hear steaming water gurgling in the radiator like the death rattle in a dying man's throat, and the rush of the wheels and squeaking of the springs and chassis. The engine spat out a feeble cough or two when Ed threw it in gear on the opposite side of the bridge, the car leaped gallantly, bucked weakly a few times, and died.

"We're through now, all right, all right!" said Ed resignedly as he climbed stiffly out and stood ruefully kicking the front tires.

It was getting lighter. Along the river bank to the left we could dimly make out an apparently interminable expanse of rusting tin, tar paper, low sheds, and grounded houseboats. We thought at first that it must be a tangle of debris washed ashore, but gradually the nebulous units assumed definite shape, fell into ordered rows. The farther end of the collection of huts was obscured in the morning mist off the river. One of the little winds that accompany dawn shook a fallen billboard forming the roof of one of the sheds. The billboard displayed a shapely feminine leg and advised spectators to take a good look at the bottle of Nehi soda pop standing near.

We pushed the Chevrolet from the pavement and guided it to rest beside the first hovel. "Welcome to Hoover City. Two Car Garages. A Chicken in Every Pot," read a roughly painted sign nailed to a post. Then we knew we had found a colony of the dispossessed such as were springing up in every industrial center as factories closed, savings dwindled, and banks crashed.

Packing crates, bits of tar paper, tin advertising signs, discarded automobile bodies, ancient delivery wagons, and small houseboats dragged up from the river had been fashioned into the semblance of homes. Some of the huts had glass windows with dingy curtains, but most of them were designed for shelter and nothing else. The owners had ceased to be particular before they were reduced to the colony of the down-and-outs. A hound slunk from behind one of the huts, sniffing our heels inquiringly. It threw back its head and howled dismally. Then a grey-beard thrust aside a flap of rotting carpet and emerged from the hut. He called sharply to the hound, gawped widely, and blinked his pink-rimmed eyes at the rising sun. His toothless jaws stretched in a noisy yawn. He set to work at scratching vigorously on his chest and under his arms, then he reached for the inaccessible regions of his back.

"Good morning, mister," Ed greeted him. "Looks like you got quite a town started here. Don't suppose a man could *buy* a job around here, could he?"

"A job! A job!" the old man cackled derisively. "Jobs went out o' style, son, two years ago. Most folks in Hoover City has forgot they *ever* had jobs."

Then he paused reflectively, looking Ed over from head to foot.

"You look like a bull, though," he resumed. "Jesse Gillespie jist got a job at sand hoggin' in the river. A man can only stay an hour or so at a time. It's a nigger's job, but times has got so hard the white men is chasin' the niggers away and takin' the job theirselves. Most of the men in our fair city here has got so g'ant they got to stand twicet t' make a shadder. They got bellies wrinkled up like washboards, so's they can't cut the mustard on a sand hoggin' job."

We knew how sand hoggers were lowered in hollow tubes to the bed of the river, how they dug frantically at the wet sand for a while, and then had to be hoisted to the top again. We weren't well-nourished ourselves, but we were bound to make it home somehow.

"I can stand it—for a while, anyway," Ed said resolutely. "Where does Jesse live?"

"In the next to the last bungalow on this side of the boulevard."

The old man was barefoot. He sat down and began to pick mud from between his toes.

Snores or the whimpering of babies sounded from some of the shacks as we walked along. Tousled heads popped out, withdrew hastily, or regarded us with hostility tempered by curiosity. We could hear people moving inside the shacks—muttered voices. The smell of smoke and cooking pervaded the air. Already clouds of flies were waking to life, for garbage lay everywhere—in the streets and behind the huts.

When we reached the shack designated by the old man, we thoughtlessly pulled aside a canvas strip masking the doorway and stepped within. In the faint light we saw a heavy, bearded man sprawled across a pallet of filthy blankets. His boots were still on his feet, and damp sand clung to the soles. Beside him lay a frowsy woman suckling an infant. The woman seemed to be asleep, but the baby rooted away avidly at her breast. The woman's thin legs were bare and mottled with varicose veins. The baby turned its head and allowed the teat to slip from its lips with a smack which startled us. Its eyes searched us fearfully and it wailed gently. The mother stirred in her sleep and thrust the teat back in the baby's mouth. Ed and I shook off our inertia and backed out.

"Oh, we oughtn't to 've done that, kid!" Ed whispered hoarsely. "Someway it didn't seem like this was a house for a human, did it? Seemed like it was O. K. to walk in without knockin'. More like a barn or a hog pen. Most hogs got better pens than that, eh? But we didn't have no right t' walk in there like a big horse!"

"Jesse! Jesse!" the woman within called shrilly. "They's been somebody in here! I *know* it! I c'n *feel* 'em!"

The man growled unintelligibly, but almost instantly he appeared at the doorway. He glowered at us, his fingers rasping through the matted stubble on his face.

"Was it you jist in here?" he demanded pugnaciously. "If you was, I don't see what you cal'lated t' find, 'less you figgered on rapin' my old woman."

"We wanted t' see about the sand hoggin' job," Ed spoke up. "Whether they're hirin'. We gotta have a job."

"They'll hire a man in my place, I reckon," Jesse responded sullenly. "I'm one man that ain't a bit picayunish about what I do, but when I gotta have my guts twisted up like a corkscrew, when my haid aches like it would split, when I can't even undress of a night I'm that tard, I'll try a little starvin' first. I'm not goin' back. They c'n take the job and go t' hell with it fer all o' me. It's two miles down the river if you wanta find out about it. I'm gonna sleep fer three days hand runnin'."

As we made off we heard him plop soddenly on his pallet.

We were almost cheerful as we plodded along the river bank. The sun had risen warm and the water dimpled and shimmered. Motorboats darted here and there, sending miniature breakers lapping against the shore and throwing white spray. Hell divers slipped quietly beneath the surface to pop up far from where they dove.

We discovered the boss of the sand hoggers addressing a group of overalled white men: "You needn't chase the niggers away no more, men. Get me right. I ain't no nigger lover. I come from Peachtree, Georgia, where niggers step off the sidewalk and take off their hats when they see a white man comin'. I tried my best t' use white men, but they play out on me. So I gotta use the niggers. I'm sorry as all hell."

When we returned, the inhabitants of Hoover City were returning from their morning foraging expeditions to the commission houses and garbage cans. They salvaged over-ripe bananas, half-rotten potatoes and apples, stale bread, wilted lettuce, and moldy beans.

"D'ya know what the chain stores is doin'?" exploded a ragged crone. "They're pourin' coal oil over the grub in their garbage cans so's we can't eat it. Sometimes you c'n find a loaf o' bread that ain't soaked, but all of it smells and tastes like coal oil. Some of the kids grabbed it and eat it anyways, and it made 'em sicker 'n a dog."

We were so hungry we accepted the greybeard's invitation to join him at breakfast in his hut. The *menu* consisted of slightly decayed bananas, but we gulped them down voraciously, spitting out the spots that were too sour. The den was even more horrible than Jesse's. The greybeard's couch was a pile of musty straw flung in a corner and the room contained nothing else in the way of furniture. It smelled like a dank cellar. Yellowish oat sprouts were springing out of the damp earth beneath the straw.

"It's a wonder you don't die of rheumatism," Ed commiserated as he frugally nibbled a banana skin.

"I do have it purty bad in my jints," the old man answered. "Lookut the knobs on my fingers. My knees and elbows git the same way. But it's heaven now to what it was last Winter. I like to 've froze more 'n once and I sure praised God t' see Spring come ag'in."

Ed glanced at me significantly. He was always twitting me about the docility of the poor and deriding my predictions that they would rebel against the degradation being forced upon them.

The population of Hoover City grew daily. Refugees from the city were arriving constantly with some of their possessions salvaged from the wrecks of their homes.

Others came empty-handed. A preacher drifted in and rallied enough modern Jobs to erect a church which was slightly more pretentious than the dwellings. It had a pickle barrel for an altar.

Ed and I kept searching the city for some odd jobs. The police harried us and made us keep moving. They told us not to hang around the employment agencies and not to panhandle. The sluff dished out at the soup lines made us sicker than the garbage off the dump. Not only that, somebody was always trying to save our souls.

At last we found a man who was willing to pay us four dollars for unloading a car of gravel. More than once I sank to my knees on the harsh rocks, my head pounding. I had been worrying more and more about Mother and about Bonny Fern, and, thinking of them, I rose again. Our hands were soon lacerated and burning.

"A man needs something that'll stick to his ribs on this kind of job," Ed gritted, but he shoveled all the faster. When we had dug a hole to the bottom and could shovel off the floor, the going was easier. When we tottered to the side of the car with the last shovels full of gravel, we sank down on the rough planks and lay for an hour without moving or speaking.

We had hired the greybeard to watch the car that day, for we were afraid somebody who knew we were working might strip it. We found the old man dozing luxuriously in the front seat, which was a great deal more comfortable than his bed of straw. Our muscles were growing stiffer and stiffer, but we were determined not to wait till morning. Something like panic seized us; our desire to leave the place was uncontrollable. We carried gas and oil from an adjacent filling station and rejoiced to hear the engine throbbing once more. We headed into the glittering maze of neon tubes and street lights. Below and behind us night was blanking out Hoover City. We were in such a hurry to get away that we had forgotten to clean the spark plugs, but the lurching motor reminded us of it before we'd traveled far.

We pulled the car to the curb, scraped the plugs, and headed west again. We sniffed the fragrance of hot dogs in a kiosk beside the way, and remembered that we had not eaten since our meager breakfast of apples which had been too mushy for the retail trade and hence the legitimate prey of the colony of the disinherited.

Fortified by five hot dogs and belching contentedly from a half dozen bottles of pop, we set out afresh. The Chevrolet had apparently decided to lead a better life, for it ran along with utmost docility. As we cleared the suburbs and left even the trolley tracks behind, the moon ascended the sky and we fell to singing sentimental ballads. Before morning familiar landmarks began to whiz by.

IV

Thunder rolled; lightning forked across the sky. The wind rose and lashed blinding rain across the windshield as we pulled into town.

"Some homecoming!" Ed yelled as the car went ploughing down Main Street like a motorboat dividing the waves. We peered out eagerly, looking for somebody we knew, but nobody was stirring. We drove through town without seeing anybody.

The lane to Monkey Nest Camp was flooded but it had been shaled since we saw it last. The car slipped into the ditch several times, but at length we drove into the grassy yard of the house in which I was born. It was in the last stages of dilapidation. The weatherboarding was warped and broken, windows shattered, and the doors banged to and fro on squeaking hinges at the impetus of every violent gust that whistled through the structure.

"Let's not sit here," I said impatiently. The desolation of the place intensified my dejection.

"Thought it might let up, but don't look like it now," said Ed, climbing out and squinting at the sky. He was stiff from sitting at the wheel, and he began to dance and beat his breast.

It should have been daylight, but black clouds hid the rising sun and fog lay so low on the ground that we could not make out the camp houses below us. When we drew closer, we saw that many of them were gone and no trace of them remained. They had never had any other foundation than white oak posts set in the ground, and even these had rotted away in most cases. Buck brush flourished rankly on the spot where Mike Riordan's shack had stood.

A few of the houses were still standing. They were weatherbeaten and in disrepair. The foundation posts under the house in which Staffords used to live had given way and it tilted at an angle suggesting a sinking ship poised for the final plunge beneath the waves and into oblivion. The doors and windows were gone and the wind whistled savagely through the apertures. The walls had been built of upright, unpainted pine boards, and many of these had been wrenched loose by the elements or by thrifty farmers seeking lumber for hog pens or henhouses. English sparrows had stuffed every crevice with the coarse straw of their nests.

The skies lightened slowly. We peered into each camp house, but could find no signs of recent human occupancy. The interior of each shack was littered with the pitiful trash that accumulates in the hovels of the very poor. In some places good-sized saplings had shouldered up through the broken floors and reached for the holes in the roofs. The rain fell in a steady downpour, and the small creek near the communal spring, now filled with rubbish and fallen branches, was boiling madly.

253

"There's not a soul here, kid," Ed said uneasily. "Let's us hoof it over to Ben's and find out how the land lays. Remember, we was a right smart delayed in gettin' here."

"I guess we'd better," I answered. "We've looked in every one that's still standing. Maybe they found some place else to stay. They'll know at Ben's."

As we turned to go, I chanced to look toward the shack that had housed Liam Ryan's barroom, which stood at the extreme end of the semicircle and a bit apart. A wisp of smoke was coming out of the rusty pipe surmounting the building. The wind caught it and dispersed it instantly, but I could tell it was smoke and not fog.

"There they are, Ed," I called. "They're living in the old barroom."

Ed turned about and we were soon standing before the door. It opened a crack to my knock and Mother's frightened face peered out.

"Mother! It's me! It's us! It's Larry and Ed!" I cried as we stepped inside quickly to get out of the rain. But it was almost as bad inside. We could see daylight through the roof in several places. Liam's bar was still in the place. It was not an expensive walnut or mahogany one, but built of pine. Behind it the long mirror had been shattered by marauding small boys, but some of the slivers were tacked to the wall. Against the rear wall stood a long pine table. It must have been the one on which the naked chippies had danced so long ago. When I was a boy, I had lain outside and yearned through the doors of Liam's barroom. I knew that the liquor made the miners happy for a while, made them forget for a while the cruel hours lying on their sides picking away at the coal, and the rocks overhead ready to crash down. And when I was yet very young, I knew what the attractive attributes of the chippies were.

As I looked closely at Mother and Aunt Jessie, I realized with a pang that time does not wait, and that it is especially relentless with the women of the poor. Aunt Jessie greeted us with a forlorn and toothless grin; her hair that had been so thick and wavy hung on her head in sparse grey strands. Mother had withered away like an apple bitten by the frost; innumerable wrinkles checked her face and converged upon her mouth and eyes. I decided that rheumatism brought on by living in such a dump was responsible for the huge knobs that distorted her fingers and wrists. She walked with a cane fashioned from a broom stick.

Ed and I sat down and tried to mask our dejection. A stream from the roof poured steadily down my back, but I did not mind. The floor was covered with pans and tin cans into which rivulets from overhead splattered and drummed. Now and then Mother or Aunt Jessie carried a full one to the rear and emptied it. It soon filled again.

"Come over here where there's a dry spot, boys," Aunt Jessie invited. But we sat still. I was surprised to see how Aunt Jessie's children had shot up in the air. The largest girl was almost grown and had the luxuriant chestnut hair which had made all the boys crazy about Aunt Jessie when she was a girl. The children were huddled over a mail order catalogue, playing a game of wishing. Each one had three wishes at a time, and wished for something out of the catalogue. Then it was the next one's turn. The largest girl chose clothes mostly, but the younger ones were partial to candy and groceries.

"Are you hungry, boys?" Mother asked after a bit.

"Well, a little. Not much," I answered.

"I'm not a bit hungry," Ed asserted politely, but he was.

"I've got a pot of wild greens here. They're not very good because I only had a little lard to put in them for seasoning."

"That's all right. That'll be fine," I said with spurious

255

heartiness. "Been a long time since we've had any good old wild greens."

Mother hobbled to the table at the back of the room and peered into a kettle resting upon it. She started violently and lowered her face for a better view, then burst into tears. I ran over to see what was the matter. The kettle was running over with greenish water upon which sprigs of poke and wild mustard attended by globules of cold grease floated.

"I thought I had it in a dry place," Mother sobbed hopelessly. "The roof's always springing a leak in a new place. That was all we had in the house to eat."

"Why, Ed and I'll go back to town and get some groceries," I said cheerfully. "We'll be back in three shakes of a dead lamb's tail. What do you want?"

"I know you haven't got much money, son," Mother said. "You *can't* have. So if you want to get some groceries, get corn meal, navy beans and salt fat jowl. We can make that go further than anything else. Go to the Split Nickel Cash and Carry. You'll have to learn to make every penny count."

Outside, Ed and I took a hurried inventory. We possessed two dollars and four cents between us, and we knew it might be a long time before we saw any more cash.

When we returned and Mother and Aunt Jessie set to work preparing the meal, the children began picking at things, tearing chunks out of the salt jowl and gulping them down avidly with smacking noises. Aunt Jessie asked them where their manners had gone. The children gobbled the food even more audibly when they came to the table but Aunt Jessie forgot to reprimand them. She chewed away eagerly. She had a few teeth left, but they were in the back of her head and she had to work her jaws and mouth furiously to accomplish anything with them.

After breakfast Ed and I waded through the mud to

Ben's. The sumac, buck brush and saplings had the best of it now in the clearing where Ben and the hired man had grubbed away so doggedly with axe and mattock.

Bonny Fern was in the barnlot picking up chips in her apron. The rain had subsided to a silvery mist, and it clung about her hair. "Why, hello!" she cried gladly, letting the chips fall and grasping each of us by a hand. Her hands were chapped and red and her face was tanned and freckled. She wore a shapeless cotton dress, patched in spots, and with damp splotches showing in front where she had been kneeling on the damp earth. The barnyard steamed; amber pools lay everywhere. Bonny Fern ploughed through them as though she did not mind them, but Ed and I tried to walk around. As Bonny Fern led the way to the house, we could see her bare feet through the holes in the soles of her shoes every time she took a step.

Ben was patching harness in the kitchen. His wife was sitting listlessly by the window, staring out. The children could be heard wrangling in another room.

"Come in," Ben called out as we stood wiping our feet on a gunny sack. "You can't hurt this place none. This plague-taked harness is rotten as dirt. Good thing my hoss is so ga'nt it has t' stand twicet t' make a shadder. It's so devilish weak it don't pull very hard or I'd hafta be patchin' oftener."

"Well, you was lucky you cleared out when you did," Ed offered by way of consolation as we sat down.

"Mebbe I was," grunted Ben dubiously, "but I can't see no fortune or even a livin' in this life. I borryed all I could any place I could t' git through the Winter. I still owed on that south ten acres I was fool enough to buy jist before the War, and I made out a mortgage on the hull place like a ninny. The mortgage's been due more'n a year and they're threatenin' t' sell me out any day."

"Well, why don't you start into raisin' hawgs?" suggested Ed jocosely.

"I raised me some hawgs last Winter. I figger it cost me twelve dollars a head t' raise 'em. I took a notion I needed some money a while back and I shipped one of the fattest ones off t' market. . . ." He searched the hind pocket of his overalls and produced a leather wallet from which he withdrew a sweat-stained paper. It was a check from a commission house calling for the sum of eight cents. "That's what I had left of the hawg after the freight and everything was paid."

"You et the others, I bet. You had some good pork chops offen the rest, eh?" Ed said.

"Like hell! I didn't have nothing t' feed 'em but acorns and not many of them. Their meat was tough as whit leather. We had t' pound the baby on the back more 'n once t' keep her from chokin' t' death on it." He pounded copper rivets in the harness angrily for a moment. "But I guess I'm lucky at that," he resumed. "Feller shipped a car load o' cattle t' Saint Looie not long back, they tell me, and the commission house sent him a tellygram he'd hafta send twenty more dollars than the cattle brung 't pay the freight and commission. He wrote and told 'em he didn't have a red t' his name; he'd jist hafta send another car load of cattle."

"What about the pipe line job Bonny Fern wrote us about?" I asked.

"It's comin' this way. A long ways down the river bottom yit, but I hear they're hirin' about one out of every fifty thousand that asts fer a job. You and Ed oughta be able t' git on if anybody could. You fellers got a way about you that the bosses can't say no to—or the wimmen, either."

"Well, we'd better get going. We'll see you later," I said. "If there's any job there we surely need to get it."

Bonny Fern had come in and was standing near the kitchen range drying her wet clothing. She followed us outside, and Ed walked ahead across the field. The rain had ceased and the sun was breaking through the scudding clouds.

"It's been even worse than I thought it would be," she said plaintively. "The loneliness most of all. I wouldn't mind the starving once in a while if there was any point to starving. As Vachel Lindsay put it:

'Not that they starve, but starve so dreamlessly;
Not that they die, but that they die like sheep.' "

"I'll not starve and die like a sheep," I said.

"What will you do?"

"I'll find a way to do something. That's what worries me night and day now, what to do."

"We were hungry more than once last Winter. So were your mother and aunt and the children."

"Yes, I know. That's one thing that makes me all the more determined to do something. But you've got to know where to hit."

"Come on!" yelled Ed impatiently. "We've gotta fix that roof, Larry. You're like the Arkansaw Traveler. Long as it's rainin' you can't fix it and when it ain't rainin' it don't need it. Come on!"

"Are you going to the pipe line?" Bonny Fern asked.

"Yes, and I'll see you first," I said. I bent over swiftly and directed a kiss at her face, hardly daring to look at her. She was still smiling, a little more brightly. "She didn't mind!" I told myself as I ran across the field to join Ed. My childish awe of her had never entirely dissolved.

"Goodbye, honey," I heard her say, but as I turned my head I saw her running swiftly back toward the house.

Ed and I found some aged powder kegs near the Monkey

Nest dump. Many of them crumbled away to brittle flakes of rust as we touched them, but others would still turn water. The walls of Frenchy Barbour's shack were yet standing, and we tore off a number of planks. Mr. Stacpoole, the owner of the Monkey Nest and the camp, had left the country years before, and nobody paid any attention to the property.

We patched the roof of the barroom the best we could, and persuaded a dealer to give us six dollars for our Chevrolet. Three dollars we left with Mother. She said that would be enough to keep them in groceries for a month, but we told her not to skimp too much, for we were sure of a job. We kept telling ourselves we were sure of one, and forced ourselves to believe it.

There were hundreds of men on the freight which we boarded for our trip down the valley. Bands of men and boys were roaming the country searching for work as for a treasure. In the box car with us were several women and girls.

Ben was right. The boss could not resist us, but hired us at once. In spite of the hard Winter we had been through, we still looked muscular. Many of the applicants were emaciated, and did not like to stand on their feet long at a time. They leaned against the shed which served the boss as an office, or lay about on the ground.

"I didn't wanta work, nohow," one of them said on being turned down. "I don't *never* expect to work no more."

V

The trucks roared away from the pipe line company's headquarters before the village had awakened. They swung onto the bridge over the river and a loose steel plate clanged as their wheels struck it. The men leaned over the sides of the trucks and spat sadly into the river. They were thinking of the day ahead; their muscles were stiff and sore, for most of them were not used to this kind of work. A pearly fog shrouded the river and its willow-fledged banks. A bit beyond it the trucks paused here and there, disgorging workers, until they were scattered a mile or so along the ditch. The acetylene welders were the aristocrats of the job, for they were hard to find in this sequestered hinterland. If they came in late after carousing the night before, nothing was said. But if one of the shovel stiffs was tardy, it meant his job.

The welders already had their torches spluttering, welding three lengths of pipe into one long section at the edge of the ditch. Then the welded section was swung into the ditch with a hand crane, and bolted to the next one. There were not many pick and shovel men, for the company was using a ditching machine.

The ditcher hummed along through the level land, its cutters flashing in the sun. It resembled a huge fat spider unreeling a black strand behind it. Two men could handle it nicely, and it piled the dirt neatly on one side. But sometimes it would strike a root as big as a man's leg, and then there was a job for men with axes, picks and shovels. The men, some of whom were poor farmers from nearby, hated the ditcher and rejoiced every time it broke down.

"Machinery has ruined the country," they'd say. "No sale for horses on account of automobiles, no sale for hay, no sale for oats. A stick of dynamite under that go-devil would be the best thing that could happen to it. Then they might put some men to work."

The whole region had been stricken by drought. The stock ponds had been sucked dry by the blazing coppery sun. The mud dried and cracked into squares like a flag-paved court. Most of the farmers thereabouts were share croppers, but there would be nothing to share this year.

The cane in their fields was stunted and the sap in it had dried. If we happened to find a green stalk, the juice wasn't sweet. We could see the share-croppers lying listlessly in their yards, gazing out over their blasted fields. Sometimes they appeared beside the ditch—gaunt men, slatternly women carrying babies, and beady-eyed children clinging to their skirts. They had packs of lugubrious lop-eared hounds. Usually they surveyed the ditching machine silently for a few moments and then vanished as silently as they came, but occasionally one of the men would hit up the boss for a job.

"Full up!" was the invariable reply, and after the applicant had left, the boss would elaborate: "They got their *livin'*! Can't beat 'em out of that, and what else does a man get out of life but a bite to eat and a rag to his back. If I had a farm to work, I wouldn't mess with no goddamn job like this."

Once one of the disappointed farmers heard him and wheeled about, snarling bitterly: "A hell of a livin' *I* got! I been eatin' turnip greens without any seasonin' till my belly goes wishy-washy every time I step. By God, mister, I got a fancy livin', believe me!"

Up and down the ditch the superintendent rode on a wiry cayuse, shouting orders, spurring laggards with sarcasm, and arbitrating the many disputes with the farmers over the right of way. The timekeeper checked up the men by the badges on their hats, and issued new badges to the ones who had just started.

After the welded joints had been lowered in the ditch and bolted together, tractors with slips attached filled the ditch, but some shovel men were needed to round up the earth. They couldn't do without men altogether. Ed and I shaped the continuous mound and patted it down with the backs of our shovels. Field mice had worn a labyrinth of paths next to the grass roots, and they ran squeaking as

262

we unearthed them. The men chased after them, batting with shovels. The underground dens were padded with grasses, and often they held pink and shivering baby mice, their eyes bulging like blue warts and red veins pulsing beneath their thin skins.

"I'm up a tree," the ditcher man confessed to the boss. "I can't go no fu'ther. They's a gal up the line has jumped a'straddle of me because the line goes right through a graveyard. She's got a gun four yards long, and if anybody wants to buck up ag'in it, they can, but not me. They's an iron fence around the graveyard, and it'll take a couple good men to horse it way. But far's I'm concerned, it c'n stay put."

"I'll see about that!" snorted the foreman. "She ain't got no right to hold up this here job. We got a right of way across that there place. We got the law on our side."

"Yeh, but she's got the gun," retorted the ditcher man, unconvinced. "That ain't gonna help me none if she blows my guts out."

"Awssh! ptu!" the boss spat disgustedly. "Come with me," he called to Ed and me.

The graveyard was on a small knoll. The girl leaned against the fence and held the shotgun awkwardly but determinedly. She said that her grandmother had told her to keep everybody away till her grandfather came home. The foreman stalked off toward the farmhouse, and the ditcher man sat down to doze. The delay was not troubling him.

"You'll let that gun go off and shoot somebody," hailed Ed, who was quite a kidder.

"That's what I aim to do if anybody sets foot in this buryin' ground," rejoined the girl, tossing her hair out of her eyes. But she grounded the shotgun and smiled.

"You wouldn't dast shoot *me*," Ed continued. "Besides, you look like you got too soft a heart."

"Oooh, yaw!" she replied.

"I don't suppose you'd have no objections to us just *lookin'* at the graves," Ed pursued. "I think a man ought 't spend a little time in a graveyard now an' then. It puts the fear o' God in him."

"Well, I guess just *lookin'* won't hurt none," she conceded meltingly, "but don't start no monkey business."

The dozen graves were surmounted by stones bearing elaborate designs and pious sentiments. One of them bore the representation of a hand pointing skyward, and the words "Gone Above." Also, this stanza:

> "Remember, friend, as you pass by,
> As you are now, so once was I.
> As I am now, so you must be.
> Prepare for death, and follow me."

"That's Aunt Rhody's grave," volunteered the girl. "She wrote out that verse before she died and made Uncle Hal promise to put it on her tombstone. I don't know whether she made it up out of her own head or not."

"No matter who wrote it, it puts a man t' thinkin'," said Ed solemnly, winking at me as the girl turned to prop her shotgun against the stone.

Presently the boss returned with a rheumy-eyed patriarch, leaning heavily on a gnarled cane. He was the girl's grandfather.

"I know I sold the right to go through my land, neighbor," admitted the old man, "but I never 'lowed that you'd cut through the buryin' ground. All of my folks from away back yonder lays a-sleepin' there, and it's hard lines to have their rest disturbed."

He seemed about to burst into tears. The boss started pulling his fingers to make his knuckle joints crack.

"Looky here!" he exploded. "We paid you to go through here and we're goin'. There ain't no grave in the part we cut through, nohow."

"You can't tell jist exactly where the graves is now," the old man persisted. "I moved up to Detroit in '26 to stay with my son Basil, and the dad-blasted tenants let the fence down and their cattle tromped up everything so's you can't tell nothin' about it. I found a lot of tombstones in a pile, and I jist set 'em up in places that *looked* like a grave."

"We got the law on our side," snapped the boss. "Come on, you two, nail a-holt of this fence and pack it out of the way!"

The patriarch had taken possession of the gun, and as we moved forward he raised it and squinted down the barrels. His misty eyes had cleared. We hesitated, and looked at the boss.

"If you wanta git blowed to Kingdom Come, step up," invited the old man. "I'll stand here till Hell freezes over and they build fires on the ice before I let you lay a finger on this fence."

"I'm licked!" the boss acknowledged despairingly. "The super himself has got to settle this fuss. You better knock off for today, boys, while him and me talks this thing over."

Ed and I did not wait for the trucks to take us back to the village. We raced across the fields to the railroad bridge, which made the trip two miles shorter than the highway. When we got to the bridge approach, our hearts were hammering at our ribs and our sweaty shirts were plastered to our backs. There was no footpath across the bridge, and a sign warned pedestrians to keep off. Stepping from one tie to the next necessitated a mincing gait, but skipping a tie stretched the legs a little too far. Ed remembered how a fellow had been caught by a train in the middle of such a bridge and had to hang by his arms underneath the ties till the cars passed. The engine had rained hot cinders on his hair, and he almost forgot and let go to brush them off.

Nevertheless, we paused in the middle of the span to look down the river. The stream had shrunk to a muddy creek and the willows that fringed its normal banks were parching. A stench arose from heaps of dead fish stranded on the sand bars. Farmers drove their cattle for miles to the river, for their wells and springs had played out even as their ponds had. Two overalled farmhands on ponies now herded a bunch of cows toward the water. When they smelled the water, the cows bawled and broke into a run. The farmhands drove their charges back across the plain in a cloud of dust.

In the village, farmers were gathered in the courthouse square, talking about the drought. There was a statue of an American doughboy going over the top, with menacing rifle and formidable scowl, and on the base were inscribed the names of the county boys who had died in France. *Dulce et decorum est pro patria mori* was chiseled above the names. A brass tablet set in a boulder told how the volunteer militia of the village had defended it against guerrillas in the Civil War. The low stone wall around the courthouse was polished and greasy from the buttocks of many years' loafers. Horses tied to the hitching-racks shuddered their hides to dislodge flies, and under the wagons hounds scratched fleas and panted, with tongues lolling out. One horse had set its teeth firmly in a post and was drawing in its breath with a queer whistle. Ed said it was a stump sucker and would blow itself up like a balloon.

We entered the solitary beanery. Soon the short-order counter was jammed with pipe line huskies. The proprietor was overjoyed, and the two waitresses, enlivened by the rough sallies directed at them, dashed from table to table.

"Roas' beef. Roas' pork. Catfish dinner. Apple, peach, raisin pie!" one of the waitresses recited, sliding two glasses of water along the table and spilling half their contents. As she bent over we could see her heavy breasts flopping beneath her loose dress. Ed called her back time and again, and each time she came willingly enough, though with feigned exasperation.

"Call this coffee?" he complained jovially. "Tastes more like crick water. And I bet you this fish is the one that swallered Jonah."

"You're awful pertickler," she countered saucily. "I bet your wife has to kiss you good-night and tuck you in bed every night."

"Gwan! You know I ain't married," Ed grinned. "It's worry over my money that has turned my hair grey. How do you pass the time in this place? Is they a liberry or a movie?"

"A liberry!" mocked the girl. "They never heard of a liberry in this burg. The Bijou Dream's pretty good, though, tonight. 'A Passion in the Desert.' They say it's keeno."

She lingered expectantly for a while, but Ed did not pursue his advantage.

"We told the old coot," said the boss next morning, "that if we run into a grave we'd stop and figger some other way. But I don't aim t' run into no grave, see? If we should, accidentally, and he ain't about, he can't prove nothing if the ditch is filled. The fillers caught up with us yesterday, and inside of three hours after we pass through the pipe'll be in and the ditch closed."

So we laid the iron fence aside and set down planks on which the ditcher could climb the knoll. Its caterpillar treads bit into the planks and the shovels tore into the loose sandy soil—good digging. When the machine got to the cemetery it began bringing up chips of rotten wood and white bits that looked like fragments of bone. The engineer pretended not to see them for a while, but an especially large chunk caused him to shut off the engine.

"We're in a grave, all right, I guess," he said uneasily. "Maybe we should stop. We ain't got no right to fool the old man thisaway. Besides, I ain't anxious to churn up no dead man's bones."

"By the holy jumpin' Jesus," howled the boss, "we gotta get away from this place! Lemme take it through if you're yeller!"

Almost the whole crew had gathered to watch, but neither the old man nor his granddaughter was on hand. When the ditcher had passed through the graveyard, the end of a coffin protruded from the side of the ditch, six feet down. Silently and hastily we lowered the length of pipe and several men sprang down to adjust it and to bolt the connections. At the crest of the knoll the ditch was ten or twelve feet deep. When any of the men passed the place where the coffin showed, he shied gingerly and hugged the other side of the ditch.

Suddenly a piece of the coffin fell on the pipe with a ghastly thud. This was too much for one of the men. He shrieked and clawed his way up the side. The earth was loose and crumbly, and almost at once the sides buckled and filled the ditch to the top. Some of the men struggled out from where they stood; others ran to the shallower sections. One man was buried to the waist, and we worked frantically digging him free. A panic had seized us.

"Everybody in the clear?" bawled the boss, who had shut off the ditcher and run back when he heard the shouts. "If it's only a few wrenches lost, we'll call it a job."

The timekeeper checked all the men by his book and

268

the badges on their hats, and found everybody accounted for. At that moment the water boy ran up and bellowed:

"There's a man with a fit over here! He's been settin' on a grave and just now he hopped up and hollered something about somebody bein' covered up. Then he fell over and went to thrashin' around like a chicken with its head cut off." He pointed to the back of the graveyard.

The stricken man, evidently not much more than a boy, writhed on the ground, frothing at the mouth. Guttural sobs shook him.

"An epileptic!" cried Ed. "You better jam a stick between his jaws or he'll gnaw his tongue off."

"Mos' all these rubes got a cripple or idiot in the family," said the boss, grabbing the water bucket and drenching the prostrate sufferer. "I saw one back in the next county born without legs. Jist rolls on the floor and whines like a pup. Has to wear a didy like a baby."

Soon the epileptic quit struggling. His face had turned dark blue and his breath came in whistling gasps. But his glassy eyes closed, and he seemed to be sleeping peacefully. He lay for an hour or so, then sprang up suddenly and sped across the fields.

Ed and I got lodging at the home of the patriarch whose graveyard had been defiled, but apparently he had heard nothing about the violated grave. His middle-aged son, Basil, was at home from Detroit, but he lived in hope that the automobile industry would presently revive and call him back to the fleshpots of city life. He spent a great deal of time behind the barn, moodily surveying the rusty automobile which had brought him home. The tires were flaccid and cracked by the weather, and enamel was flaking off the Michigan license plate. Chickens roosted in the back seat, whitening the cushions with their droppings, and wallowed luxuriously in the velvety dust between the chassis. Basil shooed them away with a stick. The car's weight was sinking it in the soft earth.

"No use o' plumb ruinin' that car," he grumbled. "With some top dressin', new tires, and a little tinkerin', she's good fer fifty thousand miles yet. Wisht I had some licenses for the scoundrel. The automobile business's *gotta* pick up *some* day."

The family gathered in the evening beneath the honey locust tree in the yard. The patriarch was fond of recalling how his skill with the fiddle had been acclaimed when he was young. Now youngsters danced to the yapping radio, with its barbaric clamor of traps and saxophones.

"One thing I don't like is this new-fangled music," the patriarch said. "This gol-darned boopa-de-doop and vo-de-o-do. If *that's* music, I'm a Chinyman. Now, something like this. . . ." His doleful voice accompanied the merrily squeaking fiddle:

> "Buffler gals, aintcha comin' out t'night?
> Comin' out t'night? Comin' out t'night?
> Purty little gals, aintcha comin' out t'night
> Fer t' dance by the light o' the moon?"

When the fiddle quieted we could hear katydids shrilling in the honey locust's branches, and a whip-poor-will crying farther afield. A hoot owl's maniacal laughter sounded from the barn lot. The moon raced for ragged black clouds, plunging within them to emerge on the other side and go chasing a flying wisp again. After Basil's silent wife and daughter went into the house, the old man's art assumed a more Rabelaisian flavor. With many mournful quavers and a great deal of adagio scraping, he cackled a ballad:

> "As I come up to the purty maid's winder;
> As I come up to the purty maid's winder;

As I come up to the purty maid's winder;
Sing toor a la loo, sing toor a la bum.
There she lay a-snorin' and sleepin';
There she lay while I come a-creepin'.
Sing toor a la loo, sing toor a la bum."

The remainder of the ballad related how the venturous swain debated aloud with himself as to whether he should advance boldly or retreat. The maiden apparently spoke in her sleep to dissolve his inhibitions. The climax was tragic:

"Come a sad day when she fell a-weepin';
And then she recalled that snorin' and sleepin'.
Sing toor a la loo; sing toor a la bum."

On Sunday the shops of the village were closed. Only the churches were open. Ed and I ranged the woods aimlessly, throwing stones at squirrels and chipmunks. Heavy rains had broken the drought, but too late to do the farmers any good. In the woods falling leaves were carpeting the ground. This was a region of drift mines, burrowing horizontally into the hills.

The hills were honey-combed with them, but they were all abandoned now. Some of them had caught fire; others were flooded with water. The burning mines had been known to smoulder for months and even years. Their soapstone and culm heaps exuded a phlegmy white liquid.

We were standing before one of the mines, sniffing the acrid scent of coal smoke and casting rocks within, when we heard a weird cry down the shaft and the patter of feet. Thinking we had aroused a wildcat, we started to run; but paused when we saw the epileptic half-wit of the graveyard come blinking out of the dark. His clothing was tattered and his matted hair studded with cinders. One jaw was swollen so badly that his lip lifted in a snarl, exposing inflamed gums.

271

"You hit me!" he accused, more plaintively than belligerently.

"I didn't aim to, buddy," Ed apologized. "Didn't expect nobody to be in that hole."

"I live there," the half-wit confided. "I live there since they covered my brother Paul up in the ditch. Before it turned so cold, I slept under the trees, but it's warmer back there. My tooth hurts, but if I heat a rock in the fire and lay my face on it, it feels better. But I wish Paul was here. I have to find something to eat around farmhouses at night, and the dogs chase me. They tear my clothes and bite me."

"Nutty as a coon!" Ed whispered to me. "Ain't you got no place t' stay, buddy?" he asked the half-wit.

"I guess I *am* crazy," was the reply. "Once they had me in a big house with bars, and when I had spells and cried they beat me. My head felt funny and I couldn't help it. But Paul got me out. He promised then he'd take care of me. We walk and walk places and he works on roads and jobs like the ditch. When I had bad spells, he hid me in the woods. Yesterday he started working on the pipe line. No, it wasn't yesterday! A long time."

Suddenly his face contorted fiercely and he shouted: "He's in that ditch! I started to tell them, but I had a spell. When I woke up I was afraid and ran away. But I know things sometimes. I went in the night to dig him up, but I happened to think he was dead and it wasn't no use. The dogs from the farmhouse came chasing me, and I ran away again."

"He's goin' off in a fit," muttered Ed, grasping the half-wit's arm. "Steady, buddy! We aim t' help you. Take hold of yourself."

The half-wit relapsed into a throaty sobbing, and stood docilely.

"First thing off the bat," pursued Ed, "is t' do something for that tooth, and shave you. You need grub." He stood pondering. "You wouldn't like t' go t' town t' a dentist?" he ventured cautiously.

The half-wit backed rapidly toward the cave. "No!" he screamed. "If they see me in town, they'll take me back! Let me alone!"

"Okay! Okay!" Ed soothed. "We'll fight 'em till we're sweaty as a bull before we'll let 'em take you back."

The half-wit sat down on a flat stone and began probing inside his mouth, fingering the sore tooth.

"It hurts awful," he whimpered, the tears coursing down his cheeks and trickling among his whiskers.

Ed went to the farmhouse, returning presently with some food, a pair of pliers, shaving soap, and a safety razor. Ed laid his patient down and placed a knee on his chest. "Open your mouth, buddy," he commanded. "This will hurt like billy hell, but try t' keep still."

"I know it," said the half-wit firmly. "Paul pulled a tooth for me before. And you must keep your tongue out of the way or the pliers may slip and pinch a big blue blister on it."

The half-wit winced as the tooth tore out, but he arose quietly and spat blood in the creek. Then Ed lathered him and shaved him. He held his head obediently the way Ed put it.

By this time the Autumn rains had set in. Every day sodden earth and leaden sky seemed to merge in a sheet of water. "Cloudy all over and pourin' down in the middle," Ed said dejectedly one morning as he pulled aside the blind and prepared to draw on his still damp overalls. "They's sand in my joints. I feel it grit in my kneecaps and in my elbow joints. This goin' wet all the time is enough t' kill a mule."

The relentless rain chapped our faces, filled our shoes,

273

and wadded our sox in hard ridges. When we wore oilskins, we were steamed with sweat. Some of the men had rubber boots, but they puckered the feet till they resembled a washerwoman's thumb after a hard day's scrubbing. If we stood a moment in one spot, we kept slowly sinking in the muck. When we drew our feet out, the mud yielded reluctantly, making a sound like the fadeout kiss in a talkie. The ditcher gummed up, and vibrated the spongy ground so that the ditch was always caving. Trucks mired down, their back wheels impotently spinning and throwing slush. One day the triumphant farmers saw the useless ditcher pulled to the gravelled highway, and they came swarming, their judgment vindicated.

Miles away across the valley we could see a low range of hills. The superintendent would ride up on his cayuse and try to encourage the faint-hearted. He pointed his quirt toward the misty ridges.

"Yon's the High Ground, bullies," he would say cheerily. "Up there in the High Ground they's a sandy soil that don't stick like this gumbo. Looks a little lighter there in the West, don't you think? These clouds are gonna break away. It won't rain no forty days and forty nights like it done in Scripture days. Lord promises you that every time you see a rainbow."

Then he would spur briskly on to another gang, but his cheerfulness didn't dry our clothes or lessen the weight of our soggy brogans.

Ed and I were carrying food to the half-wit regularly. One rainy night I awakened to hear something scraping over the window sill. A lightning flash revealed the intruder as our protegé. I arose hastily and lit the kerosene lamp. He stood shamefacedly, rivulets trickling from his dank hair, his clay-plastered feet hesitating in a pool of yellow water.

274

"Tonight I got to thinking of Paul in the ditch," he began. "Paul was always more particular than me. He wouldn't like that sand in his hair or the mud on his face. He made me wash every night. I felt like a spell coming on, so I come here. I didn't know any place else to go."

"Let him sleep here," Ed yawned. "Give him a pair of my pants and a shirt, but we'll have t' get him out early so nobody'll see him."

With dry clothes on, the half-wit curled up in a blanket on the floor. Soon his cloudy eyes closed and he snored peacefully.

"What we gonna do with him finally?" Ed wondered miserably. "He smells like a wet dog, and he might wake up in the night in a fit and murder both of us."

Still pondering, we fell asleep. When we awoke in the morning, our guest was gone, leaving the borrowed shirt and pants and taking his own clothes. He had painstakingly scraped all the mud off the floor.

The ditch now caved in so frequently that the men who bolted the joints worked feverishly, their eyes riveted on the sides. Ed and I were working away when a loose rock plinked on the pipe.

"Better jump!" I cried. "That's a sign it's coming in."

"I got my eye on it," said Ed, manipulating the wrench rapidly. "Soon's I tighten this nut, it can cave and be damned."

But I clambered out. Suddenly the sides buckled, leaving Ed buried to his neck. He feigned unconcern. Fortunately, the dirt was loose and sandy.

"No harm done," he wheezed, "but dig me out, kid. It ain't right by the company I should be standin' here idle."

A dozen men had gathered, but the boss waved them back.

"Two!" he decreed positively. "Two can do more good

than twenty. Just be in one another's way. Is it squeezin' you, lad?"

"Naw!" Ed scoffed valiantly. "Gimme a cigarette while I'm restin'."

Two of us set to digging furiously. Ed's eyes bulged and I thought that the blood would burst out of his face. Then his tongue protruded and pushed the unlit cigarette off his lip. But when we uncovered his chest, he breathed more freely.

"Keep that shovel outa my ribs!" he cried gaily.

But when he was completely uncovered he could not walk. We carried him to the farmhouse. The next morning he could hobble around, but he was unable to work for two days.

The farmers didn't seem to mind the mud. They spat on their calloused hands and dug like gophers. At noon they ate a pone of cornbread and a fruit jar full of blue skimmed milk. They sold the cream. We older hands were playing out, and we resented their energy. Only the prospect of the High Ground and better digging roweled our jaded spirits.

"I just wanted to show you this," said the half-wit next Sunday. He had led us to the graveyard. The ditch had been levelled to leave a symmetrical mound, and at the head of it there stood a flat sandrock carried from the creek. "Paul Stafford" was scratched on it.

"You got the S backwards," Ed said critically, but he was more agitated than he appeared. A suspicion that the half-wit's brother was really buried in the ditch had been growing on him.

"This must be Willy Stafford, the idiot. Don't you remember? Don't say anything to him about it or you'll scare him," muttered Ed to me.

276

"I never saw anybody in that ditch that looked like Paul Stafford," I whispered.

"There was lots of men. Besides, he's had plenty of time t' change," returned Ed in a low voice.

"I carried sod from the creek because the clay looked so bare," the half-wit went on. "Now all I want to know is that you believe he's here. I know things sometimes. I saw him buried. But he's in a graveyard, anyway, and I wouldn't have known how to get him a nice funeral, anyway."

"Sure, buddy, we believe he's here," reassured Ed with a sickly smile.

"That's all I want to know," cried the half-wit joyfully. "I been wanting to give you something, but I didn't have anything. But I looked for these, and they were hard to find because so many are wormy. You can tell the wormy ones because there's a little black hole in them."

He paused and fumbled in his coat, withdrawing a greasy paper bag in which we had once carried food to him.

"Maybe you'll like these," he said hesitatingly, as though afraid of being rebuffed. The sack was full of hickory nuts.

"Sure, buddy, I like 'em swell. Much obliged," said Ed, picking up a rock and cracking one of the nuts on a tombstone. A fat white worm with a yellow head squirmed out of the kernel. Ed swept it quickly into his hand and held it so the half-wit could not see. He had turned away, and was walking quickly.

"Goodbye, then," he called back, breaking into a run. "Water broke in the mine and put the fire out. It's cold in there now. But I know how to keep hid. I know things sometimes, and my head's quit buzzing."

"Hey!" shouted Ed. "Wait a minute! Hey, Willy!"

But the half-wit was gathering speed. He vanished in the brush, and Ed came back to resume his nut cracking.

"Maybe his brother *is* buried here. If he is, he must be the Paul Stafford we knew," he said after a while.

"The timekeeper said nobody was missing," I reminded him.

"Supposin' he just started that morning. A new man don't have a badge till the timekeeper makes his first round, and he hadn't checked up yet that morning. He goes by the badges."

"What can we do?" I asked, troubled.

"Why should we try to do anything?" said Ed, cracking another hickory nut and finding a worm in it, too.

"I wonder which is the more comfortable death"; I said, "being smothered in a ditch or squashed in a coal mine."

"Hey!" said Ed indignantly the next morning. "You know what? That High Ground business is just a fake. Old Pus Gut's been horsin' us to a standstill with that boloney. A floater just pulled in and he come by the way of the High Ground. They's another crew over there with a ditcher, and they're about to the top of the hill a'ready. I'll be cow-kicked if I waller in this mess another hour!"

I was cleaning the gluey clay off my shovel with a putty knife, and I threw both down. All of the old hands palpitated with righteous wrath; they gathered in gesticulating knots. When the optimistic superintendent rode up to upbraid us for loafing, we confronted him with the evidence of his perfidy. At a loss for an answer, he cantered away. We pelted him with mud balls and hurled sulphurous curses after him. He flung back a Parthian shot: "If you don't like the job, there's plenty of other men anxious to work."

And so it turned out. The farmers stuck sullenly to their posts. Along the muddy banks of the ditch the shovels

278

rose and fell. The farmers worked grimly to show that they could succeed where the ditching machine had failed.

"You city guys c'n quit if you want to," said one of them. "You think this job is a tough titty, but we got worse the year round and we never see a cent of money. Come a good crop year, you get nothin' for what you raise; come a year like this, when everything's burned to a cinder, and still you got nothin'. Fight the cussed chinch bugs! Fight the corn borers! On this job you can anyway rest at night and know what you made is yours."

The farmers humped resolutely to their shovelling. The phantasmagoria of the High Ground had never excited them; they never expected anything and were never disappointed. We old hands were standing aside—spectators now. The job moved on without us and left us cleaning the mud off our shoes. Our feet were pounds lighter as we sloshed across the fields, but we were still sore about that High Ground hooey the super had fed us.

VI

"Winter comin' again, Larry," said Ed ruefully, gazing out of the box car door. We were on our way home. The raw air whipped in, and the weather did not match our clothes. We had saved all we could during the Summer and Fall, but we were going home without much money.

We were the only ones who left the freight when it slowed down for the grade near Monkey Nest Camp, the population of which had dwindled to the occupants of Liam Ryan's barroom. The other bums huddled in a corner, scratching the loose straw about them like a hen making her nest.

That Winter was harder than the one before. The slow worm of monotonous poverty gnawed at us daily and by night, for Ed and I often lay awake till almost morning

279

talking about what should be done. There was nothing to do, nowhere to go but to Ben's, and that was always a melancholy experience. Ben and his wife were always submerged in apathetic despair. I was terrified now by Bonny Fern's attitude toward me. She seemed possessive, accepted the food I occasionally brought with a thankful but complacent air which indicated that she considered it a matter of course and right. I avoided her sometimes, and she begged me humbly and tearfully to tell her what was wrong. I could not forget Rollie Weems and his advice about marrying, and it was apparent to me that I was in an infinitely worse position than Rollie ever was. Aunt Jessie and the children daily reminded me of him.

Ed had become expert at snaring cottontail rabbits, and when the snow was deep he could kill them with a club as they floundered impotently in trying to escape. We usually ate the rabbits stewed, for that saved lard. Before Spring the rabbits grew scarce. Though the cottontail is one of the most prolific of beasts and the dry Summer had been kind to them—few of the young ones drowning in the burrows as was usually the case—there were too many hungry people ranging the woods for meat. Ben's wife and Bonny Fern had canned a hundred quarts of wild greens.

"It's danged funny how many things a man c'n eat if he has to," Ben said. "You watch what a cow or horse eats, and if they c'n eat it, so c'n a person. I bet I learned more about wild green and such last year than anybody else. It's hard on the women and children, though, 'cause they get the bloody flux jist twicet as easy as a man."

"Do you remember how horrible Father thought it would be if I went into the coal mine, Mother?" I asked one day. "In the old days when we tightened our belts during a strike, there was a prospect ahead of going back to work. Now there's nothing . . . nothing! The Monkey

Nest is gone; they scoop up coal with a steam shovel in the strip mine. The steam shovel does the work of 500 miners. The factories even during the good times in '28 and '29 were all the time doing away with men by putting in labor-saving machinery."

"I wish your father was here. I wish you were more like him," Mother answered sadly. "He always knew what to do to straighten things out. But he always knew how to keep the miners back of him; that's what counted. They lost out after he died, you remember."

I had to smile at that. Mother was getting childish. Yet I could remember how my father, the magnetic Irishman with curly chestnut hair and mustache, could play upon the emotions of a crowd as a skillful harpist plucks the strings of his instrument. He could plead subtly as a violin or stir his hearers like a militant trumpet blast.

"Father always wanted me to be a lawyer or a doctor, you know," I said, "and now I've turned out to be nothing."

"I want you to be a fighter like him. We've got to have more fighters."

"Rollie was a fighter, too, but he lost. He didn't do any good."

"You've got to know who to fight, how to fight and when to fight."

"I think I know. It's starting in the cities; it started before we left. But the farmers are different. They came in and took our jobs at the railroad shops when we struck. They were glad to stay on the pipe line ditch after we quit."

"Some farmers are that way, but not all of them," argued Mother, stubbornly. "They're more ignorant than anything else. They just need somebody like your father to talk to them and explain things."

The snow drifted high around Liam Ryan's barroom

that Winter. We had patched the cracks as best we could, but the planks were full of knot holes and porous from lack of paint. Ed and I agreed that this was a harder Winter on us than the one before.

Factories did not open in the Spring, but the tides of the disinherited began to flow again. Hoboes captured freight trains and rode boldly through populous cities, defying both railroad bulls and city police. Flivver tramps clattered along the highways, breaking down, begging gas and spare parts. Usually the police would not allow them to light; often they were given gas and food in order to get them to move on. Like vagrant tumbleweeds they drifted along the highways from state to state. They had no place to stop.

The highway that was to be built near Monkey Nest Camp drew job seekers from hundreds of miles around, even before the surveyors had finished driving the stakes. In hundreds of free tourist camps the word was spread that a new highway was going through, and boomers gravitated to the site to squat till the work began. Dozens of floaters piled off freight trains and camped stolidly near the spot. The nights were lighted with their jungle fires; you could hear them muttering low and earnestly as they ate their mulligan stew or drank java brewed in smoke-blackened tomato cans. It was apparent that most of them were not professional bums, but men who had held jobs as machinists, carpenters, bricklayers, painters, railroaders, and "white collar" workers.

When grading began, so many were assembled that it was almost impossible to get near the boss. After the *furore* of selection, the disappointed applicants dispersed. Spring had extended into early Summer before Ed and I were finally hired. The concrete base had been poured and was ready for the paving blocks.

We were a varied lot. Most of us were prodigals back from the industrial plants of the East, and those who had never left for the lotus lands resented the invasion of the homing wanderers. "They'll hire an out of town man every time," they grumbled.

The paving gang swept along as slow as Time—as a mountain glacier grinding its way toward the sea. The concrete base ahead of us was dotted with piles of sand, the cushion for the bricks. Gangs of workers attacked the sand with shovels, and it swished as they spread it fanwise. Two men pulled a template that extended from curb to curb, smoothing the bed to a uniform thickness.

Then came the bricksetters, back and forth, swiftly laying the paving blocks in rows across the road. Three Negroes and two white men, bending from the waist, reaching for the bricks carried from the parking on each side. A streak of yellowed grass showed where the bricks had pressed. Plucky weeds rose up slowly, their spines uncrushed by the bowing down, but they were blanched like a man trying to walk erect after a prison sentence. I felt like the weeds when I straightened my aching back with a quick jerk at the ends of my rows. It was monotonous and gruelling work—three rows, an alternate half brick to break the joints. Click! Click! We butted the bricks together. The tongs clanged as they dropped their burdens, often enough on our heels. Mostly we were lost in bitter silence, but sometimes the Negroes sang softly. Bricksetting is no work for a man with a bay window, and some of the stouter ones puffed and reddened as they stooped.

"Poor back!" said a familiar voice, as somebody stroked my bent spine. "I 'lowed I'd find you here. I knowed this was your home town and when I heerd of this job way up in Wisconsin I headed this way."

"Why, hello, Nat!" I said, looking over my shoulder. "Where's your wife and the kids?"

"Out here in the bresh. I'm gonna make a bresh arbor and camp out there this Summer. I'm on the go now, Larry. Got a flivver I travel around in. You heerd about me losin' the little home in Rosewood Manor?" He sighed deeply.

"Yes, Jasper wrote us about that. Where's Jasper?"

"Well, sir, the last I heerd of Jasper he was headed for the West Coast. Thought maybe he'd git a job pickin' cucumbers or apples in Oregon."

"Hey, fella!" hollered the boss. "You ain't startin' out like you'd set the world afire. More brick! Bring 'em the brick or they can't set 'em! Keep 'em piled around their ears!"

Heat waves blurred the sand piles ahead; behind us a smoking tar kettle warmed the stifling air. Ed carried coal scuttles full of smoking hot asphalt and poured it in the cracks between the rows of bricks. His shoe soles had collected a six inch layer of tar. But his worst job was cutting the stuff in chunks, preparing it for the heater. In Winter asphalt splits like stovewood—it "crriiicckks!" ahead of the ax as a ripe watermelon does before a sharp knife. Now it was like molasses, and cutting it was as exasperating as trying to hew a hole in water and expecting it to stay.

Ed pulled on the ax handle and swore weakly. He was saturated with sweat; in the morning his clothing would be stiff with white salt rings. He started to walk across a pile that had melted and spread out and his feet gummed like those of a fly on Tanglefoot. Some of the bystanders roared when Ed sat down involuntarily and the seat of his pants stuck, too. But it's not so funny when you're hot enough to have a queer ringing in your ears and the core of your head is like fire.

284

"Steamboat" Mose was our pace setter. The boss paid him five cents an hour extra to speed us up. He was a huge, raw-boned Negro of sixty. "More brick!" he'd holler lustily, "Ain't had a brick today!" If the boss happened to stray away, however, he'd soon dry up. He wasn't as anxious as he sounded. He sucked grimly at an empty hickory pipe and emitted a short grunt as he set each brick. Working behind him, I noticed that his shoe soles were worn through and his brown toes were whetted pink on the bottoms by sand and gravel. He wore a heavy Winter undershirt. "The sweat soaks it and it keeps you cooler than a light one," he explained. That's what he said, but I suspected he wore the heavy one because he had no other.

The houses were set closer together as we entered the outskirts of the town. The blocks unreeled slowly. Yards disappeared and trim umbrella catalpas and syringa bushes were seen no more. As we invaded the district of shops, merchants and idle clerks came forth from their cubicles to watch us. The storekeepers folded arms over bulging paunches beneath white aprons and leaned against door jambs or hung from awning ropes.

We envied the cool looking storekeepers. It would have seemed a luxury to be able to stand erect even in the blazing sun. To sit in the shade for a minute would have been a glorious boon. At the ends of our rows we straightened as quickly as we could to ease the sharp pain in our spines. But sometimes we crossed and began the next rows before we could unkink ourselves. Women in crisp frocks trundled infants in perambulators. They eyed us curiously and somewhat apprehensively as though they were afraid we'd rape them. Roving dogs came along and sniffed at us interrogatively, wondering what the crazy men were up to—going around and around like a blind mule on a treadmill. They curled derisive tails and trotted jauntily away in search of amusement or food. Their noses twitched as they sampled the floating aromas.

"How *do* they stand it?" inquired one business man of another across the street. "I'm all a-lather jist settin' under the 'lectric fan."

"Aw, they're *used* to it! It don't hurt *them* like it would you or me. That kind of work is good for a man if you're *used* to it."

("I'd like to see *you* stooping over, red in the face, puffing like a steamboat, your belly folding into huge, hairy ridges, bursting the seams in the seat of your pants!" I thought savagely.)

I no longer felt shame at being seen at such work as I would have once, and I knew that the only way for me to rise to something approximating the grandiose ambitions of my youth would be to rise with my class, with the disinherited: the bricksetters, the flivver tramps, boomers, and outcasts pounding their ears in flophouses. Every gibe at any of the paving gang, every covert or open sneer by prosperous looking bystanders infuriated me but did not abash me. The fat on my bones melted away under the glare of the burnished sun, and the fat in my mind dissolved, too. It dripped in sweat off the end of my nose onto the bricks, dampened the sand. I felt weak as from the loss of blood, but also resigned. I felt like a man whose feet have been splashing about in ooze and at last have come to rest on a solid rock, even though it lay far below his former level.

So when Hans appeared suddenly before me I had to pause and wipe the salt from my stinging eyes to make sure that he was not an apparition. He had changed. His hair, which had always stood stubbornly erect, was iron grey, his face lean and scarred. His right cheek was concave, as though the teeth might be gone. He threw up his mutilated hand in greeting.

286

"Is that you, Hans?" I said wonderingly. "Everybody in the United States must have heard of this job. But I'm afraid you're too late to get on. I'll ask for you if you want me to."

"I'm not looking for a job; I just wanted to stop to talk to you. They found an excuse to kick me out at the rubber heel plant. It's never difficult when they really want to. I've got a job now; the best I ever had."

"What are you doing?"

"Organizing. First in the cities; now among the farmers. I've found again what I lost when Liebknecht died and I thought the world was ended."

"I hear that things are stirring in the cities."

"Yes!" His swarthy face beamed. "Listen, Larry! In St. Louis fifteen thousand marched to the City Hall, demanding relief. The police began throwing tear gas bombs. The workers stood their ground a long time. A gigantic Negro caught the gas bombs, threw them back among the police and several of them keeled over. The Negro's arms were burned to the shoulder, but he kept catching the bombs and hurling them back. It was glorious. They won their demands, the authorities rescinded the cut in relief which had been ordered."

"Excuse me, brother!" broke in the foreman. "This is a job of work, not a place t' make speeches. If Donovan wants t' hold his job, you fellers had better break up the meetin'."

A hot answer hammered at my teeth, but I held it back. Nothing could be gained by quitting, I thought, so I bent over and resumed my work. I gave Hans directions for reaching the camp, and he promised to come out that night. I told Nat to come, too, and to bring Emma and the kids.

Nat appeared first, but Emma was not with him. "She

wouldn't come," Nat explained, "because she ain't got no Sunday-go-t'-meetin' togs, and the kids is half-nekkid. I told 'er they wasn't no use puttin' on dog, but she said she'd ruther stay there even if she is a little skeered out in the bresh. Dog my cats, if she ain't gittin' so she's as bad 'bout chewin' the rag as poor Lena was—God rest her poor soul! I look fer Emma t' git the female complaint yit."

He was still grumbling fitfully when Hans appeared. Ed and I were so tired we lay on the long bar and propped our heads up with our hands. Mother sat near by on a box and listened to Hans as he told us all that he had experienced and seen within the last three years, since he'd been let out at the rubber heel plant.

"Some of the workin' men may be wakin' up, but not many," Ed conceded as Hans told of the work among the unemployed. "Give 'em a coupla meals so's their bellies won't be flappin' agin their backbones and they'll be hunkadory and to hell with the hindmost."

"When I was a boy in Germany," Hans said, "there was a nobleman's estate close to our cottage. He had a splendid orchard, and we boys were always hungering for the fruit we never had at home. We used to steal over the high stone wall when the gardeners were busy elsewhere to eat our fill of the fruit and even fill our blouses to take home with us. We liked the pears best. They were huge and sweet as sugar. Sometimes we'd start to grasp one in a hurry and it would crumble between our fingers. Wasps had entered it through a tiny hole near the stem, a hole not evident to a casual eye, and eaten all away but the rind and seeds. Things that seem as solid as a rock may be fragile enough to collapse at a pinch. But you've got to pinch first."

"The city workers may do it, but not the farmers," contended Ed. He told Hans about the farmers who had

288

taken our places on the pipe line, about Ben who was about to be ousted from his farm. How he sat about dejectedly, waiting for the blow to fall.

"When a man's asleep," said Hans, "you can't awaken him by deploring the fact that he *is* asleep or silently wishing he were awake. You must shake his shoulder, shout in his ear. If he doesn't awaken at once, you must keep on shouting till others join in and make such a hullabaloo that everybody's bound to listen whether he wants to or not."

> " 'Rise like lions after slumber,
> In unconquerable number. . . .
> Ye are many, they are few. . . .' "

I quoted somewhat uncertainly. I had never outgrown my passion for poetry. During the War and immediately after I had thrust life away from me—lived in books, and I had read more verse than anything else.

"You talk like Larry's father used to," Mother said to Hans, sadly. "He was the best talker there ever was in this country. He could persuade the miners to do anything he wanted them to."

"Larry could be a good one if he tried," Hans said.

"I?" I cried in surprise.

"Sure. Most of the Irish are good talkers. You used to moon about the rubber plant and reel off poetry by the yard. Here's living poetry for you—an epic as vast as the earth. Feet in broken and worn-out shoes beating the streets of cities like a drum; clenched fists storming toward the sky! I can take you and show you poetry with a rhythm that shakes the earth!"

Aunt Jessie came in, and the two younger children were yawning. The oldest girl was ashamed of her torn dress and passed quickly to the rear of the room to hide behind the stove.

289

"I'm keeping you up too late," Hans said, rising. "I'll go now, but you'll see me again. Think of what I've said, Larry. When does the sheriff auction off Ben's farm and goods?"

"The date's been set a dozen times and they gave him a little longer. He says he's had to talk to them like a Dutch uncle, but it's no use this time. They've told him positively that they must have the money by November 5th or the sale will come off and no fooling."

"I'll see you again before then," Hans said. "I'm going down the valley for a while." Nat followed him pensively from the room.

The pace of "Steamboat" Mose never slackened. I was finding it more and more difficult to keep up with him.

"For Christ's sake, slow down," I whispered over his shoulder. I didn't want the boss to hear. "Are we running a race with one another? Job'll be finished soon enough as it is."

Mose was getting along in years, but bricksetting was his job and it pleased him to know he could still make the young bucks beg for mercy. He remembered when bricks were laid on the sand without any concrete underneath. Then nothing heavier than beer wagons drawn by massive-hooved Percherons taxed the paving. Victorias hitched to high-stepping thoroughbreds were the vehicles of the aristocracy.

Proud of his craft, Mose chuckled, and the bricks clicked faster. I fancied I could hear the segments of my backbone creaking; my wrists had swollen and my fingers puffed till my knuckles were dimples. But I had to keep on. I grew conscious of the foreman's accusing eyes. I was fumbling the bricks, finding it hard to lay them straight and true. The bricks had to be dropped perfectly flat; if they fell edgewise they had to be raised up and the sand cushion smoothed out again.

"You handle them brick like a cub bear does a roastin' ear," the foreman observed caustically. "Mose is way ahead of you when you ain't holdin' him back. So shake that thing, and show me what you can do!"

I got to thinking of a cool, dim warehouse where I'd worked, and of a lumber yard fragrant with pine where a man could hide under a pile of lumber and blow for a spell. The sun puts funny ideas in a man's head. Sometimes the voices roared like a mighty magnavox, then they dwindled to a whisper. My ears felt as if they were stuffed with cotton. I thought how, if the carrier dropped a load of bricks on your outstretched hand, groping while you were keeping your eye on the row, your fingers would blossom on the ends like unfolding roses and the nails turn from white to red to blue-black. The back of my head ticked like a clock. Cold shivers ran over me and goose pimples sprang out. Iridescent spots rose before my eyes, floated languidly away, and burst like pricked bubbles against buildings and the bystanders, who seemed to be grinning like prize fight fans panting for the knockout punch.

I was thirsty enough to spit cotton, but my stomach was sick from drinking too much of the tepid, brackish water. When I bent over, I could hear a sloshing inside me. The boss said a man couldn't drink ice water and work in the hot sun, and, besides, ice cost money.

Even a prize fighter has to have a respite now and then. My buckskin mitts were worn out at the thumb and the crystal sand clinging to the bricks ate into the flesh. I began to tape my thumb and to pull myself together.

"Water!" I hollered in a croaking voice. The cry was caught up and hurled down the line.

"Water jack!
Oughta been here
And half way back!"

The water boy came hurrying with a pail of lukewarm
water. Two rusty tin cups were wired to the side. I seized
one eagerly; even the scalding liquid would assuage thirst
a little. The water seemed to boil in my throat as it
descended.

"Hey!" shouted the horrified water boy. "*That's* the
nigger's cup. You got the wrong cup!"

"What of it?" I asked, more fluently now that a furrow
had been cut through the sand and dust in my neck.

"Damned if *I'd* drink after one of the black baboons,"
muttered a proud Nordic clad in a ragged sweater and
patched overalls. I noticed that several flakes of smoking
tobacco, pinch hitting for "chawin'," adhered to his pendulous lower lip and fluttered into the pail, gyrating to
the bottom and staining the water with amber. And often
I heard some of the men before drinking inquiring cautiously which was "the nigger's cup." But I could no
longer withdraw into my fantastic inner world and despise
these men. I did not aspire to be a doctor or a lawyer any
more. I was only as high or as low as the other workers in
the paving gang.

Mose began slowing down one afternoon. His motion
became as deliberate as one of the "slow camera" movies.
The boss noticed it and hurled some witticism at him, but
it was no use. At the end of the row, Mose staggered
blindly but doggedly to the other side to begin anew. But
at last he stumbled and struck his head against the curb-
ing; he raised on all fours, tried to rise to his feet. His
knees buckled under him and he fell like a tree at the last
stroke of the ax. The men gathered about him, more in
curiosity than in sympathy. He lay there, a tired and for-

lorn figure, a tiny blue vein pulsing rhythmically on his temple.

"A blue gum nigger!" exclaimed one of the workers. "By Jesus, boys, if that bastard was t' bite you, it'd be the same as if a rattlesnake had. Poison as hell!" He probed beneath Mose's gaping lips with an inquisitive forefinger, but—evidently fearing the imaginary virus—drew quickly back.

Well, it was only an old nigger played out. That was the way it appeared to the boss and many of the others. But here also was the death of a life and the setting of a sun.

"He won't be no good on this job no more," grumbled the foreman. "Never no good any more once they get over-het." He gave another Negro, a young one, Mose's mitts, and the crew moved slowly forward.

"Wait a minute!" I called. "What are you going to do with Mose? Are you going to get a doctor for him?"

"Hell, no!" snorted the foreman in incredulous disgust. "He'll come to." He drew closer and muttered in my ear: "A doctor for a nigger that got a little touch of the sun? You must be dippy, sure enough!"

"I don't lay another brick till you get a doctor for him," I said loudly. Ed heard me and came up.

"Get a doctor!" he demanded. Others began to shout or murmur, according to the degree of their boldness: "Get a doctor!"

"All that fuss over a nigger!" grumbled the foreman. "Donovan, I swear t' God, if you couldn't lay them brick down so fast, I'd tie a can t' your tail so fast it'd make your head swim."

Nevertheless, he fetched a doctor.

The Summer advanced. Ed and I had roofed the barroom and chinked the cracks. Crops had been better, and

Ben had more food than he had the year before, but no more money. It was impossible to sell anything. Bonny Fern complained that I never came to see her. I was always tired at night, and I didn't want her to take things too seriously. I heard that she was hinting about that she and I might marry soon. To me Bun Grady and Rollie Weems had become symbols of the unmarried and married worker respectively, and it struck me that it would be better to remain single even if I ended as a bald and destitute boomer, harried from day to day by the spectre of unemployment and the prospect of dying among strangers. And I looked forward to Hans' return eagerly. A man who did the work Hans had undertaken needed to be free.

When scarlet and yellow leaves began drifting down into the sand, we could see the end of the job a mile or so ahead. We had passed through the town and into the open country beyond. Ed's asphalt split readily now, but he had trouble keeping the tar from cooling too quickly and solidifying in the buckets. Our fingers were frost-nipped at the ends, and we had to bundle up so that the free swinging of our bodies burst the seams in our garments. Ours was a cruel and undesirable lot, but the expectation of being jobless once more was more terrifying still.

Snow spat insolently in our faces the day of the final payoff. Great blobs of it clung to everything. The road was opened for traffic, and we couldn't move spry enough with our stiffened muscles. The drivers honked at us indignantly.

Nat and I were walking together down the road. As we reached the first houses of the town a car nosed into him gently and pushed him off the slab. The car was traveling slowly and Nat was more angry than hurt.

"Yeah!" shouted Nat, shaking his fist at the indifferent driver, who stepped on the accelerator and sped away.

294

"We're no good on this street now. The tough part is done and only the good part left. I've sucked the hind tit all my life, by God, makin' it light on somebody else. There's Emma and the three kids out in that bresh arbor in the grove with their butts hangin' out. What the hell 'm I gonna do with 'em and Winter comin' on?"

I couldn't tell him. I walked silently beside him, the damp snow beginning to crunch a little underfoot. A squirrel barked defiantly from the fork of one of the giant elms that arched the roadway. Nat stooped and picked up a small stone to cast at the saucy animal. It popped back in its hole, but thrust out its head to chatter afresh.

"That critter," mused the involuntary rover wistfully, "he has got a warm hole in that air tree, and likely a raft of nuts stashed away fer the Winter, but look at me. . . ."

"The foxes have dens, the birds of the air have nests, . . ." I began oratorically.

Nat had read the Scriptures, too. "And this son of a bitch hath nowhere to lay his goddamned haid!" he supplemented ruefully.

I parted with him at a street corner, but before I had gone far I heard somebody running behind me, and turned to see Nat hurrying up.

"I clean fergot t' ask you t' he'p me," he panted. "My car's h'isted on boxes and my old jack ain't no more good. Me and my old woman and all the kids at once has tried t' pry it up till we could git the boxes out, but we're too light in the poop."

The brush arbor had shed its leaves long ago, but it had been patched into a makeshift shelter with wooden boxes and tin asphalt containers carried home from the paving job.

"Off to the races again, mama," Nat said to Emma. "I think I'll hit it fer Arkansas and hole up there fer the

Winter. Then I'll be in time fer the early cantaloupe harvest."

"After livin' in a place like this all Summer and bein' et up by chiggers and mosquitoes, a body don't mind movin'," Emma said, almost brightly. "I'm always thinkin' maybe Nat'll git a steady job som'eres so's we c'n live in a house again. We ain't lived in but one house sence we lost our little home in Rosewood Manor, and then only for two months."

"A man gits tired of buyin' furniture and then givin' it away when a piddlin' job plays out," Nat explained. "It's worse on account of the biggest girl. She ain't never been t' school, don't know 'er a-b-c's yit. Plenty of people, though, couldn't read their own names if it was writ in letters high as a box car, and they seem t' git along good 's anybody elset. I do think that too much schoolin' makes a fool outen a poor man's kids. Makes 'em expect things they can't never have. They's always plenty of rich man's kids fer the soft snaps."

"Learnin's a great comfort even if a body don't make money offen it," Emma observed wistfully. "Anybody that can't neither read nor cipher don't have much chancet in this world. I do hope by the time the boys is old enough we'll be able to send 'em. If I could git story books to read in a place like this where there ain't no company the time would pass faster."

"Better be studyin' 'bout fillin' yer belly 'stid of wastin' yer time with story books," broke in Nat sourly, returning with a stout white oak pole.

The car was a touring model of the vintage of several years back, and it supplied mute evidence of its many trips in search of the elusive job which, even when captured, soon petered out.

Using a wooden block and the pole, we raised the car off the boxes and let it down on the earth. Nat regretted

296

that he had not pumped up the tires while the weight was off them. The children hopped about as chipper as sparrows, though their lips were blue with the cold and their teeth chattering. Wherever they might be going or whatever might befall them, they were not likely to look back to the brush arbor home with nostalgic pangs.

"We'll start fust thing in the morning," Nat said. "Gettin' too late t' start out now. Good luck t' you, Larry if I don't see you again, and much obliged till you're better paid."

As he mentioned my name, Emma started slightly and gave me a rather unfriendly look. I thought she must be remembering the bacchanal in Rosewood Manor from which she had chased us with a broom.

VII

Ed and I walked to town the next morning. We met Hans darting down Main Street as though he might be in search of somebody.

"Hello," I said. "Where have you been gone so long, and what's your hurry?"

"I've been busy," he returned. "I've been looking for you, too. Do you know what day this is?"

"Sure. It's the sixth of November."

"And today Ben Haskin is going to be sold out at auction."

"Yes, I suppose he's reconciled to the idea by now."

"Will you be there?"

"I suppose so. Though I don't like to be around at such times."

"You'd better be. You'll see and hear something that'll interest you. I've been back here over a week, but I've been too busy to see you before."

"We'll see you there, then," I said as Hans hurried away.

The streets were crowded with idle men. They dawdled on the corners or haunted pool rooms, pocketing hands that were softening from disuse. In many of the shop fronts "To Rent" signs appeared—the ubiquitous spiders were at work filming the edges of the windows and the spaces between the shelves. Ed and I paused to watch a mouse entrapped in one of the vacant windows. It dashed about headlong, butting against the plate glass and scratching impotently. Its beady eyes glittered madly and its whiskers twitched. A cat came stalking from the depths of the store, and, deliberately raising a front paw, sent the mouse spinning with a sharp blow. A large crowd gathered. It was a better show than the goofy looking fellow in another window down the street who was demonstrating with pantomime and placards the merits of EZ Way Shaving Cream.

Nat came coaxing his spitting flivver down Main Street. At the traffic lights he worked the gas feed up and down frantically, the engine responding with a mounting roar. Vile-smelling smoke poured from the exhaust. The chauffeur of a swanky town car behind sounded a haughty protest on his suave musical horn. Milady within buried her nose in a filmy handkerchief and looked distinctly annoyed.

Everybody was distracted by the racket as Nat advanced spasmodically from one light to another. Sometimes the engine died before the light flashed green again, and then Nat would hop out and spin the motor hurriedly, shouting agitated directions to Emma as to the proper manipulation of the spark and gas levers.

At the traffic light near which we were standing the car refused to budge, and no amount of cranking would wake it to life. Nat became more and more rattled. He dashed to and fro, adjusting the spark and cranking with desperate fury. He was drenched with sweat, though Winter was already in the air. Emma was trying to comfort the baby, who had set up a disconsolate wailing. The tools were under the back seat and Emma and the children had to stand up and dislodge bundles to get at them. Nat grabbed a wrench and raised the hood, at a loss.

Meanwhile, other motorists were honking irritably. The strident klaxons of huge trucks mingled with the minor tootling of musical horns. The inexorable lights flashed their alternate signals to stop and go. Some of the exasperated motorists jerked at their wheels and passed around the stalled car, hurling back witticisms and invectives. Others joined the crescendo of blatting protest, which soon extended a mile and brought merchants and clerks forth from their cubicles to see the fun. A policeman strode up and stood with arms akimbo, watching Nat's unavailing efforts in silence for a moment or two.

"Whenever you get that coffee grinder wound up, buddy," he suggested with exaggerated mildness, "get it offen the street. They's others wants t' use the street, y' know. This ain't no free parkin' lot. So move on."

He glanced sidewise at the bystanders on the sidewalk, relishing the appreciative guffaws of some of them. Others regarded Nat sympathetically and glowered at the cop. Nat had been rocking the car back and forth, thinking that something which had become stuck might be shaken loose. He turned his agonized steaming face to his inquisitor and shouted bitterly:

"O you go t' hell! Ain't I doin' all I can?"

"You get that can offen the street and do it quick— quick as hell could scorch a feather! Savvy!" snarled the cop, enraged at the affront to the majesty of Justice. He folded his arms grimly. The implacable lights winked red and green, red and green, red and green. Nat sat down heavily on the running board and mopped his brow.

Dogged defiance cropped out all over him. Emma was sobbing and the children were sniveling.

I had been waiting to see what Nat would do. I stepped into the street, calling to a group of men—some snickering and some silently watching—standing on the corner.

"Come on, you guys, and give this man a hand instead of hanging around and making fun of him."

"Yeh," said Ed to the cop. "He'd like t' have one of these new models himself. Ain't no picnic for him t' have a laughin' stock made of himself. He'd like t' have a car that starts off fine and peppy when the light turns green."

"Don't get cocky! . . ." the cop began pugnaciously, but, seeing a bunch of men pouring into the street, he sauntered away, twirling his stick. The chauffeur of the town car had been playfully nosing his massive bumper into the flivver's rear, not hitting it hard enough to push it, merely enough to jar it.

"Back up! Back up!" I shouted bellicosely. The alarmed chauffeur complied. Milady in the back seat was frozen stiff with horror and disdain at the presumption of the hoi-polloi. Ed unscrewed the gas cap.

"You're out of gas," he announced to Nat. "Ain't no use of a man gettin' rattled over something like that light, or a bull-dozin' cop. We all get a-scared of things that don't really amount to a hill o' beans. Get in and we'll push you to a filling station."

Nat climbed in. When the light turned green our feet gripped the bricks and the car moved forward smoothly and silently. Emma's tragic, tear-stained face cracked in a smile. The children whooped with elation.

"A silent six!" Nat cried joyously. "I got a better runnin' car than I've had fer many a day! Makes all the difference in the world having some he'p when you need it most."

We pushed the car up to a filling station and stopped it beside the pumps.

"Maybe you got a long way t' go," Ed said to Nat. "You don't know where you're goin', so the treat's on us." We made up a collection of pennies and nickels among the men and paid for the gas.

"I don't know where I'm goin', but I'm on my way," Nat replied. "I got nothing t' lose wherever I go. Good luck to all of you, friends! When you all need a friend, I hope you'll find 'em like I did. And ever' time I get a chancet, I'm gonna be a friend to somebody else. That is, t' them that's friends to me, not t' cops and sich like."

"It's a fact," Ed said as the car moved away. "They's millions in this country jist in his shoes. One flophouse is about the same as another; one garbage dump smells jist as sweet as the next one. They've lived on promises and hot air fer over three years, and that gets so it ain't very nourishin'. Jist as that old German guy you're always talkin' about said, they got nothing t' lose but their chains, and most of 'em ain't even got any chains t' lose, because they have a hell of a time persuadin' anybody t' chain 'em to a job."

"Did you hear Nat cuss the cop?" I asked.

"It was like a mouse spittin' in a hungry cat's face and sayin': 'Put 'em up, big shot, I aim t' take you to a cleanin'!' " said Ed thoughtfully. "When a worm like that begins to squirm and turns sassy, something *is* gonna break loose."

"I think it was a character of Balzac's that said there is nothing more terrible than the revolt of a sheep," I remarked. An idea struck me.

"Say, fellows," I called to the men still standing about. "How many of you are ex-Boy Scouts and are behind on your daily good deeds? Wouldn't hurt to repeat in one day. There's a man going to have everything he owns sold this afternoon. It's near noon now. In other places where there are enough men with enough guts, such sales don't come off. Are you that kind of men? It isn't far out there."

Some of them slunk off, but more than half followed us. As we left the city limits, the men chatted cheerfully and began to sing.

"It's good to have something to do, know you're doing some good," said a studious looking chap wearing glasses. "We've just laid around and let the flies blow us so long we're withering away from dry rot."

Ed picked up his feet and laid them down briskly, cut a caper now and then. When we reached the lane, we were surprised to see dozens of men, evidently farmers, hastening towards Ben's. Many of them carried rifles, pitchforks and clubs.

VIII

Ben's yard was jammed with buggies, saddle horses and a few cars. The household goods were piled in a shabby heap under an elm tree. A few chairs with rungs broken and seats scarred, a table or two, a bureau with splotched mirror, some rusty iron bedsteads, a mattress with straw bulging from rents in it and checked into squares where the springs had rusted upon it, and a few other pieces of furniture were to be seen. Ben and his family were not in sight. Ben's solitary horse stood with drooping head, tied to a post. Several farmers came up to it, peeled back its lips to guess its age.

I saw Hans moving about among the farmers. They were nodding their heads grimly, leaning upon their rifles or pitchforks, hefting stout hickory shillelahs in their sinewy hands.

"You brought these men from town?" Hans asked me.

"That's great. Now watch and see whether *these* farmers are as docile as Ed thinks they all are."

Ed was looking on and grinning somewhat shame-facedly.

At the appointed time, the auctioneer shouldered his way through the crowd. He was to sell the household goods and implements before the sheriff arrived to sell the farm. The auctioneer was a horsey fellow dressed in the style of an itinerant medicine show spieler.

"Gather up closely, ladies and what you brought with you," he yelled. "So all can see and hear. This is where your money does double duty. You see what I hold in my hand? A bee-e-au-tiful cut glass pitcher, and there's six glasses to match goes with it. If you want to know what this gen-u-wine cut glass would set you back in any merchandise emporium in this fair county or any other for that matter, just step in somewhere and inquire. Pass the lemonade! Lemonade, made in the shade by an old maid, stirred with a rusty spade. Brrrr! A little nippy to talk about lemonade, friends! How would this bee-e-au-tiful, splendiferous, all-wool-and-yard-wide cut glass pitcher look foaming over with egg nog, good old yaller egg nog, with the fresh country eggs and the corn—syrup! Shame on you, I know what you're thinking!—in it. That re-minds me of a story. A certain young man, who is in this crowd—and I may call his name out later—was approached by a friend who asked this certain young man to mix up some good old-fashioned egg nog. 'I would,' replied the young man, *'but where in the mischief will we get the eggs?'* All right, ladies, gents, children, and bob-tailed houn' dawgs, what am I bid? If you start off with less than a silver dollar, I'm going to be ashamed to own that I'm a resident of this fair county."

He paused expectantly and gulped a glass of water, slushing it about in his mouth and spitting it out. The farmers stood with folded arms. They had not laughed at his sallies as they usually did, and the auctioneer was bewildered.

"I bid a dime," a farmer standing apart from the others called. Instantly a lanky fellow strode over to the bidder and muttered something to him, twirling his shillelah suggestively.

"Did I hear a bid?" asked the auctioneer, cupping his hand behind his ear and leaning forward.

"No," said the slim farmer. "He just made a mistake. Didn't you make a mistake, pardner?"

"Sure," answered the bidder, sullenly but submissively. "I reckon I just made a mistake."

"I like t' see a man own up to his mistakes. Gee Whiz! I wonder if that limb would hold up a two hundred pounder." The slim farmer raised his eyes to the branches of a hickory tree near the house. A rope knotted in a hangman's noose dangled from one of the high limbs. Several farmers held the loose end.

"Put up the whole shootin' match, auctioneer!" ordered the slim farmer. "No use of you wastin' yer time on one article at a time."

"I see we'll have to wait till the sheriff gets here," said the auctioneer, his urbane manner deserting him. "I know what you're up to, but you're not going to work any snide like that on me."

"We'll bid on the household goods *now*!" insisted the farmer firmly. "Come on!" He thumped on the ground with his cudgel and several of the others drew closer.

"How much am I bid on all these household goods?" muttered the auctioneer hurriedly.

"Well, without all the high-falutin' palaver you used tryin' t' sell the pitcher and glasses, it oughtn't t' be wuth much. I bid eight cents. Does anybody else wanta bid?" As he said this, he glared about him. Nobody spoke.

"Sold to this gentleman for eight cents," said the auctioneer mournfully.

"Now the implements and the hoss."

The horse and implements fetched twelve cents. Just then the sheriff drove into the yard and four armed men climbed out of the car. They were hefty, magnificently muscled youngsters, and as they walked they slapped the pistols swinging in holsters at their sides. The sheriff climbed on a table.

"I'm talking to you as law-abiding citizens," he began. "And I hope that's what you are. Those that haven't any respect for the law are not wanted here. The Communist organizer we tarred and feathered a year or so ago here found that out. There's another one in the crowd here, a German named Hans. He's an ex-soldier, and like as not he shot down American boys, raped Belgian girls. I call on you law-abiding citizens to catch this Communist Hun and give him what he deserves—I don't need to tell you. Now I'm going to sell this farm to the highest bidder, and if there's any interference, we know how to take care of that. . . ." The deputies eased their guns about, and scowled menacingly.

"Listen, sheriff," called the slim farmer. "You ain't bluffin' us any. Neither are we a-skeered of bogey-mans any more. We helped you tar and feather that organizer, yes, but we know better now. I see yer deppities. Right smart lookin' young fellers. Let's have a little friendly shootin' match t' see who kin shoot the straightest and oftenest—two or three hundred of us or you and yer four deppities. Set up yer target some place. They's men in this crowd kin knock out a squirrel's eye as fur as they kin see it or even its shadder." Rifles clicked ominously and sun-burned knuckles whitened as they gripped gunstocks or pitchforks. Many of the rifles were the old-fashioned long-barreled ones.

Suddenly one of the deputies whipped out his pistol and fired into the crowd. A man fell, and women screamed. But the farmers closed in. The man who was hit arose, holding his arm. It hung limply and blood was dripping off the ends of his fingers. "I'm all right," he said, between clenched teeth.

"Don't shoot, comrades!" shouted Hans. "It won't be necessary."

The sheriff had been trying to use the butt of his revolver as a club, but the press was too close. He and his four deputies were soon helpless, farmers hanging on to each arm.

"See that white oak log, sheriff," said the slim farmer. "Now you put up the place fer sale, or, by doggies, we aim t' use that little log fer a batterin' ram and run it clean through yer purty autymobile. Pick 'er up, boys!" Ten men grunted as they raised the heavy log and started swinging it.

"All right," said the sheriff. "You win, this time. But the law will be respected if they have to send out the militia and keep it out."

"They'll hafta keep a squad of militia at every corn shock, then. We ain't a-skeered. Put up the place."

After the place was sold for fifty cents, the sheriff and his deputies drove away. Ben and his family appeared from within the house. Ben was looking happier than he had for a long time, and his wife and children were cheerful, too. Bonny Fern began carrying things back into the house. The slim farmer called Ben to his side.

"Brother Haskin," he said gravely. "We've decided t' sell you back yer goods and chattels and the farm fer 99 cents. If you think that's too steep, we might shave it a little. I'll loan you the 99 cents."

The crowd cheered. Ben thanked them in short, awkward phrases. He fumbled with his greasy felt hat. At last rage, determination and an awful exultation exploded from his face. "I'm not a speechmaker," he shouted. "Couldn't make a speech if I was to be hung the next minute. All I wanta say is, by God, I know what it takes— *I'm ready!*"

Speakers mounted the table one by one. They were farmers, habitually stern and taciturn. Silently, they had plodded behind the plow, watching the fat furrows curl away. They had burned brush in the fence corners, merely nodding at their acquaintances as they rode by. They were not speakers, but some vital force flowed from them as they talked. I was standing near the table when Hans nudged me. "Now it's your turn," he said. I did not demur. I had been thinking of things I'd like to say to these men.

I was frightened a bit at first, but I was soon at ease and enkindled by the response of the crowd. I thought happily that I must have inherited some of my father's gift. After I had finished, a weather-beaten veteran sought me out.

"The best talk we've had in these parts since Tom Donovan usta be alive," he declared. "It seems like old times. I was one of the Monkey Nest miners, but I hadda go t' farmin' when they locked out the union men. Keep up that kind o' work. You're sure a chip offen the old block."

I looked for and found Hans. "I'm going with you, Hans," I said positively.

"What about your mother?" he said. He appeared to be pleased.

"I can let her have what money I have. I wouldn't make anything here this Winter anyhow. I'm going."

"Look here, Larry, feel that lump on my head." He guided my fingers to a bump the size of a hen's egg. "A policeman's club did that. Could you stand that?"

307

"I'm going."

"Look at this." He drew back his lips and showed that most of his teeth were gone. "I used to have splendid teeth, remember. The police didn't get the teeth. Some workers did that. Sometimes they are confused; they fight those that are trying to help them. Could you still want to fight for them if they did you like that?"

"I still want to go."

"Your curly hair will turn grey, fall out before long. You'll probably have your white, strong teeth knocked down your throat before six months have passed. Sometimes the jails are full of crabs and graybacks. They're hot in the summer, and cold in the winter."

"What's the matter, Hans? Don't you want me to go with you?"

"Sure," he laughed, "I just wanted to make sure you had no romantic ideas. You used to live in a world of poetry, you know. The kind of poetry we live and see is terrible as well as majestic, sometimes it's bloody and grim and it takes a stout heart to keep knocking away."

"I sweated away my illusions long ago. I'll keep knocking."

Mother was crying softly inside the littered house. Bonny Fern had gone to fetch her. I was a little hesitant about telling her I was leaving, but I did so.

"I can make it all right," she said. "Your father would want you to do something like that. Don't you worry about me."

"I'll take care of her, Larry," said Bonny Fern. "You must be careful."

"I can't promise to be careful," I replied. "In the kind of work I want to do, that would mean to be cowardly."

"Well, be as careful as you can," she amended tearfully. Her eyes appealed almost frantically, but I turned my head. I didn't want her to take anything for granted. I thought she looked prettier every year, even if she was tanned and freckled and her hands rough and red. But I had to be free.

"I'll be right here," she said.

Nat was standing outside the door with a tire tool in his hand. "I thought you were across the state line by this time," I said.

"Naw! Been here all the time. Heerd about this from some farmers we passed on the road and thought I might be some he'p."

"You headed west?"

"Sure!"

"Then Hans and I will ride with you for a stretch. I've no clothes worth taking beside these I have on."

"Is there room for me?" It was Ed. "I wanta go with you, Larry. You and me's been together too long t' split up now. I ain't much at the speechin', but I got this." He bared a bulging arm.

"We throw the spark," Hans said as we chugged out of the yard. "Sometimes it splutters and goes out, but again it will light a mighty blaze. The farmers are stirring. And merely to jar the farmer out of his lethargy is a great deal."

"Them farmers is like a suckin' calf," observed Nat. "A suckin' calf you try t' wean in a bucket. Be danged if you don't hafta pull its ears off t' get it started, but you gotta pull its tail off t' get it stopped."

Mother and Bonny Fern were waving and blowing kisses at us. Ben waved his hat. A bend in the road obscured them. We watched the spot where they disappeared soberly for a moment.

We drove on till twilight began to gather in the low places. Emma whispered into Nat's ear and he halted the car, climbed out and began to tinker with the spark plugs.

"Hope she ain't gonna act up like she did on Main Street," said Ed.

"She'll be all right in a minute," said Nat. Emma and two of the children got out of the car and slipped into some bushes beside the road.

We were off again. Ed stretched. "Another hard Winter comin' on, Larry," he said. "But I won't mind it like the others. I'm beginnin' t' get some kick out of livin'. You and me both got a different spirit."

Hans' dark face could scarcely be seen now. His eyes were bright as coals. The flivver wheezed on into the dusk. It was chilly, but I did not mind. Emma and the children huddled shivering under a dingy blanket. The cold air rushed against our faces.

END

AMERICAN CENTURY SERIES

Distinguished paperback books in the fields of literature and history.